SAY TO THIS
MOUNTAIN

Say to

This Mountain

THE SHILOH LEGACY SERIES ★ BOOK THREE

BODIE & BROCK THOENE

TYNDALE HOUSE PUBLISHERS, INC.
CAROL STREAM, ILLINOIS

Visit Tyndale's exciting Web site at www.tyndale.com

TYNDALE and Tyndale's quill logo are registered trademarks of Tyndale House Publishers, Inc.

Say to This Mountain

Designed by Dean H. Renninger

Edited by Ramona Cramer Tucker

Published in 1993 by Bethany House Publishers under ISBN 1-55661-191-9.

First printing by Tyndale House Publishers, Inc. in 2006.

Scripture quotations are taken from the *Holy Bible,* King James Version.

Library of Congress Cataloging-in-Publication Data

Thoene, Bodie, date.
  Say to this mountain / Bodie & Brock Thoene.
    p. cm. — (The Shiloh legacy ; bk. 3)
    ISBN-13: 978-1-4143-0122-8 (pbk.)
    ISBN-10: 1-4143-0122-7 (pbk.)
    1. Shiloh (Ark. : Imaginary place)—Fiction. 2. Depressions—Fiction. 3. Country life —Fiction. 4. Arkansas—Fiction. I. Thoene, Brock, date. II. Title.
  PS3570.H46S28 2006
  813'.54—dc22   2006005607

Printed in the United States of America

11 10 09 08 07 06
7 6 5 4 3 2 1

This story is for
Margaret Tait

My dearest Margaret,
who climbed my mountains
with me . . .
You were always there.
You are still here.
A miracle, I think.

The world took little note of the tornado that touched down near the village of Shiloh, Arkansas, in late October of 1929. Two people were killed. One house was completely destroyed. A few barns and out-buildings were damaged. Telegraph lines and a mile of railroad track were uprooted.

What was that compared to the great Wall Street crash? No natural disaster in American history had ever matched the catastrophe of a thousand stocks tumbling into the abyss in one black day!

News of the Shiloh tornado was reported as a footnote in a handful of small-town newspapers. A Tulsa news photographer, delayed at the Fort Smith terminal, hired a biplane to carry him above the path of destruction. His pictures appeared on the front page—not because the twister was particularly newsworthy but because they were well-done photographs taken at great expense. The next day even those had almost been forgotten.

The Wall Street catastrophe, however, was still fresh and bloody news. The list of financial casualties extended into every city, town, and village across the country. Each passing hour brought the unhappy word that another well-known financier had jumped from a window or put a bullet in his head after leaving a note: *Tell the boys I can't pay.*

Postmen, shop clerks, street sweepers, and factory workers watched as their own small Wall Street fortunes turned to ashes or their banks shut up tight. They read the words of John D. Rockefeller and President

Herbert Hoover declaring that the worst was over. The market was basically sound, they said. Everything would be right again in no time. But few believed those words. The bubble had finally burst, and a general gloom settled over the land.

Illusions of prosperity and easy money vanished on that single black day just as surely as the house and barn of J.D. and Maybelle Froelich had disappeared when the Shiloh tornado touched down. Like the debris that littered the hills and fields between Hartford and Shiloh, Wall Street was strewn with the remnants of a million broken dreams and buried beneath the mounds of ticker tape. The fortunes of a nation had been sucked into the maelstrom of financial panic. What was one little twister compared to that?

To the folks of Shiloh and Hartford who had witnessed the descent of the ominous funnel cloud, however, the Wall Street news took a backseat. After all, it was reasoned, New York City was a faraway place run by the sons and grandsons of Yankees, wasn't it? It could have crumbled and dropped into the Atlantic Ocean as far as anybody in Sebastian County was concerned.

And was it really news that the Northern carpetbaggers were throwing themselves out the windows of the fancy New York hotels over such a thing as losing a fortune? It was, in the opinion of most of the folks around Shiloh, just what they deserved. The fact that they were pitching themselves out of windows only proved what everyone in the South already knew: "Them Yankees ain't nothin' but cowards—the lot of 'em! Why, there ain't a battle they'd of won against our grandpaps if they ain't outnumbered us ten to one!"

There could be no argument on that point from any resident of Shiloh this afternoon in early November. Old men and young gathered to smoke and talk on the front porch of Grandma Amos's general store, and the conversation drifted from Yankee cowardice to the falling price of cotton to the weather and then to the odd look of the moon rising early over yonder.

Wall Street was forgotten. The fate of J.D. and Maybelle Froelich was now of reduced consideration. Even Yankee atrocities were momentarily put on the shelf, and the low price of cotton dropped from the top of the list.

It was Grandma Amos herself who started it. Ancient and withered, the old woman had seen a lot in her day. She had been alive to see the march of General Sherman's butcher soldiers into Atlanta. When she had a word from the Lord, folks mostly listened . . . if they had not heard the same story a dozen times before.

As afternoon softened into evening, Grandma Amos stepped out to light her pipe and let her watery blue eyes linger on the moon. She gave a little moan and shook her head.

At this cue, half a dozen other old-timers joined in lamenting the look of that moon. "Heap of trouble be a'comin' from the look of that there moon over yonder," one said.

"Yessir," said another.

"What's one little ol' twister t'compare with troubles a'comin' when the moon shines like that in November?" the third claimed.

Grandma Amos's head looked big and too heavy for her thin, sloping shoulders. It seemed her face had gotten bigger, her nose longer, and her ears larger while her body had shrunk, but everyone knew that inside that oversized head was a storehouse of things seen and things remembered—great events and past calamities.

She blamed the tornado on the moon. Said a moon that strong had a way of twisting up the clouds and making the whole world a little cocked off. Said she sure hoped Birch Tucker didn't aim to bury J.D. and Maybelle until the moon waned a bit, because such a thing was bad luck all around.

When she was told that the body of J.D. had not yet been recovered, the old woman shuddered, raised her eyes heavenward, and called on the name of Jesus. "Oh, my Lawd Jeeeee-sus! Have mercy on us sinners!"

Some among the bystanders chuckled behind their hands. But young'uns got big-eyed and spooky feeling. And many among her listeners agreed with Grandma Amos outright. They predicted either flood or drought would come within the year.

Grandma Amos raised a gnarled finger to point at the darkening sky and recited the years that troubles had come upon the land and the people of Shiloh, Arkansas. Every hard year had begun with an autumn twilight just that shade of purple and a full moon rising big and orange and early over the mountain. Like tonight.

Folks drifted off to supper with the old woman's words ringing in their heads. A golden light glowed on the ridges as though a forest fire were sweeping across the Poteau Mountains. A veil of smoky mist floated across the treetops and down toward Shiloh Valley. Iridescent rings circled the moon and reached like silver calipers to measure the width of the mountain, then lift it from the earth. All these signs were portents of things to come.

Before the first cloud covered the night sky, before the first clap of thunder, the moon and the mist and the mountain told it all. Such a moon as this gathered the storm clouds in. Such a moon heaped up the tides and changed the courses of the rivers. Such a moon caused hens to stop laying and milk cows to go dry. Such a moon, the old woman said,

twisted the clouds and twisted men's hearts. Such a moon could also
draw life too early from the womb. . . .

The stars dimmed. Clouds rolled in and hid the mountain and the
eerie yellow glow. The old folks of Shiloh looked toward the glowering
sky and knew the moon was up to something.

"Don't need no prophet t'tell me so," cackled Grandma Amos.
"Don't need no *Farmers' Almanac*. Trouble. Thus sayeth the Lawd! Be
written there plain on the night sky!"

SAD
MUSIC

part one

For I have learned
To look on nature, not as in the hour
Of thoughtless youth; but hearing oftentimes
The still, sad music of humanity,
Not harsh nor grating, though of ample power
To chasten and subdue....

WILLIAM WORDSWORTH

CHAPTER ONE

Trouble Comin'

NOVEMBER 1929

The storm arrived in the late evening. A slow drizzle erupted into a torrent that drenched the carpet of fallen leaves beneath the old hickory tree in the yard. Raindrops drummed a rhythm against roofs and windowpanes. A steady stream gushed from the waterspout into an enormous oak rain barrel. Single drops joined company to become rivulets in search of the low places on the rutted roads of Shiloh. The James Fork swelled and tugged at the roots of water oaks. Leaping up, the flood buried the fording place beneath two feet of rushing water.

In the hills, deer took cover in thickets. In pastures, mules and cattle clustered together and stood with drooping heads as water dripped from hides and ears and tails. In farmhouses, families gathered around kitchen tables and looked out from silver windows at the darkness that hid the storm from view. Woodstoves crackled and cast-iron kettles rattled on the burners, while outside the downpour rumbled on.

And then it was over. As suddenly as it had begun, the roar abated and the world became a melody of single sounds again. Water dripping from the eaves. The distant rushing of the James Fork. The bellow of a cow answered by the indignant croak of a bullfrog turned out of his burrow. Voices dropped to a whisper.

Jefferson Canfield stepped from the warmth of the Tucker farmhouse into the cold night. He breathed in the sweet scent of rain-washed air and raised his face toward the sky. The moon was full and bright behind the clouds, yet not a glimmer of silver light showed through. The storm was not yet spent. Soon enough rain would begin again.

Jefferson frowned up toward where the moon should have been and hoped that Birch Tucker would make it back with Doc Brown before then. He thought of the waters of the James Fork streaming across the road down at the ford. Birch had ridden toward Hartford four hours ago, before the full force of the storm hit, and even then the creek had been high. The young mule Birch rode was strong enough to handle the current, but there was no way Doc Brown's old Model T could cross over now.

It was a bad night to need a doctor. A bad night to be out. And Jefferson had seen it coming. He blamed the full moon for all of this.

"Afraid t'show your face," he muttered at the unseen orb. "Done cause all this trouble whilst you stay outta sight. Don't even have the manners t'share a little light with us poor folk down here."

He sighed. There was nothing to be done about it now—and it was going to be a long, cold night. The cookstove and the parlor stove needed a heap more wood, and Jefferson welcomed the chance to get out of the house and feel useful for a while.

Placing the lantern on the top step, he retrieved the ax and half a dozen dry oak rounds from beneath the porch. He took his time with the chore. Breaking each round with a slow, deliberate rhythm, he tried not to think of what was happening inside the house. He set his mind on praying—holding back the storm and breaking up the clouds until Birch and Doc Brown could get through. What with chopping stove wood and such earnest prayers, he raised a sweat in spite of the cold. Somehow it felt better than sitting around, waiting for something to happen.

Truth to tell, he sensed that Trudy Tucker wanted him out of the house. All evening she had been coming in and out of the kitchen, where he was playing checkers with the young'uns. She walked around him and never said a word unless Jeff asked. And her answer was always the same, until finally she glared at him and told him to go on outside and make himself useful.

This was useful. Well, at least it was something. Overzealous in his work, Jeff chopped the wood into thin slivers that grew in a heap beside the door. A few drops of rain fell to mingle with beads of perspiration and course down the ravines and crevasses of Jeff's battered face. When would the rain start again?

He imagined Birch and Doc Brown stuck on the far side of the crossing. If the creek rose any higher, there would be no hope of fording, no matter how good that mule was. And it was dark. Had Birch or Doc thought to bring a lantern?

This question stopped the ax midswing. Jefferson peered at the block, then at the pile that was more kindling than stove wood. It was enough wood for ten cold nights and several hungry stoves.

Tossing the ax back under the porch, he took the steps in one stride and stuck his head into the house. He almost called out for Trudy but then remembered what was going on and lowered his voice to a loud whisper directed at the closed bedroom door. "Miz Trudy?"

Silence. The door remained shut.

"Miz Trudy?"

No answer. He heard the creak of the rocking chair; then Trudy opened the bedroom door and glared at him.

"You are half in and half out, Jeff. Come in or stay out, but close that front door before you let the night air in."

Jeff stepped into the house and closed the door quickly behind him. Womenfolk had a way of making a man feel like a schoolboy sometimes. Miz Trudy was a pretty woman, tall and chestnut-haired and elegant like a city gal. She was mostly soft-spoken, but when her brown eyes flashed like this, her husband and her young'uns and Jefferson all snapped to attention.

"Yes'm." Jeff lowered his eyes to the floor and hooked his thumb in the strap of his bib overalls. His six-foot-five-inch frame made the parlor seem small. Compared to outside, the house felt like a furnace. He wiped his forehead on his sleeve. "Sure is hot in here. I done chopped enough wood t'get the Rock Island engine all the way t'Kansas City an' back." He thought it would have been all right to keep the front door open awhile longer. Cool the place off a bit.

"Well, don't leave the door hanging wide open when you carry wood in."

"Yes'm." He frowned. "I was thinkin' . . . don't know if Birch took a lantern. Him and Doc Brown most likely goin' t'need a light down at the crossin' the way things is t'night. Figger if y'all don't need me, I'll go down there . . . since Tommy and Bobby and baby Joe is all tucked in now."

Trudy managed a smile. "You have filled the hot-water reservoir twice and chopped more wood than we'll use all winter." She nodded, and her expression became gentle. Sympathetic. "Men are mostly of no use at a time like this."

"My mama used t'say the same thing. Me an' my pa used t'go on down t'the barn an' wait it out. But seein' as how y'all got no barn after that twister . . ." He shrugged. "Ain't gonna need me while I'm gone, are you?"

"Wear your coat, Jeff. You'll take a chill and give Doc Brown more than he bargained for."

"Lily all right in there?" He shuddered and looked past Trudy toward the soft light of the kerosene lamp on the bureau.

"We'll all be better when Doc Brown gets here. Pray the rain holds off awhile."

He nodded and took his heavy brown-canvas coat from the hook. "I'll take me a rope, too. In case the crossin' is overflooded. You tell Lily I'll get the doc here quick as I can do it."

The weary voice of Lily floated out from the room. "Miz True don't need t'tell me nothin'. I ain't gone deaf. Jus' git on now. Make me nervous t'have you pacin' an' choppin' an' frettin'."

Trudy shrugged and grinned and gave Jefferson a small wave as he scurried out of the house, careful not to open the door too wide.

The bedroom was lit by a kerosene lamp placed in front of the mirror on top of the chest of drawers. The reflection gave a single flame the brightness of two lamps with half the use of kerosene. The shade was pulled, and new blue-checked curtains had been drawn over the tall, narrow window as insulation against the cold. The wainscoting was freshly painted white, and all but one of the walls were covered by wallpaper displaying bunches of tiny blue flowers.

The fourth wall was only half finished. Lines of white plaster covered the exposed surface like a road map. Rolls of unused wallpaper lay in a heap beside a stepladder, buckets, brushes, and tools.

The white-iron bed in which Lily lay was shoved against the opposite wall, and she was covered by the flower-garden quilt that Jefferson had given to her. Curled up on her side, Lily seemed as small as a child to Trudy, who placed a hot towel against her back as another contraction gripped, tightened, clamped, and eased away.

"There now," Trudy soothed. She glanced at the large face of the alarm clock beside the lamp. The pains were fewer than three minutes apart and strong. Where was Birch? the doctor? Jefferson? It was now six hours since Birch rode out for Hartford. Two hours since Jefferson left. Why were they not back?

Lily drew a deep breath of relief at the momentary reprieve from pain. "You shore is good t'me, Miz True," she whispered. "Ain't no woman ever had a young'un in such a perty room as this. I keep lookin' at them flowers on this here wall. Pertiest walls I ever seen. Too bad we didn't finish that there wall afore this young'un figgered it be time t'come out."

The very thing Trudy had been feeling guilty about. She had let Lily do the washing and then asked her to help hang the paper. They had been almost done when Lily's water broke. "I let you work too hard, Lily."

"Ain't nothin' . . . washin' . . . hangin' paper ain't nothin'. Y'all treats me like a queen, Miz True. Last baby I borned done got borned in a tent on the side of a cotton field. I done picked me a sack of cotton on that day. Poor lil' thing look at this hard ol' worl' an' jus' go on back t'Jesus, I reckon. Now this young'un—" the vise of a contraction began again and she gave a small gasp—"this . . . gonna . . . see blue posies . . . Jeff's mama's quilt . . . gonna want t'live."

Trudy grimaced in empathy as Lily's words gave way to the quick panting breath of labor. She replaced the towel on Lily's back with a hot one from the kettle and put her hand on the rock-hard abdomen. It would not be long now. What was keeping those men? She was at once angry at their delay, worried that there had been an accident, and terrified that she would be left to deliver this baby alone.

Lily made no sound, although this was the strongest contraction yet.

It was Trudy who made a little moan and then said in a pained voice, "Oh, Lily, you deserve better."

Seconds passed like hours as the rain ticked against the window and the clock clanked like a bird pecking against a tin can. Then there came a big sigh of relief from Lily and from Trudy, too.

"Won' be long, Miz True," Lily croaked.

"The doctor will be here soon."

"If he ain't here—"

"Hold on, Lily. They cannot be much longer."

"Young'uns comes when they wants. Don't be scared none. Ain't so much t'birthin' a young'un, Miz True."

Trudy put a hand to her forehead in dismay. Not much? Trudy had delivered all three of her boys in a hospital and under a doctor's care. All sorts of fuss about it. And Trudy herself had been such a baby about it all. Thought she was going to die. The only thing she remembered of any use to poor Lily was the fact that it had felt good when the nurses put hot towels on her back and stomach.

Now here was Lily. No hospital. No electricity. No doctor—not even a nurse. A howling gale outside and Trudy feeling as if she wanted to howl inside. This was no good. In the modern world of 1929, was such a thing possible?

"Lily. Hold back." Trudy tried not to let her terror show in her tone of voice.

"Knowed it be comin' t'night. Big ol' moon. My mama say when the moon be full—" Again the gasp. The panting breath. Two and a half minutes since the last one!

✳ ✳ ✳

The long, shrill wail of the locomotive whistle echoed across the moonlit hills of the countryside.

It was a lonely sound, answered only by the silence of the night as the train slipped away. Max Meyer gazed out from the unlit Pullman compartment and wondered what the passing world beyond would look like in daylight. The leaves would have turned to scarlet and gold by now. Crops would be harvested. Hay gathered into big red barns. A white church steeple would tower through the autumn colors. Narrow lanes would crisscross the hills, leading from one neighbor's home to another. Come morning, the washing would be done and hung on lines to dry and soak up the sweet smells of November. There would be stock to feed and stumps to pull and children to get off to school.

The light from a distant farmhouse caught his eye. Like a bright star, it gleamed to mark the spot that some man's heart called center of the universe. Home! A warm, familiar beacon for someone else.

But for Max tonight, the light was simply a reminder of everything he had missed.

Just as surely as if he had spent his years traveling through one long, lonely night, Max had never seen the colors of his own autumn. Never slept on sheets stiff from drying in a country breeze. Never rejoiced in hearing sons call to one another across a field. Never looked at a distant light and called that light home.

And yet he knew about all these sweet things. He brushed the open letter beside him and reached across to touch the small hand of his sleeping son. Here was his light. Here, the center of his universe! This boy—*his* boy—had suddenly become the beacon calling his heart home.

Max had spent his lifetime in the skyscraper canyons of Manhattan—a shadowed, sunless world of blaring horns and rattling jackhammers. All this time he had been trying to be somebody, trying to make his mark on the world. Tonight he knew that the only worthwhile thing he had ever done had something to do with this kid asleep in the berth across from him.

How different their lives might have been if he had married Irene. If he had held their baby in his arms and known all the things he knew now. Nothing in all the world was worth the heartbeat of this one sleeping child!

"David," he whispered, as though the name were a city and a street and a house with a warm fire inside and food on the table.

The boy stirred. Small fingers moved like a bird beneath the warmth of Max's big hand and then grew still. "Mama?"

"No, Davey. It's me. Dad . . . Max."

Silence. A long, contented sigh, and then the boy's fist opened and grasped Max's forefinger as though to pull him along into some pleasant dream. "Where are we, Dad?"

"Arkansas."

"Will we be in Shiloh soon? With Trudy and . . ."

"A while yet." Max did not want to break the spell of color and warmth that David's touch brought to him.

"Will you wake me then?"

"Yes. Go back to sleep now, Son."

Son! Speaking that one word was like suddenly understanding a new language. Max sat, unmoving, as the gentle clacking of the train on the track lulled the boy back to sleep. He did not pull his hand away but felt the pulse of David's heart beating through his fingers. A fragile thing, this heartbeat—and there were plenty of people back in New York who would like to stop it. Max knew they were far from safe even now. He had spotted what he imagined to be FBI men standing on the platforms of half a dozen train stations. Boss Quinn's gangsters could not be far behind. A New York Jew, a blond boy, and an enormous dog named Codfish would be easy quarry if the scent was ever picked up.

Max reached down to touch the head of the black Newfoundland sleeping at his feet. No one who saw Codfish failed to comment. The dog stood out like a circus bear on a leash. His huge size and great lumbering gait made heads turn to look when Max wanted only to be invisible . . . to melt into the crowd. Max imagined Boss Quinn's goons asking the conductors of every train, *"You seen a man and a kid with a big black dog?"* Codfish would not be quickly forgotten.

Codfish raised his head at the touch of Max's hand and then, with a contented sigh, let it fall back across Max's feet.

"What am I going to do with you, you stinking mutt?" Max whispered.

Codfish licked his chops, sighed again, and thumped his tail against the compartment door. The loyal dog had been David's friend, bodyguard, and salvation. But now the animal's presence was a danger.

Max paid the porter extra to walk Codfish. Never at layovers in larger cities. Only at the smallest, most obscure whistle-stops. "If anybody asks," he had instructed the porter, "tell 'em the mutt belongs to an old lady, okay?"

So far, so good. Max had watched from behind the half-drawn shade a dozen times as Codfish strained against his leash, pulling the scrawny black porter from pillar to pillar in tiny stations like Gerberville and Halcyon and Pikestown. Stationmasters and luggage handlers raised their eyebrows and offered the beast water to drink or half a sandwich to gulp down without chewing. Max had read the lips of the porter: *"B'longs to an ol' lady . . ."* No G-men or gangsters stepped forward to challenge the statement.

In the great cities like Philadelphia and Baltimore, Codfish remained locked out of sight in the first-class compartment with his young master. Max hung out the Do Not Disturb sign and hoped that the FBI and bootleggers were still chasing one another around Manhattan. Perhaps Boss Quinn believed the boy was already in FBI custody. Maybe the Feds thought David and Max had been nabbed by Quinn.

No, it was too much to hope for. No doubt those two warring factions had crossed paths at Grand Central Station while David, Max, and Codfish had quietly slipped onto the train at Pennsylvania Station. Max would have liked to see the fireworks. Maybe one day he would call the *New York Times*, ask for Harry Beadle, and get the whole story of that day.

"Hey, Maxie!" Beadle would say. *"Where ya been, Maxie?"*

"To the ends of the earth, Beadle," Max would reply. *"To another century! To Shiloh, Arkansas. . . ."*

CHAPTER TWO

A Parting Promise

The full moon glowered down on the black Atlantic, outlining the schooner's swaying masts. The *China Doll* was riding at anchor alone now at the spot known as Rum Row. Like a flock of migrating birds, all the other rumrunners had headed south for the winter. Only the *China Doll* remained behind, hidden from Manhattan by a thick bank of fog. Soon enough her owner, Boss Quinn, hoped to follow the bootlegger flock to a warmer climate.

But first there were old scores to settle.

Yellowed photographs, brought here from Max Meyer's hotel suite, were fanned across a desk like a deck of playing cards. Names and dates scrawled in the margins identified each image. The bootlegger studied them like captions in a picture book.

From left to right the story read:

October 1892. A young couple stands together, stiff and unsmiling, among the crowds and baggage at Ellis Island. *Papa and Mama* reads the ink on the edge of the snapshot, but there are no children in the picture yet. She is not more than seventeen years old; he is in his early twenties. Her sweet face is framed by a ragged shawl. His dark, angry eyes glare out from beneath the broad brim of a black hat. The plain gray dress she wears is topped with an overcoat much too large for her small frame. The cuffs of his collarless white shirt protrude three inches from the sleeves of his too-small suit. *Alphonse und Ruth Meyer in Amerika* declares the old German script on the back of the photo.

September 1898. The face of Ruth Meyer seems fuller now. Dressed in a pale cotton summer dress with puff sleeves and lace at the high collar, she no longer has the look of an immigrant. A small boy with a sober expression stands beside her high-backed chair. A baby is in her lap. She gazes proudly at the camera, and it is plain to see that things have gone well for the little family since their arrival in the New World. *Mama Ruth Meyer. Son Frederich, age 4. Son Max, age 1.*

January 1900. Papa Alphonse Meyer sits surrounded by his wife and two small sons to commemorate the arrival of a new century. Alphonse's suit fits him well. A silver watch chain across his vest testifies to the beginnings of prosperity. His expression, like those of his wife and sons, displays contentment. The Promised Land must be all it was promised to be.

There are single photos in the collection as well. Frederich at five. Max at three. Max at five. Frederich at seven with his pet cat in his arms. These were the photographs Ruth and Alphonse must have showed to friends at the market or the bakery or the synagogue, with words such as: *"My sons, you see? Born right here in America, both. Citizens, they are already! Frederich? He will make a lawyer one day. Max, the youngest, he will make a doctor!"*

Such dreams might have come true. If success could be measured by the number of visits made to the neighborhood photography studio, then the family of Alphonse Meyer was doing quite well in 1900.

But then one single newspaper clipping placed in the center of Quinn's broad desktop interrupted the happy sequence.

June 15, 1904. "Tragedy on the East River! 1,000 Die as Steamboat *General Slocum* Burns and Sinks!"

The brittle newsprint told the whole story of the disaster. Men, women, and children from the Lower East Side neighborhood known as Little Germany had boarded the boat for an outing. Fire broke out in the second cabin and spread rapidly through the ship. There were few life preservers, and the lifeboats capsized. Those who jumped from the blazing ship found fire in the oil-coated river. They burned and drowned while thousands of citizens watched helplessly from the banks. One thousand died. Only five hundred survived. Most of the dead were women and children. An entire East Side neighborhood was decimated in a single afternoon.

The victims are listed alphabetically in long columns. Three familiar names are circled in red:

Alphonse S. Meyer, aged 35
Ruth A. Meyer, aged 29
Frederich D. Meyer, aged 10

Of the Meyer family, only little Max had survived. And at that point, the story of Max Meyer's life suddenly became bleak and spartan. Like

many of the broken survivors of Little Germany, Max left the neighborhood to live with relatives in the tenement neighborhood on Orchard
Street.

From there the photographs picked up the tale with the picture of an
elderly couple dressed in grocer's aprons outside a dry-goods store.

Zeyde Fritz. Bubbe Fritz. 1906. At the old Orchard Street store reads the
childish scrawl.

Other pictures dutifully trace the boy's progress toward manhood.
Max at his bar mitzvah. Max graduating from high school. Max looking
remarkably like his father, with a darkly handsome face, black hair, and
broad, square-set shoulders. Max in the army with Ellis Warne and Birch
Tucker. Max with Irene Dunlap. Irene. Max and Irene at Coney Island.
Irene, and Irene again. Cousin Trudy at her wedding to Birch Tucker. Max
with Joseph and Sadie, Trudy's parents. Max in cap and gown at Oxford.
Max shaking hands with President Warren G. Harding. Max with Herbert
Hoover in 1927 at the conference on European Financial Affairs.

Pretty heady stuff for an orphan kid from Orchard Street. Anyone
taking the time to study the record could not help but admire Max
Meyer.

And so it was tonight for those on board the rummy mother ship as
she lay at anchor off the coast of New York. Five men had crowded into
the opulent cabin of Boss Quinn.

Bootlegger, gangster, owner of the *China Doll*, Boss Quinn had also
grown up near Orchard Street. He remembered well the sinking of the
General Slocum. He had stood among the thousands of spectators on
the bank of the East River and watched with horror as little specks of
humanity flailed in the flaming, oil-coated waters and disappeared
beneath the surface. The scene had been something like he imagined
hell to be. After watching the bodies float down the East River, Quinn,
at twelve years of age, had entertained thoughts of becoming a priest.
One thing had led to another, however, and the career of Boss Quinn
had taken an entirely different turn.

"You did not tell me that Max was on the *General Slocum*, Keenan,"
Boss Quinn said as he tapped the nib of his pen against the image of Max
Meyer and then on that of President Hoover.

Mike Keenan, founder and president of the now bankrupt Cunard-
Keenan-Meyer Seagoing Brokerage, shrugged a reply. What did such details have to do with the issue at hand, anyhow? Keenan had been drunk
when he'd been hauled out of bed and brought to the *China Doll* against
his will. Forced to endure the cold Atlantic crossing in an open boat,
Keenan was now sober and sullen. Beneath all that, he was frightened.

The groaning timbers of the ship were the only sound as Quinn once again contemplated the photos before him. "This kike has come a long way from Orchard Street. He has come so far that he has forgot the code of the old neighborhood. Trust. It is everything or it is nothing, Keenan. I will tell you the truth: Maxie Meyer will wish he went down with the *General Slocum* when I catch up with him. And I *will* catch up with him."

He hefted a bundle of bound letters, all addressed to Max Meyer at the Plaza Hotel. "Our pal Max is a very sentimental guy, as you can see. He keeps everything. Snapshots. Letters. Lots of letters. Letters from people he most cares about. He has left us a map, see? Left the names and addresses of relatives. Of friends. The sort of people a guy goes to for help when he is on the lam and needs a place to hide out."

Like a blackjack dealer, Quinn broke the string that bound the correspondence and dealt the envelopes onto the photographs. "Meyer's aunt Sadie and uncle Joe in Montreal. Good. Canada. Out of the country. Maybe Max took the kid to Montreal. Maybe he thinks the Feds cannot reach him and the kid if they are not in the country. And maybe he thinks I will not look for him in Canada." Quinn smiled at that thought. He had connections in Montreal.

A second letter was placed beside the army photo. "Ellis Warne. Akron, Ohio. A doctor. Who can a man trust if he cannot trust an old army buddy? And a doctor to boot."

A third letter was tossed over the wedding photograph of Trudy and Birch Tucker. "Cousin, huh? His cousin Trudy married an old army pal. They got three little kids. Boys. I have read this letter. This cousin Trudy of his wishes that her dear cousin Max would come visit sometime. Maybe Max is thinking he can take his kid to visit."

Quinn pointed to the return address. "Tulsa, Oklahoma. Well, well, if it ain't a coincidence. Tulsa, Oklahoma, where Sabre Oil Company used to be—that is, before Sabre Oil went bust and swallowed up my million bucks. Tulsa. Maybe a guy like Max is thinking this would be a good place to take his kid. What do you think, Keenan? You are supposed to know our old pal Maxie so well. Where do you think he has gone? Where do you think he is hiding that little rat kid of his?"

With a gesture of contempt, Quinn added one last portrait to the collection. Now the face of nine-year-old David Meyer smiled mockingly at him. Quinn stared back, noting the similarity between the child and Max Meyer and Irene Dunlap. It was as though the photographic negatives of Max's and Irene's features had been overlapped to make one photograph in the face of the boy.

"David Meyer." Quinn muttered the child's name. "Max Meyer's kid, huh? This is the same kid what saw the two Swedes get bumped off.

The same kid I let go after he seen Joey the Book get worked over in the warehouse. The very same one we wish to remove from circulation so he cannot rat on any of us. The very same kid who has disappeared off the face of the earth while every G-man in New York is looking for him to testify against me and the boys so as we can fry in the electric chair at Sing Sing.

"Where would Max Meyer take this kid, do you think, Keenan? He knows the FBI would like this kid in court to send me up. He also knows that I would like to see this kid good and dead. And that I would like to see Max Meyer dead, too, on account of all the dough he has lost me. So, Max *and* the kid. Kill two birds with one stone, I say."

Quinn coughed into his hand and dabbed a kerchief over his forehead. There was a nervous rustle in the room as his three thugs anticipated an imminent explosion from the Boss.

"This very kid belongs to Max Meyer," Quinn went on. "Max, who has also double-crossed me. Max, who has cost me a million bucks! Hard-earned dough down the drain with all of lousy Wall Street! And now Max and this kid have taken it on the lam. Tells Miss Rutger to meet him at Grand Central and also sends every federal agent in the city to the same place while he has no intention of showing up. He pulled a fast one on me. On me! Boss Quinn! I do not like having a fast one pulled on me. Not by a lousy Orchard Street Jew and his brat. Do you know what will happen to my reputation if word gets around that I have been beaten by a kid and a lousy Jew scribbler? Do you understand my meaning, Keenan?" He raised his steely eyes to Mike Keenan, who sat perspiring beneath the light of the lantern.

"I don't think much of this either, Quinn." Keenan tried to sound tough, as though he were the injured party, but the bluff fell short.

"I trusted you to invest my million. Made you my personal stockbroker." Boss Quinn's cheek twitched as he fought for self-control. "I trusted that you had bought off this Max Meyer, this newspaper weasel. You said he was on our team. On our team, you said to me! Print anything we want him to print, you said! But what does this newspaper weasel do?" Quinn leaned forward on the desk. His fist tapped hard against Max Meyer's photos and letters.

"He double-crossed us," Keenan blustered. "Like you said. He pulled a fast one. Got away. Him and the kid. They got away."

Quinn shook his head slowly. "Look at this, will you, boys?" He waved a hand toward the ugly group of his henchmen. "The one time I go legit and it costs me a million bucks. Nine years I have been running rum past the Feds. Greasing the Coast Guard. Greasing the coppers. Greasing city hall. And now will you look? I am crossed up by a two-bit news hawker and a nine-year-old kid." He paused and smiled slightly. "And a slick Wall Street hustler." His eyes shifted to the face of Mike Keenan to emphasize his point.

Color climbed to Keenan's plump cheeks. He managed a feeble laugh of denial. "Me? Quinn, what are you saying? I have lost as much as . . . I am broke. See? The margin calls cleaned me out. You think that I—?"

"Max Meyer was in your pocket, you said." Quinn's expression hardened. He toyed with the edge of David Meyer's picture.

"How was I to know?" Keenan pleaded.

"You cost me a million bucks. Not only that, there is a little kid running around who knows enough to sink the *China Doll* and her cargo and me with it, if you take my meaning. If the Feds get to the kid first, I am done for. . . . So, where is Max? Where is your old Orchard Street friend Maxie Meyer?"

The reply burst from Keenan's mouth. "How should I know?" The color drained from his face as fear took hold. "I tell you he double-crossed me, too! You cannot blame me for this!"

"Blame you? My stockbroker? Lemme tell you, Keenan. You know, when I sell a few cases of booze to some juke joint down in Harlem, I deliver it. You get my meaning? It does not matter how many cops I have to pay off or what bother to which I am required to go. When Boss Quinn gives his word, it is as good as gold. I expect the same from those I deal with. Trust. You know? This is the basis for all business. Trust."

Such noble words coming from the mouth of one of New York City's most prominent gangsters might have seemed laughable to those who had done business with Boss Quinn. Freely translated, Quinn's discussion about trust meant this: If Boss Quinn promised he would break a man's legs, then that man should immediately go out and buy crutches. If Boss Quinn declared that he would not be undersold by some two-bit bootlegger, then that bootlegger should retire quickly and move to Florida. If Boss Quinn stated that he did not like being double-crossed and that he would fit the traitor with concrete overshoes, the traitor could trust that there was a place waiting for him at the bottom of the East River. It was that simple.

"Trust." Quinn squinted at the pictures and slowly raised his head to smile serenely at Mike Keenan. "I trusted you, Keenan. Trusted your good reputation. And now I am a million in the hole. I ask you, was my trust misplaced?"

Silence. The *China Doll* rocked gently on the Atlantic swell. The richly paneled office of the bootlegger seemed too warm and close. Keenan tugged at his collar, suddenly aware that it was drenched from his sweat. "It–it is too warm in here," he stammered.

All eyes were on his face. All waiting for his reply. The bow of the boat rose and fell again.

Keenan felt the tightness of nausea in his throat. "I need a little . . . It is so hot in here. . . ."

Boss Quinn drew a deep breath and leaned back in his leather chair. He inclined his head and considered Keenan's discomfort the way a cat considers a mouse caught beneath its paw. "The tide is changing. Going out to sea. A little seasick, are you, Keenan?" Quinn lifted the lid of a teak cigar box and removed a long green cigar. Striking a match on the bottom of his shoe, he lit the thing and puffed smoke across the desk into Keenan's face.

Keenan choked. "Some fresh air." He looked longingly at the slatted door and rubbed a hand across his face. "Quinn, I—"

"Trust. That is what we were talking about." Quinn stroked the cigar thoughtfully. "I can see that the subject makes you a little nervous, Keenan." He gestured toward his thugs. "Makes him hot, see? Makes him queasy." A chorus of low chuckles came from the trio. "Boys, what do you think of a man who gets nervous when the subject of conversation comes to trust?"

"No!" Keenan protested. "It's the smoke. The heat—"

Quinn blew another cloud of smoke toward Keenan. "The heat is on, all right. And the jig is up. You have my million bucks, Keenan? Can you pay me?"

"Your million? Why, how could I?"

"Just asking." Quinn shrugged. "Sure hate to kill you if you could pay me what you lost me."

"Kill? Me?" Keenan's face went another shade paler. He moaned and put a hand to his mouth.

Quinn motioned with one finger, and at the signal the thugs grasped Keenan and jerked him to his feet.

"Mister Keenan says it is too hot in here for him," Quinn said lightly. "You boys should cool him off."

"No!" Keenan struggled against his captors, only to have his arm wrenched backward and twisted until he fell to his knees. "Please—no! Quinn! I will pay you! Sell my estate! Just a little time."

"No good. No good, Keenan. I have already checked into little matters like your assets. Your mortgage. You do not even have enough life insurance to pay me back."

"My wife . . . kids . . . please!" Keenan was sobbing now. Begging.

"Trust. You see? Citizens about town need to know that Boss Quinn is good for his promises. That no citizen can cross me and get away with it. Like you, for instance. We just fit you with concrete overshoes, drop you overboard, and nobody knows where you have gone to. But they know you ain't no place to be found, and this thought makes them wonder. Makes them shudder and think twice before they think about crossing me. You see, Keenan? It's nothing personal, but if you get away with this, it would create difficulty for my business."

"Not me! Not me! It's Max Meyer who crossed you! Crossed me, too, Quinn! Max! Kill Max Meyer, not me!"

"I fully intend that Max Meyer will be likewise dead. But where is he? Until I find him and his kid, what am I supposed to do?"

"I can help you find him!" Keenan moaned. "Please, Quinn. Not me!"

Quinn shook his head in mock sympathy. "I make you a parting promise, Keenan, and my word is as good as gold. Max Meyer and his kid *will* be found. They will pay for your untimely demise. Trust me. I will tell Max how you died. That you died because of his neglect to play the game by the proper rules. It is not me who kills you, Keenan. It is Max Meyer, and I promise you that I will take vengeance on him for your death. Trust me."

A slight nod of Quinn's head indicated that the conversation had come to an end. Keenan was gagged and dragged from the cabin to the deck, where a small rummy ship with an adequate supply of wet concrete was tied alongside.

CHAPTER THREE

Stations and News

The train station had stood on the corner of Rogers and South Seventh since 1911. Even in the pouring rain of a dark night, it was still the most glorious building in all of Fort Smith, Arkansas.

Schoolteachers brought their young students on pilgrimages to the great edifice. And it was here that simple country folk learned the meaning of the word *grandeur*. Yes, Rome had St. Peter's, Paris boasted the Eiffel Tower, and New York gloried in the Chrysler Building. But Fort Smith had the KC—the Kansas City Southern Railroad station— and only a blind man or an arrogant fool would deny its majesty.

The entire structure evoked a feeling of awe. The doors were twenty feet tall, making even a big man seem small as he passed through. The rotunda towered one hundred feet above the polished tile floors. The wide, echoing corridor that led to the waiting trains seemed a mile long. In the back, huge locomotives huffed and chugged and smoked impatiently. Whistles shrieked, and conductors shouted across the platform as passengers scrambled to board.

Ever since the KC first opened, Leroy Johnson had been a fixture there. Each evening at five-thirty, come rain or shine, he rode his bicycle three miles to the station and proudly took up his vocation. He was a railroad man. His children grew up giving that answer proudly whenever they were asked what their daddy did for a living. He had always been a railroad man, just like his daddy before him! He worked down at the KC station!

Leroy's family had always been proud of that. They had never known a hungry day nor gone without proper clothing. And when the big Barnum

& Bailey circus had arrived at Fort Smith's KC station back in 1913, Leroy had gotten the whole Sunday school passes to the show. They had sat in their own section of the bleachers under the big top. And not one of the white folks in the audience had made a protest, because everyone in Fort Smith liked Leroy and considered him an asset at the KC station.

That was a proud day. But then, the years had been full of proud days. Wearing the uniform of a railroad redcap, Leroy had carried the luggage of some mighty important folks. On an average day, he made as much as one dollar in tips. Twice as much in busy seasons, holidays, and such. Between trains, it was Leroy's responsibility to keep the mosaic tile floors glistening and the white porcelain sinks and toilet bowls shining bright. For these duties he earned two bits an hour and the promise that one day he would receive a pension from the Kansas City Southern Railroad.

Security. No matter if the crops were good or bad. No matter that Prohibition law closed down all the saloons on Garrison Avenue. No matter that the New York stock market came a'crashing down on everybody. Leroy Johnson had no worries. The railroad was *forever*! Folks were always coming and going and coming back again. Luggage always needed toting. Taxis needed to be hailed. People needed recommendations of hotels: "Yessuh. Best ho-tel in the town be the Gold-man Ho-tel, suh. Ain't never stayed in it myself, naturally, but it gots the KFPW radio broadcastin' station up on the fift'floor. I listens t'the music it play, and it sound real fine."

Leroy had long ago learned when to offer such additional items of information and when to keep his mouth shut. It all depended on whose baggage he was toting. Some white folks looked at a man of color and naturally expected him to shut up and tote the valise just like in the slave days. Those folks usually did not offer a tip. Not even a penny.

Such folks had never learned to say, "Thank you kindly" from their mamas. And Leroy recognized them right off when they called him "boy," even though he was an old man now. With such as these, he pretended deafness and bent his back as though he had lumbago. If he moved slowly enough, usually they got impatient and carried their own bags or tried to hail one of Leroy's nephews, who worked as assistant redcaps for tips alone, hoping one day to step into Leroy's position after he retired. They were young yet and had much to learn of the skills that their uncle had long since mastered.

It was well-known that Leroy was a champion at judging the parade of humankind that marched to and fro across his clean tile floor. Mamas and papas, children of all varieties—Leroy could take one look and pretty much tell what sort of folks they were behind closed doors. Sometimes the rich ones were poor and mean in spirit, while others who dressed less fine were rich and generous-hearted. Clerks, shopgirls, businessmen, and bankers—were they honest or crooked? Did they cheat, or were they true? Were they at peace in spite of great wealth or poverty?

Leroy had only a few years of formal schooling, but he had spent his life as a student of human nature. This was his hobby, his entertainment, his true calling. It was, he often told his nephews, a gift from God, a great responsibility that the Lord had given him to serve and observe folks and then to pray for them according to what they needed. Kind folks and mean-spirited alike got prayed for as Leroy scrubbed the floor and polished the fixtures. He reckoned he would find out one day in heaven just what effect his prayers had taken on the lives of all those strangers. It gave him something to look forward to beyond his pension. The thought pleased him very much.

It was cold tonight. Cold enough that Leroy wondered if the rain might turn to snow. But the sky was beginning to clear. The moon peeked through the clouds. The plume of smoke rose from the stack of the express locomotive arriving in Fort Smith from St. Louis.

Three redcap nephews stood at attention along the platform like an honor guard. Leroy stood behind them and scanned the windows of the passenger cars as the people within stirred and shuffled toward the exits.

By reason of rank, Leroy had first choice of whose luggage he would place on the hand truck. With a nod, he directed nephew Pearcy to the well-dressed woman and her three sleepy stair-step children. There were at least half a dozen suitcases there. Nephew Toby assisted the elderly cleric with his battered case. Nephew Hank moved toward the traveling salesman who hollered, "Hey, you boy!" There would be no reward or thanks there, Leroy judged. But young Hank had need to learn patience even with gruff folks.

It was a sparse crowd arriving—a mere handful planning to stay on in Fort Smith. Most everyone else was traveling on south, maybe as far as New Orleans.

Leroy draped his arm across the hand truck and took in the crowd at a glance. Who needed his assistance? Not the young flapper with the carpetbag. She charged right by and embraced a tall young man who had been pacing the platform for twenty minutes before the train arrived. Not the old woman who stepped from the train to be mobbed by grandchildren and embraced by daughter and son-in-law.

Leroy turned his attention to the small boy who leaped from the train as though he were plunging into a swimming hole.

"Come on, Codfish!" the young'un hollered. "Come on, Dad! It's Arkansas!"

An instant later, the head of an enormous black dog poked out from the car. Pink tongue lolled to one side as the beast smiled at its young master. A bright red bandanna was tied around its neck to catch the drool.

"Come on, Codfish!" the boy called again.

The dog nodded, examined the stop, then picked his way cautiously down to the side of his master. A tall, darkly handsome, well-dressed man in a brown suit followed. Overcoat across his arm, expensive brown fedora shoved back on his head. No luggage. Not even one small case. Now here was a curiosity.

"End of the line, they say," ventured the man, patting the dog on his broad head.

It was the biggest dog Leroy had ever seen. Bigger than the bear cub at the Barnum & Bailey circus. Such a dog made the grandchildren of the old lady turn and stare admiringly and then nudge one another at the strange accent in the man's voice. *Big city folks.*

"We are strangers in a strange land, Davey," said the man to his son.

Plain as anything, this fella talked more like a Yankee than anybody Leroy had ever heard. Had they come all the way from up North without so much as even one valise? Impossible. Improbable, anyway.

Leroy wheeled his hand truck toward the odd little trio. "How-do, suh." Leroy tipped his cap. "Y'all needs help with y'all's bags? My, my! That be the biggest dog I ever laid these ol' eyes on!"

The dog wagged. The boy beamed. The man rubbed his chin thoughtfully.

"We've . . . lost our luggage, you see," explained the man.

But Leroy knew the man was not telling the whole truth. He just knew it. "Don't say! How many bags, suh? The company don't like for bags t'miss connections like that. We find 'em for you," Leroy offered sympathetically.

"We . . . no, don't worry about it. It's that we left them all behind, you see."

The boy's eyes were bright in spite of the late hour, his lips tight together as though he was holding back from telling something that was not supposed to be told. *The truth.*

"Ya'll come far?" Leroy smiled gently and patted the dog Codfish on the head. He knew they had come *very* far. But why?

"Several days!" the father answered, not wanting to say more. There was an unspoken story here that even Leroy with his great gift could not figure out.

"You don't look none the worse, suh. Nobody know by lookin' that you ain't got but one suit of clothes on your back." Indeed, the suit was pressed, shirt clean, shoes bright.

"Top-notch stewards," came the reply. "An excellent railway line, this is. Except now we hear that we will be unable to travel the rest of our journey by rail."

"Where y'all headed?" The platform had begun to empty out now.

"A little town . . . Shiloh, it's called."

"Shiloh! Why, that's right. Had a twister out that way t'other day. Ripped up a mile of track. Killed two people. Trees down all over the road. Lucky thing more ain't dead or more damage weren't done. But no, suh, the train ain't goin' out Shiloh way 'til they gets the track laid down again, I reckon." He jerked his thumb toward a heap of freight. "That there is a'waitin to be hauled, as y'all can see. Folks who wants t'go out that ways are hirin' mules or else catchin' a ride with somebody happens t'be headin' out yonder."

"Yonder?" The tall man leaned forward thoughtfully, as if he could not quite understand plain English.

"Yessuh." Leroy waved a hand toward the track where the Rock Island Line usually left in the morning for Hartford, Mansfield, and a water stop at Shiloh. "Rock Island ain't runnin'. Got her over yonder in the yard, suh."

The boy held the dog by its collar as it snuffed along the platform and lifted its leg against an iron pillar. Leroy struck out his lower lip in disapproval. Something to clean up later. Maybe he would give nephew Pearcy the job.

"Maybe a taxi, then?" asked the man, evidently not noticing the boy and the beast as another pillar was marked.

"No taxi go out so far. What's in Shiloh that a gentleman like yourself be wantin'?"

"Family."

Leroy's eyebrows rose in surprise, and he stifled a startled laugh. "Fambly, suh? You sure y'ain't got the *wrong* Shiloh?"

"My cousin lives there. Is there a telephone? She doesn't know I'm coming, and I'd like to ring her—"

"*No, suh!* No telephones in *Shiloh!*"

"Of course. The twister—tornado?—take out the lines?"

"No, suh! There weren't no lines t'take down, I reckon. But if'n there was, I reckon they'd be down all right. It was a sight t'see. Out t'the airfield, folks is payin' a penny a pound each for one of them aereo-contraptions t'take 'em up over top of it. A sight to see, all right, suh. But there ain't no telephone lines down, nor electric neither, I reckon. You sure you gots the *right* Shiloh, suh?"

"You have an airport here?" The gentleman rubbed his chin again as if some Yankee idea lit up his brain. He frowned and glared at Codfish. Then, with a shrug, he dismissed his doubts. "Can you call a taxi?"

"Yessuh. Gold-man Ho-tel is a fine 'stablishment, suh."

There was much about this strange encounter that Leroy Johnson could not figure out. In the first place, he was tipped an entire hour's wages—twenty-five cents! Such a large tip had only come his way a few times in all his years as a redcap, and to earn this one he had only called a taxi and recommended a hotel. There was no luggage to tote. These two were obviously foreign in speech and dress. How could such folks have family out in Shiloh?

Leroy figured they had just come to the wrong Shiloh. He guessed that there was some terrible mistake and that the man and his son would certainly be disappointed after such a long trip from the North.

Fingering the two bits in his pocket, Leroy returned to his mop and his praying. "Them folks has lost more'n their luggage, Lord. Them two is jus' plain lost. Well now, Jesus, suh, I reckon You knows who they is and where they is and where they be goin', don't You, suh? So I jus' leave them right in Your good hands, an' I 'specs You be ex-plainin' the whole story t'me when I sees You."

Three short whistle blasts erupted from the long, sleek locomotive of the Baltimore & Ohio passenger train.

"Akron! Next stop, Union Depot! Akron!" called the conductor as he alerted Willa-Mae Canfield and the other colored passengers that they would reach their destination tonight at ten minutes after the hour of eleven.

Akron. Boomtown of the Roaring Twenties. Rubber capital of the world. The tire empire of Firestone, Goodyear, and Goodrich. Home to one hundred thousand laborers whose sole purpose in life was to build round rubber shoes for the automobile. It was a rowdy place in the beginning, stinking of rubber and packed to overflowing with laborers recruited from worn-out mining towns and worn-out hardscrabble farms and from the flood of new immigrants that had passed through Ellis Island and kept on going west.

From seventy thousand in 1910, the population had tripled in a decade to over two hundred thousand. By the tens of thousands young, single males took jobs in the "gum factories." Young women followed to become wives; then children arrived in need of homes and places to shop and schools and churches. Houses shot up. Streetcar lines carried the "gummers" to the factories and wives and children to shop at Polsky Company or O'Neil's Department Store. And for a while there was great prosperity. Until October 29, 1929, the smell of rubber in the air had been the sweet smell of success.

Then came Black Tuesday, the day Wall Street collapsed. And on that day there was only the smell of fear hovering above the rubber capital of the world. Fear in the factory houses of Goodyear Heights and Firestone Park. Fear in the middle-class frame houses of Kenmore. Fear in the enormous mansions of the Portage Path millionaires. Fear in the North Howard Street apartments of the maids and gardeners who served the wealthy.

Willa-Mae fit into this last category of Akronites. She was employed in the service of Mr. and Mrs. Edward Weldon, who had made their fortune selling Packard automobiles and playing the stock market.

At first Willa-Mae had been hired on as a domestic maid for their Portage Path mansion, but Mr. Weldon had commented that she was too big and too black to be trafficking through the house all day. Having Willa-Mae carry a basket of laundry down the hall, he declared, was like having a Packard roadster drive through. "I like her well enough, Evelyn," he had said to his wife. "Find something else for her to do where she has room enough to do it."

The kitchen of the Weldon mansion had proved plenty big enough for Willa-Mae to move around in. And she could cook! She could cook anything at all and make it taste like something from heaven. Perhaps that was why she was so large, Mr. Weldon speculated. Pineapple upside-down cake. Fried chicken a man would kill for. Mashed potatoes whipped to lumpless perfection and heavily laced with sweet butter.

As Mr. and Mrs. Weldon ate Willa-Mae's cooking, they cursed their expanding waistlines but proudly served their guests. Willa-Mae had cooked for the likes of Harvey Firestone and Henry Ford and state senators and city civic leaders. Not that they ever saw her or would have spoken to her on the street. But they had eaten her cooking all the same, and she was proud of it.

For nine years straight, Willa-Mae had cooked fourteen hours a day, taking only Sunday as her day of rest. Never missed a day from illness. And never asked for a vacation until two weeks ago, when Big Hattie had given birth to her third child in far-off Harlem and sent a wire begging Willa-Mae to please come see these beautiful grandbabies.

And so Willa-Mae had gone off to New York City. She had left her husband, Hock, and daughter Nettie and Harry to tend to themselves. She had personally instructed the temporary cook on every detail of the Weldons' way of eating and what schedules should be followed.

Declaring that he would eat out every night until her return, Mr. Weldon had driven her to Union Depot in a brand-new 1929 Packard automobile. He had carried her one small valise and escorted her to the third-class railway car reserved for coloreds. Willa-Mae had thought he was going to climb onto the train and go to New York City with her as well, but then she had told him about the pineapple upside-down cake waiting for him on the sideboard back home. She had promised she would be back in one week, and he had promised that he would be at Union Depot waiting to drive her to her little apartment on North Howard Street. It didn't matter that it would be after eleven at night when she arrived.

Mr. Weldon was a fine gentleman, Willa-Mae mused as the clacking of the train slowed and the lights of Akron slid past the window. Yessir, Mr. Weldon had treated her kindly and fairly. No matter that he was a rich man and she was just a cook. When he had a hankering for her to whip up some dish, he was not above putting her in the backseat of his fine automobile and driving her to the market. When she worked late, cooking for some high-toned dinner party, he would often take her home in that long black Packard. Like a gentleman, he would wait until she was inside, safe from the brawls of rowdies who frequented the speakeasy around the corner. Only then would he pull away.

Willa-Mae gathered up her valise and the paper sack containing precious oranges, which she had purchased in New York and brought home as gifts for Hock, Nettie, and Harry. She took a deep breath and smiled. Yep, it was Akron all right. Didn't need no train whistle or conductor to tell her where she was! She could tell she was in Akron just from the smell. Blindfolded she could tell the sweet, burned smell of the rubber smoke and coal.

Harlem had been an interesting place to visit, full of sinners and saints, gin joints and jostling crowds. The grandbabies sure enough were beautiful, and Big Hattie was good to see again after so long. But it would be good to be back home in Akron all the same. Too much had happened back there in New York City. That Wall Street place had all kinds of white folks moaning and shaking their heads and some jumping out of windows. A terrible thing, it seemed to be, although Willa-Mae was not certain what it all meant. Back there in New York, folks thought it was the very end of the world!

Willa-Mae considered that New Yorkers were prone to hysteria. They were also rude. She was not sorry to leave Pennsylvania Station and head for home. No sir.

Of course, she had hated leaving Big Hattie and Philbert and those grandbabies in such a place. She had told them she would ask and see if maybe a town so well-off as Akron might have a good job for a young, strong man like Philbert. And she had promised Hattie that there were lots of places she could sing and make money.

Willa-Mae did not tell her she had been thinking of Hattie singing for weddings and funerals and church and such. No use Hattie knowing that Willa-Mae did not approve of all this newfangled music Hattie was singing. No use telling Hattie she should not have changed her given name and called herself D'Fat Lady so she could sing in the gin joints. Hattie was making good money and would not listen to her mother. It was best that Willa-Mae lure the little family out of Harlem and into a nice, mostly respectable town like Akron.

Hattie just needed her mama nearby to straighten her out, Willa-Mae reasoned. It was New York City that had pulled sweet Hattie into singing such music! One week here in Akron and Big Hattie would be back in church singing for Jesus again. One week close to her mama and that girl would straighten up and do right like she was raised.

Willa-Mae had considered all these things on the trip home to Akron. *My!* How the world seemed upside down from the way it had been on the farm! She couldn't say she liked the modern times much. She thought some about her boy Jefferson. How he had come home from the war thinking everything would be different and better for him. Well, it hadn't been, had it? The Klan had run him off, and then Old Mister Howard had thrown Willa-Mae and Hock off the farm. No. Those days in Arkansas had not been better. Now was better.

Willa-Mae sighed contentedly as Union Depot came into view. She might ride on the coloreds' car, but Mr. Weldon would be there waiting at the station in his big Packard. She could hold her head high. A steady job. Plenty of good food to eat. Working in a fine gentleman's house. And there surely was no pleasure for Willa-Mae like going for a ride in Mr. Weldon's elegant automobile!

The train crawled forward, shuddered, stopped, and hissed with relief. Union Depot was all lit up. The shape of its gray slate roof looked to Willa-Mae like a big tent for a revival meeting.

"And I sure is revived to be back," she muttered. "Thank You, Lord Jesus! Amen."

Peering out the window at the station, she could make out folks waiting beside stacks of luggage and other folks looking for somebody to get off. She could not see Mr. Weldon among the crowd. He would not have trouble finding her, she knew, because there was only one car for coloreds, and Willa-Mae was hard to miss even in a big crowd.

The night air was crisp and cold as she stepped from the train. The warm, sweet scent of oats drifted over from the Quaker Oats factory and filled the air. The scent made Willa-Mae instantly hungry. She had packed a lunch before leaving New York, but that had been a long ways back. It would sure be good to be back in the Weldon kitchen again, she thought as she searched the faces for her employer. Sure enough, it would be mighty fine to bake a cake for Mr. Weldon and have a piece when he was done.

The image of the gleaming tiled kitchen and the pantry full of food mixed with the aroma of oats made her mouth water. She hoped that temporary-hire cook had done a good job for the Weldons, but not too good.

Now, where was Mr. Weldon?

Willa-Mae stepped forward as the crowd on the platform began to thin and drift away. She pulled her coat close around her and shuddered. It was plenty cold, all right. Maybe Mr. Weldon was waiting inside the depot. No use in him standing out in the cold.

Willa-Mae was used to it. She had ridden all the way from New York with her coat on because there was no heat in the third-class car. It didn't bother her. She had been colder than this lots of times in her life. But Mr. Weldon was a pale, soft sort of man. He had been skinny and sickly before she had gone to work for him, and her home cooking had done him a world of good. All the same, Mrs. Weldon was always warning him about taking a chill and made him dress in woolen underwear at the first hint of autumn. No doubt he had taken that advice and waited inside on such a cold night.

The snack counter inside the terminal was closed. The long wooden benches were empty except for a young couple who slept sitting upright with their legs stretched out on a battered trunk. The last of the travelers hurried out the exit to catch the one remaining taxi at the curb.

Willa-Mae frowned at the empty waiting room and decided that Mr. Weldon was most likely parked out front.

"What you thinkin' of, Willa-Mae?" she chided herself. "While you dallyin' round in here, poor Mister Weldon's waitin' out in the automobile for you." She hurried toward the exit and burst through the double doors as the last cab pulled from the curb.

There was no sign of the black Packard. Willa-Mae clucked her tongue and shook her head in disgust at her own foolishness. "Mister Weldon done come and gone, Willa-Mae, while you waitin' like you 'spects he gonna tote your bag."

She sat down on a bench to think what to do. No use calling Mr. Weldon and telling him she had been waiting for him by the train. Such an admission would be shameful. Prideful. She didn't want Mr. Weldon thinking that just because she had been to New York on a train she had come home too proud to go look for her ride. No. Better just to show up for work in the morning like usual and tell him she had gotten in late last night and that she hoped he hadn't waited long for her.

"He *didn't* wait long, neither," Willa-Mae muttered. It had not been more than five minutes before the train arrived and everyone cleared out. If Mr. Weldon had been here, he sure hadn't let any grass grow under his tires.

For the first time, Willa-Mae wondered if her employer had not come to Union Depot at all. But it sure wasn't like the man to forget a promise. It sure wasn't like him to leave Willa-Mae to find her own way back to North Howard Street at such a perilous late hour. He was usually mighty good about such things.

There were only two explanations. Either Mr. Weldon had taken sick, or that temporary cook was better than Willa-Mae had thought she would be. Maybe she made a cake the likes of which Mr. Weldon had never tasted. Maybe it was such a cake as to drive Willa-Mae's pineapple upside-down right out of his mind—and Willa-Mae with it!

She drew herself up, indignant that such a lying thought could enter her mind. Straight from the devil, such a thought! Her Mr. Weldon and Miz Evelyn thought the world of her. They would not disremember her and her nine years after only one short week! *They would not!*

And furthermore, Willa-Mae reminded herself, if Mr. Weldon said he would come to pick her up, then he would come if he could. And he would wait until the train pulled away and the whole place closed down. Indignation turned to worry. Something was wrong. Bad wrong.

The B&O train whistled farewell to Akron and slid away from the depot at the same moment Willa-Mae chugged across the deserted street to catch a streetcar home. Hock would be waiting up for her. Nettie and Harry would have missed her, too, although she knew they had gotten along fine while she was gone.

But what about Mr. Weldon and Miz Evelyn? Them all alone in their big, old, ratty house with nobody to look after them but Katie the Irish maid and that temporary-hire cook! No doubt the change in routine and strange diet had upset Mr. Weldon's bowels and left him unable to even drive.

For the first time since she left Akron, Willa-Mae felt guilty. Those folks were like children in a way. They depended on her to keep things regular. And now look what had come of it!

"Lord, Lord!" Willa-Mae shook her head sorrowfully as she paid her nickel for the streetcar. "Oh my, my! Poor ol' Mister Weldon. Poor Mister Weldon." She swung into her seat as the streetcar driver eyed her curiously.

"You know Mister Weldon? The Packard king?" he asked as the electric car hummed and whirred up the nearly deserted street.

"I work for him and the missus," Willa-Mae admitted. She did not explain all the facts about how Mr. Weldon had promised to meet her but had not and what that must mean.

"Yes?" He sparked with curiosity as the wires sparked on the top of his car. "The papers say it was an accident. If you ask me, there's gonna be a lot more of them sort of accidents up there with them Portage Path millionaires."

"What you sayin'?" Willa-Mae felt giddy. "What accident?" Had Mr. Weldon been in an accident? the Packard? fallen down the stairs? "Accident?" she asked again.

"That's what us fellas said: 'What accident?' How can a man cut his own throat shaving? Cut it so bad he near bleeds to death?"

"What you sayin'?" Willa-Mae cried and clutched her sack of oranges to her. "What you *talkin'* 'bout? Mister Weldon? You say *Mister Weldon* done such a thing?"

"Go on," mocked the driver, a florid-faced Irishman with a belly as round as his face. "You don't work for him, Mammy."

"Tell me what you sayin' 'bout my kind Mister Weldon!"

The streetcar was empty except for Willa-Mae. The driver smirked. "You can read it in the paper same as me. Guy lost just about everything in the crash."

"Crash? His Packard done had a wreck?"

He laughed gruffly. "You don't know much, do you, Mammy? The stock-market crash is what I mean. Weldon lost a bundle, I hear. Of course, they don't write that in the paper. Just that Mister Weldon had a freak accident. Cut a vein shaving. Woulda died if the maid hadn't found him. He'll recover." The driver shrugged. "Or at least he'll live. Don't know who is gonna recover from this Wall Street deal. Everybody lost something—me and my old lady included. Had our savings tied up, and then what do you know? *Pow*—that's what! Wonder how Mr. Weldon is gonna like being poor like the rest of us?"

For fifteen minutes as the streetcar slid down the rails, the driver talked on. Willa-Mae did not listen. Sometimes she heard her own voice say "Uh-huh" or "Hmmm," but she was not really hearing what the man said. Her mind was humming like the streetcar, rumbling down its own tracks, making frequent pauses to grieve and worry and wonder. What was to come of the world if a man like Mr. Weldon could do such a desperate thing?

CHAPTER FOUR

Emergency at Plant One!

The moon was a dim orange ball behind the pall of smoke issuing from factory smokestacks. Its light seemed especially distant and cheerless tonight to Dr. Ellis Riley Warne as he loosened his tie and stretched out to rest for a few minutes on the examining table of the medical infirmary of Titan Tire and Rubber Company. He was a long way from the harvest moon and the sweet autumn air of his boyhood home in Guernsey County, Ohio, and every step away from the farm had seemed more painful than the last. Tonight, as he closed his eyes, the situation seemed even more hopeless than it had in broad daylight. Perhaps it was because he was so tired. Perhaps, come morning, things would not seem so bad.

The stump where his left leg had been amputated was aching, and for a moment he contemplated removing his prosthesis and letting himself fall into a deep sleep. He thought better of it, remembering that Jack Titan's car was still in its parking place. The old man was still prowling around his factory and was as likely to pop into the medical office as any place. Titan would not take kindly to one of his swing-shift physicians being asleep and legless on the job. No matter that Ellis had been on his feet at his own clinic since early this morning. Titan expected his company doctors to be alert at all times, and Ellis could not be caught being otherwise—especially not now that he needed this moonlighting position so desperately.

Ellis yawned and turned his head to look out the soot-blackened window toward the massive silhouette of the factory. The three-room infirmary was located on the second floor of the large redbrick building that had been the original tire factory in 1895. In the early days, Jack

Titan had manufactured bicycle tires with the help of twenty-seven employees. The second floor had been for offices and storage.

Thirty-four years later, Titan Tire employed more than ten thousand workers in competition with the Goodyear and Firestone tire companies. But unlike Harvey Firestone's factory, the plant of Jack Titan was far from modern.

Titan called the drafty brick infirmary "our company hospital." The space was poorly heated by the same old potbellied, coal-burning stove that had warmed it in the bicycle-tire days. No matter how many times it was scrubbed, it continued to reek of rubber.

Ellis Warne was one of four Akron doctors who practiced medicine at the Titan Tire Company Medical Dispensary. Three, including Ellis, were fresh out of medical school, flat broke, and trying to establish a private practice. Part-time shift work at the rubber factory helped them make ends meet. The fourth physician, Dr. Keller, was the only full-time doctor on the staff. He was seldom in the office these days, however. Dr. Keller was a well-known customer in the speakeasies just beyond the factory gates.

Twenty years ago, Dr. Keller had lost his private practice in Cincinnati when he operated on a child after an all-night binge. A routine tonsillectomy on an eight-year-old girl had ended in her death when she choked on her own blood. In spite of the disgrace, Jack Titan, an old and sympathetic school friend, had hired Keller as chief medical administrator at the Titan plant. It was a lofty title that, thankfully, meant little or nothing in the day-to-day operation of the infirmary. When left to his own devices, old Dr. Keller referred any condition more serious than a cold to a staff nurse, who then directed more urgent cases to one of the three part-time staff physicians.

Though forgiving of his old classmate Keller, Jack Titan was a tyrant to the young doctors who oversaw the operation of the Titan medical dispensary. He continually offered them his own prescriptions for good health, advising his "inexperienced" staff doctors that with every illness a laxative be administered to the patient. Countless boxes of purgatives were kept on hand along with regular medical supplies. Ellis guessed that the old man was hoping for the day when an epidemic of colds might sweep through the plant and then be purged from ten thousand workers by doses of castor oil.

Hundreds of bottles of laxatives were handed out free of charge to the Titan factory gummers each month. By this act, Jack Titan came to believe that there was no employer as generous and good-hearted as himself. But while the overflowing sewers of Akron may have been proof to Jack Titan that he was good to his employees, Ellis Warne knew better.

The lack of ventilation in the Titan plant left men choking for want of fresh air. Emphysema, bronchitis, pneumonia, and tuberculosis were not uncommon. Preventable accidents were frequent. Compared to the modern plants of Firestone and Goodyear, conditions here were deplorable.

Ellis also knew that the factory worker who complained was considered ungrateful, and ways were found to send that gummer packing. This policy also extended to idealistic young physicians who had been hired to patch up broken men, not amend the way tires were manufactured. For this and other reasons, the staff turnover in the medical infirmary was frequent. Just last week, Ellis had considered giving up his three nights a week as a swing-shift physician and concentrating entirely on his neighborhood practice. But all that was before Black Tuesday. Before Wall Street had betrayed him.

Things were slow tonight in the infirmary. The usual cases of colds, headaches, influenza, and hangovers simply did not fill the waiting room. Suddenly every slacker in the plant was filled with the realization that leaving work for a minor illness could now result in the permanent loss of his place on the line. Already rumors were flying thick and fast at the factory that Old Man Titan was up in his lair, trying to figure out ways to trim production costs. The logical conclusion was that Titan would simply trim back the workforce. Desperate times meant desperate measures.

It was after eleven o'clock. Ellis closed his eyes and pulled a rough gray-wool blanket up under his chin. It felt like an army blanket, he mused. Most likely Titan had purchased it through army surplus.

The distant booming of the factory sounded like artillery. This was a new kind of war in which men were fighting for life and only barely managing to survive. Exhausted, Ellis shuddered at that thought. He, too, was only just managing. He and Becky had imagined that all their struggles would be over once he finished medical school. He was thirty-two years old, and now he was worse off than when he had just been beginning.

"The trenches," he murmured as the stink of rubber and sulfur swirled through his senses. As he drifted toward sleep, a phantom pain ripped through his missing leg. He felt a searing in the toes that were buried somewhere in France. He dreamed of those toes wiggling beneath the bomb-scarred soil of Belleau Wood.

He heard again the faraway voice of Max Meyer as Max carried him across the battlefield: *"Hold on, Ellis! Hold on, you crazy Irishman! Don't die on me now, you Mick! Think of Becky! Think of Beck! Think of home, Ellis! You'll make it if you think of home!"*

The hard plank operating table at the field hospital cut into his back. *"That leg has got to come off, son."*

"No! Don't cut it! Not my leg!"

"You will die if we do not take it off, boy!"

"Don't take it! Don't—my pop is a doctor! Don't take it! Leave me my leg!"

"Hold him down. Nurse! Get his other arm. . . . Tie him down. . . . We need some help here."

"Think of Becky! Think of home!" cried the voice of Max through a thick fog. *"Home. . . ."*

Far away, the wail of sirens split the night and covered the screams of Ellis's nightmare. Was this the sound of celebration in the front lines? Had the war ended?

Rough hands shook him toward consciousness. The wailing sirens continued, and Ellis realized the sound was not part of his dream. He was hearing the whistle at Titan Tire.

"Doctor Warne?" The voice of Nurse Giselle Kowalski brought him back to reality. "Wake up, Doctor! An emergency at Plant One."

Ellis sat bolt upright and shook his head, trying to clear exhaustion from his brain. "Sirens?"

"An emergency in Plant One," she repeated, helping him on with his lab coat and lifting his black medical bag. Giselle Kowalski's name suggested a slender, antelope-type creature, but the name *Bison* would have been more appropriate. Strong and stern, she was a large, woolly-haired woman of forty. Ellis had seen her heft an unconscious gummer onto the exam table without batting an eye. Tonight she used her strength and gruffness to propel him out the door and into the cold night air.

He had left his coat in the infirmary, and the biting chill accomplished what sleep had not been able to. He was wide-awake. "Did they say what—?"

"There's a gummer with his arm caught in the calendering machine. Hurry."

The antiquated company fire truck was already at Plant One when Ellis and Giselle arrived two minutes later. Several hundred men milled around outside the doors. The usual booming roar beneath the enormous roof was ominously absent. All faces turned fearfully to stare at Ellis as he passed into the vast building. The screams of the trapped man resounded from the metal girders, directing Ellis toward the scene of the accident.

"Get me out!" wailed the man. "Don't let them cut it! Don't let them take it off! My arm! My arm!"

"It's the doc!" someone shouted, and suddenly Ellis was surrounded by men, all talking at once.

Jack Daugherty, the shift foreman, ran over to join them. He was a thick-trunked, leather-faced man, but his eyes held the terror of a small child. "It's my sister's kid!" He was shaking all over. Sweat poured from his face in spite of the chill inside the building. "I got him the job, see? Isaac was beside him. Said he stumbled and fell just after the machines was switching on. . . . His arm's in the rollers! Right up to the shoulder," he managed to explain. "We can't—can't get him out!"

The story was punctuated by the boy's screams.

"How long ago?" asked Ellis.

"Five minutes." The foreman broke down. "Forever. He ain't but seventeen. My sister's kid. How'm I gonna tell her? *How?*"

This was not the first time Ellis had seen men trapped in the calendering machine at the plant. Its giant cylinders were stacked like the rollers of a wringer washing machine. Thin cotton cords passed through them to be coated on each side with hot rubber. The acrid smell of sulfur combined with the smell of hot rubber to give the place a hellish atmosphere. The towering machines looming on all sides seemed like gloating enemies, dwarfing the men who passed by.

Ellis spotted the huge rollers of the calendering machine in the far corner of the building. Men swarmed over it in frantic helplessness, searching for some way to pull the arm free from the bone-crushing steel. It had been the same each time Ellis had witnessed it. Whatever went between those rollers came out in pieces. He knew it before he ever saw the boy. The arm would have to be taken off. He had come with his chloroform and his tools . . . like a grim mechanic come to fix the machine so the plant could get on with business.

"The doctor's here—listen to me, John! The doctor's gonna get you out."

This information sparked new terror in the boy. "*No!* Don't let him take it! Don't let him take off my arm!" Now Ellis was the enemy.

How well Ellis remembered that same stark terror. He did not speak to the young man. He could not bring himself to say even one word of comfort. There was no comfort at such a moment. There was only the reality of what must be done and the peace of the chloroform.

The boy lay stretched halfway across the sheet of gum-dipped cotton cords that had been feeding into the rollers. His toes still touched the ground, although his arm had vanished to the shoulder and his head rested against the upper cylinder.

He was lucky. Another instant and his head would have been crushed as well. But this was no time to think about luck. Later, when it was over, Ellis would tell him how near it had been. . . .

"Lift him up." Ellis ordered two men to lay the boy on top of the corded sheet. Waist high, it made a makeshift operating table. "Have you called an ambulance?" He took the boy's pulse. It fluttered like a bird.

"Don't cut it!" screamed the patient. "Leave me my arm!"

Curiously, no one had yet called an ambulance. "Just you. We just called you."

"We'll need to get him . . . to People's Hospital." Ellis directed his gaze to the foreman, the boy's uncle. "Go on. Call the ambulance and get his mother. We'll meet you at People's Hospital on West Market Street." At this the man began to sob. "Get going," Ellis commanded. Then he thumped the grieving man on the back. "He'll want his mother when he comes around."

Giselle had already prepared the anesthetic—chloroform dripped on a cotton cloth. Ellis took it from her, and only then did he speak to the boy. "You'll make it, John. Your uncle Jack has gone to fetch your mama." He slipped the chloroform mask over the face of the boy and counted slowly as the screams and the struggle ceased. And then there was profound silence, the peace of suffering at rest.

"If any of you are squeamish, get out now." Ellis's command echoed hollowly in the vacuum of stillness. One by one, the men who had crawled helplessly over the machine backed away as Ellis began cutting away the boy's coat.

In the end, only he and Giselle and two firemen remained. And then the ambulance arrived to carry young John Daugherty to the hospital. Ellis did not doubt that the plant would be back on line before the boy had even awakened. And somewhere in his executive suite of offices, old Mr. Titan would judge the success of the operation not by whether an arm was lost or a life was saved but by the time lost while the plant was silent and by how many tires the arm had cost him.

✳ ✳ ✳

The cry of a distant siren echoed across the rooftops of Akron. Dragging his clubfoot, six-year-old Frank Penn limped over to look out the second-story window of the one-room Howard Street apartment.

"Don't see what it is," he reported to his mama and his four-year-old brother, Jim.

"Prob'ly nothin' at all," said his mama. "Akron's full of such sounds in the night. Train whistles. Police cars. Sirens. One shift comes on, and the next gets off. Ain't nothin' for you boys to worry yourselfs about. Mama told you. It ain't like the whistles at the mine—not at all. Not like when the mine fell in. Nothin' for you boys t'be scared of. Pay it no mind," she said, painting her lips more heavily than she had ever done back home when they lived in Coal Town. She had told Frank that wearing lip rouge was important for her job. He did not like it all the same, because she could not kiss him and Jim good-bye without getting the red stuff on them.

"You gonna be gone long, Mama?" Frank asked as she adjusted her stockings.

"Depends. Just you never mind, Frank Penn. Watch your brother. Don't go out in the hallway. Don't speak to them niggers who live across the hall. And don't open the door until you know it's me come home. You hear me now?"

"Yes'm." He nodded and looked out the window at the dingy street below. "I'll do good."

"That's my little man. Help me take care of your brother. Since your daddy died, you're my little man, ain't you, Frank?"

Mama seemed nervous tonight. Was it because the factory whistle had blown early?

"Yes'm," Frank said again, wishing there was not so much stuff on his mama's face. He had liked it better when she was trying to just be a waitress, because she hadn't had to paint herself up like that, and she hadn't been nervous about the factory whistles and the men.

The men had something to do with her new job, Frank supposed, because his mama always had to be there when they got off work, and sometimes she brought different ones here to the apartment for a while.

"That's good, Frank. It ain't gonna be like this forever; you'll see. Soon as I get enough money saved, we'll get out of this dump. We'll take a train all the way to California, where there ain't no coal smoke and the air don't smell like burnt rubber and the sun shines all the time. Then I'll get a better job. You'll see. We'll get your foot fixed even, and you and Jim can play ball like other kids." She ran her hand over his light brown hair and caressed his cheek like she used to do in the old days back in Coal Town. Back when she was just a mama and when Frank's daddy had not been killed in the mine.

"That'll be good, Mama," Frank said, certain that his mama was the prettiest lady anywhere. "Maybe you can be in movies." He said this because his daddy had always said it to her and it had made her laugh.

Tonight she only smiled sadly. "I'm an actress all right, ain't I?" She did not say this to Frank but to the walls of the bare, grimy room. She looked at the white-iron bed in the corner and then at the mattress where Frank and Jim slept together beside the steam radiator. "It'll be better soon," she whispered before she looked at the window and pulled down the shade. Pointing her finger at little Jim, she warned, "Don't cry when I go. You know how I hate it when you cry."

"He won't," Frank promised for his baby brother, even though Jim usually did cry awhile after their mama left.

"Good." To Frank she said again, "You remember what I said about not talking to those niggers. Soon as I get some money, we're moving to someplace where there ain't any colored folk. Just don't dare speak to them meantime, lest they think they're good as a white child."

"Yes'm," Frank agreed seriously, although sometimes he did say how-do to the skinny little man who kept chickens out in back of the apartment building. Once the little man had given him and Jim each a lemon drop, and he had looked at Frank's bent foot with sad eyes and said kind words to him. But Mama didn't know all this, or she would have whipped Frank good.

"I can count on you, Frank." She blew a kiss to Jim, waved good-bye, and hurried out the door.

Jim began to whimper almost as soon as the lock clicked.

"Shut up, baby," Frank said. "Crybaby. Listen!" He held his finger up, and Jim fell silent as the click of their mama's high-heeled shoes tapped on the stairs and then on the tile foyer before vanishing out the door and onto Howard Street.

Frank pulled Jim to the window. Below in the dark shadows, they could see Mama hurrying to catch the streetcar down the block. She wore a close-fitting hat over her short brown hair. Her best blue Sunday dress had been shortened until her knees showed. This was also because of her job, she had told the boys. Her old brown coat looked black in the night. She looked to the right and to the left, then dashed across the street.

She did not look over her shoulder, even though Frank hoped she would. "Maybe she'll look. Wave to her," he said to Jim. The two small boys raised their hands in unison to wave good-bye, but their mama did not look back to see them framed in the window.

It was after midnight when Harry Beadle stepped into the *New York Times* building elevator. For about the fiftieth time that day, he thought how much simpler his life would be if he could disappear like his friend Max Meyer.

The FBI goons would not leave him alone. Agent Burns was convinced that Harry had somehow tipped Max off about the trap in Grand Central. Burns had grilled Harry for the better part of two days: "Where is he headed? What's his plan? How does he contact you? What is your code?"

To all these questions, Harry professed to be as baffled as the Feds—

which, of course, he was. But his inability to answer only served to infuriate them more. At one point, he had even considered making up a story to see if he could get them off his back, but then he had decided he was in enough trouble already.

The Feds were asking questions around his apartment building and his office, Old Lady McCreedy was giving him the eye, and the city desk editor seemed to think that Harry was about to be arrested for bootlegging. It was all so distracting. How was he supposed to get his work done? After all, there were still deadlines to meet, or he would be out of a job.

Harry supposed he could not blame everyone for being uneasy, with the six-footers who looked like linemen from Notre Dame standing across the street from his home and haunting the *Times* lobby at all hours. He sighed heavily and pondered again how cruelly life was treating him.

At the deep, sorrowful sound, Wally, the night elevator operator, looked over. "Mister Beadle, I must have been drivin' dis elevator in my sleep. I almost fergot I got a message for youse."

"Yeah?" said Harry without interest. "What is it?"

"I don't know, on accounta it's sealed, see?" Wally pulled an envelope from his uniform pocket and passed it to Harry. "A guy come in about five o'clock and says for me to give you this. He slips me a finif, too," he added, to prove that it was an important message and by way of a hint.

"Do you know this guy? What'd he look like?"

"I dunno. He was all bundled up, see? And he talked really low and growly-like, like he was tryin' to disguise his voice. Anyways, all he says was 'Give this to Harry Beadle;' then *whoosh*, he's gone."

The elevator stopped moving. They were already at the lobby level, and the vision of having the message torn from his hands by an overzealous G-man flashed through Harry's mind. "Thanks, Wally," he acknowledged, passing the elevator operator a dollar. "Hold the door for a minute, will you?"

He ripped open the note and scanned it hurriedly. Printed capital letters spelled out: *LOU'S. TONIGHT. IMPORTANT.* Thrusting it into his overcoat pocket, he nodded to Wally to open the doors.

Harry stepped from the elevator into a completely deserted lobby. Amazing! He wondered if it was possible that the FBI had finally given up. More likely, the defensive tackle who normally hung out here had gone to answer a call of nature. What luck!

Lou's, a little speakeasy favored by newspaper scribblers, was just a few blocks away. Tucking the ends of his wool scarf into his overcoat and pulling his hat down firmly on his head, Harry thought what a good suggestion the meeting place was. The November wind swirling through the canyons of Manhattan had pneumonia written all over it, and Harry did not wish to chance catching his death. He needed a little drop of something to fortify himself against the chill.

Halfway between streetlights, as he was pondering whom the note could possibly be from, he felt the familiar sensation of being followed. He turned abruptly, hoping to catch the FBI man unawares. One of Harry's few pleasures in life these days was embarrassing the agents by waving at them.

No one was in sight. At first he was surprised, then chagrined that he was so conditioned. "I am acting as guilty as the kid with his mitts in the cookie jar," he muttered, "and I haven't done anything!"

Ten more strides into the cold, damp wind and Harry turned a corner onto Broadway. There it was again, that prickle on the back of his neck. The newsman spun around, but nobody else was out on this raw night. "It appears that even G-men have the brains to be indoors," he observed. "In fact, I seem to be the only mug dumb enough to be out."

The path to Lou's speakeasy led him past an alleyway. He gave it no more than a glance until, out of the shadows, a voice called his name. "Harry Beadle," it rasped.

"Who's there?" Harry demanded. "Who's calling?"

The voice did not speak again. A tin can or something clattered somewhere deeper in the shadows. Who would have suggested that he go to Lou's, call him by name, and then be afraid to be seen? "

Max? Maxie! Is that you?" He advanced hesitantly into the alley. "It's okay, Max. Nobody has followed me tonight. Come on out, Maxie. Let me see you."

Nothing. Silence, except for the wind-stirred debris of the alleyway.

"Max?" Harry repeated, stepping in farther and peering into the gloom. "I give you my word of honor there's nobody but me. You can come—"

Something hit him from the side and threw him across the narrow passage. His head crashed into a brick wall. He stumbled over his own feet and fell down in a heap.

Hands yanked him around by the back of his overcoat. He tried to yell for help, but the attacker was twisting the scarf tighter and tighter around his neck. A foot between his shoulder blades kept him down as the hands went on twisting and tightening.

Harry strangled, and his eyes began to bulge.

A fraction of an inch before his scarf choked him into unconsciousness, the pressure let up. "Where did he go?" growled a cement-mixer voice.

"Who?" Harry managed to gasp. "Where'd who—?" His words ended in a gurgle, and his arms flailed wildly as the scarf knotted again.

"Don't crack wise with me," the rasping voice demanded. "Where is Max Meyer?"

"I don't know! I swear I don't! This ain't legal, you know. I already told Agent Burns." The stars exploding in front of Harry's eyes were not as bright as the light that suddenly came on in his head. "Hey," he choked, "you ain't with the Feds, are you?"

A gravelly chuckle. "If that makes any difference to what you knows, youse had better give me the straight skivvy. I ain't as easygoin' as the Feds." The knot began to crank down again.

"Hold it!" Harry pleaded. "I don't know—really. Maybe he went to some island someplace. You know, skipped the country."

The man with the sandpaper voice seemed to consider this for a moment. "Out of the country, eh? All right, scribbler, not a word of this to anyone; got it?"

Harry actually tried to nod in agreement, but the size-ten brogan that kicked him in the temple put an end to any movement for about an hour.

CHAPTER FIVE

Hope and Worry

Moonlight broke through the clouds, bathing the Tucker farm in a silvery sheen. Lamplight glowed golden from the small, square farmhouse—a cheerful sight to four approaching riders who were hours later than they'd expected to be. The great hickory tree in the yard had lost all its remaining leaves in the driving rain. Bare branches now reached up in stark silhouette against the sky, and the old tire swing creaked back and forth in the breeze.

Rubble from the barn looked as though a giant fist had slammed down on the roof. It was this sight that caused both the doctor and Pastor Adams to forget for a moment why they had ridden out with Birch Tucker on such a night.

"I heard it was a close one." Dr. Brown shook his head in amazement.

"I had not realized how very close," agreed Pastor Adams in his clipped British accent. London born and bred, the Methodist preacher had come to America five years before to serve as a circuit rider. "Every year one hears of such things, but one never expects it to be so close to one's own home. The first such devastation I have ever seen."

"You should see 'er in daylight, Reverend," Birch said.

"I shall write my mum about the way you braved the storm and saved the boys, Jefferson," said Pastor Adams. "I assure you, such a tale will be read with great fascination at teatime in Mayfair. And of course I will write about the bell being torn from the belfry of the church. Remarkable. Quite."

The pastor was a good man, but he still had not learned to speak proper Arkansas English. And folks could tell he was a foreigner even before he opened his mouth. A diminutive five-foot-five in height, he was not much taller than a schoolboy. Prematurely balding and ruddy-skinned, he looked a decade older than his thirty-three years. He dressed all in black, complete with a clerical collar, no matter what the occasion. He rode his circuit of five Methodist churches on a stocky bay mare with the tiniest little postage stamp of a saddle perched on her back.

"Twister ain't nothin' compare t'when a woman's time come to bear her young. Ain't that so, Doctor? We best git on up the lane or we gonna miss the main event." Jefferson nudged Old Bob to a slow, gentle lope through the water-filled ruts. The others followed, approaching the house like a troop of cavalry.

Pastor Adams volunteered to lead the animals to their makeshift pen while Birch, Jefferson, and the doctor stomped the wet and mud off their boots and burst into the parlor ready for action.

"Trudy?" Birch called quietly and rapped on the bedroom door. "I brought the doc."

The three boys, asleep on the mattress in the corner, raised sleepy heads to peer unhappily at the intruders.

"Dad?" Tommy croaked. "Where you been?"

"Go back to sleep. Where's your mother?"

Trudy opened the bedroom door. Her eyes were red-rimmed from tears and exhaustion. With sleeves rolled up and an apron tied over her coveralls, she looked as if she had been hard at work.

"I brought Doc—"

Soundlessly, Trudy stepped aside and let Dr. Brown pass into the bedroom. She looked past Birch and straight at Jefferson, who stood back, wringing his hat in his hands.

"Tried to hurry, Miz True . . ."

Birch plunged ahead with an explanation. "Missus Palmer had her baby tonight. I had to go fetch Doc there. Had to wait. Then his car wouldn't make it, what with the roads being so upturned. Had to borrow him a horse from Dan Palmer. Then we met Pastor Adams on the road." Birch jerked his thumb toward the front door, as though that explained everything.

"Quit your babbling, Birch Tucker." Trudy did not remove her eyes from the pained expression on Jefferson's face. "Can you not see that we have a man in agony here?" She reached out and took Jefferson's enormous hand, tugged the crushed hat free, and tossed it toward the hat rack.

"Yes'm, Miz True." Jeff looked near tears. "How's my Lily? I come back soon as I could. That ol' mule wouldn' go on over the creek. I jus' sat there a'waitin' an' a'prayin' 'til they come. Birch done brought the preacher so's I can marry that gal, an' . . ."

His voice trailed away as the healthy wail of an infant penetrated the thin wood of the door. "Oh," he breathed, as though he had heard a chorus of angels. "We wasn't late, then. Doc made it jus' in time."

"You were late all right, Jefferson." Trudy nudged Birch. "Lily did all the hard part." She smiled as she gave Jeff's hand a squeeze. "Jefferson Canfield, you have a beautiful baby girl."

Jeff staggered back, sinking onto a fragile-looking parlor chair. He raised his hands and head and cried, "Thank You, Jesus! Oh, Lord! A baby girl!" Then he stopped midpraise and looked curiously at Trudy. "You say it's a gal-baby? I figgered 'twas s'posed t'be a boy."

"Not at last check. A girl. Tiny and perfect." The wail continued as Dr. Brown checked the baby behind the closed door. "And outraged."

Jefferson shook his big head, spilling water drops on the floral rug. "I had me a dream, see? Jus' as clear as anythin', Miz Trudy. I seen that Lily's baby was a boy chil'. Heard the Lord say I got t'be that baby's pa."

Birch laughed. "Next time you'll have a boy. Or the time after, Jeff. First you ought to marry Lily and make it legal." At that moment, Pastor Adams knocked to be let in. "And here is just the man to set it right."

Birch opened the door to the dripping circuit rider, who took too long wiping his boots for Trudy's liking. "Better late than never, I say." Birch grinned broadly. "Although a wedding and fatherhood all in the same hour is cutting it a mite close. What do you think, Pastor?"

The reverend simply smiled and dripped and dallied on the porch as though he was afraid of getting Trudy's floor wet. "Well, well. I say, I say. It is quite a night, isn't it?"

"Come in." Trudy grasped his arm and pulled him firmly past the threshold, then closed the door hard against the cold night. "You are late, Pastor, but a welcome sight."

"The child is born, then?"

"Me an' Lily gots us a gal-baby, Preacher," Jeff replied.

Doc Brown's voice interrupted as the one wail divided into two distinct cries. "This one's a boy! A big, strong, strapping boy! Twins, by heaven! Well done, Miss Lily!"

✳ ✳ ✳

Trudy brushed Lily's tousled hair and tied it up with a blue ribbon. Tucked in the top drawer of the bureau was a white-cotton nightgown that Trudy's mother had sent all the way from Montreal for her thirtieth birthday. Tiny mother-of-pearl buttons glistened in the soft light as she held it up for Lily to see. Soft lace trimmed the high collar and the cuffs of the long puff sleeves.

Trudy had never worn it. She had saved it, still wrapped in soft pink tissue paper, for some special occasion with Birch. But tonight Lily had need of a wedding dress, and this would do nicely.

Lily touched the fine material with wonder. She admired the tiny stitches and cooed over the perfect pleats in the bodice. "Such a thing is too fine for the likes of me," she declared. She could not take such a fine thing from Miz True after all that had been done for her.

"Stuff and nonsense," Trudy replied firmly, helping Lily with the little buttons and plumping the pillows behind her back. The crowning touch was provided by a pale blue silk shawl draped over the shoulders of the bride. Only then did Trudy hold the round hand mirror for Lily to see her own reflection.

Lily put her hand to her mouth in wonder. "Is it me, Miz True?" she questioned softly. Turning her shining eyes to Trudy, "Ain't nobody never treat me so good. Ain't nobody ever—"

"You are beautiful, Lily, and that is the plain truth of it. You make a beautiful bride. Jefferson will make a fine husband to you and a father to your babies."

At that, Trudy opened the door wide to reveal the waiting groom dressed in Birch's brown-tweed jacket. The cuffs of his shirt protruded three inches from the too-short sleeves of the coat. He wore a yellow bow tie, also new, which the boys had given to Birch last Christmas. His black hair was heavily pomaded, parted in the middle, and slicked back. He stood beyond the threshold, self-consciously tugging at his left sleeve and fiddling with the bow tie. The doctor, the preacher, and Birch, who would be best man, stood behind him.

"Why, Jefferson," Trudy said in a kind voice, "was there ever a more handsome bridegroom than you are tonight?"

The big man smiled gently, revealing teeth that were jagged and broken from a decade of hard toil and abuse in the prisons of Oklahoma. His muscled arms strained the material of his jacket.

Trudy remembered how those arms had held the limp body of Latisha, his first bride, on that terrible night with the Ku Klux Klan. How his gentle eyes had wept for his bride. Who could have imagined this moment or dreamed then that someday Jeff Canfield would find happiness again?

"Only the Lord . . ." Jefferson whispered the answer to Trudy's unspoken question as his gaze rested on Lily. He turned to the sleeping babies tucked snugly into bureau drawers that served as cradles. A smile of wonderment cracked his scarred face. Years of hardship and grief fell away from him. He straightened his shoulders and lifted his head proudly.

For an instant Trudy glimpsed the brave young soldier returning from the battlefields of France on a train so long ago.

"You be beautiful, Lily," Jefferson said softly. "Never seen nobody so beautiful as you. . . . If I had a bunch of flowers, I'd give 'em t'you, gal." He spoke these tender words as if no one but Lily could hear him.

Lily inclined her head as though he had anointed her with oil. "You done brung me flowers, Jeff." She placed her hand on the flower-garden quilt. "A whole field of flowers t'cover me, t'lay me down in. Don't need no more t'make me happy. Jus' needs my Jefferson, is all."

The holy silence that filled the room knit the souls of two lonely people in a moment.

"Weeping may endure for a night," recited Reverend Adams after a time, *"but joy cometh in the morning."* He patted Jefferson on the back and nudged him forward to Lily's bedside. He opened his small, well-worn Bible and continued in a confident voice, "Dearly beloved, we are gathered here in the sight of God. . . ."

✳ ✳ ✳

And so it was that Jefferson Canfield was repaid in an hour for ten long-lost years. In one night he became the father of two babies and the husband of the young widow Lily Jones.

A baby in each arm, he sat at Lily's bedside as Dr. Brown filled out two birth certificates.

"Full name of mother?"

"Lily Hope Canfield," Lily whispered, letting her fingertips rest gently on Jefferson's arm.

"Age?"

"Figger I be nineteen year or so."

The doctor did not seem surprised by the vagueness of her reply. "Date of your birth, Lily?"

"Don't rightly know. Can't rightly say. My mama tell me the lilies of the field was bloomin' the day I come."

The doctor held his pen above the document as he considered this information. "Well, that would be spring of 1910 as I reckon it. Let's see. And the lilies in bloom, you say?"

"So I been told."

"April or May, then. Which do you like?"

"April come first."

"Well now, Lily—" he wrote down the date—"if anyone asks from here on out, you were born April 30, 1910. The day the lilies bloomed brightest."

Lily repeated the date wistfully. "April 30, 1910. Yessir. I will remember that."

"Good." Now he turned his attention to Jefferson. "Full name of the father?"

Mindful that the babies had been fathered by William Jones, who now lay buried in a shallow grave in the woods near Shiloh, Jefferson hesitated. Whose name should rightfully be on such a paper?

Lily answered for him. "His whole name be Thomas Jefferson Canfield. Go on and write it down. Named for a pres'dent, he is."

"Well now." The doctor smiled slightly as he filled in the blanks. "Age? Date of birth?"

To this Jefferson spoke right up. "I'm twenty-nine. Born July 22, 1900, in Mount Pisgah, Arkansas. My pappy is named Hock Canfield and my mama Willa-Mae." There was not space for all of that on the form, but Jefferson wanted to say it anyway. This was a proud moment. He wished his mama were here to see it. He wished old Hock were here to shake his hand and take him out on the back porch to have a serious talk about what it means when a man becomes a father. He wished he could stand up in the pulpit of the old Mount Pisgah Church and tell the folks what the Lord had done for him on this night. Like Joseph in the Bible, he had been redeemed from prison and given a family!

But he could not speak openly of such miracles. Instead, he contented himself with holding these babies and feasting his tired heart on the sound of Lily's voice. "Lord Almighty! I am fit t'bust!" he finished. "If only my mama could see this! Ain't no one man ever had such blessin', I reckon. Not all in one heap like this."

"And now important decisions to be made," the doctor continued. "Names."

"Names?"

"For the babies. They can't go through life being called Boy and Girl. Have you thought of names?"

Lily knit her brow in consternation. How could she admit that she had never expected any child she brought into this hard old world to live long enough to have a name recorded on a paper and registered at the Sebastian County Courthouse? "I ain't give it much thought." She looked to Jefferson for help. "Jefferson? You name your son."

Still mindful that the husband of Lily had been called William Jones, Jefferson looked down into the wrinkled face of the boy and knew what was right. "His name is William Jones Canfield."

"That was quick," said Dr. Brown. "A strong name."

"Oh, Jeff." Lily squeezed his arm. "You be a fine, good man." She blinked back tears. "William would be right proud. Right pleased by what you done."

"Now, Lily—" Jefferson shifted in his seat—"you name our little girl. Ain't she perty? Looks jus' like you, Lily. Never seen such a perty little gal. An' I know somethin' 'bout gal-babies, too. I had a whole cabin full of baby sisters when I was growin' up. Always laughin' an' singin' like a nest of songbirds, they was. I always wanted gal-babies around my own place. My mama used to say that sons is raised to go away, but daughters almost always stay." His words fell silent as the baby sucked her fist and he remembered his little sisters.

At this, Lily ran her hand over the quilt and explained, "Jefferson's been tryin' t'locate his mama. Sent a letter hopin' somebody know where she be. But so far we ain't got no word back."

There was much in this story that remained unspoken—much that could never be explained. How had Jefferson lost touch with his family? Where had he been for ten years? The good physician asked no more than required, just focused on the task at hand: the naming of the baby girl.

"Jeff's mama made this here quilt, which Jeff give me when we come to our understandin'. Her name Willa-Mae. We gonna call this young'un after Jefferson's mama. Gonna call her Willa-Mae Canfield."

✳ ✳ ✳

Jefferson's mama, Willa-Mae Canfield, hardly noticed when the streetcar clacked to a stop at the end of North Howard Street.

"North Howard you said, Mammy?" the driver asked in a bored-sounding voice.

Willa-Mae simply nodded and stepped off the car and into the dark, not saying that she did not like being called Mammy by this Irishman. No matter. The streetcar moaned away to roam the nearly empty streets of Akron until the 3 AM shift change at the factories. Then the driver would have plenty of gummers coming and going to Firestone and Goodyear. No doubt they would all have plenty to talk about in spite of the late hour. Worries most often looked more worrisome late at night.

North Howard Street seemed unchanged since Willa-Mae left last week. Little old houses and apartments above storefronts all seemed to be sleeping peacefully. No sign of the disaster that this great crash had brought upon Akron. And Mr. Weldon.

Most all the streetlamps were lit, making puddles of light on the cracked sidewalks. A few decrepit automobiles were parked along the curb. Not many folks on North Howard Street had automobiles, but there were some who had earned their money at the factories and others who had made a bundle on bootleg gin and gambling.

"Bad apples," Willa-Mae called that sort. They lured the menfolk into sin with loose women and took their paychecks and stole the food right out of the mouths of their babies. Such goings-on were common in the neighborhood and much worse down in the shanties under the North Hill Viaduct.

With a sigh that extended all the way from North Howard Street to the troubled mansions of Portage Path, Willa-Mae hefted her valise and her luggage and ducked through the shabby doorway.

The steam radiator hissed and rattled in the corner of the one-room flat. Curled up together like two spoons, Frank and Jim Penn slept on the mattress and waited for their mama to come home. Soft light shone through the ragged tear in the window shade. Just enough moonlight seeped in that the bare room was not entirely dark.

The sound of coughing emanated from the flat above. Little Jim removed his thumb from his mouth just long enough to cough a reply. His thin body convulsed as the hacking seized him until it seemed he could not find a breath. Frank sat upright and patted his brother on the back until Jim finally relaxed and shuddered, put his thumb in his mouth, and fell instantly to sleep.

The cough was nothing to worry about, Mama had told Frank. Just a stubborn cold, she said. After all, she had the same thing, didn't she? Everybody caught it back in Coal Town, and it never hurt anybody. It was in the air, like coal dust and soot from the factories.

It seemed that Frank was the only one who never caught a cold, never felt sick. Only hungry sometimes. Mama told him that maybe God was making it up to him because he had been born with his foot turned in. Frank had often thought that, given the choice, he would just as soon hack all night like Mama and Jim.

Footsteps sounded in the hallway outside the door. Frank sat up, careful not to pull the blanket off his little brother. "Mama?" he whispered. "S'that you, Mama?" The footsteps kept on going past, but Frank waited, hoping his mama might have just missed the door like she did sometimes when she had been drinking.

But it wasn't her. Probably just the old colored lady, Mrs. Canfield, coming home. Frank listened to the heavy tread on the stairs as the old woman climbed to her apartment on the third floor. She had wonderful big feet that flapped on the floor when she walked. Frank admired her feet and the way her toes pushed against the leather of her old shoes like they wanted to break the seams right out. He had watched those big feet from a distance when they walked past in the morning and in the night, but he had never spoken to Mrs. Canfield because of what his mama had said.

A few moments passed; then the boy turned his eyes upward to the cracking plaster of the ceiling. His ceiling was the floor of the old woman's apartment. Frank could hear her open the door and close it again. The timbers above him creaked and groaned as she walked. Muffled voices penetrated through the plaster, and words seeped down to make him feel better somehow. As if they were the voices of his family. As if somebody big had come home to take care of him and his brother. Like when he and Jim used to stay overnight at Grandma and Grandpa's house before they passed on and Grandpa would come in from checking things in the barn.

"Willa-Mae! Where you been, gal? You come later than I thought. Been worried 'bout you!" This was the crackly voice of the spindly little man named Hock. He began to cough.

"I missed y'all somethin' terrible, Hock Canfield." Willa-Mae's voice was stronger and louder than that of Hock. "My, that cough ain't got no better, I see."

"It's nothin'. Just got me all excited t'see you is all."

Frank liked to hear Hock and Willa-Mae talk. Their accents were like the folks in Coal Town. Everybody in Coal Town, black or white, sounded like the Canfields. Back home, before Frank's daddy died in the mine, all their neighbors said "how-do" and "y'all." Frank had been homesick for such talk since Mama brought them here to Akron so she could get a good job and earn enough to pay to have his foot made straight like other kids.

Mama told Frank that the Canfields were beneath them. But on nights when he was lonely, Frank was real glad that the Canfields were above them so he could hear them talk through the ceiling.

"I waited down t'the depot . . . ," Willa-Mae was saying. "Mister Weldon didn't come. . . . Heard all 'bout the tragedy when I was a'ridin' home on the streetcar."

Usually Willa-Mae Canfield sounded happy when she talked. Hardly ever was there a time when Frank did not think she was singing out a story when she was just telling about what she'd done and what she'd cooked and what Mr. and Miz Weldon were up to. But tonight she sounded different. Maybe just tired, Frank thought. His mama sounded that way most all the time now that they had come to Akron. When he asked her if she was feeling all right, she said she was just tired. The cold made her tired, she said.

The ceiling squeaked loudly as big feet moved from one side of the room to the other, then stopped right over where the mattress lay. Right over Frank's head. Sometimes he wished the boards would break and all those people up there would fall through and fill this empty room and stay awhile. Maybe that was what it meant to "drop in." Only he didn't want big Willa-Mae Canfield to land on him.

He put a hand protectively over Jim. "She'd squash us like a bug," he whispered.

Little Jim paid no mind to his brother's warning. His thumb was still plugged into his half-open mouth. This thumb sucking was going to ruin Jim's mouth. Everybody back home had said so. Grandma had said so. Mama had said so before she stopped caring about it.

Frank scowled at his baby brother, then hooked his finger around Jim's wrist and tugged the thumb out of his mouth. There now. Frank figured he was supposed to do such things, since their mama had asked him to look after Jim.

It made no difference. As soon as Frank turned his eyes upward again, Jim whined in his sleep and stirred. In went the thumb for half a dozen frantic slurps before he relaxed.

"Willa-Mae . . ." Hock sounded worried. Frank knew all about the sound of worry. Since his daddy died, Mama sounded worried all the time.

Willa-Mae answered him. "I thought those Wall Street folks up in New York City was jus' gone crazy. Now . . . and my poor Mister Weldon, poor Miz Evelyn! Don't know what that woman gonna do. She ain't no more than a chil' in her mind! Helpless-like. Mister Weldon tell her what t'do. He tell her ever'thing. I takes care of the shoppin' and the cookin'. Katie takes care of the cleanin'."

"Folks say y'all ain't goin' there no more. Say you an' Katie best start lookin' for someplace else t'work. They say Mister Weldon done lost most ever'thing. He can't keep no maid like Katie, no hired cook like you. They say he ain't gonna have no food to cook. No house t'clean. What we gonna do if'n that the way it is, Willa-Mae? How we gonna get along what with Nettie in school and Harry t'raise since his mama and papa died?"

"I ain't leavin' Mister Weldon an' Miz Evelyn in the hour of need. No sir, I ain't. Not 'til they tells me I ain't welcome no more."

"But Willa-Mae—" A long, hard cough interrupted.

"You quit frettin' 'bout me, Hock Canfield. 'Pears t'me we best worry 'bout you gettin' over that cough, or you ain't gonna have no job down t'the Titan plant. You get inta bed. I'll fix a poultice."

Now this was the Willa-Mae Frank liked to hear. She was telling the old man what to do. Telling him she would fix a poultice and everything would be all right.

Frank smiled and snuggled closer to his brother as he listened to the clank of pans and the creak of her big feet on the floorboards. This was what he liked best of all. It made him feel better when Willa-Mae said that no matter what happened, everything would work out fine.

Frank liked to pretend that she was saying these things to him and to Jim. Nobody ever said such things to the brothers in real life. So it was good to make believe that Willa-Mae Canfield was telling him he would be all right. Jim would be all right. Willa-Mae would fix a poultice for Jim, and he wouldn't cough anymore.

The boy sighed and closed his eyes. No matter what his mama said about Willa-Mae being an old nigger lady and beneath them, Frank was secretly glad that the old woman was above them . . . just a thin floor away.

☆ ☆ ☆

As tired as she was, Willa-Mae could not sleep. She lay beside Hock and listened to the deep rattle of his labored breathing. In the front room, Harry was snoring. She could hear the restless tossing of Nettie, who slept behind the curtain in the alcove.

Hock, Harry, Nettie . . . this small, shabby space was home to Willa-Mae because those three were here. She concerned herself with their daily troubles. She worried about Hock's cough and Nettie's schoolwork and Harry's going out with girls now with all the temptations there were these days. But the little flat on Howard Street did not—could not—hold all the children Willa-Mae loved and prayed for tonight.

All were grown and gone now except for Nettie and Harry. Most had young'uns of their own to work for and worry about. That fact did not diminish Willa-Mae's concerns about them.

Hock wheezed and coughed beside her. He was awake tonight as well.

"You okay, old man?" she asked.

"Hmmm. Jus' thinkin' 'bout all the chillens."

"Me too."

"Thinkin' 'bout how when they was all little an' we crammed all of 'em inta our little cabin down yonder in Pisgah."

"I was thinkin' 'bout that, too."

"I used t'wonder what it'd be like when they was all growed an' on their own. What it'd be like when I didn't have t'worry no more 'bout how we was gonna feed 'em an' put clothes on 'em. How we was gonna get 'em schoolin' an' keep 'em healthy . . . all them such things."

Willa-Mae chuckled. "I figgered when we got 'em 'long that far, you and me wouldn't have no more worries, Hock Canfield. I kept askin' myself when things was gonna get easy."

"Hmmm. That's what I was a'thinkin', too. We didn't know much, did we, old woman?"

"Not much." Another low chuckle. "Them was the easy times. In them days we worried 'bout what we gonna feed . . . but there was always food. Worried about what they was gonna wear, but they was always dressed. When they was little we kept 'em fed. Kept 'em warm in the winter and fanned in the summer. Loved 'em and saw to it they knew 'bout the Lord and what was right and wrong. Got 'em t'school and taught 'em how t'work."

"That was all the easy stuff," Hock agreed and rolled over to wrap his spindly arm around Willa-Mae's broad girth.

"I thought I'd stop worryin' when they all growed up. But we jus' changed them small worries for big'uns is all." She stroked his head. "Now they mostly got their own famblies. Hard times comin' for all of 'em, Hock. And here we is, layin' awake in the middle of the night frettin' 'bout all of 'em. Jobs. Young'uns. This mean, sinful world. It seem harder t'me now 'cause we can't take care of 'em no more. I lay here and wonder what's t'come of 'em. Tell you, Hock, it *was* easier when we was back there with all of 'em crammed inta that little cabin and alls we had was corn bread and buttermilk t'feed 'em on."

"We done the bes' we could for all our babies, Willa-Mae," Hock whispered. "There jus' come a time when we gots t'know the Lord is their daddy and their mama even more than we is. Gonna have t'be the Lord who help 'em get through whatever is a'comin'. They gonna have t'lean on Him for understandin'. Ask Him for daily bread. Guess He loves 'em most as much as we does, old woman."

"He loves 'em more, the Good Book say, though I don't rightly see how He's got so much love."

"But He do."

"Knowin' that makes the worry less."

"Makes it tolerable, anyhow."

"But now . . . what we gonna do for all of 'em, Hock? Trouble's comin'—I feel it deep in my bones. And I ain't scared for me or you, 'cause we done had our turn at livin'. But our young'uns?"

"Guess we got t'let 'em know troubles come an' go, but life don't end," Hock answered as visions of a thousand sorrows mingled with images of good times before them both. "Aside from that, most important thing we old folks can do is pray. We can't fight their battles, but we can pray for ever' one of 'em by name. Mebbe that's most important, Willa-Mae. Mebbe we is old now. Can't feed 'em no more nor put clothes on their backs, but we can pray. Then the Lord gonna answer even when they don't know how t'do what they got t'do t'get on with livin'."

Willa-Mae felt better after they talked. She closed her eyes and held on to Hock as the two of them prayed aloud, naming children and grandchildren alike. So many souls. So many troubles. And as always, they ended their prayer with the name of the son they had not seen or heard from in ten long years.

"Don't know if our boy be dead or alive, Lord, but I reckon You know all that. If he's livin', Lord, let him know You're near. Bless his soul, sweet Jesus. Stand beside our Jefferson. . . ."

✳ ✳ ✳

For a long time Jeff lay beside Lily's bed. He held her hand and stared into the darkness.

Like old man Job in the Good Book, his troubles seemed to have vanished at last. And yet he was still a wanted man. Still on the run. All it would take was for one man to suspect that Jefferson was the escaped convict they called Cannibal. One telephone call back to the Oklahoma prison and Sheriff Ring would be here with his shackles and his dogs to take Jefferson back to prison. Birch's cousin J.D. Froelich had threatened to call the lawman with his suspicion about Jefferson. Now J.D. was dead, but this country was full of men just as mean and ugly inside as J.D.

The folks around Shiloh and Hartford all took the word of Birch that Jefferson had worked for him for ten years. But what if someone happened by who had seen Jeff fight in the prison matches? Someone might look at his broken teeth and battered features and say, *"I know you, Cannibal! I seen you whip that nigger from the Missouri chain gang last year."*

The possibility was troubling. It kept Jefferson awake. After all, now he had more to worry about than just himself.

He squeezed Lily's hand and listened to the babies' soft breathing. "You give me blessin's, Lord, but a heap of worry, too. Got me a woman and two young'uns t'love and care for. But I got the law after me. Got no land of my own t'work so's I can keep food on my table. Got not table, no roof t'put over their heads . . . not even beds t'sleep in." He squeezed his eyes shut and conjured up the image of his childhood cabin in Mount Pisgah. The rough-hewn logs. The bare plank floor. Wooden boxes for storage in the rafters. His cot beside the stone fireplace. His mama at the cookstove and his daddy milking the little Jersey cow.

"And the smell of cotton growin' in the field," he whispered. "It weren't much, but it was ever'thing, Lord. I don't need much. Won't ask for much, except now I got me a reason to live again—Lily and these here babies. See, Lord? I don't want t'always be lookin' over my shoulder. Always hearin' dogs an' chains an' goin' cold inside for fear they comin' t'take me from my fambly."

He listened to the quiet breathing of Lily, and he loved her with his whole soul, even though he had never slept with her, never lost himself in passion with her the way a man does with a woman. It was a holy love, he knew. It made him want to do right for her. At the same time, it made him scared that he could not do enough.

He figured this was something like what Joseph must have felt about Mary after she had her baby boy in a stable. "You wasn't Joseph's chil', Lord, but what a powerful load You done put on that man's shoulders."

Jefferson sighed. "Jesus, sir, I need help myself now. World always been a hard place, always gonna be. Yessir, Lord. Lovin' Lily an' these babies mean a whole lot more than what I feels about 'em. I got lots t'do t'make love somethin' real. A place to live. Food in their bellies. Clothes to wear. Schoolin'. Church on Sunday. Tuck 'em in at night . . . You got t'help me love 'em right, Lord. I'm askin', please, sir, for Your help."

CHAPTER SIX

One Pumpkin Missing

Ellis knew from the huskiness in Becky's voice that his phone call from People's Hospital had awakened his wife from a deep sleep. Young John Daugherty was hanging on, he told her, but there was a long night ahead for the boy and his family. Ellis would not be home until morning.

"Oh, Ellis," she replied. "I am so glad you were there for him. Who better than you?"

He replied that he wished it had been anyone but him. Then she reminded him of the day his father had been called to cut Pat Hicks out of the threshing machine back on the farm. She was right to remind him of Doc. It helped prepare him for the long hours ahead. Tonight Ellis wished that his pop was around to talk to. Doc always seemed to have the answers before Ellis even knew what questions to ask. Beyond the numbing tragedy of the day, the strongest emotion Ellis felt was the ache of missing his pop.

As if in sympathy for the lost arm of young John Daugherty, the phantom pains in his leg awakened as he walked down the quiet hospital corridor to face the mother of his patient.

Ellis gathered his courage as he took in the scene on the other side of the glass-paneled door. The waiting room was painted a sterile pale green. Wooden chairs lined the walls. A square coffee table in the center was littered with half-filled ashtrays, magazines, and newspapers with headlines still displaying the grim banners of the Wall Street disaster and subheads proclaiming the chaos it would bring to the rubber factories of Akron.

None of that meant anything now to the plump, middle-aged woman who sat next to Jack Daugherty in an otherwise empty room. The headlines could have proclaimed that all of New York City had fallen into the Atlantic Ocean. What would that have mattered when her child's life was threatened?

Ellis could tell at once that the two were brother and sister. Like the shift foreman, Gladys Daughterty was squarely built, and her mouth was set in the same grim line. Pale blue eyes stared unseeing at the heap of magazines. Her light brown hair was peppered with gray and done up in a bun on her head. She had not taken off her frayed tan coat, although she had been waiting for hours in this room for news of her son. She had waited long enough. Ellis drew in his breath and opened the door.

Jack and his sister looked up sharply in unison. They stood, and a rosary clattered to the floor at the feet of the woman. For an instant their faces betrayed the fact that they had been expecting the worst. At the sight of the professionally reassuring smile Ellis fixed on his face, their fear melted into relief, and the woman dissolved into tears.

"Oh, Doctor . . . my Johnny! My Johnny . . . will he live, then?" The unmistakable Irish brogue reminded Ellis of his own mother and father.

"He's a fine, strong boy," Ellis soothed, unconsciously taking on a touch of the soft lilt he had grown up hearing. "A fine, strong boy. He has had a rough time of it, but he'll pull through all right, Missus Daugherty."

"I am no missus, Doctor Warne," she corrected. "My Johnny and I are alone. I without a husband. Him without a father. Except for my brother, Jack, here, he is all I have in the wide world, sir." She clung to Ellis's hand as to a lifeline. "I do not know what would have become of me had I lost my boy! Oh, thank you, sir! I thank you with all my heart! I will have a word with Father O'Malley and have a Mass read on your behalf."

Ellis did not tell her that he was in need of more than a Mass—that he needed a miracle, a thunderbolt from heaven to deliver him from the pit he had dug for himself and fallen into. No, tonight he was the doctor. Self-assured and professionally compassionate, he spoke in comforting tones about how life would go on for John even with the loss of his arm.

As they lingered over stale cups of coffee in the hospital cafeteria, Ellis even lifted the cuff of his trouser leg and gave his prosthesis a solid knock as proof that a man's future did not end with the loss of a limb. Very well done.

Gladys nodded solemnly and thanked God for the blessing that it was only an arm lost, not her boy's life.

Very convincing, Dr. Warne, Ellis told himself. Yet all the time, he was feeling just as false and hollow as his bum leg.

Then the subject turned from hope to more practical matters. Jack Daugherty shifted uneasily in his chair and caressed his cup of cold coffee thoughtfully. "Johnny was only a part-time gummer," he began hesitantly. "High school in the day. Worked at the plant three nights a week. His medical bills, Doctor Warne . . . you know the policy on part-timers."

Yes. Ellis knew it well. Titan Tire would not be bothered with them. Whatever pay the boy had coming would no doubt be used to cover the cost of calling the ambulance. All the rest would be the responsibility of this mother, who had spent a lifetime on her knees scrubbing floors to raise her fatherless son.

Ellis managed to shrug as though payment of medical bills were of little consequence to him. "In a day or so I will have him moved to the public ward." This was a kind name for *charity ward*. "My practice at Titan is a part-time position. Three nights a week." He did not add that he earned more in three days as a swing-shift doctor at Titan than he did in three weeks of private practice. "Here is the address of my clinic." He fumbled for his card and slid it across the table to rest beneath Gladys's fingers.

She picked it up and stared at it a long moment, her eyes filling with tears. "'Twas no accident you were on duty tonight, sir. And you with your leg and all. To give a mother hope. You will give my Johnny hope as well," she murmured. "No, it is not by chance that a man such as yourself was there for my boy."

Ellis did not reply that he wished it would have been any other doctor but him. He did not speak the truth that his own future looked anything but hopeful tonight. He simply nodded in acknowledgment. "I often take special cases. Like your Johnny." By this he meant that most of his patients could not pay him. "I will do what I can for your son, ma'am."

"I cannot pay you much. But if you would care for my boy—ah, you would have the thanks of a mother's heart! A mother's gratitude, sir! God bless you, sir! God bless you!"

Ellis could not help but wish that God would bless him with patients who paid medical bills with something more than gratitude. Perhaps then he would not be working eighteen hours straight and cutting young men out of Titan's machines. Saving the life of someone else's child—he who had been unable to save his own son.

But what was the use of thinking such thoughts? What was the use of wishing things could be different? Nothing had turned out as Ellis and Becky had planned. They had not been blessed like Gladys Daugherty with a living son. No. There had been no happy ending at the Warne home. For them, hope and joy had vanished in a night.

* * *

Halloween had come and gone this year as only one black day in the dark week when America stumbled and fell into a financial abyss. Now, just a short streetcar ride away from Akron's Howard Street slums, Titan Tire and Rubber Company, and People's Hospital, the middle-class suburb of Kenmore was still decked out for a holiday that had never come.

In the soft light of dawn, Ellis walked stiffly from the streetcar toward his home and clinic at 1064 Florida Avenue. Everything looked exactly as it had a few days ago, with pumpkins carved and neatly arranged in family groups on the front steps of nearly every house. Yet everything was different now. In less than a week, everything had changed.

On the porch of the Benjamin family, the big orange faces of Mama and Papa Benjamin beamed down on the grinning round heads of their five sons. A long, green cigar stuck out from between the spaces of Papa Benjamin's teeth—the same kind of stogie that the real Mr. Benjamin smoked one after another in his office at National Bank.

A second cigar had been divided up and placed between the lips of his pumpkin sons—the largest piece in the mouth of the oldest, and so on down the line until Gordon, the youngest, had only a tiny stub. By this it was easy to tell which pumpkin head was which. The pumpkin head of Mama Benjamin seemed unperturbed by the fact that her youngest child was chewing a cigar like his papa. (Everyone knew that the real Mrs. Benjamin would have walloped her sons good if she had ever caught them smoking their father's cigars.)

It had been the intention that the cigars would be lit on the night of Halloween. But after Mr. Benjamin came home from the bank and told his family that everything had been lost in one day, the plan was forgotten, and the carved heads remained dark and gloomy on the stoop.

Next door, six orange Fitzgerald heads perched on the porch rail: Father and Mother Fitzgerald, two femininely carved pumpkins with dimples like the girls, and two identical boy pumpkins carved just like the twins—down to the missing front teeth.

The candles inside the Fitzgerald pumpkins had also remained unlit on the appropriate night. Mr. Fitzgerald, who sold insurance policies, had invested heavily in the stock market. He had gambled and lost and spent what pocket change he had left at a speakeasy on Furnace Street. He had been brought home by an off-duty policeman two days ago and had not been outside since.

And so it was all along Florida Avenue, where Ellis walked. Pumpkins up one side and down the other—all except for the empty front step of Old Maid Ruptke and her grouchy mother, who everyone said lacked any sense of humor whatsoever. (The Benjamin boys had added that the two women were so ugly that there wasn't a pumpkin in all of Ohio that could do their faces justice.)

This morning, of course, so soon after the crash, all the world had lost its sense of humor. To Ellis, the cheerless step of the old women seemed much more appropriate than the comically decorated porches of their neighbors.

But one other pumpkin was missing from the block this year. It should have been here at this house—on the Warne porch. Ellis let his gaze linger on the three jack-o'-lanterns his little family had carved last week. On the top step sat Papa Ellis Warne in his natty straw hat. Mama Becky was crowned with a crumpled Easter bonnet. Between them both was little Ellie, whom everyone called Boots. Smiling sweetly, her carved eyes looked coyly up and away from the cigar-chewing Benjamin brood.

But her baby brother, Howard, was not beside her. After only one year of four pumpkins on the porch, now there were just three again.

"We are still here, folks," the images seemed to say. *"Picking up the pieces. Still smiling. Still right here at home on Florida Avenue. Here to stay."*

The Warne jack-o'-lanterns were too cheerful. Painful to look at for those neighbors who remembered that a family of four had perched there last October. Ellis knew that children had been warned not to mention it—not to say one word to Boots about her little brother.

Everyone had been quite careful of the Warne family. When Becky walked down the street to catch the streetcar, neighbors waved to her and chatted with her about the weather and the roses and the latest news about gangsters and bootleggers and such—ordinary conversation, as though Becky's life were no different from before. Yet after she had passed by, they leaned on their rakes to stare after her and shake their heads in a sort of fearful awe. How did she manage?

Her shoulders were always back, her head held high. Always there was a slight smile on her lips. Becky carried her grief with dignity that defied all reason. Everyone on Florida Avenue knew what little Howie had meant to her.

She appeared to handle the baby's loss much better than Ellis did. He discussed this only with himself, but it seemed to be so. His arms always seemed empty now that there was no baby Howie to lift up. He hid the sorrow in his eyes behind a false smile. His hellos, how-are-yous, and I-am-fines did not ring quite as true as Becky's.

Ellis told his heart it was because he had been with the baby when he died. Here he was—a doctor—but helpless to stop the deadly progression of the meningitis in the little boy he loved. Ellis had known it was hopeless from the start, and knowing it had somehow made his heart more bitter with every passing hour of the ordeal. Who could ever be the same after something like that?

And Boots? Well, for a six-year-old, she was handling the loss quite well. Accompanied by her shaggy white mutt, Snowball, she wheeled her baby dolls around the block in a little wicker pram, just as she had pushed her baby brother in his carriage last year. But she did not stop to talk to the neighbor ladies much anymore. She had no little brother to show off now. After all, a doll was only a doll. No voice. No smile. No little hand to close around her finger.

People often asked her, "How is your mother? How is your father? And how are you?" Implicit in these simple words was the unspoken question that Boots understood all too well: *"How are you all making out since the baby died?"*

Could anyone answer a question like that? Ellis wondered.

"Fine. We're fine. Did you see the pumpkins on the step? We're fine. Fine. Fine. Fine. I am going to be a princess at the party. Mom made my princess dress. My crown has real glass rubies. Mom is fine."

If the truth had been spoken aloud by pretty Boots Warne, it would have sounded different:

"Sometimes I hear Mom crying through the door of the bathroom. She turns the water on so Pop and I won't hear. Sometimes Pop sits with the paper and stares and stares and then pretends he's thinking 'bout something else, but I can tell he's thinking 'bout Howie. And me? Sometimes I sneak into the nursery and stand just where the crib used to be. I close my eyes and pretend he's still there, and then I open my eyes and the place is empty. So empty . . ."

These were not the sort of things that one discussed with curious neighbors, however. Ellis had made it a point to tell his daughter, "No use in making anyone else feel bad about what cannot be changed. So, chin up. That's it! Shoulders back. Eyes straight ahead. Sometimes there is nothing else to do but march ahead like a soldier. . . . Now give me a hug. Here's my hankie. Blow. Yes. You try very hard to be brave for your mother, and so shall I."

And Ellis had pretended to be brave for Becky. He had not burdened her with the details of the financial difficulties at the clinic. He had bought her a new car on credit, then taken a job moonlighting at the Titan Tire Company Medical Dispensary three nights a week to pay for it. When Mr. Fitzgerald spoke to him about the great fortunes to be made in the stock market, Ellis had mortgaged the house and put every spare cent into RCA and Anaconda Copper. At last he thought he could see a way to get out of debt!

Now everything was lost, and Ellis had not burdened Becky with the terrible news of his stupidity. Even now she was fixing breakfast, waiting for him to come home after a long and terrible night. He knew she would be listening to the radio news, which proclaimed that the stock market was only correcting itself. That things were really fine. That the disaster was not really a disaster.

Maybe for J.P. Morgan the crash was only a minor adjustment. But for Ellis, every hope seemed to have fallen over the brink of a yawning chasm. Like the rest of Akron, he had taken the news of the crash in stunned silence. He had ridden home from the Titan plant on a streetcar filled with grim, pale faces. He had come into the house, and Becky had thrown her arms around his neck and said, "Oh, Ellis! Thank God you were not so foolish to put our money into Wall Street! I have just heard that the Fitzgeralds have lost all their savings! Mrs. Fitzgerald is at the end of her rope! All those children to feed! Whatever shall they do?"

As the hours had passed, a hundred similar stories poured in. Some of their friends said that the tire factories would close within months. Others predicted that Akron would be a ghost town in less than a year. After all, if America could no longer afford to buy cars, then what need would there be to make tires? And again, Becky had praised him that he had not been so foolish as to purchase an automobile on credit. After all, the Smiths had lost their automobile. The three Smith children had been told at school that they would soon be in the poorhouse and had come home in tears. How fortunate Becky was—she said—that her husband had not been a fool!

This morning as Ellis passed, the grinning pumpkins on Florida Avenue seemed to mock his every dream. They alone knew that he had been just as empty-headed as any jack-o'-lantern in all of Akron. Now the bank owned a mortgage on his house, and Titan Tire Company owned his very soul. Without the extra work and the steady paycheck from the factory clinic, Becky and little Boots would wake up one day and find that they were much worse off than anyone else on the block. Without that job, they would wind up paupers on the street.

This morning the world looked normal. The smell of frying bacon filled the air. In the sunshine, the big yellow stop sign on the corner looked like a giant lollipop. Old Lady Ruptke swept the dust from her front walk and waved to Ellis as he passed by. Nothing at all had changed . . . and everything had changed. Real fear settled on his shoulders until he felt as if he carried the weight of a mountain on his back. And no matter what happened, he knew he must carry the burden alone.

He entered the little frame house quietly, thinking that Boots might still be sleeping upstairs. He stood a moment in the dim light of the front room and listened for the sounds of Becky at work in the kitchen.

Silence. No smell of coffee or bacon frying. Becky had overslept, and

Ellis was relieved that he would not have to talk to her right now. He was too tired to put on his brave face. Too tired to tell her that the grief she saw in his eyes was simply weariness from a long night. Too tired to lie convincingly. If he had to look her straight in the eyes across the breakfast table right now, no doubt she would see through his charade and pin him down until the truth tumbled out of him.

The clock ticked loudly on the shelf of the hutch in the dining room. It was almost five-thirty. He had already made his early morning hospital rounds. His clinic did not open until ten o'clock. That meant he could have almost four hours of sleep if he went straight to bed. The thought of sleep sent a cold shudder of relief through him. Until this instant, he had not realized how tired he was. The stairs reared up before him. He gripped the banister and pulled himself up past the smiling family photographs that lined the wall like little windows looking out on a distant and pleasant world. Or were those smiling faces looking in at him, witnessing his fear and failure?

One photograph featured all his brothers in baseball caps, bats and gloves and baseballs in hand. Ellis paused to stare at the image and at his own pale black-and-white face among the others. So young. So whole. Untouched by war. Full of hope. Unconcerned about the future. Back then there was only the joy of the present. He had never imagined what the future held for him. . . .

The war. The loss of brothers and friends. The loss of his leg. The joy he had found in Becky's love had made every loss seem unimportant . . . until the loss of their son.

When the baby died, something had died inside Becky. Yes, she still smiled and talked and kept on living, but she held Ellis at arm's length. She looked at him but did not really see him. She kissed him without desire, held him without passion. He had told himself for months that she only needed time to heal. But when he reached for her in the night, she pretended to be sleeping, or she stiffened at his touch and turned to face the wall. Even worse were the times when she gave herself to him out of a sense of duty and resignation. Did she think he did not know, that he could not tell she was just pretending?

Later, when they lay together in the dark—he alone with his thoughts and she alone with hers—loneliness overwhelmed him. As it did now, as he stared at those smiling faces on the wall.

It was good that back then he had not been able to see into this bleak moment. If he had, he would not have taken even one halting step toward his future. He would have happily sighed once and died on the battlefields of France. He would have been buried with his shattered leg, and his heart at least would have been whole. Not like now. Fragments of yesterday, pieces of dreams, tattered remnants of hope smiled back at him from those pictures on the wall.

More was missing from the life of Ellis Warne than his leg.

"Ellis?" Becky's voice whispered down from the landing.

Her presence startled him. He glanced up at her, and only at that moment did he realize he had been crying. He wiped his cheeks and leaned heavily against the banister as though his leg was bothering him. "I didn't mean to wake you, Beck," he said hoarsely, grateful for the shadows and the dimness on the stairway.

"You didn't. I was awake. I thought I heard you come in, but when you didn't come up . . ."

"Sorry," he said, although he did not know what he was sorry about.

"The boy?"

"He'll live." Ellis did not look at her face. He did not want her to read his thoughts or guess at his loneliness. Instead he let his glance sweep over the white-cotton nightgown and her bare feet on the top step. Such small, perfect feet.

"His family?"

"They'll live through this, too. Although it is never easy."

She did not reply to this because they both knew that yes, people did live through tragedy. And no, it was never easy.

"You can catch a few hours' sleep."

"Yes." He wanted to ask her to come back to bed with him, but he did not. Instead he looked again at the baseball-team photo and took the last few steps slowly, brushing past her without offering an embrace.

"Or would you rather I fix breakfast first? Are you hungry?"

He smelled the faint aroma of lilac on her skin. Her red hair was tousled from sleep. She swept a curl back from her brow and tossed her head. He looked everywhere but into her eyes. Yes, he was hungry, but not for food. "No thanks. I showered at the hospital. I'll just sleep awhile. Is Boots all right?"

"She got an A in spelling yesterday. Brought the paper home to show you." False cheerfulness stiffened her voice.

"Send her up to give me a kiss before she leaves for school, will you?" Ellis limped to the door of their bedroom and stood looking at the empty bed. The blankets on Becky's side of the bed were mussed, while his side was smooth and unrumpled. She had not reached out for him in the night. She had slept unmoving, not caring, and he knew it.

"You sure you don't want to just sleep? She can see you after school."

"No!" Ellis snapped, startled by his own harshness. "I want to see her! Don't you understand? I don't want another entire day to get by without her seeing me!"

"Fine," Becky replied coldly to his rebuke as she swept down the stairs past the gallery of wood-framed onlookers who had once been living witnesses to their happiness.

Ellis put a hand to his head in instant remorse. But there was no calling his sharpness back. No calling Becky back to the top of the stairs to tell her that he loved her and needed her to look at him today—needed her to see him, to hold him and kiss away the leaden weight that pressed on his soul. No calling Becky back. No calling back the past, the better days . . .

He stripped and fell into bed, contenting himself to sleep on her side, to lay his head on her pillow and drink in the sweet scent of her perfume.

CHAPTER SEVEN

A Place to Call Home

There was a fat, juicy orange beside each place at the breakfast table this morning. In addition to these treats, Willa-Mae had brought handkerchiefs from New York embroidered with an *H* for Hock, another *H* for Harry, and an *N* for Nettie.

"The red hen died while you were gone, Mama," Nettie said as she poured milk over her cornflakes. "I know how fond of that red hen you were. Papa said he didn't know what got into her. I went out to feed her on Wednesday, and she was dead."

Little Nettie, who was eighteen and no longer little, told the tale in practiced English. She had long since shed the stigma of her Arkansas accent. No longer did she drop her *g*s or put an *s* on the end of a word where it did not belong. She had gone to high school and graduated last June with honors. Now she attended Akron University on an endowment and worked part-time at O'Neil's as an elevator operator.

Tall and slender, Nettie moved with an athlete's grace. She walked and talked and ate with the manners of one who had sat apart from the crowd and watched until she learned just what was proper and what was not. To Willa-Mae, Nettie seemed sometimes to have grown into a white girl in dark skin. Yet for all of that, Nettie was not above tending Willa-Mae's ten chickens in the coop behind the Howard Street apartment building.

It was only seven o'clock in the morning, and Willa-Mae was already dressed for work. She had decided last night that she would go to the Weldons' just as she had six days out of every week for the last nine years. It was not her place to act as if she had heard bad news. Not her place to question the story that had been given out. If Miz Evelyn said that Mr. Weldon had cut his throat by accident, then that was the way Willa-Mae would play it. All the same, she found it difficult to talk to Nettie and Harry and Hock about family things this morning—about Big Hattie and her stage name and her singing career in Harlem, about the babies and Philbert, and now about the chicken.

Willa-Mae cracked eggs into the skillet as Harry staggered out in his nightshirt and sat down at the plain wooden table. Just like always.

"Hi, Gramma." He rubbed his hands over a face that never failed to remind Willa-Mae of her son, Jefferson. At seventeen, the boy was as big as Jeff had been at that age. Harry, like Nettie, talked with the untainted accent of a child born and raised in Ohio, but something about the resonance of his voice conjured up memories of Jeff. Sometimes Willa-Mae caught herself looking twice at him, drawing her breath in sharply as though she were seeing the son she had lost so many years before.

This was one of those times. Her spoon poised above the skillet, she stared at him for a long moment as he stretched in the chair and popped the knuckles of his big hands, then reached out to snatch a biscuit off Hock's plate.

"Willa-Mae!" Hock growled. "Feed this chil'! He like to steal ever'thing on my plate whilst you been gone! I'll waste away t'nothin' if he don't get fed proper."

At Hock's protest, Harry gulped the biscuit in one bite and laughed at the disgusted look on Nettie's face.

So much like Jefferson. . . . Willa-Mae could not scold him. She and Hock had taken Harry in after the boy's mama and papa died within a year of each other in 1920. Eight years old he had been. It had seemed to Willa-Mae as though the Lord had given her back her boy to raise some place where life was not so hard.

Akron. A tiny cold-water flat on Howard Street. Electric lights. Three rooms. A gas stove. Icebox. No matter that Harry had to carry the ice up three floors two times a week. This was a good place to live.

Once Willa-Mae got over missing the farm, she had decided she never wanted to go back to the old way of life. It was not so easy for Hock, but he had come to accept the city. Ten chickens in the coop out back and a ten-by-twenty-foot plot of garden made his life nearly complete.

Life in Akron had been nearly perfect. Never a thought of fear. No worries about too much rain or not enough rain for the cotton. No trouble with the straw boss or The Man. Life was plain and simple. Would all that change now? Willa-Mae wondered.

Nettie and Harry bantered playfully across the table, and Hock carefully poured gravy over his three remaining biscuits. The skillet hissed and popped. Eggs and bacon sizzled. There was enough for two grown men, but Harry would eat most of it by himself. He made a joke about how these eggs were the last ones that red hen ever laid and how he would eat them with respect. Nettie talked about school and work, and this led to how glum the faces seemed around town these days.

But no one mentioned Mr. Weldon. No one brought up the most obvious question: Would Willa-Mae still have a job after this morning? She made one dollar a day since Mr. Weldon had raised her pay last year. That was six dollars a week, twenty-four dollars a month—six dollars more than Hock, whose pay as a grounds-maintenance man at the Titan Tire and Rubber Company totaled only eighteen dollars a month. Of course, there was Nettie's part-time job, but that only provided enough money for an occasional movie after the cost of her clothes and school-books was figured in.

This morning the little family spoke of nearly everything but what they were really thinking about. There was Willa-Mae, fixing breakfast as usual. Nettie eating cornflakes as usual to keep her figure. Hock talking about hunting hogs back in Arkansas—how there never was ham or bacon flavored like that from an Arkansas razorback. Nettie and Harry listened but were not overnice about Hock's nostalgic memories of those hog days in Pisgah. Hard times—that's what those good old days were. Back-breaking, heartbreaking *hard times*!

As Willa-Mae left the little flat and hurried to catch the streetcar, she wondered if maybe Hock had brought those days up to remind her that no matter what happened this morning, they had all made it through hard times before. If they had to, they could make it through hard times again.

The Tucker household was awake and breakfast had been eaten when Mary Brown rode up the lane.

"Hello, boys!" she called from atop her tall bay. Bobby and Tommy returned her greeting with curiosity. They had not met the daughter of Dr. Brown before, and even though they had heard that a nurse was coming, Mary Brown did not look like a nurse. They each responded as they had been taught: "Good mornin', ma'am." And then, casting wondering looks over their shoulders, they raced toward the barn, leaping over mud puddles with only partial success.

Suppressing the urge to shout after her sons about splashing, Trudy wiped her hands on her apron and smiled. "You are Miss Mary Brown."

Mary looked nothing like her father. She was quite pretty, Trudy thought, wondering what Mary's mother must have looked like to produce a daughter so different in every way from her father. Her hair was blond and bobbed short according to the fashion. Her skin was as fair as Dr. Brown's skin was swarthy. Her eyes reflected the clear blue sky of the morning. Dressed in a navy blue, cable-knit sweater and a midcalf riding skirt, she sat her tall mount with accustomed ease. She returned Trudy's smile, looking as young as a schoolgirl instead of her actual age of twenty-three.

"And you are Birch's wife, Missus Tucker. Papa said you were pretty and much better than Birch deserved." This she said loudly and with a laugh as she spotted Birch and Jefferson on the other side of the shattered barn. "Hey, Birch!" she called to him with a familiarity that belied the fact that she had not seen him since before the war.

"Hey, Mary!" He raised his head and tossed away a broken plank. "Is that you?"

"It's me."

"Last I saw Mary, she was a skinny little . . . you've grown up, Mary. Look good!"

"You look old, Birch!" she replied. To Trudy she said, "When I was a child—oh, my, didn't every gal in these parts just die for Birch Tucker? Well, you've got him, Missus Tucker," she said with a laugh.

Trudy liked her instantly. "Call me Trudy."

"Call me Mary." She swung from the saddle.

"We have something in common. You loved him first, but I loved him longer."

"He was the meanest thing . . . called me Corncob 'cause I was as tough as him and I could lick any kid up through the seventh grade."

"Hey, Corncob!" Birch called as an afterthought, as though the memory had bubbled up in him and just popped out of his mouth.

"See what I mean? You're welcome to him. I was glad to see that one go." The cheerfulness of her face was so unlike her father's serious countenance that Trudy could not help but be surprised.

"I have a pot of coffee on to take off the chill, if you like. Tie your horse there." Trudy indicated the rusted iron ring set deep into the old hickory tree.

"Papa would have made me bring the automobile, but the roads—"

"Terrible that you had to ride horseback."

"Oh no. I love it. Love the quiet of it. So much better than the dreadful noise and smell of these automobiles. Any excuse to get on a horse, Papa says. I was adrift in the big city. I used to go out and talk to the dray horse that pulled the milk wagon, and then they sold him and got a Ford. It was a sad day for me."

Trudy did not admit that she loved the city—clanging trolleys, rattling Model Ts, electric lights, paved streets, neighbors close enough to say good morning to from the porch. "Well, Mary, come on in. Lily and the babies are doing beautifully."

Mary followed Trudy into the house and gasped happily. "Oh! Papa said you've put everything back right! Made it just as pretty as when Clara lived here!" She touched the new green sofa and let her fingers glide along the oak table. "What a gloomy, terrible place this was for years. Just for years! I stopped by once—by accident, when my horse threw a shoe. Wretched. That Sam Tucker! Smelled like the inside of a whiskey still all the time." She caught herself with that, remembering that this was Birch's father she was speaking ill of. "Well . . . I mean . . . you know. . . ."

"Yes, we know."

"Well, someday Birch will have to get you electricity out here. Papa and I do have electricity. I allow myself the luxury of listening to the radio from time to time. I don't suppose when I go to China I will be able to have a radio." Before Trudy had a chance to respond, Mary leaped ahead. "Papa says you delivered the baby girl. All alone. Bravo. Fine, fine."

"I did not have a choice."

"Babies do that sometimes." Mary whirled around. "Are they sleeping? Shall we let them sleep awhile, then? Coffee, you said. Let me wash my hands first."

Mary Brown had barely dried her hands when the lane and the yard were filled with the sounds of horses and men and dogs. Trudy watched from the window as Birch walked up to meet a group of two dozen men.

Jefferson continued his work, sorting out salvageable lumber. He did not raise his head or seem to notice.

"A search party," Trudy said.

Mary joined Trudy at the window.

"All looking for J.D., I expect," Trudy continued. "A different bunch than went out with Birch yesterday. I do not recognize these men."

"J.D.'s friends." Mary turned away in disgust. "Not the sort you want to know. Most of them will use this as an excuse for getting rip-roaring drunk. Stagger back after eight hours with empty hands, empty hip flasks, and empty heads. Not that they are starting with full heads, mind you." Mary reached for the coffeepot on the stove and poured herself a cup. "Take a look. They're Kluxers, most of them. J.D. was one of those cross burners. Bet you didn't know that, did you?"

"I could have guessed as much."

"I recognized him by his horse one night. Riding around in his bedsheets with Bob White and Harry Farmer. Drunk as skunks. I saw them coming, and I said to J.D., 'Hey, J.D., how's Maybelle? Is she feeling better?'" Mary laughed. "He was flapping around in his sheets. Supposed to be incognito, but the fool said, 'Fine, thank you kindly.' They had been out to Frog Town to pester some sharecropper out that way."

"He had some words with Jefferson over Lily."

"The meanest, most ignorant bunch in the county. He made some remarks to me as well. My great-granddaddy was John Brown—you know, the abolitionist. I've always been proud of it. But to someone like J.D., the fact that I am related to an abolitionist is like my being descended from the devil himself. They're all like that. They don't think much of the fact that your ancestors crossed the Red Sea on foot, either, from what I hear." She made a face. "Don't look at them too long, Trudy. They'll show up in your nightmares, honey. . . . J.D. is one less to worry about, if you ask me. Wherever he is, may he stay there and amen."

Birch was talking quietly to the leader of the group. Trudy caught bits of the conversation as her husband gestured at the rubble of the barn and shook his head. No, he would not be going out to cover the same ground in search of J.D. this morning. He and Jefferson had been out twice. Followed the path of the twister for eight miles and left no stone unturned. Jefferson's wife just delivered twins last night, and there was plenty to do around the place.

A young bull of a man, dressed in a broad-brimmed hat and a tan canvas jacket, peered at Mary's horse and then rode right up to the front steps of the house.

"Hey, Mary! Mary Brown! You in there, Mary? Come on out an' say howdy!"

At the sound of his voice, Mary jumped up from the table. "Oh, drat that man! I can't get away from him no matter where . . ." She opened the window and hissed, "Will you shut up, Buck Hooper!"

"How-do, Mary!" Buck beamed and touched the brim of his hat, absolutely undaunted by her harsh words and the scowl on her face.

"I am here on a call—official business—and I'll thank you to keep your bellow down, you insufferable ox!"

Now others in the party smiled and greeted her as if she had remarked on how fine it was to see them all and asked them in for tea. "How-do, Mary . . . Mornin' to ya, Mary . . . How's your pa, Mary? . . ." and so on.

"We have a woman in a delicate state here, and you are all baying like a pack of hounds. Kindly shut your traps."

"You goin' to the dance on Saturday night, Mary?" asked Buck pleasantly.

"Not with you, Buck Hooper. Not if you were the last man in Shiloh." She closed the window, cutting off his still-hopeful reply, and said to

Trudy, "The clod! He shows up everywhere I go. You would think he was quintuplets the way he's everywhere!"

Now, this was something. It seemed the men of Shiloh were used to Mary Brown's giving them a piece of her mind. "Well, he seems like a nice-enough fellow," Trudy offered.

"They'll expect Birch to ride out with them." Mary sat down and warmed her hands around the cup. "Don't let him go. They'll get him drunk."

Is she joking? Trudy wondered. "Birch would never—"

"Well then, they'll get him mad, and that's almost as dangerous as drunk around here. They dearly love to make folks angry. The best way to handle them is to give them a belly laugh, I say. To get mad at those Kluxers is a good way to get lynched. Anyway, let them go look for their dear old J.D." She smiled. "I personally think that the Lord got sick of that scoundrel and blew him to the four winds. Anyway, we can hope. And as for that wife of his . . . well . . ."

Mary said all this with such openness that Trudy turned to look at her with astonished admiration. She was saying everything that Trudy wanted to say but did not dare. "I like you, Mary Brown," Trudy said. "I certainly hope you never get angry with me, though."

Mary laughed. "I guess I'm not known for holding my peace, but don't worry. I'm leaving. Going to China next spring, where I will have to learn to preach against the Chinese Kluxers, if there are such beasts, in an entirely new language. There are some in Sebastian County who do not believe I will make the transition gracefully. I understand that they do not burn crosses there—only an occasional missionary. But growing up here has prepared me to meet opposition. Out of the frying pan, as they say . . ."

"Into the fire," Trudy muttered, watching with concern as several men leaned their heads together and then turned in unison to stare at Jefferson. "Why are they looking at Jeff?" Her question was barely audible.

"Because he's there. That's all the reason they need to hate. It's like asking a mountain climber why he climbs a mountain. Because it's there. Ask these fellas why they hate a colored man, and that will be their answer. Because he's here. They think every Negro ought to be in Chicago or Africa or someplace far away. Actually, extinct would be better yet. Now your Jefferson and Lily have added two more black babies to the population of the county—*and* they are right here under your roof. Well, you have made some social blunders according to Kluxer etiquette, Trudy Tucker, and you have done so fearlessly. I love it. Papa came home this morning quite pleased that Birch had married you. I approve as well. I can tell we are going to be good friends, you and I."

If Mary Brown said it, Trudy was quite certain she meant it. "I do not doubt you." Trudy smiled, turning away from the window and pouring her own coffee.

The two women talked and laughed like old friends for nearly forty-five minutes after the Kluxers rode off into the hills. By the end of the conversation, they knew each other well. It was a fine beginning.

By that time, Lily had awakened, so Trudy and Mary went in to check on mother and babies. Mary cooed and fussed happily as she examined them. She said she had never seen such healthy and beautiful children.

Lily frowned, bit her lip in consternation, and asked the question that had been on her mind for months. "You mean my babies gonna live, Miz Mary?"

"Live! Why, little William will be president of a university one day! See what a sober, serious little fellow he is? A scholar if I ever saw one. Little Willa-Mae will sing. . . ." The baby girl was squalling through this prophecy. "Just listen to that. What lungs! What a voice! Oh, honey. Sweet little Willa. You will sing in an opera in St. Louis, I bet!"

"Ain't no colored babies gonna grow up to do such things, Miz Mary. But I don't mind. Long as they gonna live."

"That they will, Lily, and much more besides. You'll see!"

"What I see is that you is just like when I lights a candle in the dark. You gots a gift from the Lord, Miz Mary." Lily blushed and laughed. "Makes folks t'b'lieve near ever'thing that come outta your mouth! Makes folks feel sorta happy-like inside."

It seemed to Trudy that spending a few hours with Mary was more than lighting a single candle. Her presence was like pulling open all the window shades in a dark house. Light flooded in. The view of distant mountains became clear. Dark-hearted and evil men became almost laughable in their foolishness. Darkness fled in the face of such brightness. Good things seemed very near, and all things seemed possible. Lily was right. Mary had a gift that she gave freely to others.

More than anything, Trudy thought as she watched her new friend ride away, Mary made Shiloh feel like a place to call home. It had been a long time since Trudy had felt that way about a friend. Between breakfast and noon the whole world had changed.

Jefferson had felt the presence of evil as the search party milled about the Tucker yard. He had breathed a sigh of relief as they rode out, but now he worked in troubled silence at Birch's side.

"I got me a fambly of my own now t'care for." Jefferson spoke at last.

He lifted a board and threw it onto the discard pile as Birch pried bent nails from the usable lumber.

"That you do, Jefferson."

"I don't intend to live here off your hospitality for long."

"This ain't exactly what I call hospitality, Jeff. We ain't exactly sittin' in our rockers on the front porch, now are we?"

"Well now, Birch, I been givin' it some thought. What with the season as it is and all. And that field jus' about cleared altogether. There ain't gonna be much work for me to do."

"Not unless you count rebuildin' the barn and breakin' that colt I'm gettin' from Brother Williams. Huh! Not much!"

Jefferson pried up a broken board and tossed it away. "I was thinkin' I might go on over t'Greenwood. See if'n I could get work in the coal mines."

"You're too big, Jeff. And too black. First of all, those minin' bosses don't like sending men down with shoulders so big they'll get stuck crossways in a tunnel. Second, even with a lamp the only part of you they'd see would be the whites of your eyes." Birch laughed, but Jefferson knew his friend was not really joking. "You know that's bad country for a black man these days. The brush is thick with Kluxers on a Saturday night, I'm told."

"Then the railroad. Guess I can lay track good as any man. Better'n most. Big shoulders worth somethin' t'the boss over there. I could work awhile. Earn enough. Take Lily and the babies somewheres t'live so's y'all won't have no worries 'bout the law showin' up here on the front step an' arrestin' you an' Miz True for helpin' a convict."

"Jefferson, if you've got a desire to be a railroad man, then you're welcome to give it a try. Those gandy dancers out layin' track on the Rock Island would probably be glad to see a man your size and strength come along. That's your right. But if you're worried about me and True—"

"Them walls is mighty thin. I wasn't listenin' intentional, but them walls is thin, and there wasn't a thing I could do about it. . . . I hear what Doc Brown say—'bout how mebbe there are folks round these parts be lookin' at me and wond'rin'. You gots your own fambly. Those chillens. Wouldn't be right if me bein' here among y'all brought trouble on your kin."

"The walls *are* thin." Birch smiled regretfully. "But nothin' Doctor John Brown said will go outside them. Your secret is safe, Jefferson. As safe with us as anywhere. We got to get your teeth fixed, though. And until we build you a proper place of your own to live, I was thinkin' . . . "

Birch straightened his back and looked over the field to where the woods sloped to a rise on the other side of the James Fork. "See there?

Look yonder." He pointed. A small log structure was just visible through the trees. The roof was partially rotted away, but the thick log walls were strong and undamaged by time or the elements.

Jefferson raised his head and followed Birch's gaze. "The cabin."

"It's all that's standin' of my granddaddy Sinnickson's place. It was the first thing he built here when he came back from the war. Good, solid log cabin. Later he built my grandmother a fine house after the eastern style. White clapboard and green shutters and a big porch for sittin' on in the summer evenings. It truly was a fine place. . . ."

Birch smiled as if he could see it still. "The big house burned down the year he passed on, but that cabin is still there. The roof needs attention. Well, I reckon the truth is that it needs a new roof entirely. But the chimney is good, solid stone. It'll be here 'til Jesus comes. Between the two of us, we could have it fit for habitation in a week or so. Until we can get you and Lily some place better, y'all are welcome to it."

Birch pressed his lips together as if there was more that he wanted to say. He shrugged in an embarrassed way. "True and I need your help makin' this place go again. Trudy would dearly hate to say good-bye to Lily and the babies, and I really need an extra hand. That is . . . I'm askin' you . . . don't go join the railroad."

"Growed up in a cabin somethin' like that," Jefferson mused. "Been dreamin' on havin' just that sort of cabin for myself an' Lily an' our young'uns. Didn't know that was your place."

"Ten acres on the other side of the James Fork belongs to this farm," Birch explained. "My pa just let it go to seed—like he let everything go, I reckon. It's of no use as it is, but if y'all think it's worth the work to scratch out a living . . . Trudy and I were talkin' about it . . . well, it's yours." Birch gave his head a shake. "'Course, if you'd rather work on the railroad or scoot around in one of those coal mines like a mole . . ."

Jefferson was dumbfounded. "No sir. I had my eye on that cabin. I surely did. Yessir. We can make it shine, you an' me. By the time my Lily is up, we'll have it a place to live—right nice. My daddy lived as a sharecropper an' his daddy before him. Ever'one before that belonged t'The Man—Mr. Bundy Howard. I reckon I can sharecrop jus' like they done."

"No sir, Jefferson." Birch stood up and scowled. "No more sharecroppin' for you. We mean for y'all to *have* that land, you and Lily. We mean for it to be your own piece. It ain't a gift. We ain't offerin' ya'll charity, now. No, not that. We'll have a contract. You can work it off. The land, the cabin. Those two old mules you're so fond of. Seed and a plow and . . . whatever. I need your help here, like I said, and if it's agreeable to you to get paid in land—"

"Agreeable?" Jefferson blinked at Birch in disbelief. To raise his young'uns on a piece of land they could call their own? "Ten acres, you say? A man could grow two bales a year on ten acres. Why, a man could . . . and a garden. Plenty enough . . . and hogs . . ."

"Right. We'll have the deed drawn up." Birch grinned broadly at Jefferson's expression. "That is, unless you'd rather go on over to Greenwood and work in the mines?"

CHAPTER EIGHT

Trouble's on the Way

"He didn't know nothin'!" Boss Quinn's henchman reported of his encounter with Harry Beadle. "If he had the tune, he woulda sung, Boss. I'm positive about that."

Boss Quinn soberly regarded the man called Smiley across the desktop in his office on the *China Doll*. "It was partly a misjudgment on my part," Quinn admitted in a rare display of humility. "One cannot treat the Wall Street mob as one would pay back them that has heisted a beer truck. So I'm thinking of contacting a business associate in Chicago. Perhaps he will send someone to assist us who will not be known to any of the parties or to the Feds. What is more," Quinn added, rubbing his hand over his bullet-shaped head, "I am told that this new boy is not such a mug and will therefore be able to move amongst the citizens of Peoria without a wholesale raising of eyebrows."

"But, Boss—," Smiley objected.

"No *buts*," replied Quinn. "You are not in a position to give me no lip in this regard."

Smiley nervously fingered the purplish scar on his throat—the gruesome source of his nickname. "But, Boss," he said again, failing to heed the storm warning as rising color darkened Quinn's face, "youse got no call to bring in outside muscle, see? I can handle this business without no help. I know I can. Gimme another chance."

Boss Quinn's hands pushed down hard on the flat surface of the desktop as if to prevent the furniture from jumping up to strike Smiley. "It is clear to me that your ears are not in communication with your mouth. Kindly do not interrupt whilst I explain the situation one last time."

Now Quinn picked up his meaty hands and began numbering points on his stubby fingers. "First, you did not scrag the kid, Mice, in his hospital room, which mistake has left me in jeopardy with the Feds.

"Two," he continued, as a tick in his left eyelid began to blink at Smiley, "you failed to intercept the kid's dad, one Max Meyer, even though we now know that he was on Wall Street in the company of the Swedes' gigantic black dog, right under your nose."

The tick became more pronounced, and the puckered scar on Smiley's neck seemed to gesture back as he gave several agitated swallows.

"Three, as a result of these two mistakes, Meyer and the kid have taken it on the lam, causing me additional expense and worry. What is more, what with Ham and Sal being detected packing rods in Grand Central Terminal, they are at present of no use to me, being housed in the slammer!"

Flecks of foam appeared at the corners of Boss Quinn's mouth, and Smiley backed up until he bumped into the mahogany wall of the cabin. "Okay, Boss, okay," Smiley rasped in a placating tone. "Youse is right, like always. I just want to make it up to youse, see?"

Quinn settled back into the leather chair, from which he had halfway risen in his anger. "Smiley," Quinn said in a calmer tone, "this is much better. Now give me your attention whilst I explain the plan."

"Yes, Boss, whatever youse says."

Quinn waggled a warning finger at his henchman. "Do not presume further on my easygoing disposition," he cautioned. "It is important for our future business relationship that you do well in locating the missing Meyers. Now, here is where you should begin. . . ."

Quinn tapped a stubby finger on the photograph of Joseph and Sadie Meyer. "Since my city hall mugs tell me that Mister Max Meyer has also played fast and loose with the Feds, I am of the opinion that he would think skipping the country might be wise. Therefore, I want that you should start right there." He made a pistol shape with his fingers, with which he shot Joseph Meyer through the heart. "Montreal, Canada."

"One moment and I'll connect you," the tinny, faraway voice of the long-distance operator said in Max's ear.

Max drummed his fingers impatiently on the oak paneling of the telephone cubicle and thought again of David, alone in the room upstairs. Codfish stretched the leash around the corner of the booth inside the lobby of the Goldman Hotel. The dog was giving a good imitation of his namesake at the end of a fishing line, pulling first one way and then the other. Every change of direction yanked Max's drumming fingers away from the wooden wall. He struggled to stay balanced and keep the receiver pressed to his ear.

"*New York Times* newsroom," he heard at last. "May I help you?"

"Harry Beadle," Max demanded.

"Whom shall I say is calling?"

"Ma—Mike," Max caught himself. "Tell him Mike Stock is calling."

"Yes, Mister Stock. And may I tell him what this is regarding?"

"Just get him!" Max exploded. Then he apologized. "I'm in a hurry," he explained.

"Certainly," said the secretary in a frosty tone. "I'll see if Mister Beadle is available."

Across the black-and-white-tiled floor, Max could see the day clerk pulling out a large silver pocket watch. The man adjusted a pair of round spectacles on his thin nose and studied the time, then snapped the cover of the watch closed as he eyed Codfish with distaste. Max had said that he and the dog would be in the lobby only long enough for a phone call. Five minutes at most.

"Harry Beadle," said a weary-sounding voice. "I do not know any Mike Stock. What is this about?"

"Harry!"

"Maxie? Is that you?" Harry's excited greeting dropped to a hoarse whisper. "Where are you?"

"Harry," Max said, "I only have a minute. I am at the end of the earth, okay? I only called to apologize for tricking you. There were FBI men following you, right?"

"Maxie," Harry whispered urgently, "you got big trouble. You gotta get to the nearest FBI office as quick as you can!"

"Can't do that," Max argued. "You know they'll take David away from me."

"Max, you should hope they take the both of you somewhere with high walls and mean dogs."

Max glanced down at Codfish, who was suspiciously interested in the corner of someone's steamer trunk. "What's up, Harry? Give it to me quick."

"Okay, try this: Boss Quinn is not happy with you over the little matter of two of his boys getting pinched in Grand Central. Furthermore, I wish to state that even knowing you can cause a citizen great difficulty."

"You, Harry? Have Quinn's goons been after you?"

There was a wince of pain in Beadle's voice as the reporter continued. "I have an eighty-caliber goose egg behind my ear, courtesy of someone wishing to meet you in a dark alley."

The day clerk was now drumming his fingers on the counter and staring pointedly at Max. Even though the lobby was deserted this early in the morning, the man was obviously worried about what damage the huge black dog would do to the establishment's reputation. "Harry, I gotta go. I—I'm real sorry. I need to ask for one more favor, anyway. I've mailed copies of my résumé from every whistle-stop between New York and—"

"Between New York and where, Maxie?"

"I can't tell you that, Harry. But listen, will you? I gave my return address care of that rathole in New York that you call your apartment. Hang on to the replies. I'll get back to you."

"Maxie," Harry urged one last time, "run—do not walk—to the nearest branch of the Feds. For the kid's sake at least."

"Gotta go, Harry," Max concluded, dragging Codfish away from a nearby potted palm. "Good-bye."

The Weldon home was an imposing, steep-gabled Tudor structure of red brick and half timbers. Enclosed by a high iron fence and set among tall old trees, in summertime it was not visible from the street. This time of year, however, the house showed clearly through the bare branches, and this morning it looked particularly forlorn. Through the bars of the fence, Willa-Mae could see that the grounds had not been raked. The yard, the walk, and the broad driveway were all covered with a soggy carpet of leaves, as though no one had walked in or out of the house since Willa-Mae had left to visit Hattie.

Drawn curtains presented a blank front to the world—not unusual for eight in the morning in this neighborhood, but somehow permanent-looking, as though Evelyn Weldon had closed those curtains for good this time. Four rolled newspapers lay unretrieved on the front step. Soot from factories and coal fires clung to the stucco and tarnished the bricks, giving the house a deserted appearance.

Had the house looked so gloomy before she went away? Willa-Mae wondered. Or was it just that she knew everything had changed for the people who lived inside? And if life had changed for Mr. and Mrs. Weldon, what would that mean to Willa-Mae and Hock and the young'uns?

Set back from the main house was a Tudor-style, six-car garage that Mr. Weldon called the carriage house. In that building he kept his six favorite automobiles, including the first Packard he had ever owned. He had no chauffeur, preferring to drive himself and his wife everywhere in his big black touring car.

Miz Evelyn did not know how to drive an automobile. Without her husband close at hand, those six Packards were of no use to her. Willa-Mae had marveled at the times when Miz Evelyn would call for a taxi just to take her shopping.

It was obvious that the cars had not been driven in a while. Fallen leaves lay in drifts before the closed doors of the garage. Further proof that something terrible had happened to poor Mr. Weldon.

"Lord, Lord," Willa-Mae uttered softly as she trudged up the long drive and around the side of the house to the back door. "Oh my, my," she said in dismay as she spotted the full glass milk bottles from yesterday's delivery still on the step. The milk had frozen in the night, and the paper caps had popped off the containers.

Where had Katie, the maid, gone in all of this? No doubt the temporary cook had bailed out at the first sign of trouble, but Katie had been with the Weldons almost as long as Willa-Mae. Would Katie just pack up and skedaddle, leaving the beds unmade and the milk on the back porch? Who would tend the coal furnace for Miz Evelyn if Katie was not here to do it twice a day? Who would make the beds and do the washing and the ironing or push the carpet sweeper and dust the dark, heavy antique furniture?

Poor, helpless Miz Evelyn hardly knew how to draw her own bathwater. She just talked on the telephone all day and went to ladies' bridge club and did her charity work—bazaars and auctions and fancy luncheons. What would such a woman know about being poor? She would not know what to do with herself without money.

Willa-Mae shuddered and inserted her key in the lock. The door swung inward to the white-tiled hallway that led to Willa-Mae's kitchen domain.

She hung her coat and hat on the rack, then paused to listen for some sign of life. The distant grumble of the furnace indicated that not everything was neglected. At least the house was warm.

"Katie?" she called to the maid's quarters, knowing that Katie would surely be up and about her work if she was still here.

There was no reply. Willa-Mae knocked lightly on the door to Katie's tiny room, opened it a crack, waited, and switched on the light. The bed was stripped. Drawers hung open. The closet was empty except for wire hangers on the rod. A faded cross shape on the wallpaper marked the place where Katie's crucifix had hung for years.

Willa-Mae surveyed the deserted cubicle and gave her head a shake. Perhaps finding poor Mr. Weldon in a pool of his own blood had been too much for Katie to take. She always was emotional underneath that stolid Irish exterior. So, she was gone.

Who had stoked the furnace? Willa-Mae made her way to her kitchen. Entering the gleaming chrome-and-white-tile space, she was amazed to see Miz Evelyn, dressed in evening clothes, slumped at the kitchen table. A fat, clear whiskey bottle was in one hand and a half-empty glass in the other.

"Oh my, my!" Willa-Mae cried at the sight. "Miz Evelyn! What you done?"

Miz Evelyn moaned and stirred slightly, then raised her head to gaze groggily around her. "So . . . you're back."

"Yes, ma'am." Willa-Mae hurried to fill the teakettle and light the stove. "Miz Evelyn, ain't you even been to bed?"

"Don't you know what's happened?"

"Where is Katie, Miz Evelyn? How come you ain't in bed this hour in the mornin' like usual?"

"Katie left." Evelyn Weldon ran a hand through her gray-streaked brown hair. "Or rather, I discharged her last night."

"What you sayin', Miz Evelyn?" Willa-Mae took tea from the container and sugar from the bowl while she waited for the water to boil. "Katie gots nowhere else to go. No matter how hard bad times is, she'd stay with you."

Miz Evelyn gulped back the whiskey remaining in the glass and poured herself another.

"Miz Evelyn . . . that don't do no good, ma'am." Willa-Mae wished the water would boil so she would have a cup of tea to put in her employer's hands.

"You are right, Willa-Mae." Miz Evelyn grimaced at the strength of the amber liquid, then stared at the bottle. "Nothing will do any good." She raised her eyes to Willa-Mae. "Or haven't you heard?"

"An accident . . ."

Miz Evelyn gave her a bitter laugh. "More like the sinking of the *Titanic*, my dear. No lifeboats either. As for our dear Mister Weldon . . . my husband . . . he took the easy way out." She ran a finger across her throat.

"He'll get better, Miz Evelyn. You'll see. You and him can get a new start in the car business. You'll see. Y'all gonna be fine. I can stay on and help 'til y'all gets back on your feet—"

"Then you did not hear." Miz Evelyn's voice was hard.

"Yes, ma'am. Heard Mister Weldon had an accident. That he's gonna get well."

"Mister Weldon died last night at People's Hospital, Willa-Mae." This was said without emotion, as if she were reporting the weather.

The kettle hissed and screamed as though it must respond to her words.

"Lord have mercy." Willa-Mae removed the kettle but did not pour the water for tea. The room spun around her and she sank into a chair. "Oh, not my Mister Weldon."

"And you may as well hear the whole truth. He lost everything. Everything. Savings. The business. This house. Ted and Jack will most certainly not have the funds to finish college. And as for me?" Again the bitter laugh. "Well, he laid in a good supply of bourbon and left me to face this all alone." Her dark eyes were hard with anger and grief. "When he met me, I worked in a millinery shop. He was a struggling car salesman. We were poor then, but I loved him. Did he think I could not still love him if we were poor again?"

"Miz Evelyn . . ." Willa-Mae could feel herself trembling. Silent tears rolled down her plump brown cheeks. "My poor Miz Evelyn!"

"What? Tears, Willa-Mae? Never mind. I've cried all the tears I will cry for him. He took the easy way out; that's all. And now here I am. Here you are as well." She looked around the kitchen. "I shall write you whatever references you require, of course. Although as many of us as were ruined by this, I cannot guarantee that there will be anyone left who can hire a cook."

"I can't leave you, Miz Evelyn!"

"You have no choice, Willa-Mae. When I say we lost everything, I mean I cannot even call a taxi for myself. I cannot pay you."

"No need, Miz Evelyn! I can stay and cook all the same."

"I will have nothing for you to cook. No kitchen to cook in. Do you understand?" Another drink. "Do you understand? Everything is gone!" Miz Evelyn shouted and threw the glass against the wall. "He took it all with him! He left me to face it without him!" Her rage dissolved into tears.

Willa-Mae enfolded her in her arms and stroked her head as if she were a child. "There now, honey. There, there," she soothed. "Let's put you to bed now, Miz Evelyn. You needs t'sleep some. Willa-Mae done come home. Come on now, baby. . . . Willa-Mae put you t'bed where you can sleep awhile. I'll fix up somethin' good for you t'eat. You gonna make it through this. You'll see."

Evelyn Weldon leaned heavily against Willa-Mae as they walked up the broad, curving staircase. Willa-Mae helped her undress and slip into a nightgown. She fell into bed and moaned as Willa-Mae sat beside her for a while and stroked her hair. At last she drifted into a merciful sleep.

CHAPTER NINE

Marvels and Miracles

There was a stirring in Hartford as Dr. John Brown made his way to the blacksmith shop of his brother James and placed the shiny gold coin and watch chain in his hand.

"Birch Tucker found the old man's legacy, Jim," said the doctor with a shake of his head. "I delivered the twin babies of the Tuckers' hired gal, and Birch paid me with this. I want you to put it on the watch chain for me. Hang it right on there."

"Well, I'll be . . . I'll be . . . you don't say? So it was there all the time." James gave a gruff laugh. "Hid just long enough so as to keep it out of J.D.'s grubby paws. Well, I'll be."

News of the miracle traveled quickly. In the time it took Birch and Jefferson and the two oldest Tucker boys to ride into town this morning, almost everyone already knew that California gold had once again been discovered by the descendant of old Andrew Jackson Sinnickson.

A small knot of curious onlookers gathered across the street to watch as the green-enameled FAMOUS wagon pulled up in front of the bank. Birch Tucker entered the building, stayed a short time, then left again.

Five minutes later, the assistant manager of Henry V. Smith's bank hurried over to take a seat in the barber chair of Dee Brown, another brother of the doctor's.

"He paid it off—the whole mortgage! Nearly two thousand dollars. All in gold coins. California minted. He stacked them up like poker chips on Mister Smith's desk!" Delbert Simpson trembled with excitement as he described the scene. "Mister Smith just sputters a bit like he's never seen such a thing. Then he says, 'Would you like to deposit the rest?' "

The bank officer gave a harsh laugh as he repeated Birch Tucker's response. "'No, sir!' Birch says to the old miser. 'My granddad always did think you was as crooked as a dog's hind leg, Mister Smith, and me and my wife have come to agree with him. No, sir! We will not hand over our legacy to the likes of y'all. This is exactly what we owe on our farm, which you were so eager to turn over to my cousin J.D. And this is the last you will see of Birch Tucker in your establishment!' "

There was respectful applause from the men in the Hartford barbershop who heard how Birch told off the miser banker of Sebastian County. Old men recalled how Andrew Jackson Sinnickson had detested bankers as practitioners of usury. It was a fine thing to be able to tear up a mortgage and throw it in the face of a man like bank president Henry V. Smith!

All eyes looked out through the gold lettering of the little barbershop window to watch as Birch strode up the boardwalk to enter Hartford Mortuary. Ah yes. There had been the little matter of Cousin Maybelle's funeral to arrange. Few would say it, but most hoped Birch had not spent too much of that fine gold coin on the likes of Maybelle. After all, she was only a relative by marriage, and her husband, J.D., had been the one to supply Birch's daddy with enough corn liquor to make him mean as a cottonmouth snake. Filled the man with lies about Birch, too. . . . Now here was Birch, going to foot the bill for a funeral for J.D.'s wife. Yes sir, it was observed, Birch was a good man, even if he did not have much sense.

Next stop for Birch was the livery stable owned by Brother Williams, who had a fine litter of coonhounds in the back stall of his barn. His sons in tow, Birch intended to redeem one little red hound from the bunch. It was rumored around town that Brother Williams, known as a shrewd businessman, had saved that girl puppy just for those Tucker boys.

"Boomer told me about it," said Dee Brown, snipping carefully at Mr. Winters's thinning hair. "It is not like Brother Williams to show any kind of generosity, but he saved that pup for them boys just the same. Yes. Frank Spledish tried to buy her, and George Walker, too, but Brother Williams told them she was taken. Said he took a shine to those boys and he wanted them to have one of Emmaline's pups."

"There is a God," intoned Mr. Winters solemnly at the miracle of Brother Williams's refusing to sell to the highest bidder.

"Of course, that pup won't be ready to leave her mama for another few weeks, Boomer says," the barber continued. "So I'm mighty glad Birch can pay off the puppy before Brother Williams has a chance to change his mind. You know these fits of generosity only come on Williams about once a decade, and then he usually regrets that he did the right thing."

The men in Dee Brown's shop could see the wide grins on the faces of Bobby and Tommy Tucker as they left the barn with their daddy. So that was taken care of.

Anxious to discuss the latest news about the Tucker family, an entirely new group of customers waded into the shop. Young, arrogant, and usually spoiling for a fight, Buck Hooper took his seat and prepared to argue with whatever might be said.

Now conversation shifted back around to the enormous black man who waited in the wagon. "Well, there is the bravest man in the news today," said Dee Brown solemnly. "Jefferson Canfield. My brother, Doctor John, says he's been workin' for Birch near ten years, way back before they came here. Saved those Tucker kids from the twister while Birch and Trudy were in Tulsa tryin' to get their savings out of that failed bank. He risked his own life, John said. Now that is loyalty."

Buck Hooper spit tobacco into the spittoon and looked disgusted. "Them Northern stockbroker fellers is in a bad way when a Southern Nigra is the bravest man in the news. That oughtta say somethin' about Yankees, all right. Here they go throwin' theirselfs outta winders while a darkie and his wife is savin' Birch Tucker's children from a twister. What a world it is, boys!"

Mr. Winters winked at Dee Brown and then said, "I'd sooner trust a Southern Nigra than a snowy-white, blue-eyed Yankee in a business suit, and that's the truth."

"Amen to that," said Buck with another spit.

Then Dee Brown added, "Rather trust a Southern Nigra than a Ku Kluxer in a bedsheet."

"Amen to—" Buck caught himself before he condemned his beloved Klan. He coughed, half choked on his response.

"Your brain ain't hooked up to your mouth?" asked Mr. Winters as tobacco juice dribbled from the corner of Buck's open mouth.

"There are a few good ones," Buck replied in a sullen voice. "I ain't agin one what's loyal an' knows his place. Birch Tucker's might be one of them."

"That's real big of you, Buck," said Mr. Winters.

"Real big." Dee Brown sniffed.

"You an' them brothers of yours—" Buck scowled—"ya'll jus' can't face the truth because y'all are the grandkids of ol' John Brown. But you're a decent barber, so we overlook that."

"It's best to remember I'm the *only* barber. My brother is the *only* doctor. My other brother is the *only* blacksmith." Dee Brown smiled down at Buck and snipped his shears. "And I'm the one with the shears and razors in this place."

Buck spit again but did not bother to reply. He had made his views known, and he needed a shave and a haircut if he was to attend Maybelle's funeral. Best not try the patience of the town's only barber.

No one seemed in a hurry to leave the barbershop today. Long after Birch and Jefferson and the boys left town, news filtered in about what they had bought and how much they had paid. A dozen twenty-dollar gold pieces were brought to be shown and marveled over.

The blacksmith did a brisk business soldering gold coins onto watch chains and the like. It seemed today that most everyone wanted to hold on to evidence of Old Man Sinnickson's fabled treasure. Old men in Hartford had known Andrew personally, and they rehashed all they had heard him say about the vast wealth of the California gold fields.

Long into the night, the legends about Andrew Jackson Sinnickson mingled with the current gossip about his lucky grandson, Birch Tucker.

Tattered signs tacked to trees, barns, and telephone poles marked the road to Fort Smith Airfield, which was located just across the state line in Oklahoma.

AIRPLANE RIDES

ONLEY 50 CENTS

SATURDAY AND SUNDAY

These old signs were partially covered over by new posters offering the experience of a lifetime:

WILDMAN MCKINNEY

AND HIS FLYING CIRCUS!

SEE DEATH-DEFYING FLYING FEATS

PERFORMED BY HEROS OF THE SKY!

Hand-lettered notices had been nailed to stakes and plugged into the ground along the highway. Like the familiar Burma-Shave advertisements, these were written in bad rhyme and positioned to lure customers forward one sentence at a time. David read the lines aloud as the taxi passed each one:

"AIRPLANE RIDES FOR ONE AND ALL . . .

ONLY A PENNY PER POUND!

DO NOT FEAR THAT YOU WILL FALL . . .

MCKINNEY KEEPS YOU OFF THE GROUND!"

Max finished the sentiment appropriately. "Burma-Shave . . . A regular poet, this barnstormer. A regular literary genius."

"Look there!" David cried. "More of them!"

FLY THE PATH OF THE SHILOH TORNADO!

SEE DEATH AND DESTRUCTION FROM THE AIR!

Max eyed the last proclamation dubiously. "This McKinney fellow knows how to draw a crowd."

"We gonna do it, Dad? We really gonna see death and destruction and go up in an airplane?"

"As long as it is not my death and destruction, Davey. A penny a pound seems reasonable payment."

"You think he'll take Codfish up in his plane?"

Max scowled at the dog, who raised his head at the sound of his name. "At a penny a pound, I imagine a guy named Wildman would take up the four-hundred-pound gorilla from the Bronx Zoo. Codfish will be a piece of cake. He outweighs both of us."

Wildman McKinney's Flying Circus had also been advertised in the morning newspaper and on the local gospel-music radio program broadcast live from the Goldman Hotel. So far the turnout had been stupendous. Folks came from near and far for the opportunity of spending their hard-earned cash to fly over the top of the tornado's destruction. It was not that it had been such a big twister or that the destruction was all that terrible. But the thought of sailing out of the sky and tracing the very path of the storm held great appeal.

This morning the dusty country road was a solid line of cars. All of them moving toward the airfield where the Flying Circus performed great feats of daring like flying upside down, executing loop-the-loops, and wing walking. Interesting stuff, all that, but the greatest attraction was seeing the tornado's path. Whatever damage the cyclone had done around Shiloh, it was secretly blessed by Wildman McKinney and the four members of his barnstorming troop. Business was booming today!

The roar of a biplane engine penetrated the thin cloth top of the taxi and drowned out the old Ford's rattling motor. For just a moment, the bright red aircraft passed directly in front of the sun and cast a winged shadow across Davey's outstretched hand as he hung out the window. The boy whooped and closed his fist as though he would grab hold of the shadow. As if it would pull him out of the car and carry him high above the dusty Arkansas road. Codfish barked frantically at the nearness of the enormous red bird. His flapping ears and the drooping hide of his face were stretched back in the wind. Long strings of saliva trailed from his jowls.

"We're going up, Codfish!" David cheered. "Going up in that thing!"

A hundred times on summer days, David had chased the slow-moving shadows of biplanes as they swept over the streets and yards and houses of his old Philadelphia neighborhood. To run hard and pounce on the dark shape had been the next best thing to flying in those days. Arms spread like wings, great flocks of his pals had roared down sidewalks and through sprinklers in the park. Each in his own imagination had become the great Charles Lindbergh crossing the Atlantic.

To fly! This had been a dream so wonderful in David's mind that he never imagined it could become a reality. In his loneliness and his dreams, David had pictured himself beside Lindbergh in his silver bird, the Spirit of St. Louis. He had clipped news stories of the great aviator's feats and had secretly pretended that such a man as this was his real father. He had watched the planes passing overhead and imagined that the pilot of one of those magic machines was a guy named Max who had once loved his mother. . . .

This morning David ignored Max's statement that he was not fond of airplanes. They were really going to fly, weren't they? Really going to do it. No other kid in the old neighborhood had ever really gone up in an airplane. No other kid had a dad who would take that kid on an actual flight. This was important and wonderful stuff.

David did not even care that Max worried about getting sick. Who would ever know if Max did indeed puke over the side? Max had said he would ride in back of David just in case.

"Are we close to the airfield?" The sound of the plane seemed to make Max nervous. He wiped sweat from his brow and looked up unhappily at the taxi's canvas top. "I do hate these planes. Make me seasick." He put a hand to his stomach as though he were already sick.

"Why y'all gonna ride in her, then?" questioned the taxi driver.

"I hear it's the only way to get to Shiloh."

The interest of the driver was piqued. "Well now! What's a fancy-dan Yankee like you want to get to Shiloh for anyhow?"

"A family visit."

"Somebody like you got relations in Shiloh? Why, I figgered you was some kind of a . . . one of them fancy news fellers come for a story like that feller done for the Tulsa paper. Took his pictures from the plane, put 'em in his paper, and when William McKinney seen 'em he brought his Flyin' Circus right on over here t'Fort Smith. Now you say y'all are goin' t'Shiloh to stay? Relatives, huh? Just gonna drop in on 'em, are y'?"

He laughed at his own attempted humor, then pointed across a pasture. "There's the aerodrome yonder."

Across a broad field, two hundred automobiles, trucks, and buckboards were parked haphazardly along the packed dirt strip that served as the runway for the Fort Smith Airfield. Men, women, children, and dogs sat on tailgates, climbed on running boards, or gathered on bright picnic blankets to gape at the miracle machines flying in close formation above them.

"Shore do beat the roller-coasty rides down to the Electric Park!" cried the driver. "It shore do beat all! Yessir! Like t'put them carnival rides outta business. Been up twice, m'self. Took the missus up for her forty-third birthday. She weren't so fond of it, though. Sez she wants t'live t'be forty-four, and she's not gonna get herself kilt in some flyin' contraption." He cackled again. "It's all the future, I tells her. Automobile done run the horse off the road nearly, and them flyin' machines gonna push trains right off the tracks. Now y'all are proof of that, ain't y'? Fly right into Shiloh and live t'tell about it."

He pointed at a bright yellow Curtiss three-seater as it slid down toward the landing strip. "That there is the one y'all gonna go flyin' in. See—the yeller one."

The plane seemed to dip its wings in greeting. David shouted and waved back, his eyes wide. Soon he would do more than just touch the shadow of the thing. Soon he would be part of the shadow—brushing the treetops, soaring over creeks and fields and tiny people far below him!

He craned his neck and shielded his eyes against the sun. A single building of corrugated tin marked the official airfield. This served as hangar and terminal. Above it, a fat red wind sock was stuffed with a southwest breeze.

The taxi slowed and bumped over the rutted dirt lane. At the gate, a young man in overalls stopped each vehicle and collected money for admission. David could see that plenty of people parked outside the fence and watched the show without paying. But they did not get to see the acts close up. They would not be able to get weighed and pay out their pennies to go up in the three-seater Curtiss!

"Brung y'all customers," declared the taxi driver to the gate man.

"They'll have to pay their two bits like everybody else. That'll be two bits." A hand thrust into the backseat, where Max pondered the meaning and the amount of "two bits."

The driver lowered his voice and whispered to the gate attendant, "He don't know what two bits is. Yankee."

"Well then. Ignorance ain't no excuse. Twenty-five cents each if'n y'all want in, Yankee or not."

Max paid both attendant and driver. Then they were allowed to pass into the inner sanctum of Wildman McKinney's Flying Circus.

A hot-dog wagon was doing a brisk business beside the tin building, and a photographer had set up his camera in front of a parked plane. A long line of children waited to be lifted into the cockpit and photographed wearing the leather aviator's helmet and goggles. Voices were drowned by the incessant roar of the aircraft as they landed, took off, and landed again.

An elderly man encased in a sandwich board strolled through the crowd to advertise the photographs. No matter that a picture cost as much as the actual flight. Those too fainthearted to take off in a biplane would at least have this memento of the day's outing.

David eyed the camera on the tripod and the two unhappy-looking brothers who shared a seat on the parked plane while their mother paid the photographer for a two-for-one deal.

"Y' gonna get your pichur took, young fella?" the man in the sandwich board asked David.

"Ha!" David replied with disdain. He knew from the pout on the faces of those boys that their mama would not let them go up in the plane. They had to be content to sit in the cockpit and smile for the camera. David had no need of a photograph. After all, he was here with Max! Max, who had been up in plenty of airplanes! Max, who had flown enough to know he did not like it! Max, who had even shaken the actual hand of Charles Lindbergh in New York City!

"How 'bout it, mister," the sign man asked Max. "Want a little memento of the day? Let the young'un sit up there jus' like a pilot? Six bits is all it'll cost."

"We're going for a ride," David replied sternly. "Flying to Shiloh."

"Mighty nice." The old man patted David's head. "It's a turrible wreck from what I'm tol'. A man an' wife done got kilt. They found her right easy, but he ain't been found. Ain't seen it myself, but I hear tell there's a re-ward if anyone spots that there dead feller stuck up in a tree. They found one dead one, like I said, but they ain't located t'other. Y'all keep a sharp eye for that dead man now. Might make enough t'pay the fare, if'n you spot him."

David thought to himself that this was a creepy old guy to talk about the dead man with such a happy voice. He supposed, however, that the sign man was just trying to be polite. "Yes, sir," David answered in a mannerly way. "I will look sharp for him."

"That's real fine," answered the old man, patting David's head and then Codfish's. "Y'all might tie this here dawg over t'that fence post yonder until the ride is over. Right handsome animal. I'll keep my eye out so's nobody steals him."

"He is going with us," Max explained. "We are going to stay. One-way passengers. Family business."

The old man scratched his head beneath his drooping hat. "Don't rightly know if that McKinney feller takes dawgs up in his plane."

He pointed to a large freight scale just inside the tin building. "That's where y'all get weighed. Reckon that animal weighs as much as a human bein'. McKinney might charge double. Seen him charge double for takin' up a feller who weighed in over three hunnert pounds. Wildman said he didn't know if the plane could stand the strain. Charged that fat man six dollars and two bits. Flew that fat man all around, too. Although he didn't do no fancy loop-de-loops. Got back safe, but that fat man done throwed up all over hisself."

Another long look at Codfish before the old man continued. "On second thought, I reckon Mister Wildman McKinney will do near anything for money. Prob'ly won't mean nothin' t'him that this is a dawg. Just hold on tight t'the critter, boy. That Wildman sometimes forgets hisself and flies the whole way upside down!"

Grandma Amos toddled onto the porch of Shiloh General Store. She nodded and winked at the folks who had collected there to wait for the mail to arrive. Mail deliveries were made to Shiloh on Monday, Wednesday, and Friday by Brother Williams, who owned the Hartford livery stable.

"He's late agin," grumbled Mrs. Morris. The widow counted on the mail each week to bring her pension so she could pay her grocery bill to Grandma Amos.

"He's always late." Fred Woods, the father of Tommy and Bobby Tucker's schoolmate, spit a stream of tobacco juice at a cat lolling in the sun. "But I bet he can't get here a'tall t'day."

Grandma Amos tapped the bowl of her pipe against the post and cleared her throat. She peered into the distance as though she were seeing another vision. "Mebbe Brother Williams ain't a'bringin' what is expected t'day."

"He always comes, Grandma," said Birch Tucker, who had stopped there after paying the bank in Hartford. He had hopes of finding a letter in his box that would help Jefferson Canfield find his folks. Jeff had mailed a dozen letters over the weeks, but so far his queries had brought no response. "It's just that he ain't never here on time."

"Mebbe so, Birch." The old woman still looked as though some great revelation was coming to her. "Mebbe that's the way it used t'be. But that was last week, an' this is this week. This week things is changed. There be troublin' news comin' yonder. . . ."

Every head swiveled to stare in the same direction the old woman was staring. "What you lookin' at, Grandma?" asked Mrs. Morris. "I don't see no trouble yonder."

"Huh!" snorted the old woman, as though Mrs. Morris just did not know where to look.

"She's talkin' 'bout the railroad bein' all tore up, ain't you, Grandma?" suggested Fred Woods. "The mail usually goes on the Rock Island to Hartford, and then Brother picks it up and brings it here. Now, that's what you mean, ain't it, Grandma? The Rock Island ain't runnin' no more on account of the track bein' tore up, so we ain't gonna get no mail for a while." He paused and scratched his neck when the old woman did not reply but continued to gaze across the fields.

"Well, if'n I don't get my pension, then I can't pay my bills," whined Mrs. Morris. "Who do I write to about that? The railroad? The minin' company? The post office? Brother Williams?"

"You can't write to nobody. If we ain't gettin' mail, then there ain't none of our mail goin' out from here neither. Ain't that what you mean, Grandma?" urged Fred Woods hopefully.

"No, that ain't what I mean," said the old woman in an irritated voice. Whatever she had seen was gone now. She lit her pipe and sat down in the rocking chair beside the long wooden bench. "Warm weather we're havin', ain't it, y'all?"

"What you mean 'warm weather'? . . . Now you just tell us what you seen over yonder. Some word from the Lord?"

"Is my pension money comin'?"

Grandma Amos smiled out from the wreath of tobacco smoke that encircled her head. "No, Miz Morris, I do not think that pension check is a'comin'."

"Oh, dear me." Mrs. Morris sat down slowly at this pronouncement of doom.

Birch tried to interpret. "What Grandma means is that it ain't comin' today 'cause the tracks are tore up and the mail ain't come to Hartford, so Brother can't bring it on out. Ain't that what you mean, Grandma?"

"Nope. I reckon Brother Williams be arrivin' here d'rectly. Trains ain't runnin', but all the same, the mail got to Hartford from Fort Smith in one of them flyin' machines." The old woman drew a deep breath. "What I mean is the Copperhead Mine went out of business on account of that Wall Street mess. Ain't no more Copperhead Mine. So even when the mail come through, there ain't gonna be no pension comin' to Miz Morris no more."

At this news, Mrs. Morris gasped and leaned back as if she would faint. A moment of swoon dissolved into a pitiful wailing, which was mostly ignored by all.

Of more interest to the little congregation was how Grandma Amos knew such things. There was something peculiar about the way she could predict the weather. Rain and dry spells. Babies coming one after another. She said it would happen and it did. Like some prophetess from the Good Book, she was. Had she not predicted trouble when she peered up at the moon last night? And trouble had come, sure as anything. The bad storm hadn't ended until morning.

Now here she was, predicting the mail would come by way of Brother Williams same as always. Here she was speaking of fantastic things like the mail coming in to Hartford in an airplane! She was one crazy old woman!

"There now, Miz Morris, mebbe she's wrong," consoled Mrs. White. "Who ever heard of the mail flying in an aeroplane like it were some sort of pigeon droppin's? She's just . . ." Mrs. White tapped her temple and rolled her eyes.

"Think what you want!" snapped Grandma Amos. "It's a fact. The mail flew in. Brother is a'comin' over yonder, and the Copperhead Mine done went belly-up!"

"Now, Grandma," chided Fred, "you ain't always right."

"If y'all jest turn your heads to the ridge, y'all gonna see I'm part right already. There comes Brother Williams yonder, or my name ain't Bertha Amos."

There were gasps all around. Yes indeed! It was Brother Williams coming on horseback down the ridge.

"Oh, dear me," wailed the widow Morris.

Grandma Amos was smug in her correctness. "Jest ask him when he gets here," she puffed. "He couldn't come in the automobile 'cause the roads is all tore up. The mail come a'whizzin' into Hartford in a leetle yeller flyin' machine which was drove by a wild man. And—" she cast a reproachful look at Mrs. White, who had corrected her and called her teched in the bargain—"I tell you, the Copperhead Mine is no more. There ain't no more pension comin' for Miz Morris here in Shiloh. Miz Truelove and Miz Donner in Hartford has also lost their pension. It's Wall Street what done it. I say it's them Yankees what destroyed them pensions, and the South should secede for good this time. We'd all be better off."

For several minutes Grandma Amos went on about Yankees and the injustice wrought upon poor widow-women by Northern carpetbaggers. All this time, Brother Williams drew nearer and nearer, and Mrs. Morris sobbed quietly on the bench. It was a bleak-looking group that greeted Brother Williams as he whoaed up and tied Red to the hitching post.

"How-do!" he cried in cheerful greeting. "Bet y'all thought I weren't a'comin' t'day."

"Huh!" said Grandma. "Tell these unbelievers how the mail come."

"Say! Why y'all look so gloomy?"

"Just tell us, Brother," said Birch in a low voice. "How did the mail come to Hartford today?"

Now here was news! Brother Williams leaped at the chance to tell it. "Me and Boomer was cleanin' out the stalls when all of a sudden there is a terrible *roarrrrrr*! Boomer starts into shoutin' that it must be the Second Comin'! But I knowed it was one of them aeroplanes from up Fort Smith way—"

At this, Mrs. Morris shrieked and went into a dead faint. Mrs. White gasped and put a hand to her mouth, thinking she had blasphemed for calling Grandma Amos teched when it was clear the old woman had seen a vision.

"I told y'all." Grandma Amos rocked and puffed. "The mail come by the air. On angels' wings, as it were."

Puzzled by the response to his story, Brother resolved that he would make no more roaring noises in the telling of the tale. Mrs. White got smelling salts from her pocket and waved them under the nose of Mrs. Morris so she might be fully conscious to hear the rest of the terrible news about her pension straight from the mouth of Brother Williams.

"A wild man, that pilot was. And so they call him—Wildman. He landed right on the main street of Hartford. Just when I had been sayin' to Boomer that I would not be gettin' my one dollar from the post office for deliverin' the Shiloh mail!"

Ashen-faced, the Shiloh residents considered the fact that everything Brother Williams said agreed completely with Grandma Amos's prediction.

"Oh, dear me!" sniffed Mrs. Morris. "Tell us everything, Brother! Is it *true*? It is true what Grandma Amos says about the Copperhead Minin' Company and the pension from my dearly departed Clive?"

At this entreaty from the widow-woman, the smile of Brother Williams dimmed. He doffed his hat. Bad news was like death when it had to do with money; it had to be treated with respect. "I see Grandma Amos done prepared you for the worst, Miz Morris."

"Oh, *dear*, dear me!"

"Yes'm. News is that Copperhead done bit itself in the tail like the snake it is, and it will rise no more. Several widders in Hartford is likewise stricken and now left without their pensions."

This information left everyone reeling. Men groped for a seat. Women stared at Grandma Amos with awe. Mrs. White looked as though she might fall down on her knees and kiss the old woman's hand.

"I told them all, Brother." Grandma shook her head in disgust. "But who hath believed my report?"

Brother Williams appeared mighty sorry that news of the unusual arrival of the mail and the grim fate of Mrs. Morris's pension put such a cloud over the usually cheerful group. "I been the bearer of bad tidin's, I fear." He slapped his hat back on his head. "Now, here's the mail, Grandma. I would sure like to have me a Nehi soda." He was on the step and in the store to fetch his usual drink before anyone could reply.

The rocker squawked on the porch. No one moved as the hinges of the iced cooler squeaked and the hiss of the soda sounded when the bottle top clicked off.

"Would you forgive me, Grandma?" muttered Mrs. White.

"Well, I ain't used t'bein' called teched in my own store by a customer I give credit to . . . but I s'pose."

"You are a wonder and a marvel, old woman," whispered Birch Tucker. "How do you know such things?"

Brother Williams strode out onto the porch. "I bet y'all are relieved that they got the telephone line back up here to Grandma's store. Since there ain't but one telephone in all of Shiloh, it musta been mighty inconvenient to y'all." He patted Grandma on the shoulder. "Like Grandma said real early this mornin' when I telephoned with the news 'bout the mail comin' in that aeroplane and all . . . these modern inventions done put new meanin' to the word *miracle*! Ain't that right, Grandma Amos?"

✷ ✷ ✷

Wildman McKinney did not in any way resemble the great Lone Eagle, Charles Lindbergh. If anything, he resembled a Bantam rooster climbing onto the perch of his plane. Wildman was compact at five foot eight and muscular in build. He surveyed everything in his domain and crowed a bit to a barnyard full of spectators about his exploits as a world-famous aviator.

Max observed him with the same skeptical regard as he regarded the Coney Island pilots who dragged advertising banners across the skies above New York all summer: EAT NATHAN'S FRANKFURTERS!

David's heart, however, responded to every boast of the little flier as though these were words come down from heaven.

Dressed in leather flying helmet, leather jacket, and leather riding breeches with high-topped boots, Wildman looked as exotic as any aviator ever depicted in a penny-dreadful novel. The exploits of pilots in moving-picture shows were nothing compared to meeting this genuine article!

Even though the pilot was a head shorter than Max, to David Wildman McKinney was the tallest man he had ever seen. Flashing brown eyes and a high forehead dominated the aquiline nose and finely chiseled features of his face. He had flown in battle during the Great War and carried himself with the air of a man who considered himself immortal. This self-confidence caused ordinary folks to believe that as long as they flew with such a hero nothing could possibly go wrong. The signs at the side of the road must certainly be the truth: McKinney Will Keep You off the Ground! So far so good.

The pilot personally oversaw the weighing in of Max, David, and Codfish, as though it could not be done without him. "Well, mister. At a penny a pound, that will be $1.83 for you. The kid here and the dog will be $2.46 combined. No discounts for one way. I have to land this baby just the same there in a Shiloh cotton patch as if I was landing her on a runway. Likely I'll get her landing gear tangled in a cow plop. So, full fare even for half the miles."

"You gonna take the dawg up, same as you would a human bein'?" asked the old man with the sign.

If it ever occurred to Wildman that he had come a long way down from dogfights over France to hauling dogs, he did not show it. "The dog? The dog? There will be no problem unless he figures he would like to chase the birdies when we are a thousand feet up. We got no doggie parachutes in such a case. But as long as the mutt stays put . . . well, it puts me in mind of the time in France when the mistress of a certain rich

American would not fly to the Riviera unless her leopard could come along as well."

And so it went. Each action demanded some wild story to accompany it. Every movement was accompanied with a tale of such glamour and excitement that David forgot he was standing on a grass field in plain old Fort Smith, Arkansas, preparing for a mere thirty-minute airplane ride to Shiloh. Every cock-a-doodle out of the McKinney's mouth seemed like an inspired revelation. The airfield was a heavenly cloud! The cranky yellow biplane was nothing less than the wings of the angel Gabriel!

Codfish was hoisted up and tied into the front seat with David. Definitely a fish out of water, the animal whined and dripped slobber onto Max's head. Max ascended, scowled, and slid into the center cockpit. McKinney lingered to sign a number of autographs for a gaggle of Fort Smith Boy Scouts—Charles Lindbergh himself could not have done it with more flair. Then, with a flourish and a wave, he lowered his goggles, tied his silk flying scarf, and leaped into his plane to take the stick.

Orders were shouted. The propeller was cranked. The engine coughed, sputtered, and roared to life. Through the thick, choking smoke of the motor, David could see envy on the upturned faces of the Boy Scouts. To be envied by guys his own age who wore uniforms and merit badges was a pleasing proposition. Yes, this was a very good thing, he thought as the yellow bird bumped away across the field and lifted off with a roar.

I'll Fly Away

All morning long the cloudless skies above Shiloh had been filled with the persistent buzzing of the little yellow biplane carrying city folk out to see the sights. The tornado had carved a corkscrew pattern in the earth as it skipped across the fields and hills for roughly eight miles. Broken trees and uprooted railroad tracks lay all in a tangle in the wake of the storm. It looked almost as if some giant eggbeater had come from the sky and mixed a little piece of the earth like so much cake batter.

Beyond the perimeters of the path, however, the hills around Shiloh were bright and rain washed, alive with color. Reds and golds blazed in the sunlight on Sugar Loaf and the Poteau Mountains. Splashes of orange marked the wild persimmon patches, and bright burgundy gooseberries hung thick on the bushes.

Far beneath the chattering engine of the aircraft, the scents of woodsmoke and fresh-baked bread and chicken frying filled the cool, crisp air. Folks around Shiloh breathed in the smells and took in the sights. They were all thinking how good it was to be alive. Word was that the population had grown by four in the past week. Nelda and Ed Palmer had a new baby girl. Edna Hocott had her seventh baby. The wife of Jefferson Canfield, who was Birch Tucker's colored hired man, had herself twins. Old Doc Brown was worn out from all the excitement.

And now it was time to get on with other necessary business. Young'uns were doused in tin washtubs and scrubbed pink with lye soap. They were dressed in their Sunday best even though it was not Sunday.

School was officially closed for the day—a cause for great rejoicing among the children of Shiloh. They could not show their joy too openly, however, on account of the real reason for all the scrubbing and the cooking and the dressing up.

There was going to be a big covered-dish supper this afternoon. Nearly everybody was coming to it. But before the party there had to be a funeral service for Maybelle Froelich.

"Pack the wicker hampers. Bake a pie. Close school down. It's ol' Maybelle's goin'-over-yonder send-off!" It was obvious that no one in Shiloh was overly distraught about the loss of Maybelle. Most were relieved that the twister had not dropped on their own farms. And if it had to be someone in the community . . . well, people hated to speak ill of the dead, but Maybelle was quite possibly the most deserving candidate in the county for a house to fall on. Of course, none of this was polite to say, even if it was the absolute truth.

This morning there was no tolling of the church bell to count out Maybelle's forty-seven years. The very winds that killed her had also stripped the bell from its tower and sent it tumbling down the road like a dry leaf. No matter. The bell had been found embedded in an old hickory tree and pulled out by Jefferson Canfield. Hefted onto the back of Birch Tucker's FAMOUS wagon, it had been hauled back to the church to await rehanging.

As for Maybelle, after she had been found and properly boxed by the Hartford undertaker, she had also been brought to the church in the back of a wagon. It was an ignominious end for a woman of such vanity. No doubt if Maybelle had been around to plan her own farewell, she would have insisted that her funeral be postponed another week until the new black Cadillac hearse could drive her out to her resting place in style. Too bad. Between the twister and the rainstorm, the road was likely to remain impassable to motorized vehicles for quite a while.

Birch had done the decent thing and waited to bury Maybelle in hopes that her dead husband would be found and be buried with her. But enough was enough. J.D. was just gone. No amount of searching had turned him up. As the closest living relative by marriage, Birch had declared that Maybelle would be too ripe if they waited much longer to bury her. So there was no hearse, no J.D. A buckboard and two mules were the best that could be provided under the circumstances.

If the secret thoughts of all the congregation had been spoken aloud, the consensus would have been that two mules and a buckboard made the most appropriate hearse for dear old Maybelle. As old Grandma Amos said, "A tombstone's the only thing what can stand upright and lie on its face at the same time." Funerals were, after all, the one occasion when a preacher was expected to tell whoppers without incurring the wrath of God.

Despite their unspoken opinions about Maybelle, however, folks came from great distances to attend the service and the subsequent meal. A funeral in Shiloh was not to be missed, no matter how unpleasant the corpse had been when alive.

Before the service began, men and women shuffled up to Birch outside the church and shook his hand as if to congratulate him for surviving his relatives. Nobody mentioned the mules. Nor the plain pine box. Nor the true character of Maybelle, who had been as shrill as the buzz saw at the old lumber mill. No sir. Friends paid their respects to the closest living relative, and then they filed in to take a last look at the old girl.

There was some whispering about the fact that she did not look like her true self laid out like that. The undertaker had done his best, but overzealous in his work, he had made her look too neat. Too pleasant. Too peaceful for the real Maybelle. No one could recall ever seeing Maybelle's hair smoothed back and done up so perfect. In life she always had the look of someone who had stuck her finger in a light socket.

While J.D. and Maybelle were alive, it was often said that the couple had no friends, only cronies who helped them in the making and distribution of bootleg whiskey. They also had customers. Now customers and cronies crowded into the pews beside the churchgoing members of the community.

Birch, Trudy, and their three boys took their places in the front pew. Just behind them sat the six dance-hall girls from the Hi-Times Roadhouse, which J.D. had kept supplied with corn liquor at reasonable rates. It was common knowledge that J.D. had also been paid in favors from these ladies on occasion. Maybelle had once threatened to smash a bottle of Nehi over the head of the bleached blond named Ima-Jean when they met on a street in Hartford. Now Ima-Jean sat there bold as anything, drumming her red nails on the pew. Had she come to gloat?

A confusion of perfumes emanated from the Hi-Times girls. Birch sniffed, made an unpleasant face, and wiped his eyes. Bobby and Tommy were less discreet. Bobby held his nose, and Tommy whispered, "Whooeee! Somethin' *stinks.*" He was silenced by a strong nudge to the ribs from Trudy.

Directly across the aisle sat bloated, red-nosed Leonard Jones, Hartford's town drunk. It might have been assumed that he was one of the few who would truly miss J.D. and Maybelle. But he owed J.D. money, and this fact may have tempered his grief. The scent of booze hovered around him, proof that somewhere in the hills was another maker of bootleg whiskey.

Willard Pickens, sole proprietor of the Hi-Times Roadhouse, occupied the pew behind Leonard, and the members of the house band crowded in beside him. Behind them sat Sheriff Potts, a Methodist teetotaler who had destroyed many a whiskey still in his day. He crossed his arms and scowled at Willard Pickens and his crowd, no doubt imagining how crowded the jail would be if he rounded them all up in one sweep of the funeral.

Sprinkled in among the Methodist congregation was a number of families from the Baptist side of the James Fork. One of these was Bob White, the hard-faced leader of the local Ku Klux Klaners. Bob White's presence made it clear that J.D. and Maybelle had been part of that mob.

Those families clustered around Bob White and his frumpy wife could also be surmised to be practicing members of the Klan. The Kluxers cast hard looks in the direction of Trudy, who they all knew was a Jew, even though she looked just like anybody else. They also were convinced she was just pretending to be a Methodist.

There were hard looks, as well, out the window toward Jefferson, who had dug Maybelle's grave and now waited by the buggy to finish the job when the service was over.

As the only surviving relative, Birch was not proud of the company J.D. had kept. He squeezed Trudy's hand as if to say that at last there were some skeletons on his father's side of the family that would be put where they belonged.

There was great comfort in seeing the faces of old friends and neighbors who had no truck with bootleggers or Kluxers. Those folks far outnumbered J.D.'s cronies, and they, too, seemed anxious to get this over with. Dr. Brown sat, solemn as ever, reading his Bible and only once glancing toward Bob White. His daughter, Mary, looked very pale, prim, and proper in her black wool coat, yet when she caught Trudy's eye, a quick grin and an arch of her eyebrow clearly spoke how much humor she found in the proceedings. Mr. Winters, the pharmacist, and his wife and eight children took up an entire pew. Brother Williams looked strangely deflated without the usual chew of tobacco in his cheek. Birch could only recollect a handful of times in thirty years that he had seen Brother Williams in a suit. All of those times had been funerals. And all had brought forth the same coat, same tie, same shoes.

Last to enter the church was old Grandma Amos, whose long black mourning dress surely dated back to the last century. Her black-silk bonnet, trimmed in black crepe, made her head seem even bigger than usual and much too heavy for her frail body to support. The old woman stamped her cane and tottered right up to the casket, where she peered down at Maybelle and mumbled something that looked from a distance like a sentimental farewell.

The words were only audible to the front row: "Somethin' ain't right here, Maybelle. Hmmm. That's it. Y'got your mouth shut." Being the oldest citizen in Shiloh who was still mostly sane, Grandma Amos was one person who could speak the truth and get away with it.

Preacher Adams raised his eyebrows and mopped his brow at the sight of such a load of sinners among the saints. Perhaps they had come to enjoy the meal afterward, but it was plain by the look on the preacher's face that he planned to give them plenty to chew on before dinner was served. He cleared his throat loudly and stood at the pulpit to begin the service.

"There it is!" The words of the pilot were lost beneath the noise of the engine, but his message was unmistakable. He banked to the east, gliding away from the wooded slopes of Sugar Loaf. They were following the railroad line as it connected one small town after another. Then the tracks suddenly came to an abrupt halt. Ties were scattered like toothpicks in the wake of the storm, and crews of men worked like tiny ants on the rubble. Teams of drovers and horses were busy hauling fallen trees and rubbish off the blocked ribbon of highway. From the high perspective of the aircraft, it was easy to see that the twister had skipped across the countryside—touching down, lifting off, then pouncing again.

McKinney was in no hurry to land and unload his passengers. He banked, flying low over the heads of the railroad workers. As he dipped the wings in greeting, the gandy dancers turned their faces upward and shouted hellos.

David could see their smiles even from the airplane, and he waved at them proudly, once more enjoying the sensation of being envied by earthbound mortals. Codfish barked excitedly at the sight of miniature humans beneath him.

David pivoted his head to grin back at Max, who looked green and unhappy. His eyes were squeezed shut behind the goggles. Clearly he did not think as much of the magic of flight as David and Codfish did. Max was not interested in what was going on below. He did not seem to care about finding the dead guy and earning the reward. David could see that his dad wanted nothing but to be on the ground again, while David never wanted to come down!

In hopes of earning the unspecified reward, David turned his attention to searching the trees and fields for any sign of the dead body. Bits of fabric waving from a tree branch fooled him once. A trail of rubbish followed the erratic pattern of the twister. But David could see no sign of a dead man in any of it.

Farms bordered a swollen creek that wandered through a valley. The dirt road dipped into the stream while the damaged trestle of the railroad line crossed above it. A water tower stood just beyond that. Fields swept up from the water's edge toward farmhouses and barns and pens that ran along a ridge. Here and there were smashed heaps of lumber that had been buildings. David spotted white lettering on a small, red-painted structure beyond the fork in the road.

SHILOH SCHOOL

Too bad the tornado had not taken that away. But could that really be the schoolhouse? If so, it was the smallest school David had ever seen. It looked like the shed where the school janitors in Philadelphia kept their rakes and stuff! No baseball diamond. One swing set. A teeter-totter. A slide. A lot of dirt. No kids.

This was definitely the sticks, but David could see some signs of hope. No smoke curled from the school's metal stovepipe. The place seemed deserted. David decided that maybe this was not where Shiloh kids really went to school after all. Maybe this was just some run-down vacant building.

Now, where was the real town? Where were all the people? He looked back at Max, whose eyes were open again.

"*School,*" Max mouthed and gave David a thumbs-up.

David did not feel thumbs-up about this, however.

On a low hill was a ramshackle building identified by a faded sign:

SHILOH GENERAL STORE

One market? Only one? No corner soda fountain? No movie theatre? Just a lot of trees and some fields and a few farmhouses and . . . ahead, David could see the steep green roof of another building. There was a graveyard beside it and a broad level field beyond that.

SHILOH METHODIST CHURCH

The place had horses and wagons parked all around, tied to the wrought-iron fence surrounding the cemetery. It wasn't even Sunday, either.

"There is the church, there is the steeple; open the doors, and . . ." Was this what people did for fun in Shiloh? David wondered. Trudy and Birch and their kids lived in this town, which was not really a town at all? David wished now that the airplane ride were round-trip back to Fort Smith.

This was the first funeral seven-and-a-half-year-old Bobby Tucker had attended. At first, he felt fortunate to be here. There had been a long discussion about whether he and baby Joe should be brought along or whether they were too young for the funeral.

Sensing that the tide was running against attendance, Bobby had gone outside and tossed his ball against the wall of the house while his mama and dad talked it over. Trudy had shouted out the back door that he should stop making such a racket because he would wake up Lily's babies. No doubt the thumping of the baseball had helped Trudy come to the decision Bobby had been working for. "We cannot leave Bobby and Joe here, what with Lily in bed and those two babies. Just think of the mischief they could get into—and the noise."

"Enough to wake the dead," Birch had added.

Bobby was no fool. He knew something about getting his own way. If he had wanted to stay home, he would have sat as quietly as a mouse and told his mama not to worry because he could keep baby Joe entertained for an hour until they got back. The baseball against the wall had done the trick.

Tommy, being more experienced at age nine, had gone to the funeral of his Sunday school teacher back in Tulsa and had filled Bobby in on the creepy details. This had inspired Bobby to want to see a real-live dead person for himself. The whole thing had turned out to be a disappointment, however. Except for the fact that Maybelle was lying up there in the box, nothing at all creepy or exciting had happened.

Wedged between his mother and the hard arm of the pew, Bobby had a fine view out the window. He saw Jefferson standing beside the FAMOUS wagon and the church bell. Jefferson had earned a dollar for digging the hole for Maybelle's coffin and would earn another two bits for filling it in afterward.

Sunlight glistened on the ebony skin of the big man. Hooking his thumb on the strap of his bib overalls, Jefferson studied the church bell and then peered up at the bell tower. He shaded his eyes and looked away toward the hum of the plane engine. Then, as if he felt Bobby looking at him, Jeff turned his broad face and smiled right at Bobby through the window.

"Hi, Jeff," Bobby said aloud, forgetting for a moment that the boys were required to be quiet during funerals, just like in church. This rule had been repeated to him a dozen times this morning. Now Trudy enforced it with a hard jab in his ribs. This was a sure sign that he had to pay attention to the proceedings, no matter how hot it was inside the church or how badly Miss Peebles played the pump organ.

Bobby pulled himself up straight and peered around his mother at Maybelle's coffin. It was propped up between two chairs at the front of the church, surrounded by the flowers that had arrived on horseback from Mansfield. The florist, who had run short on blooms, had sent a few small arrangements along with a large horseshoe wreath of red carnations that had been intended for the retirement dinner of a mine official. The florist had written a note saying that funerals were more important than retirement dinners, the carnations would add a lot of color, and if they placed it right, no one would notice the inappropriate shape.

Birch had decided the flowers smelled nice. And Maybelle was not going to get anything better on such short notice. So Trudy had removed the *Good Luck* ribbon and placed the horseshoe at the front of the church. Bobby had overheard his mother say that old Maybelle was going to need a lot more than luck at this stage of the game.

The flowers smelled heaps better than the ladies sitting behind them. Bobby looked at Maybelle and decided that she was less scary-looking dead than she had been alive. She just looked like a wax dummy all dressed up and sleeping. Indeed, funerals were boring. Not at all what he'd expected. No doubt Tommy had made up all that stuff about the moaning dead body of his Sunday school teacher. Tommy was always making stuff up.

Miss Peebles warmed up the little organ with a stirring rendition of "Amazing Grace." She hardly hit any wrong notes this time. Next up, skinny old Mrs. White, who was married to the head of the Kluxers, stood and began to sing "I'll Fly Away." Lots of wrong notes. Bobby could tell easy as anything.

It was somewhere in the middle of this that the roar of a plane sounded above the church, drowning out the song. Every head turned to look out the window at the retreating craft. But Mrs. White kept on.

"Some glad mornin'
When this life is ooooo-verrrrrr,
I'll . . . fly a-wayyyyy!"

Here and there throughout the congregation, a few snickers could be heard as people realized what a fitting song this was, considering what had happened to Maybelle. But the oddly appropriate lyrics might have gone largely unnoticed by Bobby if Mrs. White had not paused between chorus and verse to look into the coffin and address the deceased. "Yes, Maybelle, you done flown away, sister!" Very dramatic.

The only problem was, when she talked to Maybelle, whom everyone knew was dead, it made Bobby want to bust out with a big hoot. He felt the first tremor of Tommy's suppressed laughter on the other side of Mama as it vibrated silently through the wood of the pew. The urge to giggle filled Bobby's belly. He held it back. The need to laugh became a pain in his chest. He tucked his head and closed his eyes tight, forcing his mouth to remain closed as a great guffaw pushed its way up from his deepest soul.

"I'll fly a-wayyyy."

Trudy, sensing imminent disaster about to explode from her two sons, gritted her teeth, caught the flesh of little biceps between her thumb and forefinger, and squeezed.

Delicious pain! It held Bobby back from the disgrace of howling through his first-ever funeral. He covered his face with his hands and tried not to listen to the tender screeching of Mrs. White as she wailed on about Maybelle's flying off to some celestial shore. Bobby silently prayed that his mother's pinch would remain firmly in place. He hunched over and hoped folks would think he was crying.

"Someday we're all *gonna* fly away, Maybelle."

Behind Bobby and to the right he heard the sniffling giggle of Fred Woods and then a small cry of pain as Fred's mama, no doubt, gouged him a good one.

Now not even Trudy's pinch could save Bobby from shame. He coughed and buried his head against his mother's arm.

And then a miracle happened.

Outside, the air rumbled once again with a close pass of the airplane. It swept directly over the church, casting its shadow over Jefferson in the graveyard. It covered the singing and the wheezing organ. It drew the attention of everyone in the room.

Jefferson pointed up in amazement as the aircraft slid down just above the treetops. It was heading for the level field just across the churchyard fence!

"It's landing, Mama!" Bobby cried, then clamped his hand over his mouth.

"The thing *is* landin'!" bellowed Sheriff Potts.

Mrs. White left off singing. Miss Peebles stood up from the organ and hurried to look. Folks jumped out of the pews and crowded the windows to gawk as the plane did indeed touch down, bounce, and then touch down firmly.

Had any flying machine ever landed in Shiloh? Not to the recollection of anyone in the church today. And most likely no plane would ever land here again—not on purpose, anyway. There was something historical about the event. Everybody felt it.

The yellow craft bumped across the pasture, veered sharply to the left, and stopped. It shuddered a few times before the engine coughed and the propeller slowed and ceased its whirling.

Finally there was silence.

And more astonished silence as everyone watched the slow, deliberate actions of the passengers and the pilot.

"Must be outta gas," whispered one of the Hi-Times girls. "Is that some kind of critter in there?"

Jefferson, shovel slung over his shoulder, strolled toward the far side of the churchyard and hollered something through the wrought-iron fence.

It was Grandma Amos who broke up the funeral. She said in a loud voice, "Bet they spotted ol' J.D. hung up in a tree somewheres! Better put this on a back burner, Preacher. If it's J.D. they found, we'll all be back tomorrow."

With that parting thought, the whole congregation headed for the doors of the church. They poured out of the building like ants from an anthill.

Bobby heard the grown-ups say things like, "Mebbe they're in trouble." But he knew that no matter what trouble the people in the plane were in, it could not require the help of the whole churchful of people. He also knew that everyone mostly wanted to know why an airplane that had been passing overhead for days would suddenly land in the pasture.

"Smile, Davey. Looks like the natives are restless," muttered Max as they climbed from the plane. Columbus must have felt like this when he arrived on the shores of the New World, Max figured. On the farthest shore of the pasture, one hundred black-clad people lined up behind the bars of the wrought-iron fence to gape in solemn silence at the newcomers. Apart from the big colored man with the shovel, no one had uttered one sound.

Max gave a nervous wave. No one on the other side responded. Did the people of Shiloh speak English?

Then a high-pitched female voice squealed from the crowd. "Look yonder! Why, that there's a dawg in that thang!"

This answered Max's question about language. They spoke no brand of English with which Max was familiar. Interesting, indeed.

"Looks like you two were expected," remarked Wildman McKinney, casting an amused glance toward the mound of earth beside the newly dug grave. "Hope they ain't dug that for you."

That comment brought to mind the fate of Captain Cook, who had perished at the hands of the aborigines of the Sandwich Islands. Maybe these people did not like it that the biplane had trespassed on this field.

"Don't look real happy to see us, do they, Dad?" David moved closer to Max.

"No. We've interrupted their . . . a funeral, looks like. Be polite. Wait here. Keep Codfish in the plane until I make sure we've landed in the right Shiloh, Arkansas."

"Now I've landed here," McKinney protested. "You said one way. It'll cost you extra if I got to take you all the way back to Fort Smith. Ain't in the habit of making extra landings and takeoffs in the middle of a sight-seeing flight—"

"Just wait!" Max snapped. Wiping his sweating palms on his overcoat, he added, "I just want to make sure we don't get left out in the middle of . . . Arkansas . . . if this is not the right place."

"Cost you extra."

"Sure. Sure. Just hold on, will you? Don't leave until I check this. . . ." Turning up the collar of his coat and tugging down the brim of his fedora, he turned to face the sober crowd.

Could his own cousin Trudy live in such a community? His own dear cousin, who had earned top honors at Columbia University? Progressive, bright, and modern, surely Trudy would not stay long in a place where actual horses and mules provided transportation, where there were no telephone lines to be knocked down in a tornado because there were no telephones—no electricity either.

He felt certain that there had been some terrible mistake. No doubt there was some other Shiloh. She had written that things were a bit behind the times, but this was downright quaint—like something out of Mark Twain.

He spotted a fellow wearing a cleric's collar standing beside a tall man who looked a little like Abraham Lincoln. Beside Lincoln stood an angelic-looking young woman. For an instant he had the odd thought that perhaps when his eyes were closed, the plane had crashed and this was some sort of celestial welcoming committee. Grave and all . . .

Giving a nervous laugh, he started toward them.

"He's a'comin' this way!" croaked an old lady in a bonnet.

There was a general murmur among the group. Individual words were lost in the babble.

The priest—or whatever he was—spoke up in precise King's English. "Lost your way, have you? Is everything quite all right?"

"He ain't lost, Parson," argued a rotund fellow wearing a badge. "That there flyin' contraption been flyin' all over these hills fer days. Why would he get lost now?" Then he called to Max, "Did y'all find the body?"

"No," Max shouted in reply. "Sorry to trouble you. But you see, my son and I are looking for—"

He was interrupted by a squawk from the back of the crowd, and then a familiar voice cried out, "Oh, my! Oh, Birch! Oh! It's Max! Oh!"

Trudy. Max recognized her voice in an instant. So this really was *the* Shiloh. The very same Shiloh where his old army buddy Birch had grown up. The very same place Trudy had written him all about. Only it was more so—

"Trudy? Is that really you?" He swept off his hat and walked quickly over the furrows toward the fence.

"Max!" The astonished crowd fell silent once again and fell away to let her come forward. "Why . . . it's my cousin . . . Max! I can hardly believe it!" She was chattering. This was not like Trudy. He had seldom known her to chatter about anything.

It came to him that he had made a terrible mistake. He would say hello. Maybe stay for a while. Pay Wildman McKinney to fly him and David and the dog back to Fort Smith, where they would catch a train to Tahiti or some place less primitive than this.

"Yes. Hello, Trudy, Birch." There was Birch, looking as confused as only Birch Tucker could. "Yes, it's me. Just . . . dropped in . . . for a while . . . to say hello. Brought my boy."

"Your boy?" Trudy squinted incredulously at David. Since Trudy did not know he had a boy, this would take some explaining. Later. Maybe by mail. What could he say? That they just happened to be in the neighborhood?

Wildman shouted, "You want me to take you back to Fort Smith or not?"

"Hold it!" Max called over his shoulder to the pilot. "Just give me a minute here."

"Oh, Max!" Trudy was reaching toward him through the fence like a prisoner reaching through bars. "You cannot mean that you have flown all the way out here only to turn around and go back! Surely you mean to stay with us a day or two! You *cannot* leave when it's been so long."

Max took her hands. "We were just passing through," he lied. "In the neighborhood. On our way . . . south. Like the birds. And I thought . . ." A likely story. Now what?

"Well now, Max." Birch shook his hand, then turned to introduce Max to the rest of Shiloh. "This here's Trudy's cousin Max all the way from New York City!"

Again, more impatient now, McKinney shouted, "Are you coming or what, Mister Meyer? I can't wait all day, you know."

"Oh, Max!" Trudy pleaded. "Can't you stay? Just a day with us?"

"Well I . . . we . . ."

A small voice piped up from behind Trudy. "Are you Uncle Max? Did you remember to bring my mama's writing paper from New York City? Like we wrote you and sent the money for?"

In fact, Max had done that very thing. He extended the vox of stationery, presenting it to the boy he knew was Bobby Tucker. A miniature Birch. Blond hair. Fair skin. Clear blue eyes and a shy smile. Big brother Tommy, holding baby Joe, crowded in and smiled broadly at Max. He had seen them all in photographs, and now here they were in the flesh. It was a very pleasant experience, even if it was a bit out of the ordinary to hold a family reunion beside a cemetery fence.

"I'm leaving!" cried McKinney, leaping onto the wing.

"Stay with us awhile, Max," insisted Birch. "Tell him to come on back in a day or two."

"Well, we really should be getting along—"

"Are you coming?" McKinney sounded shrill.

"Max! Please!" Trudy seemed near tears.

"Looks like we've dropped in on something important here." Max gestured toward the shovel and the mound of earth.

Now the old woman piped up. "Y'all jest made the day more int'restin' is all, young feller. Now why don't y'all stay fer the potluck? Bring the boy. Y'all better git him an' that dawg outta that there flyin' contraption yonder, though, before that fella leaves with it."

Abraham Lincoln nodded. The beautiful angel smiled softly and looked away. The priest indicated that the funeral would be over in no time. A bevy of flappers nudged one another and eyed Max with interest.

"A Yankee . . . all the way from New York City! What do you think of that! And he brung his dawg and his kid along, too!"

Once Wildman McKinney's yellow biplane had puttered away overhead, after everyone in Shiloh had gotten a good look at Trudy Tucker's Yankee cousin and his boy and his dog, there was still the matter of Maybelle's funeral to tend to. Reverend Adams hurried the service right along. He cut out the unnecessary parts and avoided telling the whole truth during the eulogy.

The pine box was lowered into the grave, a few more words were read, a prayer was said, and that was that. Jefferson filled in the dirt over Maybelle and headed back to the farm while friends and relations and even a few strangers dropped by Shiloh Church to enjoy a meal in her honor.

The girls from Hi-Times formed a semicircle around Max as he munched his fried chicken and made polite and inane conversation.

"He's either a banker gone bust in the crash or he's a gangster," whispered Ima-Jean in Trudy's hearing.

"A gangster," Trudy said cheerfully. She no longer felt all that cheerful, however, when she saw Max eyeing Mary Brown across the room.

"Trouble, Birch," she whispered, observing that Buck Hooper had also noticed that Max could not keep his eyes off Mary for longer than one bite of potato salad at a time. Trudy took her husband's arm and led him to the corner of the room. He juggled plates and baby Joe, arranging everything on the organ bench.

"Mary's a grown woman," Birch soothed as he spooned tapioca into baby Joe's mouth. "She can take care of herself. Besides, he's only going to be here a few days."

"He has always been a fast worker, this dear cousin of mine." Trudy's glance swept to David, who was likewise surrounded by a group of little females from Shiloh School.

"Like father, like son." Birch laughed.

"No. No, Birch, this son looks like his mother."

"How would you know such a thing?"

"I went to the university with her. I knew her well. Max ruined her. Left her. David is the result of that; I am certain."

"You're jumpin' a mighty wide ditch to say such things, girl," Birch warned.

"That may be, but it is the truth, in any case. Look at him." Trudy shook her head in wonder as the boy laughed and rubbed his cheek with just the same gesture Trudy had seen Irene make. "I tell you, Birch, that is Irene Dunlap's child, or I am not Gertrude Meyer Tucker." She bit her lip and narrowed her eyes as Max excused himself from the Hi-Times girls and made his way toward Mary, who was speaking to Reverend Adams. "Now what is he up to?"

"If he's still old Max, I can tell you what he's up to."

"That's not what I mean. I mean . . . *what* is Max up to? Why is he here, of all places?"

"You were happy to see him and the boy an hour ago."

"Shocked out of my mind is what I was. Now I have come to my senses enough to remember what Max is like. And now I wonder why in all the world Max would come here." She drummed her fingers on the box of stationery he had brought to her. "He knew he was coming here from the minute he left New York. Or else why would he bring me my writing paper?"

"Well, you've got a couple days to satisfy that curiosity of yours, Trudy Tucker. You'd best ask him right out before he flies away and leaves you forever unsatisfied."

"If I were a betting woman, Birch—which I am not—but if I *were* a betting woman, I would lay odds of one hundred to one that Max has no intention of leaving us in three days." She gave Max a small wave and he waved back, raising his glass of punch in an awkward toast.

"Max come to Arkansas?" she continued. "Birch, I tell you, he is in some sort of trouble—big trouble. Him and the boy. Max gets his nourishment from the noise and fumes and corruption of New York. He has not come here for a vacation."

Trudy lifted her chin regally and gave Birch a knowing look. "No, Birch, I am absolutely certain of it now. This is definitely not a pleasure trip for our dear Max!"

CHAPTER ELEVEN

Part of the Truth

Smiley stood in the shelter of a stone cornice across the street from Joseph Meyer's place of business in Montreal. He stomped his feet against the cold and fidgeted with the knit scarf wound around his upturned collar.

For the last half hour his unconscious routine had never varied: stomp the feet to get the blood going, adjust the scarf around his throat, check the .38 caliber Smith & Wesson in his right overcoat pocket. Smiley had started across the street earlier, after an hour's patient observation had shown no new customers entering the store. But at the exact moment Smiley's foot left the curb, a tiny woman bundled up in an immense fur coat and wearing a babushka had turned onto the avenue with a determined air and marched straight into Meyer's Emporium.

Thirty minutes later, the only thing warm on Smiley was his anger, and it was increasing explosively. Smiley recognized his temper as a danger to his success and had just decided to give up his post for the night when the diminutive lady emerged into the violet twilight. Into her fur muff she stuffed the smallest of paper sacks, the size Joseph Meyer offered when selling needle and thread.

"Half an hour ta buy a spoola thread!" Smiley exhaled in a steamy burst of frustration to the empty sidewalk. He rechecked the scarf and the revolver one last time and crossed the road.

Joseph Meyer appeared outside his store with a long metal rod in his hands for rolling up the green canvas awning that overhung the sidewalk. Smiley was pleased to see this tangible evidence that closing time was at hand.

Positioning himself directly behind Joseph, Smiley entered the store. His sudden appearance startled Sadie Meyer, who was polishing the top of a glass display case. The hand holding the cleaning rag flew toward her mouth in involuntary alarm.

"What? What is it?" Joseph asked. "Did you see a mouse?"

Sadie said nothing. She merely gestured toward Smiley with the cloth.

Joseph turned. "Eh? What do you want?" he said abruptly. "We're closed."

Smiley put on his best ingratiating manner. "I'm sorry to cause youse any bother. But I hope youse can help me locate an old army pal of mine, Maxie Meyer."

Sadie, speechless, simply stared at Smiley.

His fingers picked at his scarf while he waited for a reply.

"You were in the Great War with my nephew, Max?" Joseph asked.

"Yeah, that's the ticket. Maxie and me was buddies, see? Only I lost track of him, and I was hopin' youse could help me find him again. He told me about his Uncle Joe, see, and I looked youse up."

"And what did you say your name was, Mister . . . ?"

Smiley's grin froze above his pointed chin. "Smil—Smith. Yeah, that's it, Al Smith."

"Really, Mister Smith?" commented Joseph in a broadly sarcastic tone. "What an unusual name."

"Yeah, well, enough chitchat about me. Where can I find Maxie? I ain't seen him since the war."

Out of the corner of his eye, Smiley saw Sadie still staring at him. He suddenly realized that his scarf had slipped down, revealing the jagged line of his scar. "Yeah. Maxie boy saved my life, see? Shrapnel . . . almost cut my head off."

Sadie shuddered, but Joseph clearly was not convinced. "What great and lasting friends are made by men who share the dangers of war! What was the name of your outfit again?"

Smiley's right hand dropped from the muffler to his overcoat pocket. He resisted pulling the revolver with great difficulty and mumbled something.

The movement was not lost on Joseph, however. "Sadie, I'm sure Mister Smith will understand that you were just leaving to see to dinner."

Sadie nodded mutely and started toward the door.

In a flash of inspiration, Smiley noticed a row of pictures hanging on the wall above the oak countertop. One was a photo of Max. Hanging next to it was a recent picture of Trudy, Birch, and the boys. It matched the one Smiley had seen in Quinn's office. "Say, Missus Meyer," he said, pointing, "there's Maxie. And that must be your daughter and her fam'ly. What are your grandkids' names?"

"Joseph," Sadie burst out, "the officer said—"

Joseph took her arm and hustled her toward the door. "Ah, Sadie, you don't want to burn the pot roast."

By sheerest good fortune—at least for them, Smiley thought—Sadie had said exactly the right thing. At the sound of the word *officer*, Smiley also started edging toward the door. "Youse don't know where I can find Maxie?"

"We have no idea where he is," Joseph said firmly.

"Ain't that a shame?" Smiley observed before he disappeared into the evening.

☆ ☆ ☆

David Meyer had the distinct feeling that he had met the citizens of Shiloh somewhere before. Or at least he had heard about them the summer his mother had read *Tom Sawyer* aloud to him.

When his country cousins spoke, the air around them seemed to twang like a banjo in a minstrel show. Without too much effort, David could imagine Bobby and Tommy Tucker dressed in straw hats and smoking corncob pipes. No doubt their lives were filled with great adventure.

But David knew at a glance that neither brother had ever been to a big-league baseball game or stolen rides on a tramcar or snuck into a Saturday matinee at the Bijou. They were not the type to steal and lie and sneak like David was. And even if they were the type, what opportunity did they have to commit such crimes out here in the sticks?

David might have called them hicks, except for the fact that they were relations. He viewed Cousin Tommy with confused admiration, as if this were the real Tom Sawyer just stepped out of the pages of a book. Scrawny, with a freckled face and straw-colored hair, Tommy took on attributes of literary proportions in David's eyes. David could visualize this kid lost in a cave with little Becky. He could imagine Tommy fighting off Injun Joe amid jagged rocks and heaps of bat droppings.

As for Bobby, he was a typical runt kid brother who wanted to tag along and participate in important conversations. No matter what David said, Bobby had something to add. Like about the size of certain dogs . . . like about what it was like to fly in an airplane . . . even about what life was like in the big city of New York.

"My mama was in New York City, too," chirped Bobby. "She lived in the same place as your daddy did. Orchard Street. She told us all about it."

David wanted to tell Bobby that he should shut up and listen because he was about as far from knowing about the real New York City as Cod-fish was from playing a fiddle and singing on the radio. But David did not have to tell Bobby.

"Shut up, Bobby," ordered Tommy. "You don't know nothin' about New York City. Bet you don't even know what state it's in."

"Bet I do too," Bobby defended, but he did not name the state, which proved that he did not really know. The humiliation silenced him for a while, anyway, and left David and Tommy to their conversation.

Between Shiloh Church and the Tucker farmhouse, the two boys had found out everything of importance about each other. David was nearly a year older than Tommy. They liked dogs . . . hated school . . . thought girls were stupid and annoying. Here, thought David, was the basis for a great friendship. A meeting of like minds. Hands across the water and all that.

In a very few hours, David sized up Shiloh and decided that, all in all, it had great possibilities. Of course, his country cousins could use a little city education. Had they managed yet to play hooky from school and get away with it? David decided that if he and Max hung around long enough, he could open up a whole new world for his relations.

"C'mon, David," Tommy offered. "We'll show you around."

Bobby nodded enthusiastically. "Bring that big ol' dog of yours, too."

David's eyes were wide at the prospect of roaming in a countryside wilder than any place he'd experienced in Baltimore, Philadelphia, or New York. The idea of exploring had already seemed exciting from the cockpit of the biplane when the straight ribbon of the railroad track and the curving lines of creeks seemed to beckon with adventure. It was even more exciting from a kid's-eye level. The big trees and the wild persim-mon thickets seemed to close in around the little house, adding an air of mystery and danger.

What they seemed to have the most of in this part of Arkansas was a whole lot of green brush! No matter how hard David peered at the coun-tryside from the front porch of the Tucker home, he could not spot even one other house, only some sort of hut, half buried in the foliage.

"That there is Jeff's cabin," Tommy said, following David's gaze. "He's fixin' her up to live in. Wanta go see?"

"Go on, Davey," Max suggested. "Do a little scouting for both of us."

"Don't be gone too long," Birch cautioned. "It'll be dark soon."

The boys scooted off the porch as if let out of school. Down the hill toward the James Fork they tumbled. Bobby was pointing so many dif-ferent directions at once that his arms looked like windmill blades. "There's the James Fork, and over yonder are the Poteaus, and up thataway is . . ."

Codfish ran alongside, waving his tail with every bound and barking for no reason except pure happiness. When a cottontail rabbit jumped from the path, Codfish charged ahead of the boys, stopping only when the critter darted into the safety of a bramble of blackberry vines.

Jefferson was on the roof of the tumbledown cabin. Or rather, he was balancing himself on the few remaining rafters that spanned where the roof had been.

"Hey, Jeff," Bobby called.

"How-do, boys," Jefferson's deep voice rumbled. "Come t'see your great-granddaddy's place, have you?"

"You gonna be able to fix it?" Tommy asked.

"Shore 'nough. This time t'morrow, she'll have a roof on again, and I'll go t'cleanin' out the inside."

Tommy was struck with a sudden thought. "Say, Jeff, do you suppose we could spend the night here tonight? We wouldn't wreck nothin'."

Jefferson looked down into the gutted cabin and laughed. "Reckon it'd be all right, if'n yo' daddy say so. Not likely t'be rain enough to bother none. Why don't you run on back an' ask your mama an' daddy?"

✳ ✳ ✳

Seventy-five years ago, the Howard Street apartment building had been the house of a rich man. Willa-Mae had heard tales that he was a merchant and a Christian, active in the fight against slavery. It was told that the famous John Brown had once slept in the great white frame house and had paced the veranda for hours as he talked with his host of his abolitionist dreams.

Sometimes in the night, Willa-Mae imagined she heard the footsteps of the great man echoing through the corridors of the white house. It must have been a grand place back then—full of folks with big ideas who mapped out plans for the Underground Railroad and listened to lectures about the evils of the slave trade.

Such thoughts were comforting to Willa-Mae, even though the elegant rooms of the fine old mansion had been divided and subdivided to house a dozen different families now. All the current residents of the building were poor, like Willa-Mae and Hock. All but two families were black, and the white ones obviously wanted to be elsewhere. In spite of the glorious history of the structure, no white folks would *choose* to live in it these days—not unless they had no choice. Only the most destitute would live on Howard Street.

Euola Peek, who lived with her husband and five young'uns across the hall from Willa-Mae, described the new tenant and her children like this: "Cracker. White trash if'n y'ask me. It don't cost a body nothin' to wash and keep clean, but that woman! Lordy, Willa-Mae! She get herself all fixed up t'go on down t'the bawdy houses and speakeasies on Furnace Street, and she leaves them two unwashed young'uns in that room t'tend for theirselfs! Why, I never seen a mongrel dog treat her pups so neglectful as that woman treat them babies! Not none of my business, though! No sir. I ain't gonna say one more word. I stopped las' week t'speak t'one of them little whelps. Jus' ask how they doin'. The little'un look me right in the face, and he say his mama say they ain't supposed t'talk t'no nigger! *Well!* I say . . ."

Willa-Mae had heard the new neighbor hollering at her boys. She had heard the raucous laughter of more than one man in the room. Nettie had told her that she had come home from a picture show and seen the two boys huddled in the dark hallway one night while their mama "entertained" a guest. It was a sorry situation that such things went on within the very walls where John Brown had once slept.

Willa-Mae clucked her tongue and shook her head at the shame of it. Even though she had never seen the two little white boys, she remembered they were around every time she trudged up the stairs and passed the battered green door of 2B.

There were other things on her mind today as she puffed up the steep stairway. Terrible, serious things. The stairs seemed steeper than usual somehow because the load her heart carried was so heavy. She grasped the old oak banister and pulled herself up to the landing, then stopped to catch her breath before facing the next climb.

Thirty seconds passed with Willa-Mae standing a few steps from the green door. She mopped the perspiration from her brow and looked up the stairwell with reproach. How had her home gotten to be so far up?

"You gettin' old, Willa-Mae," she whispered to herself. At that moment the latch clicked on the green door. Hinges groaned, and two small towheaded boys peeped out at her hopefully. Their blue eyes were wide as they observed the huffing giant outside their flat. Faces were dirty. Hair too long and uncombed. Tattered clothing too big for their fragile bodies. There was no light in the room behind them, even though the sun had been down for over an hour.

"You're not Mama," said the larger of the two, and his eyes betrayed his disappointment.

She understood at once what they had been thinking. They had heard footsteps outside in the corridor. The footsteps had stopped in front of their door. Shouldn't that mean their mama had come home?

"No, I ain't," Willa-Mae said with a slight smile. "I'm Willa-Mae Canfield."

The little one's eyes got wide. He smiled back at her and absently plugged a dirty thumb into his mouth.

"I know who you are," said the older brother. He looked at the shopping bag in Willa-Mae's arms. His eyes lingered on the loaf of bread protruding from the top. He was hungry—that was plain to see.

Willa-Mae raised her chin regally. "Well, I don't believe I know who y'all is. Y'all got names? We be neighbors. It ain't fittin' not t'know names."

The serious eyes clouded at her question. The little one shook his head as if to deny that he had a name.

The older brother frowned as though remembering some command from his absent mother. "My mama says . . . she says . . ." He paused and looked at Willa-Mae's feet. A slight smile brushed his lips for an instant before his gaze swept up to Willa-Mae's round face.

Willa-Mae knew what the child's mama had said. She did not want to hear it again. "How you know ol' Willa-Mae's name?" she jollied.

He pointed a finger at the ceiling. "We hear y'all." He suddenly brightened, and the little one nodded vigorously in agreement.

She laughed big in mock amazement. "What you say?" Now she looked over her broad girth at her feet. "Y'all mean you can hear ol' Willa-Mae and us all up there?"

"Uh-huh. Hear you walk. And talk, too."

She tapped her foot on the floor in a move that made both boys laugh. "Well then! Well, well! I'll jus' tap y'all secret messages!" She tapped her toe three times, which brought a delighted howl from the brothers. "But I got t'know what y'all use for names!"

Fair skin blushed bright pink beneath the grime. "Frank." The big one screwed up his mouth, trying to hide his great pleasure at the thought that someone cared enough to ask. He jerked a thumb at his baby brother. "This here's Jim. He's four. But he sucks his thumb all the same. Don't mind him. He don't know no better. I been tryin' to break him of it 'cause Grandma said it'd ruin his mouth, but he don't pay me no mind."

"I see," Willa-Mae nodded sincerely as though she were discussing the matter with a concerned young mother. "Reckon y'all shouldn't worry 'bout it none. My baby girl Nettie sucked her thumb 'til she went t'school. Other young'uns broke her of that right quick."

Frank looked relieved. "That's real good."

"You go t'school?"

"No'm. I was right ready to go last year, but it was too far. And this year Daddy—"

Downstairs the glass in the entry door rattled as the door opened.

The child's eyes widened, and he looked past Willa-Mae fearfully, as if to say, *"What have I done?"*

Willa-Mae read the terror in his expression. He had done just what his mama had told him not to do. He had spoken to a nigger lady and even told Willa-Mae his name. What price would the child have to pay for such a terrible sin?

"I'll be gettin' along now," Willa-Mae whispered.

The boy nodded frantically and jerked his little brother back into the gloom, then slammed the door behind him.

Willa-Mae shifted the shopping bag in her arms. She shook her head sadly at the green door and walked on. Another minute and she could have talked the children into taking part of the loaf of bread. Peering over the banister she could see that Charlie Gibson was the culprit who had come in from the cold. For an instant she considered knocking on 2B, then thought better of it. Maybe her kindness would bring trouble down on the heads of the young'uns. Best to let it go.

"The world is a place of troubles, Lord," she muttered, once more trudging up the steps and humming the tune of "John Brown's Body."

The moment of truth arrived, but Max was not ready for Trudy's direct gaze and probing questions.

She gave Birch a nudge and a not-so-subtle hint. "Birch, I know you have work to do. Max and I have some catching up to do."

Birch gave Max a pitying look. "Sure. I'll just be out—well, it's great to see you, Max." It might have been more accurate to say that it had been nice knowing him and don't forget to duck. Instead he grinned sheepishly and sidled out of the kitchen.

Trudy pulled out a chair from the kitchen table and pointed. "Sit," she directed.

Max obeyed. "Has anyone ever told you how much you sound like Bubbe Fritz when you say that? She was always telling me to sit and listen."

"If you had done so, no doubt life would have been easier for you."

"Yes, well . . ." He nodded and laughed uncomfortably. She knew him too well to be fooled for long. "Somehow I feel like a schoolboy sitting here with you looking at me like that."

"We have always been honest with each other, you and I."

"You never gave me a choice."

"I will not give you a choice now either." She leaned against the sideboard and crossed her arms, as if daring him to lie to her.

"I'll bet you keep those kids in line. Bet they don't get away with anything. Birch either, huh?"

"I learned early in life what sorts of things little boys try to get away with. I learned by watching you, Maxie dear." She looked out the window to where the boys darted in and out of the birch trees at the bottom of the hill. "But I see that in the end you have not succeeded in getting away with anything." The silence in the kitchen was broken only by the soft hiss of steam from the cast-iron kettle. Then she added in a gentler voice, "David. He is a handsome child."

Max cleared his throat and shifted in his seat. "Yes, I think so. A good kid, too."

"And his mother?" It was plain by her expression that she already knew. "Irene?"

"She—she's dead, Trudy. Cancer. Left the kid. What could I do?"

"I am glad you have done the right thing, Max." She did not add that he was long overdue in meeting his obligations, but Max heard the unspoken reprimand all the same.

"I wanted him to meet the family. You are really the closest thing to a sister that I have ever had, you know . . . and your boys call me Uncle Max. You should be Aunt Trudy. So I got on a train and here we are."

Max did not want to tell her any more than that. She did not need to know.

"Well then."

Had she accepted his simple explanation? "I would have called but—"

"No telephones here."

"Yes, but I should have telegraphed. Should have let you know. I apologize. This was a whim, really. Manhattan is like a morgue after the stock-market crash—gray and depressing, like the whole world is collapsing around us. I got your letters . . . about this place and the boys, and it sounded so . . . idyllic. I wanted the kid to meet you, see a normal kind of life and family. I was hoping we could rent a place, stick around for the holidays maybe. You know . . . a real Christmas for the kid. With cousins. But now I see I should have taken a little more care with you. We'll just stay a few days and travel on south. New Orleans, maybe. A little vacation . . . get to know each other."

Max had the uneasy sense that Trudy knew everything, that nothing was hidden from her. Like their grandmother had used to claim: "*I have eyes in the back of my head!*" Max almost believed that Trudy had inherited the extra pair of eyes.

She softened visibly and sat down across from him. "Oh, Max!" She took his hands. "Of course . . . of course it was right for you to come here.

I just thought . . . I imagined you were in some sort of trouble. I could not imagine you, of all people, coming here to little Shiloh."

Max breathed a sigh of relief. Hook, line, and sinker, she had swallowed every word. "It wasn't Shiloh I brought him here to see," he said. "It was you. Family, you know. Something I have never really had myself. I thought maybe you and Birch could teach us what it's all about."

CHAPTER TWELVE

A Glow in the Cabin

At first, Trudy doubted the wisdom of letting the boys sleep out in Jeff's cabin. "I don't know, Birch. Who's going to keep an eye on them?"

"Now, True," Birch countered, "who said they need an eye kept on 'em? Boys need to be boys. 'Sides, Bobby and Tommy want to show their newfound cousin a good time."

In the end it was none of these arguments that convinced Trudy to let the boys go. The reasoning that carried the day was the simple matter of space—there was just nowhere to put them all. "All right," she agreed at last, "but I don't want you out running around after dark."

"We won't, Ma," Bobby and Tommy promised, and they scattered to gather up blankets and lanterns for the great adventure. "Besides, we'll keep David's big black dog with us, so nothin' will bother us. Not even old Lucifer."

Trudy fixed each of them four thick ham sandwiches made from ham Grandma Amos had smoked in her own smokehouse and pickles brought to the potluck by Mrs. Winters. Tommy claimed some leftover fried chicken. Half a pumpkin pie disappeared into the hamper, along with two dozen persimmon cookies, leftover biscuits, fresh butter, elderberry jelly, and quart jars of milk. Whatever might happen on their one-night campout, they would not go hungry.

The kitchen table was crowded enough without the three boys. Tonight Lily was up and dressed in a pretty blue dress that Trudy had given her. She declared that at no time in her whole life had she ever been so spoiled. She had picked cotton in Louisiana the day after her last baby was born—and buried. Now Trudy had made her rest in bed as if she were the queen of Sheba or something. She attempted to get past Trudy just to take up the corn bread, but Trudy made her sit—on a chair with a pillow, no less!

"Lordy, how you do go on, Miz True!" Lily giggled and blushed. She giggled again when Jefferson sat down beside her and declared that she was the prettiest woman he had ever seen.

Max sat across from Jeff, and the two former soldiers fell into a lively discussion about their days in Paris after the war. Just to think that they had been in the same city and never met each other!

"Yessir," Jefferson said. "A man as big an' black as me was hard to miss walkin' round Paris, I reckon! A black sheep is what I was, an' that's the truth!"

It was a noisy, raucous mealtime. Then Lily and Jeff brought out baby Willa and little William to be passed around and rocked and admired by all. Baby Joe got jealous and cranky and had to be put to bed. There were dishes to be done, and talk turned serious as Birch asked about Wall Street and discussed the banks closing down and tycoons pitching themselves out of windows and such.

In the wake of such talk about disaster, both William and Willa got hungry at the same moment, and Lily's milk came in like a flood, so she had to hurry back to the bedroom. Jefferson followed her to hold baby Willa while she fed William and then the other way around.

But Birch and Trudy and Max lingered a full hour more in the kitchen, talking over old times.

Two kerosene lamps glowed in the ancient little cabin across the creek, and bedrolls were spread on the corner of the floor under the greatest remaining expanse of roof.

"Ain't that a sight?" Tommy mumbled around a mouthful of fried chicken. He was gesturing through the gap in the roof toward where a lopsided moon sailed toward its setting place behind the trees atop the ridgeline.

"Yeah," David said, "but you should see it come up out of the pitch-black ocean sometime. It looks just like the water is blowing a big silver bubble or something."

Bobby frowned with the thought that the sky over the humble Poteau Mountains of Arkansas might not be as dramatic a sight as the Atlantic Ocean.

Tommy tried again to impress his city cousin. "We're gettin' a redbone hound puppy. When she grows up, we can track and hunt with her."

"That's great," David said. But he spoiled the compliment by adding, "Do you s'pose she'll be able to swim? Codfish can swim. He saved me from drowning."

The big dog, curled up at David's side, opened his eyes at the sound of his name.

"Yes sir," David affirmed, "I betcha Codfish is the best dog in the whole world. He's the quill."

"The what?"

"Come again?"

"You know," David said, replaying his comment in his head to see if he had stuttered somehow and not known it. "I said, he's the quill!"

"What's a quill?" asked Tommy suspiciously. "I don't see no—any," he corrected himself. "I don't see any quills laying around here."

David looked surprised. "Don't you know anything? The quill is the best. You know, tops. Why, they say that all the time on *Dixie's Circus and Novelty Band.*"

Tommy and Bobby still looked blank.

"On the radio," David explained. "Don't you even have a radio?"

Bobby's lower lip stuck out. He was afraid that failing to meet their city cousin's expectations had branded him forever as a hick. But while David was helping himself to another persimmon cookie, Tommy punched Bobby lightly on the arm and slipped him a broad wink.

In a loud and deliberately casual voice, Tommy remarked, "We'd best not be too loud out here. Old Lucifer might hear us."

"But, Tommy," Bobby protested, "we heard—" He shut up quickly at a warning scowl from his brother.

"Old Lucifer?" David questioned. "Who's that?"

"Not who, what," Tommy explained. "The biggest, most ferociousest bear in these parts. They call him Lucifer 'cause he's meaner than sin. Got hisself caught in a trap and had to gnaw part of his own foot off to get loose. Ever since, he just loves to catch folks out in the woods."

"Well, I'm not scared," David proclaimed, but the quick looks over each shoulder that accompanied his words spoiled the declaration.

Tommy appeared to have a new respect for his city cousin. "Really? Do you mean it? You wouldn't be a'scared if old Lucifer poked his nose right in that door?"

Tommy pitched a biscuit through the open doorway. The yellow light from the lanterns created a half circle of illumination that pushed back the darkness for only a few feet. Beyond the glow, heavy shadows seemed to pile up in mysterious layers.

David wished there was a big, solid door to bolt across the uncovered entry into the cabin, but he didn't want to say it right then. "Nooo," he went on doubtfully. Then, with greater force, he added, "No, I wouldn't. Codfish can handle any old bear."

Tommy thought quickly. "Old Lucifer is just death on hounds, and nothin' makes him madder than a dog barkin'. You'd best keep your dog real still."

"Tommy," offered Bobby, "I'm scared."

"It'll be all right," comforted his big brother. "Old Lucifer is prob'ly miles from here right now. You know we heard he carried off that red-haired kid over to Mansfield just last week."

"Carried him off? Killed him dead?" David asked. He pushed himself as far back into the corner of the little cabin as he could, until his back bumped against the rough-hewn beams that had stood since before the Civil War.

"Yup," Tommy agreed. "Ate him clean up. All they ever found was his shoes and a little patch of red hair no bigger'n one of these." With an underhand toss he pegged another biscuit out into the darkness.

David gulped a last swallow of cookie, which for a moment had refused to go down. "How do you know Lucifer isn't around here?"

"Why, shoot," Tommy explained, "we'd hear him. He'd come crashin' through the brush like a steam locomotive, with his great sharp claws tearin' up the ground and his big red eyes blazin' with hate and awful foam drippin' from his razor-edged fangs. It's a sight I don't ever want to see; you know it would be the last glimpse of this earth you'd—*wait!*"

The last word was spoken with such urgency that Bobby and David both jumped and knocked over the remaining biscuits. Codfish began to happily crunch them up.

"Did you hear it?" Tommy asked anxiously.

"Hear what? Hear what? I didn't hear anything," David vowed in a voice more hopeful than certain.

"A sound outside in the brush," Tommy warned. "There it is again."

From the middle of the darkest shadowy tangle of brambles came a crackle of brush and a snort.

"What was that?" David breathed.

"It's him! Now, be quiet! Don't get him riled!"

There was a greater commotion in the weeds, and a low grunting sound moved closer to the boys. The hackles on Codfish's neck stood up, and he gave a menacing growl as he stared into the darkness outside the cabin.

David looked around with a panicked expression. "What'll we do?"

By now Codfish was barking furiously. "Keep your dog still—that's what," Tommy ordered. "Don't make old Lucifer any madder. Bobby, you hold on to him."

Bobby threw his arms around Codfish's neck while David tried unsuccessfully to shush him.

The grunting and snorting outside became even more pronounced, and a hulking dark shadow could dimly be glimpsed in a tangle of vines. David's mind painted in the blazing eyes, the slavering jaws, and the daggerlike claws. "What can we do?" he pleaded again.

Tommy seized a handful of cookies. "Maybe we can distract him while we make a run for it," he said, pitching the sweets into the brush with an underhand toss.

David's eyes were wide and his body practically rigid as he glued his attention to the moving form. Tommy stepped just to the side of his cousin. In an explosively loud and terrified voice, he yelled in David's ear, "Oh, my goodness! Here he comes!"

The black shape turned toward the sound of Tommy's voice as if drawn by a magnet. Branches crashed and snapped as the snorting beast accelerated directly at the boys.

"Run for your life!" Tommy shouted, expertly managing to leave his right foot where David would trip over it and fall sprawling in the dirt.

David scrambled to his feet and took off toward the house. His heart was pounding so hard that he thought it would jump out of his chest. His fists pumped furiously in rhythm with his feet, as if he were trying to get airborne. But four leaps into the brush was as far as he got before he tripped again over a log and fell hopelessly tangled into a heap of vines.

He could hear the fearsome creature snorting right in his ear and feel its hot breath on his neck. He tried to scream, but only a tortured squeak came out of his throat. How close was the bear? Where were his cousins?

David rolled free of the weeds at last and shot a look over his shoulder toward the cabin. His glance took in Tommy, who was rolling on the ground next to his brother, consumed in a fit of laughter. Bobby was giggling, too, while trying to keep a grip on Codfish. The dog was barking furiously at the snorting, grunting, and rooting shape of . . . a dark red hog. The porker was busily engaged in gobbling up the rest of the biscuits and the persimmon cookies that Tommy had so thoughtfully been tossing outside.

Tommy didn't get his voice back until after the spasm of humor had gone away. He wiped his eyes and said with an enormous grin, "Guess I musta made a mistake. It weren't Lucifer after all. It was just the old sow. Come on back in, Davey. There's some things about Shiloh that New York City ain't gonna have to offer."

David felt his fear become anger at being fooled, but the rage was quickly replaced with admiration at the success of the trick. "Say," he said, "I bet you guys have never heard of the Subway Spook. Pass me one of those ham sandwiches, and I'll tell you all about it."

Even with the boys spending the night in the log cabin, the Tucker farmhouse was packed like a tin of sardines. Jefferson, Lily, and the twins were in one room. Baby Joe was now sleeping in Birch and Trudy's room, and Max had been assigned to the sofa. Only the boys' room remained empty.

No announcement was made that it was bedtime, but Trudy had begun to stir around in preparation. Gales of laughter mingled with Codfish's barking drifted up from the field where the boys were playing some game in the dark. Trudy gave Birch one of her "go see" looks as she took an extra set of sheets from the linen drawer. Hot water for washing had been drawn from the reservoir on the woodstove. Birch lit a lantern and invited Max to walk out with him to check the animals and whatever two-legged critters might be prowling around tonight.

All was quiet now. Whatever had been going on at the cabin was settled, it seemed. A layer of clouds collected at the base of the mountain, creating the illusion that it was floating above the earth. The moon had already gone down, but now a shimmering canopy of stars illuminated the earth. The Milky Way made a trail across the sky that seemed to end in one point of earthbound light sparkling from the old cabin. The men stood awhile on the rise and looked down across the darkness at the tiny glimmer. No stars, distant worlds, or planets could mean more to Birch and Max than the three boys in orbit around that lantern's glow.

"Those boys," Birch said tenderly, as one father to another. "When a man's got kids, just watchin' them grow is like growin' up yourself all over again, ain't it? There they are down there in that old house. Enough food to last a week. Me and my brother did the same. It just takes me back, that's all."

Max did not say what he was thinking. That he had never slept out under the stars for the fun of it. That his brother had died before they had time to make such memories. He did not say that this night and this place and watching Birch and Trudy together with their children made him ache inside for what he never had. For what he could not have now.

"This is a wonderful place," he said simply.

"This little old rock farm . . . it ain't much, I guess, but it's home. Gives me a chance to do better for my boys and for Trudy than my own father did for us. Guess I'm livin' my life now the way I wish it had been when I was a kid. Let them have some fun. Make sure they know I love them. . . . Just want to make it better—you know what I mean?"

"Yes." Max wanted to ask his friend where to begin. How could he make up for all the wasted time with David?

"It might be good for David to go to school with the boys," Birch suggested unexpectedly. "Let him get acquainted, fit in with the rest of the kids." He shrugged. "I figure when you get back to New York, you got some fine school picked out for him. Our little school ain't much—one room, sixty kids, one teacher, and a couple of helpers. But I bet David would like goin' all the same."

"Birch . . ." Once again the question, the longing for advice, stuck in Max's throat. "I'm all new at this business. Fatherhood. I'm not so sure I know how to do it right, see? I look at Bobby and Tommy with you and . . . I have a lot to learn."

"Ain't so hard as all that. Mostly it just takes lookin' at a kid right in the eyes when he tells you somethin' he thinks is wonderful but maybe to you it don't amount to a hill of beans. You gotta remember that everythin' is new to a kid, Max." He waved toward the glow of the cabin. "I slept out down there. I know what it's all about. Tellin' spook stories and eatin' enough in one night to feed Cox's army. Come mornin', they'll tell me all about it like they invented it, and I gotta let them think they surely did."

Birch was smiling with anticipation. "Now, see, my dad . . . he stole that away from me. When I hunted my first possum, it was not as big as the first possum he hunted, and he let me know it. He let me know I never plowed a furrow as straight as he did. Never rode a horse as good. Never was as smart. Never fought like he could fight."

He turned away from Max and looked at the rubble of the barn. "I'm gonna put hammers in the hands of my boys. I'm gonna let them help me build up this place again, and they'll feel good about what they done, too. I think a kid—any kid at all—mostly wants to do good. Sure, they ain't gonna do everything right the first time, but that ain't a sin. That's what learnin' is all about. Make a mistake. Try again. Do a little better next time—and better yet the next time.

"Everythin's new and wonderful to a kid," Birch repeated, almost under his breath. "They think they can sprout wings and fly. They believe everything they imagine is possible." He gave a low chuckle. "I reckon that's what the Lord meant when He said we ought to be like little children. They have faith still. They still believe they can move mountains. Maybe their souls remember what it was like to be in heaven, where maybe they really could fly. Then we grow up and learn about gravity, and we become grave in our hearts. And then we stop believin'. I almost did."

Birch shrugged in an embarrassed way, as though he had not meant to talk so much. "Well, life will turn hard for them soon enough. It has a way of doin' that, I reckon. But I do not want to be the one to tell my boys they can't move mountains. No sir. I look at my sons, and I think . . . yes sir, Lord, maybe all things really are possible. Maybe man *was* meant to fly. Meant to build great cities. Meant to say to this mountain 'be moved into the sea' . . . and then find a way to make it happen. That's what I want to give my boys. If I can do that . . ." His words trailed away as he gazed at the distant lantern light and imagined what the boys were up to down there.

Max pondered his words. "Where do I begin, Birch?"

"Right here." Birch tapped his heart. "Listen to him. Look at him. Teach him what's right, but give him room to make mistakes, just like you have made mistakes. Someday he may hurt you. Kids do, sometimes. It's part of it, I expect. There will be times when you gotta forgive him, like maybe he has to forgive you. It ain't easy, Max. But it's worth it. Live every day like that, and love will just happen."

When they got back to the house, Trudy had made up Max's bed on the sofa. The sheets were sweet smelling, like the air of Shiloh. Lamps were snuffed out. Bedroom doors were closed.

Max lay in the dark and listened to the muffled voices of Birch and Trudy, then Jefferson and Lily. A soft chuckle as they shared tender words that only a man and a woman in love could share with each other.

Alone, on the outside of their intimate world, the heart of Max Meyer was filled with a longing he had never known before. He had seen the world. He had had his pick of beautiful women. He had racked up accomplishments in the business world that men like Birch Tucker and Jefferson Canfield could not imagine. Yet, he admitted to himself, he was a poorer man than either of them.

The House of Morgan was a fashionable if technically illegal jazz-and-booze business in midtown Manhattan. The name was an inside joke, based on the well-known Wall Street financial firm of J.P. Morgan and Company. Helen Morgan's clientele included bankers, brokers, trust officers, and company presidents, as befitted the club offering the hottest music and the most potent bootleg whiskey in the most stylish surroundings. Many a gullible wife sent her husband off to the night-club believing he was on his way to a very accommodating bank that kept unusually late hours for important clients.

Smiley parked his car around the corner from the club and walked into the alley behind the House of Morgan. An unmarked steel door opened at a combination of raps and pauses. A very large man, his belly straining the buttons of his size-fifty-four tuxedo jacket, escorted Smiley through the kitchen and to the rear of the bandstand.

Helen Morgan's club was only moderately crowded tonight, and the music lacked enthusiasm. Since the crash, a number of the usuals had stayed away, some because of guilty consciences and others because of death or imprisonment. Ever since the day that *Variety* had carried the headline "Wall Street Lays An Egg," business at the House of Morgan had been off. Customers had even begun a practice unthinkable only weeks before: They were asking the prices of goods and services!

Even the normally snooty college-student waiters in their starched white coats sounded subdued as they poured rotgut into porcelain tea-cups. The waiters and the crockery maintained the whimsical fiction that Helen Morgan's was a respectable dance club, but nobody was very amused these days.

Smiley did not need to be told where to go. A curtained alcove, half hidden from view by the bandstand, was the special accommodation reserved for Helen Morgan's liquor supplier, Boss Quinn.

"The Boss is waitin' for youse," said a brutish man in a dark brown suit who was almost as large as the doorman. "I hope for your sake youse come up with somethin'."

"Nice to see you, too, Ham," Smiley growled out of the corner of his mouth. "How long you been out?"

Behind the curtain, Boss Quinn was waiting. "Since you did not phone me no news," he said bluntly, "I infer that you were not successful."

"Yes and no, Boss," Smiley whined. "They ain't in Montreal, and they ain't been there. But I seen another pitchur of Meyer's cousin, the one what lives in Oklahoma. You want I should go there next?"

Quinn thought for a moment. "No," he said at last. "We need a different angle on this job. Leave the newshawk be for the present, and focus your attentions on the kid. Go back to that priest in Philly and see what you can uncover. . . . And Smiley," Quinn added as the killer turned to leave, "do not be too long about it."

CHAPTER THIRTEEN

Coming Up Empty

Funeral services for Mr. Weldon were a private family affair. Although Willa-Mae had been considered one of the family by the late Packard king of Akron, she was not included in the gathering. Instead she contented herself with remaining behind at the Weldon mansion to cook one final meal for the mourners before she left her job.

Shortly after the meal, Mrs. Evelyn Weldon packed her bags and headed for the train depot with her sister from Kansas City. She promised that she would write letters of recommendation for Willa-Mae as soon as her nerves settled down and she had a chance to rest a bit, but Willa-Mae doubted that Miz Evelyn would remember her promise. She had always been the nervous, delicate type, and now whatever nerves she'd had before her husband's suicide were altogether shattered.

There was a list of rich folks who had always purely admired Willa-Mae's cooking skills. In the old days, when prosperity and a good cook seemed to go hand in hand, some had even come back to the kitchen to try to steal Willa-Mae from the Weldons. She had always wrapped up extra cake for her admirers and sent them on their way with a firm but gentle no. She had always been happy cooking for the Packard king. She liked the way Mr. Weldon drove her to the market and drove her back to Howard Street after a late-night dinner party.

Well, now all that was finished. Mr. Weldon was gone. Miz Evelyn was mostly crazy and probably drunk in Kansas City. And Willa-Mae heard up and down Howard Street from former maids and kitchen help that most of those fancy, rich white folks who had raved over her cooking were now firing their cooks and maids and chauffeurs as well. Those who were not completely bankrupt were cutting back on domestic help. This meant that Howard Street unemployment suddenly soared. Times had changed. Even if Miz Evelyn somehow remembered her promise to write all those letters on Willa-Mae's behalf, there would be no position open for Willa-Mae to fill. And that was that.

Willa-Mae had been mighty proud that her cooking talents had been so admired by a man like Mr. Weldon. She had been overproud of the fact that she had her own back-door key to the Weldon mansion. That she sometimes rode in the front seat of a brand-new Packard automobile. All of this had made her secretly despise those hard times back in Arkansas.

When she had written Delpha Jean Jones down in Pine Bluff last Christmas, Willa-Mae had told about Hock's having a fine job at the tire factory, about Little Nettie's growing up and going to college, about Harry and how smart he was. She had told how much he looked like Jefferson and how he was going to graduate from high school. Along with all that, Willa-Mae had made sure she mentioned the Packard car and the running water and the big gas stove she cooked on in the Weldon kitchen. All of this was described almost as if it were Willa-Mae's own.

Delpha Jean had once lived for a while in the big city of Chicago with her sister, but unlike Willa-Mae, she had hated the North. Hated the big city. She had married her dead husband's first cousin and moved back to an Arkansas farm as soon as she could. She had never ridden in an automobile, not even one time. She washed her hands in well water. She cooked on a woodstove and lived by the old-fashioned ways that folks had always lived by.

Willa-Mae had worried after she mailed that Christmas letter that she had been altogether too prideful.

"Well, gal," she said to herself as she looked in the mirror today, "now you see what that pride brung you. What gonna happen if Hock lose his job? And what about Nettie and Harry and their fine schoolin' now, Miz Willa-Mae High-and-Mighty! Ain't gonna be no leftover pot roast and pieces of chocolate cake for you t'bring home t'Hock and Nettie and Harry."

She shook her head. "All you got t'fill up your time is cleanin' a little bitty two-room, cold-water flat and feedin' a few chickens. What else you got t'do, gal? You gonna have to walk your own self t'the store now. See how good you cook for your fambly when there ain't no fine food on the shelf and no kinda stove t'cook on 'cept a little bitty two-burner without even an oven. Delpha Jean Jones got it better'n you got it now. Leastwise she got a big garden and hogs in the bottom. You be sure and write her the truth 'bout that when you drop her a line this Christmas!"

Humbled, Willa-Mae put on her yellow Sunday dress and her blue straw hat with the yellow hatband. She put on her walking shoes and her white gloves, took up her Bible, and walked eight blocks to the old redbrick Missionary Baptist Church, where the doors were never locked.

Halfway there, it began to rain. It rained just long enough to ruin Willa-Mae's favorite hat, and then the sun came out and smiled at her. Well, now she didn't even have that hat to feel proud about, did she?

"Yessir, Lord. You got my attention," she muttered, walking up the steps to the church.

Willa-Mae was alone in the sanctuary. The place smelled musty, like damp wool coats and wet shoes. Even the pages of the hymnals and the bellows of the pump organ had begun to exhale the dank scent of winter into the room. In contrast to the heavy aroma, sunlight streamed through arched stained-glass windows, splashing a crazy quilt of red, blue, and green across walls, linoleum floors, and rows of wooden folding chairs.

Willa-Mae chose a patch of crimson light to sit in, and the tinted light turned her skin the color of the mahogany pulpit nearby. She sat for a long time, listening to the quiet.

"Well now, Lord, it's jus' me, ol' Willa-Mae. Come visitin'. Tell the truth, I don't know what else I'm gonna do now. I clean the apartment in half a hour. Make the beds up. Scrub the floor. Jus' don't know what t'do with myself now that I got no job. Nettie ain't a chil' no more. Harry's 'bout all growed. I figgered I'd live my days out over there cookin' for Mister Weldon.

"Hock and me is gettin' old, Lord. Now times gets bad, and I don't mind tellin' You, sir, I ain't easy in my mind no more. What if Hock lose his job down at the factory?"

Willa-Mae had prayed enough years to know that the Lord did not often step right up in her face and shout directions in her ears. Most times she just prayed and prayed and began to feel easy in her soul, like a mountain of worry had been lifted away. That was answer enough. It was like the Lord said to her, *Don't you worry none, Willa-Mae. You know I gonna take good care of you and yours.*

But today there was no reply, no lifting of her burdens. Willa-Mae prayed and prayed, but she did not hear the answer in her soul. The only sound was the faraway wail of the factory siren as the shifts changed.

Willa-Mae closed her eyes and let her Bible fall open. She plunged her finger to the page in hopes that some word would be there for her when she opened her eyes. Instead, she found her finger on a list of *begat*s: *the son of Amariah, the son of Azariah, the son of Meraioth. . .*

"Don't see how the begats will lead me unto understandin', Lord," she whispered in quiet disappointment. "I'm waitin'. I'm willin'. Jus' tell me what You want me t'do."

Willa-Mae sat until the sunlight through the windows grew dim. She waited and prayed and searched the pages of her Good Book, but no revelation came to her. No whisper came to her heart to say, *Willa-Mae, this is what I want you to do now. . . .*

At last she sighed and shook her head. "All right then, Lord. Guess You tellin' me t'wait. I ain't never been one t'like waitin', but now You don't give me no choice. You just gonna have t'speak up real loud when I get close to it. You jus' holler on down, *Willa-Mae! Pay attention, honey. This is it!*"

★ ★ ★

Smiley nervously studied the outline of St. Joseph's Children's Home in Philadelphia. The high gray walls that flanked the three-story brick building and the wrought-iron gate that guarded the only access to the courtyard reminded him uncomfortably of a prison.

Inside the gate, two teams of preadolescent boys were playing baseball. A crowd of even smaller children formed the rooting sections. As Smiley looked on, an argument broke out over a taunt that followed a called third strike. The batter, taller and heavier than the others, threw an awkward punch and knocked the catcher down.

The battle was joined as three more players jumped on top of the large boy and rode him to the ground. Any semblance of order dissolved into a tumbling mass of knees and elbows as everyone on both teams joined in.

Smiley grinned at one combatant's strategy. This particular boy only skirted the edge of the action, darting in to deliver a punch or a kick when his target was already down and could not retaliate.

One of the smaller children ran toward a heavy door leading into what Smiley thought of as the cellblock. "Father John, Father John! Come quick!" the boy shouted. "There's a terrible fight out here!"

Into the knot of brawlers strode a tall, spare man in cassock and clerical collar. The priest wasted no time in clapping his hands or calling for the boys' attention. Instead he waded directly into the fray and, with unerring accuracy, singled out the original offenders.

Moments later the priest emerged, an ear in each hand with a boy dangling beneath. The shouts of combat changed in pitch to less glorious cries of pain as the father escorted the two on tiptoe and posted them, nose first, against a brick wall.

Smiley examined the figure of Father John intently. So this was the man who had come to New York City in search of David Meyer. Deep down, Smiley believed that the priest had to know something. Priests always knew more than they let on, didn't they?

Smiley sized Father John up as a no-nonsense kind of individual. And that was good. But Smiley was beginning to feel anxious about his lack of progress in locating David. It might be time to play a little stronger hand than Smiley had relied on so far. He really needed to get a lucky break, or else he'd have to make one somehow.

"All right, then, who can tell me what started this donnybrook?" Father John inquired.

No one spoke. Bruised and battered though the boys were, honor demanded that no one snitch.

The priest waited, surveying the downcast heads. After an uncomfortable silence that stretched into minutes, one boy made the mistake of looking up.

"Ah—" the cleric pounced—"so, David, you tell me where it began."

David! Smiley could not believe his ears. Could it be? And why not? What better place to hide a small boy than in a whole herd of small boys?

The child in question had darker hair than Smiley remembered about David Meyer, but who paid attention to kids anyway? Of course, the fact that the young man had received a bloody nose and a swollen eye in the fracas made positive identification even tougher.

But what a chance! Smiley crossed his fingers in an unconscious return to a childhood habit of his own and began to think about how to get the boy alone for a little discussion.

Father John gathered up the two major offenders in the great baseball battle and marched them into the building. The game resumed, and Smiley noted with interest that the boy called David was posted in center field, just inside the iron gate.

Smiley weighed the options. Should he pretend to be a deliveryman? Could he call the boy over to the fence with a question about directions? Smiley did not want to be seen, but if the chance presented itself to grab the kid . . .

Briefly Smiley considered doing none of these things. Now that he had located the boy, he could alert Boss Quinn of his success and then wait till he had some help.

Smiley rejected this idea with a shake of his head. To balance his earlier failures successfully, he needed to actually have the kid in hand himself. Then, too, what if it wasn't the right boy after all?

While all these thoughts were tumbling around in Smiley's head, the batter at the plate tagged a high fast one and sent an arcing fly ball toward center field. The ball looked as if it would drop inside the court-yard . . . until a gusting breeze held it up and carried it toward the wall.

Smiley saw the hit and noted the outfielders backing up, but the potential did not register with him until the ball actually bounced on top of the stones. It caromed upward again before coming down in the street and rolling to a stop in the gutter.

Smiley retrieved it and held it in his hand as he watched the center fielder run over to the gate. "Hey, mister! That's our ball."

"Yeah, kid? So come and get it," Smiley challenged.

"Please, mister. Toss it here. We ain't allowed to go out." The boy wiped some more blood from his injured nose onto his shirtsleeve.

"Hurry it up, will ya, Davey?" the pitcher yelled in disgust as the home-run hitter circled the bases in triumph. The attention of both teams turned from the recovery of the ball to the celebration going on at home plate.

"Look, kid," Smiley said, tossing the ball up and catching it, "I need some help myself, see? Some directions."

The boy approached the gate. "Sure, I know Philly good. Where did you need to go?"

Smiley thought of the baseball's rise and fall. "Shibe Park. The ball-park."

"Easy, mister," the boy scoffed. "Down that way ten or twelve blocks. That's all. Nothin' to it."

Smiley appeared confused. "I still ain't sure, kid. Can you come out and write it down for me? It's worth a quarter, see?"

The boy cast a quick look over his shoulder. The players had located another ball, and the game was getting ready to resume. There were no grown-ups in sight.

"Okay," the boy agreed. "I guess it'll be okay." He worked the latch and stepped outside the barricade.

Smiley extended the hand holding the baseball. "Here you go, kid. Now, where'd you say to turn at?"

As the boy stepped closer to recover the ball, Smiley grabbed him by the shirtfront.

"Lemme go!" the boy shrieked. "Help!"

"Youse comin' with me, David Meyer," Smiley stated. "So shut up and youse won't get hurt." He tried to clamp his hand over the boy's mouth.

"I *ain't* David Meyer," the boy sputtered, twisting and kicking. "I don't even know no David Meyer." He bit Smiley's hand hard, chomping down on two of Smiley's fingers.

The gangster dropped the child and swore.

"Help!" the boy yelled again as he scampered back toward the gate. Smiley beat a hasty retreat.

Ellis looked at the giant face of the smiling Quaker on the billboard outside the Quaker Oats plant. It was a friendly image, warm and homey, like a steaming bowl of hot oats in the morning. A very different image than that of Titan's cold metal giant hefting a tire into the air as if to roll it over some helpless dog or passing pedestrian. Ellis wondered how different his life might have been if he had gotten his moonlighting job from the smiling Quaker instead of Titan's malevolent giant.

He yawned and settled back on the streetcar that carried him toward People's Hospital. It had been a long day at his own clinic, and the prospect of a long night at the plant loomed like a dark cloud in front of him. Even so, he had put off a visit to young John Daugherty long enough.

"Hey, Doc Ellis," Danny the streetcar driver called back to him. Danny was also a veteran of the Great War and considered himself a friend.

"How's it going, Danny?"

"Not sure yet," the man replied with a noncommittal wigwag of his leather-gloved hand. This was so out of character for the normally sunny driver that Ellis had to ask for an explanation.

"Ain't you heard, Doc? The Traction Company is fixin' to lay off about fifty of us. Rumors are flyin' about plants shuttin' down and all, and the company figgers to get the jump on fewer riders by cuttin' out some runs."

"Not you, though—right, Danny?" Ellis knew that Danny supported his wife and six kids along with his mother and an elderly grandmother on his motorman's salary. "They wouldn't let you go. You've been on this line long as I can remember."

"Eight years, come summer. Still, I ain't too sure."

Ellis got to his feet as the car slid to a stop in front of the hospital. "I'm sure it will work out, Danny. You let me know how it goes, will you?"

A soft rain had begun to fall, making the sidewalk slick. Ellis wished he had his cane. His leg was throbbing, so he waited for the elevator to the third-floor ward where Johnny Daugherty lay with his upper torso tightly bandaged.

A few family members had taken seats beside the beds of the six patients in the ward, but none were around Johnny's bed. Ellis was

relieved that the young man was alone. In the dimmed light, it was difficult to see that the dark-haired, handsome youth was missing an arm.

The boy's eyes were closed, but his pale and drawn face was screwed
so tightly into an unhappy frown that Ellis knew it was not sleep that
shut his lids.

"Johnny," he murmured. "It's Doctor Warne."

The hazel eyes that blinked open were clouded with pain, fear, and
greater sorrow than any seventeen-year-old should ever know. "Hi,
Doc," he answered in a monotone.

"They treating you good?"

"Good enough. Food stinks, though."

"So I've heard." Ellis pulled a bag of hard candy from his overcoat
and placed it on top of the bed. "Butterscotch and cherry. A whole
pound. Take at least one after every meal to get rid of the rotten taste," he
said in an attempt to lighten the mood.

"Thanks," Johnny said. But he made no move to open the bag.

"Johnny, I . . . I know what you're going through," Ellis began. "I may
be one of the few who can say that and really mean it. You know about
this, don't you?" He raised his trouser leg and exposed the bottom of the
prosthesis. "It doesn't make you less of a man to be missing a leg . . . or
an arm. It's how whole you are inside that counts."

Ellis's words sounded flat even in his own ears. He thought to himself how much lying and deceiving he had done lately. What right did he
have to talk about being whole on the inside?

"It's not just my arm, Doc," Johnny explained. "That can't be helped
now. But they are saying I was drunk. They say I was stinking, and I fell
into the machinery 'cause I couldn't . . ." Angry tears filled his eyes and
overflowed onto his pillow. "It's a lousy lie. I never had a drop that whole
day—not one!"

"I know, Johnny. I will tell Titan that I am certain you hadn't been
drinking, and I'll tell anybody else who wants to know."

"Good." The boy laid his head back and closed his eyes as if Ellis's
words were a great relief. "I been thinking about it a lot. Trying to figure
out what I could've done different." His eyes opened and fixed on Ellis
with intensity. "Don't tell Mom about the yarn from the sweater. She'd
think it was her fault, see? She told me to put on the sweater, and then
. . . well, there wasn't any way to stop it. It happened so fast. Faster than
anything, but I see every second of it over and over and over."

"I know," Ellis said, letting the boy talk it out.

"The guys must think I'm a real coward, too. Screaming and yelling
my head off."

Ellis put a hand to the boy's forehead. He and Johnny had lived the crisis together, and somehow it now belonged to both of them to deal with. "When I lost my leg," he said, "boy, did I yell! And I cried some, too, later. A man told me—he was a German—he said my loss would not make the world a better place, that it was only a waste . . . if it did not make me a better man. Don't let this stop you, Johnny. Don't let this stop you from doing whatever you set your mind to do."

"Like you, huh? Being a doctor and helping people and all?"

Ellis did not reply. Tonight at the bedside of the wounded boy, he felt like a failure. Ellis had known about the unsafe conditions at the plant, but what had he done to change them? Didn't that make him partly responsible for Johnny's arm? And what about now? Johnny Daugherty was just one life out of the thousands employed at Titan. What could Ellis do about any of it?

"Well, I gotta go," Ellis said. He was suddenly feeling very old and very tired. His leg ached, and so did his head.

"Thanks . . . thanks for coming by, Doc. It helps to talk, you know?"

"Sure, Johnny," Ellis said, starting for the door, then turning back for a final word. "You're going to be all right."

CHAPTER FOURTEEN

Titan's Strategy

"You're late, Doctor," said Giselle, thrusting a cup of steaming coffee into Ellis's hand. "The waiting room is full already."

"I stopped off to check on the Daugherty kid," Ellis explained.

Giselle's tough features softened. "How's he doing?"

Ellis frowned and shook his head. "Physically he is out of danger. Emotionally . . . I just don't know. To go from being young, healthy, and whole one minute to—" Ellis stopped as the vision of John Daugherty's arm caught in the machinery collided with his own memories of losing his leg. "It's hard to know what to say," he concluded.

Ellis raised his head and sniffed the air. For once the scent of rubber was concealed beneath the pungent aroma of disinfectant. "Somebody have an accident with the cleaning fluid?" He wiped his eyes with the back of his hand. "Rumor has it that Mister Titan will be dropping in for the visit he missed the other day. He'll probably ask us if we know how much disinfectant costs per gallon."

"You should have smelled it in here before. That new man—the Romeo in accounting I told you about—he was the first to stop in to see you, and he puked all over."

"Some lady-killer—"

"Said he felt sick, like the flu. Personally, I think it was a bad batch of bathtub gin. The girl he was out with didn't come in to work today . . . called in sick. Thelma in receivables says she saw them both last night. Them and half the men from Plant One were drinking after the shift ended. Trying to forget what happened to Daugherty."

A low groan from the waiting room next to the tiny cubicle of an office reached Ellis's ears. He held up his hand to silence Giselle. "Okay, so the official diagnosis is 'hangover.'"

"Only if you want to get them fired, you know." She shrugged. "To tell you the truth, I can't say as I blame them much. Almost makes me wish I was a drinking woman."

"There are easier ways to poison yourself than drinking bootleg gin— did you say *them*?"

"There are nine men waiting out there for you. All from Plant One, same crew as Daugherty. I'd bet a week's pay they were all at the same speakeasy. Thema says—"

"Observant lady, Thelma is."

"Her second cousin runs the joint. Two blocks from here. Thelma says business triples every time there's an accident. Folks are scared it could have been them. Besides, you know what they say: Accidents come in threes. They're all wondering who's next."

Ellis slipped into his white jacket and studied a cupboard full of laxative bottles. "Accidents come in threes because Thelma's cousin serves bad booze to men who drink too much and quit paying attention at work. If a man wants to drink himself numb, he's got no business at the plant."

"Terrific, Doctor. If you could say that with a little more self-righteousness, you would sound just like Jack Titan himself."

The telephone rang. Giselle squeezed past Ellis to answer it. "Infirmary." Giselle listened for a minute and made a face before saying "Thank you" and hanging up. "Speak of the devil," she said to Ellis. "That was Missus Fremont, Titan's personal secretary. She says the old man is on the way."

"Good thing she likes us enough to warn us," Ellis observed.

"Yes," Giselle agreed, "but now it's decision time for you. What are you going to do with them?" Giselle gestured with a meaty thumb toward the doorway into the waiting room. "You know there'll be nine fewer men working at Plant One if Titan gets even a hint of hangovers."

"It takes five minutes to walk here from the main office," Ellis calculated. "Just watch what a miracle worker I am."

The nine men in the waiting room barely glanced up as Ellis entered and promptly slammed his clipboard onto the floor. The explosion resounded against the brick walls like a rifle shot. Hands went up to cover ears and massage aching eyes and heads. A collective moan arose. Definitely bad booze.

Giselle had followed Ellis into the room. She exchanged a knowing look with Ellis, then smacked her meaty hands together. "Gentlemen," she boomed, "may I have your attention, please?"

Groans of misery replied. All they wanted was some free aspirin and maybe an ice pack. Nurse Giselle's voice made even the roar of the tire plant seem pleasantly peaceful.

"Well, Nurse," said Ellis in mock concern, "it seems to me that all these fellows are exhibiting the same symptoms. Throbbing heads, sensitivity to light and sound. Dry mouth."

At the recital of the symptoms, the heads of the patients nodded gently in agreement. "That's right, Doc," mumbled one. The man had kneaded his hat into a shapeless lump of felt.

"And your stomachs?" Ellis inquired. "A little queasy? The idea of a nice, greasy pork chop a little disturbing right now?"

The complexion of the man with the hat turned the color of the whitewashed walls, and he buried his face in the crown of the hat.

"There, you see, Nurse? An epidemic. Call Mister Titan and warn him not to come down here right now."

Heads snapped up in terror. *Titan? Coming here?*

"I'm afraid he's already on the way, Doctor."

Panic-stricken bloodshot eyes appealed to Ellis for help.

"All right," Ellis said. "Out the back with you all and get home. You've not only lost a day's pay; you came near to losing your jobs. If I see any of you like this again, I guarantee that your employment at Titan will be at an end. Understood?"

There were feeble nods and mumbled thank-yous as the men stumbled to their feet. "Much obliged, Doc."

"All of you stop in to see me before your shift tomorrow night. Now get going, and hurry it up."

The waiting room was empty in seconds. The last of the workers had just disappeared when Jack Titan arrived.

✫ ✫ ✫

Jack Titan, in contrast to his name, was a small man in every sense of the word. He stood a mere five feet, five inches, which put his head just above the center of Ellis's chest. Dressed in a plain black suit, he showed a puritanical demeanor—grim and stern. No one had ever seen him smile, except once in 1920 when a rival tire company found itself in financial difficulty.

Titan prided himself that his rubber empire extended from Akron to the rubber plantations in the jungle and that every brick and board was paid for. Although Titan stock was traded on the Big Board in New York, Titan himself owned 51 percent of the shares. He might seek the advice of his board of directors and top officials, but every major decision was made by Jack Titan himself.

Titan also prided himself that he had worked his way to the top from a life of poverty. He was proud of his early suffering, and he believed that all men should take pride in suffering. Such was his philosophy. He lived by it. This belief made compassion an alien emotion. Life had never been easy for him, he often declared, thumping his puny chest, and he was a better man because of it, was he not? Such reasoning led him to conclude that a sparse and difficult existence forged men of better character.

Titan believed with all the force of his obstinate will that men were just like tires: Those that were molded by great heat and pressure under the strictest supervision would wear the best on life's uncertain road. Those were the exact words he often proclaimed to workers and toadies alike. And that was the thinking that kept him from putting his hard-earned cash into modernizing the plant or raising the standard of working conditions for the thousands who trudged to work each day and night. Every man was expendable, he said. Those who found working at Titan Tire not to their liking could find employment elsewhere, if they cared to try.

Even the medical clinic, he confided to a member of his board, was simply a bone he had thrown out to satisfy the union dogs and the politicians. Let a man be healthy, or let him be sick while in the employ of someone else. Gummers were expected to be hardy, robust, and grateful. Otherwise they were slackers . . . or worse, drunkards. Titan had no time or inclination to coddle either one.

The accident that had taken Johnny Daugherty's arm was uppermost in Titan's mind, but not because of the consequences to the young man. The owner's concern was solely that the incident not impede the building of tires—not by downtime, not by lost morale, and not by increased union demands for safer conditions. Titan intended to see that none of those unfortunate circumstances disrupted the orderly production of his tires, and he expected that the medical staff he owned would cooperate like obedient machines.

"You are the doctor who saved the life of the young man," Titan began. "How unfortunate that you had to amputate his hand." He made this sound as if a piece of equipment in the plant had broken and had to be discarded.

"The entire arm. Clear up to the shoulder," Ellis corrected.

Titan flashed him a black look. Why make it sound so bad? Apparently this doctor would need some instruction before he wrote up a report that would be shown to the union officials or the press.

"But he was drunk, of course. So many of these young, irresponsible men are. Spend their pay on bootleg whiskey."

Ellis replied in a quiet, reasoning voice, "Sometimes the men drink, and the drinking causes accidents," he conceded, "but that was not true in this instance. The lad is only seventeen. New on the job. When I was able to question him about it—"

Titan raised his small hand in an imperious demand for silence. "He was drunk," he asserted again. "Reliable sources tell me that he was seen at a speakeasy in the company of his uncle, Jack Daugherty, and several other union troublemakers just before their shift began. Of course, you could not be expected to know such details, Doctor. It is in the best interest of the company that we keep tabs on men of this sort for reasons of safety and security. For the benefit of all our employees. I have the full report on my desk."

Ellis could not let the slander stand, despite the warning tone in Titan's words. "He had a loose strand of yarn on his sweater. The plant is cold this time of year, so he was wearing a sweater. The yarn caught on the belt. He stumbled and fell, and since there is no guardrail, his arm was pulled into the works of the machine. Alcohol was not a factor."

Titan drew himself up, lifting his chin in a way that dared Ellis to defy him further. "He lied to you, naturally. Obviously he has been coached by the union rats in an effort to make this factory look responsible for his own negligence and stupidity. Are you listening, Doctor? Tomorrow we will issue a news release that will discuss our concerns about the issues of alcohol abuse and plant safety. This case will be one example of how such weakness cuts productivity and endangers the health of our law-abiding employees. The truth *will* be told to the union and anyone else who cares to ask. John Daugherty was drunk!"

Wearily, Ellis attempted to reason with Titan. "Morale everywhere is low enough that there are many who turn to drink. But in this particular instance I do not think—"

"That's right, Doctor Warne. Do not think. You are not well-enough informed about the situation to think. It is your duty simply to act on company policy. Those Titan employees caught frequenting any of the speakeasies in Akron will be discharged immediately! This Daugherty accident will be used as an example," Titan explained coolly, as though he did not doubt that Ellis would cooperate. "Our security investigation reveals that at least one-third of our employees fall into the category of those who, because of drink or other moral weakness, endanger the plant. Three thousand men. An entire shift. We have asked for and received the cooperation of the municipal police. We have a list of offenders. And I can assure you that Titan Tire and

Rubber Company will ferret drunkards and slackers out and see that they are terminated at once. It is our duty to see that the health and safety of other employees is not jeopardized."

"And that the production quota of the plant is maintained," Ellis added dryly. He did not ask if all the names on Titan's list were also members of the union. That was understood. The gravest moral weakness of all, in the eyes of the company, was that of associating with the union.

Jack Titan's plan, while not spelled out in detail tonight, was clear. Cut manpower by perhaps one-third. Eliminate any union presence in the plant in one bold stroke and thus remove the possibility of any organized protest from the remaining gummers. Slash wages. And all the while demand that the same number of tires be produced as before. By paying less for the production of his tires, Titan could sell them for less and undercut his competition.

Titan had already determined that his company would survive whatever hard times lay ahead. He would not let the union stand in his way. Nor would he let Ellis interfere with his plan to turn young John Daugherty's tragedy into a public-relations advantage.

"You are an intelligent man." Titan smiled, certain that he had won his point. "You see why it is important that our public statement point out the fact that John Daugherty had been drinking just before his shift. His case justifies much of the action we are forced to take for the good of our business. While other companies will surely fail in the future, as captain at the helm of the Titan ship, I intend to see that we sail through the shoals safely."

"With the union third of the crew overboard."

Titan replied calmly, heedless of the sarcasm. "It is mostly a concession to the weak sisters who run crying to the union for every hangnail that this clinic exists at all. If it weren't for stupid little men like . . . whatever his name is . . . and slackards like him, you might be one of those who went overboard."

Again Titan smiled with self-assurance. "Titan investigates all employees, Doctor Warne. We were sorry to hear you had such bad luck in the stock market. Hard times. Ah well, we are all going to have to cut back. Here at the factory. And at home. Your position here is secure . . . unless you choose to go your own way. You are free to do that if you wish, but I rather think you will see things our way. Am I clear?"

Ellis opened his mouth, then closed it again abruptly. The threat behind Titan's last remark had not been veiled in the least. Nothing Ellis could do or say would bring back Johnny Daugherty's arm. What would happen to Becky and Boots if Ellis got fired now after he had already lost all their savings?

"Clear, Mister Titan." Ellis could not look the little man in the face. "It is never safe to be around heavy machinery after drinking."

Smiley studied the little brick house behind St. Joseph's. It was old and ramshackle, having already existed when the land was donated for the children's home, but it continued a useful life as Father John's residence.

While the school building and grounds were fortresslike and locked securely at night, the priest's home was laughably easy to approach. A half ring of ancient elms clustered against the back of the dwelling. In the deepening shadows, Smiley was able to edge close without being seen.

Apparently there was nothing anybody would want to steal. Smiley jiggled the latch, and the unlocked door popped open in his hand.

What had once been a parlor was now Father John's office. The shelves were jumbled with books, school papers, pipes with broken stems, dusty sports trophies, and faded photographs.

In the center of the messy desk, a space had been cleared to accommodate a small green footlocker. All around the empty metal box were what had apparently been its contents, sorted into piles.

On the top of a stack of books was one whose cover showed a balding man in a swallowtail coat leaning over the shoulder of a girl wearing a striped pinafore. *Dorothy and the Wizard in Oz*, the title read.

Another pile contained bundles of letters tied with string, balancing on top of a leather-bound photo album. Some of the letters had fallen onto the floor.

In a third heap were personal things. A tortoiseshell brush-and-comb set joined a perfume bottle, a crocheted doily, and a child-sized knit sweater.

Smiley held up the sweater. As he lifted it clear of the clutter, a single folded sheet of paper floated free and landed on Smiley's shoe.

Dear Father John, the carefully printed note read, *I am running away. . . .*

There was more, but Smiley's eye jumped to the signature. There, beneath a place where something had been scribbled out completely, was the name *David Meyer.*

Smiley chuckled out loud, a rattling sound like a Model T starting on a cold morning. Smiley had been right to come to the priest for information, and here was the proof!

Smiley was reaching toward the photo album when the front door of the cottage home rattled. He jumped back from the desk and dropped the note to the floor. His gaze swept around the room, wondering if he had left anything out of place. He decided that no one could tell anyway.

Concealing himself behind the threadbare window curtains, Smiley faded into the cluttered background. At one time the curtains had been striped with red and yellow, but they had paled to a uniform rusty shade. The tips of Smiley's brogans stuck out at the bottom, but the approaching steps were coming directly into the office. Smiley froze in place.

Through a tiny rip in the fabric of the drapes, Smiley watched as Father John entered the room. The priest switched on the single lightbulb that dangled nakedly in the room's center and began patting his pockets. He located a dark brown briar pipe, matches, and a flat red tin of Prince Albert. Loading, tamping, and lighting the tobacco was a process that consumed several minutes.

When the pipe was well lit, the priest settled himself comfortably in his desk chair with his back to the window. Father John picked up the Oz book and hefted it in his hand, as if its weight could tell him something.

Smiley's hand crept toward his overcoat pocket and emerged holding the .38. Father John was staring at the corner of the ceiling and tapping his pipestem against his bottom teeth.

Three strides and Smiley was behind the chair, pressing the muzzle of the pistol against the back of the priest's head. "Don't turn around," the hood ordered, "if youse knows what's good for ya."

Father John neither cried out nor dropped the pipe. In a surprisingly calm voice, he said, "I know why you've come, but you are wasting your time. I don't know where he is."

"What do ya mean?" questioned Smiley sullenly.

"You are after David Meyer, aren't you? These are his things, of course, and you think I can help you locate him for your boss—what's his name?—Quinn."

"Quit wid da storytellin'. I know he's here, and youse is gonna help me get him."

"Here?" Father John said incredulously, beginning to turn around.

Smiley poked the gun barrel into the priest's ear. "I told youse ta stay still. Now, I heard youse call him David, and I seen youse together."

"David? David?" the priest said in some confusion. "Oh, so it was you who terrorized Davey Rabinsky this afternoon—a different child altogether."

"Yeah, sure," Smiley said. "This is a flimflam job."

"Would I be sitting here surrounded by all his things if the boy was already here? I'm still as puzzled by his whereabouts as the FBI." Father John pointedly emphasized the last three initials.

"Yeah, but you know more than you're tellin'. I think youse is runnin' a bluff here." Smiley tried to sound forceful, but a note of doubt had crept into his voice.

"Do you want some advice? Give this up," Father John suggested. "Do you think that hunting down a child will go unpunished? Just look at this." The priest extracted a letter from the heap of papers and held it up over his left shoulder.

Smiley took the letter but twisted the revolver into Father John's ear to reemphasize that he meant business. "Don't try nothin'," he growled.

The message was on FBI stationery and was dated only two days ago. It requested that Father John please review all David Meyer's personal belongings one more time. The FBI was narrowing the search, the note said, after eliminating certain possibilities, but they would still appreciate any help the priest could provide.

"You see," said Father John. "I do not have the boy, nor do I know where to find him. But the FBI, with better resources than you or I have, are certainly closing in even as we speak."

Smiley did not reply for a time. Then, very softly, he said, "Bless me, Father, for I have sinned." With that he smashed the butt of the pistol into the back of Father John's head.

CHAPTER FIFTEEN

Miss Price Cuts the Rug

It was called the Shiloh School Dance, not because it was at the school but because its main purpose was to raise money for the school. Three times a year, the citizens of Shiloh put on this event in the large barn of Woody Woods and charged two bits a head for admission. Young single women brought boxed suppers to be bid for at auction. Young men brought cash to purchase both the boxed supper and the privilege of accompanying their gal for the evening.

Fiddle music drifted out from the open door of the barn. Folks in line for admission tapped their toes in time and strained to see who had gone in before them . . . who was already dancing . . . who was standing to the side and watching.

Homemade pies, cakes, jams, and jellies, donated by the married women and all for sale, decorated the side table by the punch bowl. A quilt made by the Women's Christian Sewing Circle on Wednesday afternoons was on display, and raffle tickets to determine its owner were available for purchase from every school-aged youngster in the valley. The proceeds of this great enterprise paid the salary of Miss Price, the schoolteacher, as well as providing a small stipend for two young assistants, supplies for the classroom, and upkeep for the building.

Miss Price was a scrawny-necked spinster in her midthirties. It was her philosophy that children responded best to absolute authority and were motivated to learn by fear of consequences. She normally displayed a bad temper toward her young charges, and those who did not fear her simply hated her. No student could remain indifferent to her for long.

Miss Price assumed that being despised by sixty pupils from the first grade through the eighth was the price of being an effective teacher, and she bore this cross with the air of stoic martyrdom. It was a rare thing to see her smile, Tommy had told David. She usually looked as if she had eaten a dill pickle. Sour and cranky, she seemed always to be looking for some reason to take the paddle down off the nail in the wall beneath George Washington's picture.

This evening, however, Miss Price was all smiles. Sitting behind a small table positioned just inside the doorway, she took money for the tickets. "Oh, how good to see you, Missus Peabody! Well, isn't this just a grand turnout?" She greeted the parents of her students as if they had not heard the truth about life in her classroom. Tonight she even spoke to the children in a civil tone. More than civil, it was downright gushy—and downright hypocritical, considering how she spoke to them in the classroom.

Most folks did not like Miss Price personally, but she had been hired at half the cost of all the other applicants. Because of this fact she was secretly nicknamed "Half-Price." The woman was not a bargain, Trudy often said to Birch, even if she was cheap.

Bobby, being younger, feared her. Tommy, now a fourth grader, had graduated to a sullen, obedient hatred with just enough fear to keep him in line and just enough anger to make him brave on occasion.

Tommy peered around his mother and raised a hand to hide his whisper to David. "There she is, the old bag of cow plop." This was a semibrave thing to say about her when she was so close. Tommy had become convinced that she had supersensitive hearing, like a bat. She seemed to hear everything that was said within the entire radius of the school yard.

The true reason for the extraordinary ability of Miss Price to pick up on whispered insults was that she believed all of her students were guilty of something. A sideways glance, a furtive turning, a mouth moving behind a hand were all evidence of that universal guilt, and she punished the sinner accordingly. Who could argue with such reasoning?

David squinted through the long line to see Miss Price's spindly hands reaching out to take money from Buck Hooper. Spiderlike, she was. Her hair was black, streaked with gray, and pulled back in a tight bun, forming a knot on top of her skull. Her face was pinched in the cheeks where she had lost some molars. Her nose was long and threw a shadow over her thin lips. Dark eyebrows, growing together in the middle, made a straight line above her black eyes.

"Holy cats, Tommy, you were right," David squeaked.

"Told ya she looks like a witch, didn't I?" Tommy said in a voice too loud. Trudy responded to her son by giving him a stout thump on the head and a warning glance to indicate that he had better be quiet or he would end up spending the whole dance outside in the wagon.

David gave Tommy a nudge of sympathy and agreement about the demeanor and looks of the schoolmarm. Then, as if she heard their thoughts, Miss Price looked up. She lifted that pointed head and held David in her steely gaze. In a flash, David could see that whatever friendliness she was showing toward the adults tonight was a performance. Her mouth twitched to one side at the sight of this new kid. Her eyes narrowed, hardened, threatened, then turned away to smile falsely at the next person in line.

David was sure Miss Price hated him at first glance. He had hoped that the head schoolmistress in Shiloh would be someone like his own mother or perhaps like Aunt Trudy, who had already spent several evenings refreshing his memory in the McGuffey reader. Instead he found himself face-to-face with the Wicked Witch right out of the Land of Oz.

David shuddered. He would stand among those pupils who feared her. "Holy cats," he said again.

"That goes for you, too, young man." Trudy gave David the kind of look his mama used to give him when he was close to violating some rule.

"Yes, ma'am." David looked nervously toward an approaching Model T with an old man behind the wheel and an old lady sitting up in the front seat beside him like an ancient queen. The old lady was dressed as she had been the day of the funeral. Black dress, black bonnet.

David tugged the sleeve of Max's coat as Max spoke to a group of farmers about the price of cotton on the Chicago commodities market and what that might mean for next year's crop. Maybe it would be wise to plant peanuts or corn or something along with cotton. Diversify in case the bottom fell out. A second cash crop to sell if the worst came over the next season. Livestock? The price of cattle and pork bellies was low and miserable as well. Max advised goober peas. Peanuts, he claimed, would be the main crop in the South in a very few years. Cotton was only headed down. He doubted that the cotton gin owned by Ned Hooper and his son Buck would pay enough for next year's cotton crop for the Shiloh farmers to make a profit. Those farmers who clung to the old ways, Max said, would go down for the count.

"Dad," David whispered urgently, pulling his father's attention to something much more dangerous than next year's price of cotton.

"What?" Max responded to David's whisper in a similar voice. "What's your scoop? Corn or pork bellies?"

"The teacher. Miss Price." David raised his eyebrows and jerked his head as if to register his amazement that the sole purpose of this gathering was to make money to pay the salary of the woman taking tickets. *Unbelievable. A woman that mean-looking ought to be happy to work for free*, David thought.

"Hmmm. Live cattle on the hoof, huh? Price just hit bottom." Max scowled and shook his head. "Bet she doesn't do much dancing."

Birch gave a loud hoot at that. He was silenced by Trudy's glare. "Well, it's true," he defended.

"I don't care if it is!" Trudy snapped. "The quickest way to get our boys on her bad side is to let her overhear."

"We're already on her bad side, Mama," Tommy replied without a trace of humor.

"You mean she has a good side?" Max nudged Tommy and then ducked as Trudy cast him a dangerous look.

"Do not encourage this, Max," she warned. "It is not a laughing matter."

Max held up his hands as if to surrender to Trudy's better judgment. The rest of their conference was conducted in barely audible whispers. "You are right, dear Trudy. A woman who does not dance when the party is given in her honor is nothing to laugh at. A pitiful situation. Pitiful."

"She wouldn't dance if President Herbert Hoover himself asked her," Birch offered.

"Who *would* dance with Hoover?" Max replied.

"Then Rudolph Valentine. She wouldn't dance with the sheik of Araby," Birch retorted.

"You mean Valentino?"

"Him either. I tell you, Max, she's got no joy in her. That woman probably never danced a step in her life, and she ain't even a Baptist. Doesn't know how to have a good time. She'd make a better lion tamer at the Barnum & Bailey circus than a teacher of kids, and that is the truth."

"Maybe she's just never been asked."

"She wouldn't dance anyhow, I tell you."

"Do you care to place a small wager on it, old pal?" Max was grinning as if he meant it.

David drew in his breath. Could his dad actually intend to ask Miss Price to dance just to prove a point? Unthinkable.

"I ain't a bettin' man, " Birch began, then went on, "but this is a sure thing. It ain't a wager. It's takin' candy from a baby. Well, yes, Mister Valentino or whoever you think you are. I'll lay one dollar on that. Miss Price will turn you down cold. Don't matter who you are. That woman will spit in your eye."

"Don't do it, Dad," David begged. The possibility that she might say yes loomed large in the boy's mind. It would be a difficult thing to be marked as the son of the man who danced with old Half-Price.

"You have a wager," Max replied quietly.

"No! Dad, please." David held on to Max's sleeve.

But it was too late. Max smiled at Miss Price and tipped his hat. She noticed and smiled back. The line inched forward.

"How do you do, Miss Price?" Max said when they reached the ticket table. "They tell me that you are the lovely object of this fine party."

Was that a blush on the pallid cheek? a glint in the steely eye?

"I am Miss Price," she demurred and extended her hand to be shaken.

Max took her hand and gave it a kiss. A kiss!

David hid his face in shame. Could he look at this? His own father had just put his lips on her actual hand! The same hand that grabbed ears and wielded the paddle and whacked kids with rulers was now held gently by Max Meyer.

"This is your party, yet you are sitting here working like a slave, Miss Price." Max motioned to Mary Brown, who was tending the punch bowl. "Miss Brown, will you take over the ticket table for a moment? I do believe that this is my dance, if Miss Price will do me the honor."

"Oh, good heavens, no, Mister Meyer. I couldn't leave my duties greeting—"

"Miss Brown does not mind helping for just a few moments. Do you, Miss Brown?"

Mary Brown gave Max a stunned look, rubbed her chin, and shook her head. She would not mind. She would take tickets if Max Meyer wanted to dance with Miss Price. Of course.

"Now you cannot say no, Miss Price," said Max, pulling the schoolteacher to her feet and onto the dance floor like a blushing ingenue.

Then the fiddle began to play "Turkey in the Straw." To the great amazement of all present, Miss Price took to the tune like a duck to water. She smiled and cocked her head coyly to one side as Max spun her around the dance floor.

David shook his head in utter amazement. Who would have guessed that the Iron Maiden knew how to cut a rug?

Tommy nudged David and gave a wink. The quick whispers between the cousins explained it all.

Watching from the sidelines, Dan Faraby, a recent widower left with nine children to care for, had just seen something new and wonderful out there. A transformation had taken place. Miss Price was suddenly more than just a spinster schoolmarm. If Miss Price could dance, maybe she could cook and keep house for a man as well. Dan Faraby had already muttered to bystanders that he was certain that if she could manage sixty children, she could probably also manage his nine mother-less young'uns. So Dan cut in.

Also watching from the sidelines, Grandma Amos predicted that those two would make a match. The old woman instantly had a word from the Lord about it, which meant that before the last strains of "Turkey in the Straw" had died away, the matter was as good as settled.

"One dollar is one dollar," Max said, grinning, to Birch. He put his hand out, palm up.

"First time in my life I bet money and I lose. That'll teach me."

The three boys went off to sulk on a hay bale behind the fiddle player. Max had disgraced them good by dancing with old Half-Price. But there was some comfort in the fact that now Mr. Faraby was disgracing his children as well. In fact, Mr. Faraby danced with Half-Price through "Clementine," "Cotton-Eyed Joe," and "Let Me Call You Sweetheart."

David refused to be consoled. He felt as if his own father had consorted with the enemy—danced with a spider, who had now gone on to trap poor Mr. Faraby in her web. Nine Faraby children sat clustered like a family portrait of dismay as their father said something and Miss Price laughed. A real laugh it was, too. No one had ever seen her laugh before. Not ever.

"Traitor," muttered David to his father when he came near.

"Well, you've done it now, Uncle Max," said Tommy with a dazed shake of his head. "Look at her and Mister Faraby. Old Grandma Amos has a word that they'll get married now, and we'll just have to break in a new schoolteacher."

"Them Faraby kids gonna blame us for this." Bobby sighed.

"A bet is a bet, boys," Max claimed. "One dollar is one dollar." He handed the silver coin to David. "Now you boys go on over and buy those Faraby kids all the ice cream you can eat. They'll forget about it soon enough."

Cheered by this, the mourning committee broke and ran for the ice-cream booth, calling the Farabys and picking up a few strays as well. . . .

After the boys had gleefully run off for ice cream, Max felt a hand at his elbow. He turned to see Mary Brown.

"That was kind of you, Mister Meyer," said Mary.

"Kids and ice cream. When I was a kid—"

"A lonely woman, Miss Price. I don't believe anyone ever asked her to dance before. Now two lonely people are enjoying each other's company. I mean, it was kind of you to make the effort."

"Ah, well . . ." Max did not explain about the dollar bet. He shrugged as if the good deed had just been a natural part of his personality. As if he came to all dances in search of lonely wallflowers who needed help to bloom. "She looked like she needed cheering up."

Mary Brown was no wallflower. She wore a pale blue velvet dress. Her sky blue eyes were intelligent and sparkling with interest in him. Her oval face turned up to challenge him. "Is that why you asked her to dance?"

"Sure," he said modestly. "Really. It was nothing. Sometimes it's just a good idea to help people out—"

"Like you helped Birch Tucker out of that dollar?" She grinned and headed back to the punch bowl.

"Ah. So I've been found out."

The band began to play "For Me and My Gal." Couples drifted onto the floor.

"All's well that ends well, as they say." Mary handed Max a cup of punch just as Buck Hooper strode up.

"Hey, Mary," slurred Buck. "My dance, sugar plum! 'Me an' My Gal!' They're playin' our song, Mary!" The smell of whiskey was thick on his breath.

"Sorry, Buck." She took Max's arm. "This one is taken. Isn't that so, Mister Meyer? Like you said?"

"I have asked Miss Brown to dance with me." Max shoved the punch into Buck's meaty paw and pulled Mary onto the dance floor.

"Wait a minute!" Buck protested. "I been waitin' all night!" He stepped after them, only to be cut off from following by the blacksmith James Brown and his wife.

"Thank you, Uncle Jim." Laughing, Mary explained to Max, "I have been dodging him all night. You have just assisted another lady in distress. I thank you, sir knight."

"My pleasure. Really." Max pulled her closer, enjoying the fact that she was an excellent dancer.

"If you will just glide me over to the door, I will be on my way now. I really am not one for dances and such."

"I could never tell."

"Oh, I come to this every year. It is a tradition, you know. The Brown family has a lot to live down, seeing how our forefathers were Yankees. We never miss a community activity. I bake my share of cakes and pies. Take my turn at the punch bowl—or the ticket booth."

"And you dance as well."

"Not usually."

"Isn't there some sort of boxed-supper auction? The boys bid for the pleasure of their special girl's company?"

"I never stay that long."

"Why not? You would certainly bring the highest bids of anyone here."

"You have not tasted my cooking, or doubtless you would not make such extravagant compliments."

"The young men here would not be bidding on your cooking, I assure you."

"You're very good at flattery, Mister Meyer. But now I've made my appearance at the school dance, and I'm ready to leave. It has been a terribly long day."

"Then what harm will there be if we make it just a bit longer?" Max asked. "You are the prettiest girl here. And the only one who does not say ain't or cain't or—"

"Y'all?"

"That's it. You're not like the others."

"You mean I talk like a Yankee, Mister Meyer?"

"If that is talking like a Yankee, I suppose. Anyway, I enjoy it."

The cool air wafted in from the open doors.

Mary pulled herself free from his arms. "We say some simple phrases the same here in Shiloh as a Yankee girl might say them in the North. Gentlemen on both sides of the Mason-Dixon line understand this one: Good night, Mister Meyer."

With an amused smile, she backed away from him and slipped out into the night.

CHAPTER SIXTEEN

Murder and Blasphemin'

This morning at 7 AM sharp, the shades were pulled up and the door to Dee Brown's barbershop was unlocked to a waiting clientele from around Hartford and Shiloh. Like a stick of penny candy offered free to a child, the red-and-white-striped barber pole beckoned to a dozen men. They crowded into the little two-chair tonsorial parlor to lick up the news others brought and to offer sweet bites of information in return.

The barbershop was the only neutral territory in town. Men were shaved and shorn by Dee Brown with no regard to religion or social status or political prejudice. Methodist, Baptist, Republican, or Democrat— each had his own shaving mug and his turn in one of the tall leather-and-chrome barber chairs. Each could speak his mind freely without fear of Dee Brown's razor.

Like his brother Dr. John Brown, who provided medicine for physical ailments, Dee Brown provided healing of sorts. For forty-three years he had been shaving the men of Hartford and Shiloh and listening to their troubles and opinions. His current middle-aged clients had been brought to his chair as tiny boys and perched up on a wooden plank for their first haircuts.

Dee had seen and heard practically everything in his day, and he was proud to state that only once had a fistfight broken out in his shop. The plate-glass window had never been smashed. The mirror into which his present patrons gazed was the same mirror that had held the reflections of fathers, grandfathers, and more than a few great-grandfathers. Three generations of menfolk had gathered here like patriarchs at the gate of Jerusalem to discuss local doings.

When nothing much was happening in Sebastian County, then the politics and state of the nation were often probed and pondered. This week, however, there had been plenty happening in these parts. There was so much to talk about that Dee Brown could cut hair until midnight and still there would be weighty matters left unexplored.

"He's her cousin," said Brother Williams firmly.

"Double cousin," added Mr. Winters as the shears snipped around his head. "Birch told me that the two Meyer brothers married the two Fritz sisters. That makes Trudy and this Max fellow double cousins."

"Yes," said Dee solemnly. "I could tell first thing when that fella stepped out of the plane that he was related to her. They look enough alike to be brother and sister. Hebrew children. Dark eyes. Dark hair. Handsome folk, if you ask me."

Buck Hooper gave a loud *Harrumph!* and sat forward in his chair. "Sneaky-lookin', if y'ask me."

"Nobody asked you, Buck," sniffed Mr. Winters.

"You just ain't happy 'bout Max Meyer on account of the way Mary has took a shine to him," added Brother Williams. "I seen the way he was a'lookin' her over and the way she was a'lookin' him over at the dance." He laughed as Buck's eyes bulged at the memory. "That Max feller's a slippery one, all right, if you count bein' able to slide right across the dance floor with Mary Brown in his arms."

"You don't say?" The barber sounded pleased by the news that his niece had been dancing with someone and enjoying it. "Our little Mary? Dancing?"

Buck puffed up like a bullfrog. "He just come right up an' stoled her right away from me while we was a'talkin' at the punch bowl. I oughta punch him right in the—"

"Stole her?" Mr. Winters laughed. "Nobody gonna make Miss Mary Brown dance unless she is inclined to."

"That's a fact." Dee Brown snipped the air for emphasis. "And mostly there's been no man around these parts that has made her *want* to dance, sit, stand, say howdy, or speak even one civil word. Her father has been worried some. She continues the way she's been, she's doomed to be an old maid, and that's a fact."

"Not from want of Buck Hooper tryin' to drag her to the preacher," jibed Brother Williams.

"That ain't none of your business," Buck fumed. "An' she has too danced with me. Lots of times."

"Lemme see . . ." Brother Williams rubbed his chin and peered into the air as if trying to remember something. "Yessir. Seems to me she did dance with Buck. Must've been when she was eight or nine. At Nelda

Palmer's weddin', it was." He hooted and slapped his knee. "I declare, Buck, she's let it be known all over town how dearly she despises you for a husband. Why, I hear tell she's goin' clear to China to be a missionary, just to get shed of you!"

A twitter of nervous laughter rippled through the barbershop. It took a lot of nerve to speak so bluntly to Buck Hooper.

"Ol' man, if you had any teeth in your head, I'd knock 'em out right now." Buck stood, stuck out his barrel chest, and clenched his fists.

"I lost these teeth to a better man than you," parried Brother. Then he added, "that dentist down in Charleston pulled 'em." He howled bravely at his own humor, confident in the knowledge that no argument ever came to blows in the barbershop. Men could be just as insulting as they dared within these hallowed walls.

"Calm yourself, Buck," said Dee, jabbing the air with his shears. "You know fightin' is off-limits here. Now sit yourself down."

Buck obeyed reluctantly. "Well, he started it."

Dee Brown puckered his mouth in thought. "Maybe he did, and maybe he didn't, but it's a sure thing that my niece is not overfond of any young buck in this county. That is the plain truth of it, and it is an occasion that she dances with any fella at all. Her father must be relieved at the news."

"He's a Yankee!" spat Buck. "Worse than a Yankee—he's a New York City Jew. Argue with that, if you can! If that don't bother y'all, well, it bothers me t'think of Mary takin' a shine t'the likes of him! He's still got his teeth for the time bein', but if he pesters my gal, I intend I'm gonna knock the dirty Jew's teeth right down that—"

The bell above the door jingled at that moment, interrupting Buck's blow-by-blow description of what he intended to do. A profound hush fell over the audience as Max Meyer himself entered the barbershop.

Snip. Snip-snip. Snip. The scissors clicked like Morse code, commanding silence from the ranks. Every man looked guilty of something. Even those who had said nothing at all one way or the other looked guilty just because they had heard.

"Good morning." Max nodded and smiled. He sounded as foreign as kosher salami at a barbecue.

"Mornin'," said the barber.

"I could do with a shave and a haircut." Max ran his fingers through his thick black hair. "It's been a while. Trudy gave my boy a haircut on the porch last night, but I didn't let her get to me. It is all right for the boy. Didn't want David to start school with his hair too long. But I am in need of a real barber and a hot towel, and Birch says you are the man, Mister Brown."

All of this was said by way of being friendly, but no one heard anything past the part about the boy's starting school. So the stranger and his son would be around awhile!

"School?" Mr. Winters's eyebrows went up in surprise.

"You mean y'all are stayin' here long enough for the child to start over to the school?" queried Brother Williams.

"Trudy and Birch asked us to stay on awhile." Max retreated to the back of the room.

Dee Brown raised an eyebrow. Evidently the Yankee assumed the back of the room was the end of the line.

"Lord have mercy," commented Brother Williams. "Bet that little house of theirs is crammed like a sardine can."

"We have rented . . . that is, Missus Amos . . . ," Max began.

"You mean Grandma Amos?" asked Buck suspiciously.

"Yes, Grandma Amos. I spoke with her at the dance." Max chuckled. "An interesting woman. We had quite a conversation. Did you know she was actually in Atlanta, Georgia, when the Union Army marched through?"

Brother Williams said dryly, "You musta been the only one at the dance that didn't know that. Grandma Amos loves to tell it."

"She and I hit it off. She owns the general store, and I was raised by my grandparents, who owned a dry-goods store. She has been kind enough to rent David and me a little cabin down by a creek. A pretty spot."

Brother Williams slapped his knee with glee. "So y'all gonna be stayin' awhile. Well that's fine, real fine. Ain't that fine, Buck?"

It was clear that Buck Hooper did not think this was fine. He inclined his head and cocked his eyebrow like a bull about to charge.

Max grinned stupidly back at Buck, as if he were unaware that his very presence was a red flag to this bull. The blood vessels in Buck's temples stood out, and his face reddened as he glared at Max.

The barber, sensing an imminent explosion and a danger to his window and mirror, stepped away from the barber chair and pointed his shears at Buck. "Now, there'll be none of that."

"Mary Brown is my gal. Everyone round here knows she's my gal," Buck burst forth.

"Mary don't know it." Brother Williams cackled. "And if she did, she wouldn't like it much, you bein' one of those cross-burners and all."

"You shut your mouth, ol' man—or I'll shut it for you!" Again Buck was on his feet, shaking his meaty fist at Max. "An' you! New York City Jew. Maybe you can fool an old lady like Grandma Amos, but you ain't foolin' me! Now, I'm warnin' ya. You ain't welcome in these parts! We're keepin' our eye on you!" He made as if to go for Max.

"That's enough!" reprimanded Dee Brown sharply, stepping between the two.

"Hey!" Max drew back. "What's your problem, friend?"

"I ain't no friend t'the likes of you! An' neither is Mary Brown! You go sniffin' round her an' that's the last thing you'll ever do!" Buck pushed past the barber. He threw the door open and escaped, untrimmed, into the street.

Wide-eyed, the patrons grinned at one another with excitement. They had come mighty close to seeing history made in Dee Brown's barbershop. What discussions of politics and religion had not done, the topic of spinster Mary Brown had nearly brought to pass!

Max stared out the window at Buck's retreating form. "What got into him?"

The barber resumed his task. "You didn't do a thing, son. It's just that my niece, Mary, doesn't usually like to dance. And Grandma Amos doesn't usually rent out that old cabin to anybody. She saves it. Keeps it empty for when the circuit-ridin' preacher comes through or in case there's a revival and pilgrims need a place to stay. I reckon Grandma Amos has had a word from the Lord about you, as she sometimes will. Especially if she saw you and Mary at the dance."

Dee shrugged. "Buck just doesn't like when someone comes along and changes the way he thinks things are or the way he thinks things ought to be." He gave Max a long, amused look. "Buck Hooper thinks Mary Brown ought to dance with him."

"No harm intended," Max said lightly. "I am just passing through. Mary can dance with Mister Hooper as often as she wants to."

"That's just the point." Brother Williams hooted. "She don't want to."

"All the same, Mister Meyer," warned the barber, "Buck is a mean one when he gets a burr under his blanket. He doesn't like Yankees. And a Yankee who dances with Mary Brown . . . well, this here shop is neutral territory, but just because he didn't take a poke at you here don't mean he won't give it a try out there."

"Y'all are pretty well matched," said Brother Williams with gleeful anticipation. "This is one I want to see!"

Max grimaced. "I haven't gotten into a brawl over a girl since I was drunk in Paris after the war. I don't intend to do it again."

Silence. Looks were exchanged across the barbershop floor. "Don't intend to fight Buck?" asked Brother Williams in a disappointed tone.

"For what?"

"For Mary. For Mary and . . . he called you a Yankee and a Jew."

"Well, I am both of those things, I suppose. If it offends Buck Hooper, I can't change it by fighting him."

"But Mary?"

"It seems to me that she made up her mind about Mister Hooper a long time before I came along. Am I right?"

"I reckon that's so."

"Then why should we fight?"

"Because . . . because Buck'll probably jump you and beat the tar outta you otherwise. Just because he has decided he wants to—that's why."

"Ah . . . I see," Max said thoughtfully. There was no way of stopping a bully bent on an ambush. He had learned that much as a kid on Orchard Street. But he had come a long way since those days, and he was not anxious to mix it up with Buck Hooper for any reason.

"Just watch your back, young feller," warned Brother Williams. "I ain't overly fond of Yankees m'self, but I'd sure hate to see a cottonmouth snake like Buck Hooper break out those pretty white teeth of yourn without you havin' a chance to knock his out, too."

Max Meyer left the barbershop that morning a shorn and enlightened Yankee. He knew he was considered an outsider, but he had discovered he was lucky enough to have the local bully boy gunning for him. Nobody much liked Buck Hooper outside his little group, and Buck's hostility put Max in a favorable light among the clientele of Dee Brown's barbershop.

Among those who watched Max stride out of the barbershop, no one opinion prevailed. The menfolk were divided on the matter.

"He don't know much, does he?"

"He'll learn quick enough when Buck gets him on a dark stretch of road."

"Hope I'm there to see it, boys. I think that Yankee might be able to teach Buck a thing or two."

"Buck's got twenty pounds on him. Buck'll break his neck."

"No sir. That Yankee's got a boxer's hands. Good long reach. And we know for sure that he's quicker on his feet than Buck. After all, look how he danced with Mary!"

Bets were made all around. Some wagered that the New York City Jew would come out on top, but the odds were two to one in favor of Buck. A few wagered that the Yankee would be taken out on the first blow, and others asserted that Max Meyer was a coward to the core and would not fight at all. Max might want to avoid a fight, but something was sure to explode if he stayed here long enough. Of course, if Max left before Buck had a chance to jump him, then all bets would be off.

Except for the preacher, the barber was the only man everyone trusted—and the preacher was not the one to act as bookie. So Dee

Brown was delegated to hold all the money and write down who bet on Max and who bet on Buck.

✻ ✻ ✻

Max had been instructed to meet Birch at Brother Williams's livery stable so the two could pick up a certain red puppy to take home to the boys. It was still early, and Max fished a Nehi out of the iced cooler at the dry-goods store with the intention of killing a few minutes.

The aproned merchant behind the counter smiled as he took Max's nickel. "You're that feller that danced with Mary Brown down to the dance, ain't you?"

Max smiled and nodded, indicating that he was indeed the guilty party. "I danced with the schoolteacher, too."

"Mary don't dance," stated the storekeeper positively, as though such a thing simply could not happen. He clearly found it easier to believe that Miss Price had blushed and giggled in Max's arms than to picture Mary Brown spinning around the dance floor. "Buck Hooper's a'lookin' for you, I hear," he said in a low voice.

"Well then—" Max popped the top off the Nehi and raised his soda in a salute—"he will not have far to look, since I am here. Have a nice day."

"Same to ya." The eyes of the little man narrowed as though he saw that Max's day might not be all that fine.

Not wanting to continue the same conversation he had heard in the barbershop, Max slipped out the groaning door and onto the board-walk, where he sipped his drink and scanned the comings and goings of the citizens of Hartford.

Rattling trucks and creaking buckboards filled the street. It only took a minute for Max to realize that nearly every passerby was looking his way with open curiosity. He had caused a stir, it seemed. Dancing with the schoolmarm and with Mary Brown had made him a sort of celebrity outlaw. Well, he had learned his first lesson about small-town life: It was wise to be a wallflower at the first social occasion attended!

Enough was enough. He had not been so ogled since a French baroness, furious at his refusal of marriage, had dumped a plate of veal marsala on his head at the Waldorf. With fifteen minutes left before the scheduled time to pick up the puppy, Max retreated down the alley to Brother Williams's livery stable.

The large barn seemed empty at first glance. Max recalled that Brother Williams was still at the barbershop, no doubt discussing the coming conflict between Max and Buck. Brother Williams would be disappointed that he had not been on hand at the stable to discuss the matter further with Max, but Max was relieved to be alone. He sat on a hay bale and finished his soda.

Overhead, in the loft, there was a rustle of straw and a creaking of boards. Max glanced upward but gave the noise no particular thought. In a stall at the rear of the barn, a horse snorted and coughed with a sharp explosion of breath. From another boxy enclosure came a puppy's yip and playful growls. Max went to take a look at the hound-dog pups.

The rafters groaned again. It sounded as if someone were tracking Max's movements—moving when he moved and stopping when he stopped.

"Who's up there?" he called out.

No reply, but a trickle of fine dust sifted onto Max's head and into his shirt collar. Max wondered if that country bully, Buck—or whatever his name was—was so anxious to pick a fight that he would set up an ambush.

"Show yourself," Max demanded. "Who is up there?"

"*WHOOOOOO-EEEEE,*" came a voice that quavered up and down the scale like a wriggling saw blade being played with a hammer. "STRANGER IN THE CAMP, BROTHER WILLIAMS! STRANGER IN THE CAMP!"

"Hey!" Max shouted. "Who is that?"

The ascending pitch of the yowl cut off in midscreech. Silence hung in the loft, followed by a slithering noise like something crawling toward the ladder. Max backed up to where he could see the edge of the overhanging platform.

A squinting, scrunched-up face appeared over a heap of hay, as if a Halloween jack-o'-lantern had been forgotten in Brother Williams's loft and popped up when summoned. On top of the contorted features loomed the thatch of an enormous cowlick, like a sheaf of wheat tied onto the back of the pumpkin. "BOOMER!" the apparition shrieked.

Max didn't know if this was a name, an Arkansas swearword, or some description being applied to himself. "Is that your name?" he guessed.

The cowlick nodded vigorously. "Brother Williams say don't talk to strangers," Boomer said reasonably. "Said to call out if I see 'em messin' about, but not to talk to 'em. Are you a stranger?"

Compared to what? Max thought. "Do you know the Tuckers?" he ventured. "Birch and Trudy and their boys?"

"Shore!" Boomer called down. "Emmaline and me been takin' care of that red puppy till they comes to get her."

"Well, I'm their cousin, Max."

At the name, Boomer slithered backward out of sight. It happened so fast that Max saw it as a kind of conjuring trick.

"Hey, where'd you go?" Max asked. "What'd I say?"

The quavering voice was back. "YOU'RE MAX?" it wailed.

"Yes. So? What of it?"

"Buck Hooper was round here blasphemin' somethin' turrible 'bout you!"

"Calm down, Boomer," Max urged. "I don't know what the matter with Mister Hooper is, but—"

"So I've got somethin' wrong with me, do I?" said Buck Hooper's voice behind Max's back.

Contrary to Max's expectations, Boomer did not soar into another long wail. Instead the loft grew instantly and dramatically silent. The coughing horse and the snarling puppies were also still. An expectant hush hung heavy in the livery stable, like the too-quiet calm before the storm.

"Look, Mister Hooper," said Max reasonably, "I don't know you, and you don't know me. What have we got to fight about?"

"Showin' your yella streak, are ya?" Buck sneered. The unnatural brightness of his eyes and the slight slurring of his speech suggested that, even this early in the day, Buck had managed to find a bottle of eighty-proof bravado. "Stealin' my gal . . . showin' me up in front of folks . . . givin' me the laugh around town. Lousy, stinkin' Yankee Jew, I'm gonna show you the road out of here!"

Buck stepped forward and threw a clumsy, sweeping right that Max ducked under and dodged easily. "Stand still and fight, you yella-livered—" Buck released a string of oaths that brought a loudly yowled response from the hayloft.

"HE'S BLASPHEEEEEMIN' AGIN!"

Buck swung a left-right combination that again missed connecting. But this time, when Max ducked under the punches, Buck grabbed him from behind.

The skills of Max's boyhood on Orchard Street came flooding back. Max jabbed both elbows into Buck's ribs. Then, as the hold was broken, he spun around and planted an overhand right that connected with Buck's left eye.

Max followed up this success by closing the gap between the two men, stepping in with a left that hammered Buck's ribs again and a right that just missed Buck's nose and thudded into his cheek. The skin over the cheekbone split.

Buck ducked his head and rammed his shoulder full speed into Max's chest, propelling both men into the wall of a box stall. The thin wooden partition splintered, throwing the men onto the straw-and-manure-covered floor. The alarmed occupant of the stall, a bay mare, lashed out with both feet at the intruders rolling under her hooves.

Buck ended the tumble on top, and he landed a clout on Max's ear that drove Max down into the straw. Buck was drawing back his fist for another blow when one iron-shod hoof whistled over his head and a second hit him in the shoulder, knocking him backward off Max and out through the stall door.

Looking upward through a haze of barn dust and flickering lights, Max saw a pair of hooves about to descend on his head. He flung himself to the side just as the mare's feet descended and planted themselves four inches deep in the straw where his forehead had been.

When Max rolled through the break in the partition again and sat up, he found himself staring into the hate-filled eyes and blood-streaked face of his opponent. Buck was seated on the floor of the barn, panting for breath. They regarded each other from no more than ten feet away.

"You jus' don't know when t'give up, do you?" Buck gasped, reaching toward the top of his boot. "I only figgered t'teach you a lesson, but now I aim t'cut you up some." From inside the boot top he produced a slender hunting knife. Scrambling upright, he lunged forward, slashing the blade in the air.

Max scooted backward, trying to get his feet under him again but slipping on the muck underfoot. He pushed himself half erect on the wall of the stable just as Buck rushed in. Max's hand closed on a broken board from the shattered partition, and he swung the piece of lumber wildly in front of him, knocking Buck's knife hand aside.

Recovering his stance, Buck blocked Max's exit from just out of reach of the board. "Now we'll see," Buck intoned. "Now we'll see who's the best man." The blade of the knife wove a figure eight in the air.

The combat had taken on a sinister tone, the stakes far higher than split lips and blackened eyes. Two nails protruded from the end of Max's improvised club. He kept this weapon between himself and Buck, using it to fend off Buck's lunges with the knife. The two men danced a jig with death, circling, driving forward, and retreating, but always with Buck between Max and the exit. The pair had moved below the overhanging loft. Max made a sudden move toward the ladder, but Buck cut him off from that escape, too.

Buck gathered himself for another rush.

Max saw the coiling of the drunk man's body and prepared himself. With luck, perhaps he could bat Hooper aside and get to the door.

But Buck had also planned his next move. He feinted toward the left, then plunged to the right, sweeping the knife edge upward in a vicious arc.

The swing of Max's club pulled him into, instead of away from, the line of the blade. All he could manage was a desperate fling backward.

But Max's city shoes had never been intended for use in ankle-deep straw and the muck of a barn. As he jerked away, his feet slipped out from under him, and Buck plunged in with the knife.

The blade sliced, skittered along a rib, and sank in. Pain seared Max's side, and the world spun crazily around as he sank to the floor.

"Reckon I've settled you," Buck said with a look of hellish pleasure. He drew his arm back for the blow that would finish the job.

That's when Boomer dropped the ice shoe. A three-pound, cleated, iron horseshoe, discarded from a three-quarter-ton draft horse. The chunk of metal bounced off of Buck Hooper's thick skull. It did not knock him out, but it did send him staggering sideways. He dropped the knife.

There was a disturbance at the doorway. "What is all this?" yelled Brother Williams.

"MURDER," wailed Boomer from the loft. "MURDER 'N' BLASPHEEEMIN'."

Buck recovered his senses enough to recognize that Boomer's screams would soon bring others to the livery stable. A look at Max's unmoving form and the cry of "MURDER" ringing in his ears must have convinced Buck that a plea of self-defense might not work after all. He shoved Brother Williams roughly aside and ran clumsily out the door toward where his horse was tied.

CHAPTER SEVENTEEN

The Only Thing that Mattered

It was not the strong smell of disinfectant that pulled Max toward consciousness. Nor was it the clink of scissors on the metal pan as the dressing on his wound was snipped free and discarded.

"See right there, Mary . . . some more dirt, I'm afraid. . . ."

It was not the sting of iodine or the probing fingers of Dr. Brown that made Max's eyes flutter open, squint against the light, and close again like steel traps after just one glimpse.

"Knife wounds, Dad. Horrible things. In school we were told better a gunshot than something like this."

"It's bad, all right. That knife of Buck's is a bad'n. I saw him kill a rat with it, wipe the blade on his trouser leg, and then stick it back in the sheath. I wouldn't want to cut a splinter out of my finger with that thing, let alone this."

It was not the details of the conversation about the blood and gore of Buck Hooper's knife that caused Max to lick his lips and try to speak.

"He's moaning—careful there, Dad. Here. You're too rough. Let me do it."

"You always have had a softer touch than I do, Mary. I'll go get another pan of hot water to rinse. It had to be Buck Hooper's knife . . . of all the knives in the world. Can't change it. Just hope for the best, I suppose. I'll leave him to you and God, then."

It was not the flame of pain in Max's side that made him cry out when Mary Brown sponged the salty sweat from his body.

"What is it? Oh, I know it hurts. I am so sorry, Mister Meyer. I am doing the best I can to be easy. . . ."

It was not the sweetness of Mary Brown's voice that made tears squeeze out from behind his eyelids and trickle unchecked down his cheeks as she washed him.

"There, now. Go ahead and cry. I know how it must hurt! I am so sorry. All of this because I danced with you. We won't let you die. My dad is the best doctor. . . ."

Max did not care for promises or sympathy or pain. The size of the knife or the depth of his wound did not come through his mind. No. Only one thought made the labored breathing of Max Meyer continue long after others thought it would stop.

He tried to speak: *"David!"*

The name came out garbled and unintelligible . . . like the cries Max had heard the dying soldiers make in France.

Now he understood. Those dying men had not been simply screaming in fear of their own deaths. *No!* They had each been calling out to someone . . . to something . . . in this strangled language that only dying men speak.

Max saw the image clearly before him day and night. The battlefields of Belleau Wood stretched out in endless devastation. The twisted bodies of friends and enemies alike lay unburied in long rows beside yawning graves. So many men!

Why had he not remembered how many? Why had this vision, which had been reality once, become so dim in his mind until this moment, when he lay at the brink of death himself?

Even when he had walked among the dead and the dying in France, he had never pictured himself among them. The thought of his own mortality had been a dream. Death came to other men. It came to the young men who had not yet begun to live. It came to men with families who had everything to live for. But never did Max believe it would come to him like this, hunched like a vulture waiting at his bedside.

"Not yet!" he managed.

"Don't try to talk, Mister Meyer. I'm almost through. I won't be a minute more, but it must be done."

"Not . . . *now!*"

Why had Death come now? Now, when he had David, who gave him everything to live for? Why now, when he had a chance—when he had found someone who loved him for no other reason than the tenuous link of fatherhood?

David had been an accident, had he not? A single summer night of careless desire had brought this child into existence! That thoughtless, selfish act had resulted in the only worthwhile accomplishment in all of the life of Max Meyer!

"*David!*"

All the great things Max had achieved meant nothing. What use were degrees at a university? What use were honors? What did success matter now? All those things for which he had sold his soul were utterly without value here at the end of his life!

So what was the truth about his own existence? What did thirty-two years of struggle mean when the only worthy part of his life had resulted from a night of passion for a girl on a tenement roof? Had he known that Irene was pregnant with David, he would have wanted to put a stop to the pregnancy. This was the truth that Max saw clearly in his vision now. This is what made dying so hard to face. . . .

I would have killed my son. And now he is all I have to live for. I would have killed him without a second thought while I went chasing after things . . . just things . . . Oh, God! he pleaded heavenward. *My boy! I would have murdered David!*

It was not the hands of Mary Brown cleaning his wound that made Max choke back a sob.

The vision of the dead on the field on Belleau Wood changed horribly. All the faces suddenly bore one likeness as Max walked among them. Every dead man became a boy, and every boy became that one boy whom Max Meyer loved.

"David!" He cried the name of his son aloud again. "I didn't know!"

"Trouble," said Grandma Amos when she heard about the stabbing of Max Meyer. "I knowed it in my bones that trouble was a'comin'."

"How come you know so much, old woman?" asked Brother Williams as he and Boomer helped her load supplies onto her buckboard.

She turned her puckered face toward Boomer, then stared at Brother's prize hound, Emmaline, who lounged in the sun in front of the livery stable. Then she raised her eyes skyward. "The Lawd whispers things into the heads of old folks an' half-wits an' dawgs who go out an' howl at the moon for reasons nobody but them understands. Ain't that right, Boomer?"

"Yes'm. Yes'm. Yes'm. Yep. Yep." Boomer gave a howl. "That's right. Boomer seen it. Boomer knowed Buck was a'comin' t'kill that feller," Boomer stuttered and wiped his mouth on the sleeve of his red-flannel shirt. "Boomer seen the dark angel, too. Didn't I, Gram—Gramma Amos? Don't nobody b'lieve Boomer, but I seen. . . ."

Brother Williams snorted and stamped his foot for silence. Boomer obliged. Brother Williams rolled his eyes. "Ah, now, Grandma Amos,

don't get Boomer goin' again, will ya? It's all a man can do to keep him
quiet awhile up there in the hayloft. And he's all the time seein' things."
He tapped his temple. "He's teched. Ever'body knows that Boomer's a
few bricks shy of a load."

The old woman raised her chin to challenge Brother. "You'd be a
heap better off if'n you listen t'what Boomer tells you. Most folks don't
'preciate it when I have a word from the Lord neither. Don't change it
none. I seen trouble. Boomer seen trouble, too. You go on an' laugh if
you like. Don't change it none, does it, Boomer?"

"No, ma'am. No, sir. No, it don't, Brother." Boomer grinned and
tossed another sack of chicken feed into the wagon.

"Well, if y'all know so much, you two, then tell me this." Brother spit
a stream of tobacco juice that nearly hit the old hound lounging nearby.
"Pardon me, Emmaline." He tipped his hat to the dog, then returned to
the question.

"Like I was sayin' . . . if y'all know so much, then why can't you tell if
Max Meyer is gonna live or die? After all, Doctor Brown says he don't
know nothin'. Can't tell nothin' from day to day. And that little boy of his
is just a'grievin' and a'pinin' away. Sleeps down there at Doc Brown's,
where they got his daddy. Won't eat much, Mary Brown says. He just sits
on down there at the side of his daddy's bed a'waitin'. That boy is
a'sufferin' near as much as his dyin' daddy is. Now, wouldn't it be best
. . . if y'all know 'bout this . . . that y'all tell that boy if his daddy is gonna
live or die so he can get over the frettin'?"

"Trouble." Grandma Amos closed her eyes in reply, then snapped
them open again and glared at Boomer. "What do you say 'bout Mister
Meyer, Boomer?"

"Well . . ." Boomer sucked his teeth thoughtfully and screwed up his
rubber face in deep thought. "He ain't dead yet, but I reckon ever'body
gonna die. Someday." He smiled broadly. "So the Good Book says."

"Huh!" Brother Williams tossed one last sack of chicken feed into
the wagon. "Y'all just playin' games with my mind. You don't know no
more what's a'comin' than ol' Emmaline knows!"

At that the dog raised her snout and let go with a long, mournful
howl. Brother Williams gave a start at the sound, then muttered to himself that such matters gave him crawly chicken skin and that he did not
want to think about it anymore at all.

"Well, you're the one what asked." Grandma Amos gave a cackle and
began to climb laboriously onto the wagon. "Don't matter if'n you believe. No, it don't, Brother. Jus' r'member I tol' you the truth—there's
trouble a'comin' here to Shiloh."

She sniffed the dry breeze. "Oh yes! Lawd! Lawd! There's more trouble a'comin than anyone could bear if they knowed what the future held. That's why most folks don't know the future. The Lawd only speaks t'them what can bear t'hear the message. He tells me this an' that 'cause I'm old as Methuselah an' I already seen ever' trouble known to man an' lived through it. I can bear it. He speaks t'Boomer 'cause Boomer can hear it an' it don't trouble his heart none. Nah. He thinks like a chil', sees like a chil'. He don't know that tomorrow is even comin'. An' the Lawd speaks t'ol' Emmaline there 'cause that dawg don't try to argue with Him.

"Now, folks like you, Brother, you all the time tryin' t'talk the Lawd outta stuff. You ain't old enough t'accept it. Ain't dumb enough not t'let it bother you. Ain't trustin' enough t'know the Lawd can make water out of wine an' He can make troubles into blessin's!"

Brother Williams conceded that this was all true. He was not old like Grandma, dumb like Boomer, or trusting like Emmaline.

"Then tell me this, old woman." He frowned and spit again. "If the Lord can make troubles into blessin's, how come you don't look at them troubles which is comin' and say, *'Brother Williams, I see a heap of blessin's comin'?* You know, Grandma, it would sure make me feel a heap better if you'd put it that way."

Perched on the seat of the wagon, the old woman nodded thoughtfully and lit her pipe. "Now, that is true, Brother. But if'n I was to put it that way, who would believe my report? When a heap of blessin's come in the form of a mountain of troubles, folks don't like to call them blessin's. No sir. To do that, a person has t'be old enough t'have seen it work out . . . like me! Or dumb enough so you can't figure out the difference . . . like Boomer! Or trustin' enough so it don't bother you none . . . like Emmaline. Or you got to jus' trust that the Lord knows what He's a'doin'. That's faith, Brother. An' not many folks have that kind of faith."

"Yep." Boomer wagged his head the wrong way in agreement. "Trust in the Lord! Troubles are blessin's. Yep! That's it, Brother Williams. Yep! I tell you—"

"Boomer! Button your trap!"

"Yessir, Brother Williams. I will do that." He made a buttoning motion over his lips and fell silent.

Brother Williams looked more confused now than when the conversation had begun. He still did not know if Max Meyer would live or die. There was no end to suffering in sight. Troubles were coming. And Grandma Amos said that no matter what happened, all this was a blessing in disguise!

"You're right, old woman," Brother Williams said. "No one in his right mind would believe it."

A
HOLY
THING

part two

Is this a holy thing to see,
In a rich and fruitful land,
Babes reduced to misery,
Fed with a cold and usurous hand?

WILLIAM BLAKE

CHAPTER EIGHTEEN

The Master Plan

The office of Jack Titan was decorated and furnished with old-world op-
ulence. Dark oak linenfold paneling covered the high walls to a height
of nine feet. Above that, cream-colored plaster was embossed in a swirling vine pattern that ringed the room and connected to heavy crown
molding another five feet up. Dominating the room was an enormous
carved-oak desk that Titan claimed had belonged to Oliver Cromwell,
the Puritan master of England in the seventeenth century.

Behind the desk, a tall, small-paned window looked out over the Titan domain: factory buildings, smokestacks, and a water tower with the
name *Titan* emblazoned across it. Bookshelves purchased from an old
Spanish monastery lined the walls, and the collection of antique books
and relics upon them testified to wealth, not to love of knowledge.

The doctors sat in straight-backed chairs from the Elizabethan
period, placed in a row for second-class citizens in front of the shelves
along the back wall. They were rigid and uncomfortable, but Ellis and
the other two company physicians took little note. They were sitting
forward on the edges of the seats anyway. The trio of physicians was
expected to listen and take note of the proceedings in Jack Titan's office,
but they would clearly not be called upon to offer their opinions, so
they were not among the group gathered around the massive oak table
that occupied the center of the room.

Jack Titan paced back and forth in front of the window. His hands
were clasped behind his back as he strutted, and when Titan stopped to
gaze solemnly out over his empire, he looked to Ellis like a caricature of
the emperor Napoleon. It was probably a conscious imitation, too.

Titan was pontificating about tires, men, slackers, and devotion. Ellis thought the doctors were like junior officers attending a great general's strategy session. Or maybe, Ellis imagined, they were like condemned men awaiting only the summoning of the firing squad.

"*Loy-al-ty.*" Titan broke the word into syllables. "That is all I ask of any of my staff, soldiers in the wars of industry and commerce. Those of you in this room are not merely foot soldiers either. You are the trusted lieutenants through whom the struggle is directed."

Not having a clue as to where this was leading or why they were included in this meeting, the company physicians were all ill at ease. The exception, of course, was the chief medical administrator, who was favored with a place at the table. Dr. Keller's florid face with its road-map-veined nose was beaming and nodding his approval of Titan's speech.

"Bold, decisive action—that's what is called for to restore confidence," Titan proclaimed. "No mealymouthed, wishy-washy half measures will do. Why, Titan stock has dropped nearly one-third in two weeks." He snapped his fingers at his head bookkeeper, seated to the right of Dr. Keller. "What's the current figure?"

The bookkeeper, a balding man whose fingernails looked recently gnawed, snapped to attention and recited, "Forty-two and a half as of noon today. Down from forty-eight a week ago. We were at fifty-seven and three-quarters on the first, which was a climb back from fifty-two on the twenty-ninth but was still much below the sixty-two and one-eighth on the twenty-fifth, and of course—"

Titan snapped his fingers again, and the ticker-tape voice stopped as abruptly as if a switch had been thrown.

"That will do," Titan commented. "I do not need to remind you gentlemen that the company has been investing heavily in our own stock over the last year, nor do I need to remind you how many of us in this room have a substantial amount of our personal wealth at stake here."

Ellis allowed himself the smallest shake of his head in silent response. Titan Tire stock was indeed one of the ill-timed investments he had made, but it was too late to be helped. Buying when the price was already too high and being unable to sell before the margin call had wiped out his holdings.

Titan was continuing: "The trend all across the country is the same. Investors will not return until confidence is restored."

Titan's attorney expressed doubts that things were really so serious. "The Morgans and the Rockefellers have both expressed the belief that this downturn was just a correction in the market. Why, they are even buying again in expectation of the next rally."

Titan shook his head. "That's what they *say*," he emphasized, "but not what they really think. Listen to this and learn."

Branford Briggs, with his tall, aristocratic stature and his mane of silver hair, was easily the most physically impressive man in the room, and he obviously disliked being lectured to. But apparently he disliked losing a major client even more. He did his best to appear grateful for the chance to be taught by the great captain of industry, Jack Titan.

Titan explained further. "Farm production is at an all-time high. That means that for the past year, farm prices have been falling faster than the grain pouring into the silos. Now, you are probably thinking, what difference does that make to us?"

Ellis found his thoughts flying out the window and back to the Warne family farm. What was it his brother John had said the last time they talked? Something about shipping and storage charges eating up all the profits? Before, the farm had always seemed so enjoyable and carefree. . . .

"Farmers who can't make a living," Titan went on, "don't buy equipment. They don't buy cars. That's been going on already. The sale of new automobiles is down for the first year ever. Now all the fools who lost their nest eggs in the market will give up their plans for new vehicles, too."

Ellis swallowed, and the pleasant memories of his boyhood life on the farm came to an abrupt end.

"Fewer new cars means less steel used and less coal *and* fewer tires," Titan insisted. "That of course means greater competition between the rubber companies—a competition I intend for Titan Tire to win with lower prices."

The bookkeeper raised his hand timidly and yanked it back down as if he feared his interruption might give offense.

Titan recognized the clerk with a condescending nod. "Yes, Birdsill. What is it?"

"Mister Titan, sir, how can we do that? The cost of rubber from our suppliers is up, and so is the price of sulfur for the vulcanizing and—my goodness—what with wages . . ."

"*Efficiency*, that's our watchword," Titan pronounced, as if this explained everything. "I intend for this plant to improve its productivity by 25 percent. If we eliminate the deadweight, then those who remain will work faster and better than before. Fewer mistakes will be made, and that means fewer interruptions of the line. Slackers and drunkards—" Titan fixed his gaze on Ellis—"we *must* and we *will* weed them out."

Now all the occupants of the office understood where all this discussion had been headed. Titan was talking about jobs now—layoffs.

Producing just as many tires with fewer workers and, by so doing, lowering the cost of producing each tire.

"Mister Morris here," said Titan, indicating a thin, neatly dressed man with a pencil-line mustache, "is our efficiency expert. He has been studying our line for the past two months and has concluded that we can eliminate one-third of all the drones here and still maintain output. Isn't that right, Morris?"

Morris spoke in a clipped voice, as if his vocation required that he economize in his speech. "Certainly," he acceded. "The equivalent of one full shift can be discharged."

"All at once?" Attorney Briggs wanted to know. "That will never get by the union. You'll have a strike here before the day is through. Over at Firestone, they are so worried about exactly that outcome that they decided to reduce the men's hours and not fire anyone at all."

"I know," sneered Titan. "*Underemployment* instead of *unemployment*. But Harvey Firestone is only postponing his day of reckoning. Does any one of you believe that having a whole plant full of workers grumbling about reduced wages is preferable to eliminating the troublemakers altogether?" Titan looked into the face of each man in the room. If anyone disagreed with him, no one spoke. "Besides," he went on, "I never said that we'd do this all at once. When I was growing up on the farm, do you know how we slaughtered the hogs?"

Ellis studied the little man curiously. Somehow it was impossible to imagine that this autocratic, dictatorial figure had ever even visited a farm.

"Do you think," Titan was saying, "that we plunged into the herd of hogs and went to slashing right and left? Of course not! That would stress the pigs and ruin the flavor of the meat. No, we'd take one hog at a time off by himself. When he would poke his head through a hole in the fence, we'd hit him with a sledgehammer and slit his throat. Never disturbed the herd at all. None of them ever even knew what was happening until it came their own turn."

Ellis shivered and wondered if he was catching a cold.

"Mister Morris has been helping me develop the lists," Titan went on.

Now George Franklin, the burly production supervisor who had once worked on the line himself, spoke up. "You're telling us that you already know who is going to get laid off and when?"

"Of course," Titan confirmed. "Drunkards, slackers, troublemaking union members . . . not," he corrected himself, "that they'll be fired for belonging to the union. Oh no, we're not stupid. But for every rabble-rousing Socialist unionite there is a weakness—a plausible and indeed indisputable reason he should be relieved of his duties. Captain Sanders here has been helping with that."

Ellis had been curious about the presence of Akron's assistant chief of police. The man was not in uniform, and he clutched a battered leather briefcase in his lap.

"Moral charges," the policeman explained, slapping the case. "I've been keeping tabs on the speakeasies and the fancy houses, and I've got quite a roster built up. We even got that shift foreman from Plant One— Daugherty, who is so tight with the union and thinks his job is so secure." Sanders laughed. "It seems he likes to hoist a few on the way home." Sanders's grin faded at the black look on Jack Titan's face.

"A senior man!" Titan exploded. "A man in leadership. One the others look up to and imitate. *Unionite!*" He said the last word as if it were something indescribably filthy and despicable. "Well, he'll find his seniority carries no water around here. Another drunk in the same family . . . not at all surprising, is it?"

Ellis felt his head spinning. He wondered if this scene was some nightmare brought on by his troubles at home and the recent tragedy at work. Was it really happening?

"But there are some," Titan went on with a touch of exasperation in his voice, "whom we have not yet been able to tie to anything illegal or immoral. Not that I doubt but that something wicked would eventually come to light." He nodded toward Captain Sanders. "But we don't want to wait unnecessarily in the case of known union ringleaders and other Bolshies. That's where you doctors come in."

Ellis's ears felt dull, as if stuffed with cotton. He knew Titan was speaking about him. But how? What? Ellis wondered if he had somehow gotten into this secret meeting by error. Would Titan suddenly notice his presence and denounce him as a spy?

"Each of you doctors will begin receiving men for examination. You will tell them about a new company benefit—a routine physical. Now listen carefully."

Ellis noticed that the other two infirmary physicians and Dr. Keller were sitting up like puppies eagerly anticipating their master's command. He pulled himself erect in time to hear Titan's instructions.

"Each week you will be given a list of names to receive medical discharges. It doesn't matter what the diagnosis is, so long as it is either debilitating or a threat to the health of others. Tuberculosis, perhaps. Be creative. Even if a few go to another doctor to get checked, we can always say it was an honest mistake—and then, so sorry, we no longer have a place for you. Doctor Keller will keep the master list in his office, but only a few names at a time will be passed to you clinic workers."

Ellis's mind was spinning so quickly that he could almost no longer hear what was being said. How could he be expected to do this? to lie to end men's jobs? to throw them out of work because Titan wanted to keep only those who were pliable and would not stand up against him?

"Ultimately, three thousand fewer men will work at Titan Tire and Rubber Company," Jack Titan proclaimed proudly. "Production will remain high because of greater efficiency. Best of all, we will have eliminated the radicals and the troublemakers along with the deadweight. Any questions?"

"I have one," Lawyer Briggs said. "What about the darkies? If you are going to lay off a third of your men, you had better not keep any coloreds. We don't want to have race riots here in Akron, do we, Captain Sanders?"

"I see no reason to dismiss our Negro workers," Titan fired back. "The union won't have them, and they already work for half the pay of the others, doing jobs the rest won't touch. No—until the bohunks and Polacks will work for the same wages, we'll just keep the coloreds on. Remember, gentlemen—" Titan nodded to indicate that the meeting was at an end—"as former President Coolidge said, 'The man who builds a factory builds a temple. The man who works there worships there.' What we are going to do is see that only true believers are attending the temple of Titan Tire and Rubber."

CHAPTER NINETEEN

They That Mourn

Layoffs had begun at every business in Akron, Ohio, shortly after the crash, and the Canfields felt the blow almost immediately. Willa-Mae had been first. Now Nettie had been served notice that she was no longer needed as an elevator attendant at O'Neil's. She was told right out that she needed to make room for some white woman who would surely be needing the job since the tire plants were cutting hours and wages and men.

Nettie came home crying. She looked at her schoolbooks and told Willa-Mae that this most likely meant she would have to drop out of college at the end of the term. At that, Hock lost his patience and told Nettie that it was not a woman's place to waste money on schooling anyway. Nettie ought to find herself a man and get married, he said. And she sure would not care about her schooling once she figured out there was nothing in the house to eat!

At this, Nettie's tears became an angry flood. She stormed out of the apartment, declaring that she had midterm exams to study for and she would be at the library if anyone cared.

Then Willa-Mae got cross with Hock. "You is one dumb ol' man, Hock Canfield! Don't you know the only way for Nettie t'live better than this is if she gets her schoolin'?"

But Willa-Mae's blazing eyes and formidable size did not cause little Hock to shrink from his stand. "We was better off sharecroppin' on a poor rock farm. Better off growin' cotton for The Man! We mighta been hungry, but at least we had us a big garden. Had us hogs t'slaughter an' a chicken t'fry when the preacher come by! Now we got nothin'!" His helpless anger dissolved into a fit of coughing. He bent over and clutched his throat as though he could not catch his breath. Only then did the argument end.

Willa-Mae helped him to the tattered sofa and made him lie down while she stomped off to fix him a cup of the blackberry tea Delpha Jean Jones had sent from Pine Bluff, Arkansas. The fragrant tea leaves were the last in the tin box. Willa-Mae silently hoped her old Arkansas friend would think to send more along, since this was the season of coughs and colds.

"I jus' don't know, ol' woman," Hock rasped when the hacking finally stopped. "What we gonna do now that you ain't workin'? How we gonna pay rent an' eat at the same time? I don't make but eighteen dollar a month by myself. Rent be two dollar an' fifty cent a week. That don't leave but two dollar a week t'feed us. An' now you ain't got no leavin's from the Weldon table t'bring home from that fancy kitchen."

"All the table scraps in the world ain't put no weight on you, ol' man. You was scrawny when we was poor and hungry and living on corn bread and beans all the time. You was scrawny when we was eatin' chocolate cake and leftover roast beef. Guess it don't matter what I feed you, Hock Canfield." Willa-Mae brought the steaming teacup and gave the bony forearm of her husband a squeeze. "If you was a hog, I'd say you was stunted, and that's the truth.

"Now me, I got a hunert pound extra round my middle, and it ain't gonna hurt me none t'shed some of it. I reckon I can cut back some. Little Nettie don't eat more'n a bird. She can finish out the school term and by then mebbe I'll have me a new job cookin' somewheres. Meantime, it's Harry I be worried 'bout. That boy can eat a boxcar full of vittles, and he ain't filled up. Just keeps on growin' bigger and bigger. Reckon he eats two dollar worth of beans each week all on his own. He just got this one year 'fore he be finished with high school. One year and that boy be makin' somethin' of hisself. But if'n he don't graduate from school, he gonna end up workin' in the coal mines! End up totin' bales of rubber for half the wages of a white man! Livin' in a place like this. Don't want my Harry t'spend his life like that, Hock. He be down there right now at the school yard playin' baseball with the white kids. Runnin' races for that school track team. Folks all like him, too. White kids like him. Teachers say he smart. No, I ain't so worried 'bout Nettie. It's Harry I be frettin' 'bout."

"Growin' boy," mused Hock. "You always been partial t'that boy on account of how much he be like Jefferson. But how we gonna feed him an' you an' me an' Little Nettie on what I be bringin' home?" Hock clasped his hands across his chest and looked mournfully upward as though he were praying.

But Willa-Mae knew he was not ready to pray yet. He was still in the worrying stage of thinking. Four people living on eighteen dollars a month gave him plenty to worry about, too. And on top of all that, he had this troublesome cough that simply would not go away!

"They givin' gummers medical exams down t'the plant these days, Willa-Mae," he said quietly. "Men what don't pass as healthy get the ax. White men they is, an' they is gettin' the ax by these doctor fellas. An' don't none of 'em have no cough bad as what I got."

"Just a cold, ol' man." Willa-Mae stroked his forehead. "They ain't gonna fire you for a little cold."

Hock did not reply. His dark eyes were troubled. His lower lip protruded with grim worry.

Willa-Mae knew what he was thinking. At least now he could bring home eighteen dollars. As meager as that paycheck was, it was something at the end of each month. It guaranteed this place to live, a little food on the table. What would happen if one day a foreman heard him coughing and gave him that little pink slip of paper to send him to the infirmary? He would be fired—that's what. And then what would they do?

"I tell you right out, ol' woman." Tears crowded his eyes. He looked past Willa-Mae at the water stain in the corner of the ceiling. "I'm flat scared, Willa-Mae. Like I ain't been scared since The Man turn us outta our farm an' tol' us t'hit the road. I'm scared like I ain't been since I seen my son Jefferson ride acrost that river in the dead of night an' I knowed I weren't gonna see my boy no more in this world."

"Don't talk that way, Hock Canfield," Willa-Mae chided. But she was no longer angry. She understood her husband's fear. They were both over sixty years old now, living from one paycheck to the next, and with two young'uns still to care for. Willa-Mae had figured that her Mr. Weldon would keep her on in that kitchen until she was too old to boil water. Now Willa-Mae was without the job she had counted on, and Hock was in real danger of losing his job as well. If strong white men could be turned out on the street without so much as a fare-thee-well from the company, then what was the future of little Hock Canfield?

Every concern had been whittled down to the pinpoint of survival. Willa-Mae held the teacup for Hock and made him drink the tea down to the last drop. There was no more, after all, and it must not be wasted.

The Broken Arrow Pool Hall in Tulsa, Oklahoma, had been stylish in 1920, when it was first built, but had gradually gone downhill. The green felt on the tables was faded and ripped in places, the linoleum cracked and lifeless-looking. The whole atmosphere reflected the depression shared by men whose jobs had evaporated faster than gasoline.

No one was playing pool when Smiley entered the joint, but the place was crowded with sullen roughnecks staring into cheerless mugs of beer. He sized up this group of recently laid-off oil workers and decided a low-key approach would yield better results than threats. His fruitless search for information about Max Meyer had carried him a long way from the waterfront of New York City, but he had never felt like more an outsider than he did here.

"I am lookin' for information," he said, seating himself on a stool next to the least grumpy-looking man there.

"So? Do I look like a library? Take a hike."

Smiley tried again. "It may have come ta your notice that I ain't from around here. I'm tryin' ta locate someone who worked in this area."

"Yeah? What for?" The man glared suspiciously. "You a bill collector?"

"I ain't nothin' of da sort," Smiley explained. "I represent da estate of a deceased party what is tryin' to locate a missin' relative for . . . ta give 'em their inheritance."

"What's the lucky guy's name?"

"Birch Tucker."

"Naw, don't know him," replied the man, turning back to his beer. A second later he swiveled again toward Smiley. "Say, I don't suppose I could change my name?"

"I don't think such a plan would work," Smiley warned. "But if youse can help me, I think it would be worth another beer anyways."

"What's the deal?"

"When I asked at Mister Tucker's former residence, they told me he had left no forwardin' address, but that someone with a company called Phelps Petroleum might know somethin'."

"Phelps? Yeah, easy enough to ask," agreed the man. "Hey," he yelled over the other conversations, "any a you guys work for Phelps?"

A brawny man with his shirtsleeves rolled up and a cigarette dangling from his lips looked up from the other side of the room. "Who wants to know?"

After Smiley had once again explained his business, the man admitted to having been employed with Birch. "Name's Johns. Leo Johns. Yeah, I used to work for Phelps Petroleum, before it went belly-up and stuck us for two weeks' back pay."

"Then youse knows where ta find Mister Tucker?" Smiley asked, his hopes rising.

"Naw," replied the man, unrolling a pack of Lucky Strikes from his shirtsleeve. "Birch was a good sort. I was in the crew the night Old Man Phelps canned him after Phelps's kid got hisself killed. Tucker took off that same night, and nobody seen nor heard from him since. Always said he was some kinda farmboy, but that don't narrow things down much."

Back at his hotel, Smiley reviewed his diminishing set of leads. Montreal had produced nothing. Neither had tracking the boy back to Philly. Now Smiley had come clear out to where he expected to see Indians behind the oil derricks, and he still was no nearer to finding Max Meyer. He lay back on the cheap, lumpy mattress and stared at the water-stained ceiling.

Boss Quinn was getting impatient. Something had better break soon.

Among the first to be laid off at Titan Tire was Jack Daugherty. Foreman of the swing shift in Plant One and an active member of the union, he made an obvious target for Titan.

Daugherty was not a hard-drinking man, but he hailed from Ireland, where the only men who did not lift a pint in the pub after work were teetotalers or Protestant parsons. Jack Daugherty was neither, so he became an easy target for dismissal on moral grounds after he was arrested in a raid on a speakeasy across the street from the factory.

His name was listed in the newspaper, along with fifty-four other Titan employees who were then summarily dismissed. The one exception was Dr. Keller, who was found passed out on the floor of the lavatory and taken to jail in a paddy wagon to spend the night in the drunk tank. He was released out the back door after a quick call to the Titan attorney, who explained the situation.

The article didn't mention that the men present were attending a wake for the father of Paddy Muldoon. Nor was it generally known that those arrested in the raid were already on the dismissal list of Titan Tire. The reporter noted that all were members of the union, but no mention was made of the bribe offered to the head of the Akron vice squad by Titan Tire for his part in conducting the operation. Rumor had it that Mr. Titan was well pleased with the entire event, with the exception of the behavior of his good friend Dr. Keller. The chief medical administrator was promptly sent on a brief vacation, lest further embarrassments occur.

The fifty-four Irishmen thus became the first casualties in the battle of Titan management against the union. They did not take their dismissal lying down. To a man, they took their places at the gates of the Titan plant, standing silent vigil as the days and nights grew bitterly cold, a reminder of what could happen to others on the line. Their ranks grew daily as the medical layoffs joined forces with further purges of men on moral charges.

Three nights a week, as Ellis entered the plant and left again eight hours later, the grim, sad eyes of Jack Daugherty followed his progress. Daugherty did not speak to Ellis, lest the line of blue-coated coppers construe conversation as harassment and haul him off to jail again. But Ellis felt the questioning stare of Daugherty on his back. He thought about it through his shift in the infirmary. And the heaviness of the times, the desperation of other men, always followed him home.

Becky was grateful for the quiet evening. She was glad that Boots had fallen asleep early and that Ellis was working his Titan shift. The wind picked up after dark, and static made the reception on the Philco more strain than pleasure to listen to. She switched off the radio, and with their little white dog curled at her feet, she began to read from the Gospel of Matthew, chapter 5: *Blessed are they that mourn: for they shall be comforted.*

This seemed a strange, almost trite saying to her tonight. She had mourned so deeply this year. And she had waited for the day when she would wake up and feel comforted, but the comfort had never come. Each day after the baby died had ticked by one long, comfortless minute after another.

She had been angry at times. When the anger subsided, the grief had still been there. She had felt betrayed somehow by Ellis, because she had not believed the child could die with him there. But she knew that Ellis had been helpless to save their son. And when the sense of betrayal eased, Becky's grief had reared up again with such fierceness that she thought she would choke.

She had found safety in one thing only. Like a person left out in the freezing night without a coat, Becky had felt herself gradually grow cold and numb. She had denied herself pleasure as well as pain and dismissed the suffering of others as a lack of fortitude. She had held her head high and taken some pride in surviving through each hour, even though she constantly wished she could have died with her baby. As long as she did not let herself feel anything, she could go on living.

Was Ellis hurting? Becky could not think about his pain, lest her compassion for him reawaken her own terrible grief. So she had denied his grief as well as her own.

The ache inside had slowly become more bearable as the cold numbness set in. Was this the comfort she so longed for? *Blessed are they that mourn. . . .* No. The shadow of a comfortless grief still tapped on her shoulder, reminding her not to feel life too deeply. If the anesthetic ever wore off, she felt she would crumble into a million pieces.

Becky closed her eyes and dozed.

The wind howled, shaking the glass panes of the windows. Snowball lifted his head suddenly as though he heard something outside. He stood and whined, then trotted to the door.

Becky sat up and sighed, unhappy at the thought of opening the door on such a night. Then she heard it . . . the sound of a crying baby.

She sat still and stared at the black window, waiting to see if the whimper was her imagination or if she would hear it again. The pitch of the storm increased, then receded . . . like a wave drawing back.

She heard it again—the distinct cry of an infant outside on the front porch. A baby? Becky's heart raced at the sound.

Again the little dog whined and scratched to be let out. Becky sprang to her feet and threw open the door as the plaintive cry resounded once more.

Switching on the porch light, she peered out and listened. The dog darted past her and bounded down the steps as the yowl drifted up again. It was not a child at all—only a stray cat wailing to be fed. Becky turned out the light but remained on the porch as the freezing wind whipped at her clothes and pierced her like tiny needles.

Grateful for the physical ache of the cold, she waited until she began to grow numb again before she went back inside to the warmth of the house.

CHAPTER TWENTY

No One to Tell

The mail brought word of financial devastation to the house on Florida Avenue from nearly every member of the Warne clan. Ellis's brothers Matthew and Mark had each lost all their savings. John had managed to get out of the market before he lost everything, but now the commodities prices had slid into the gutter, and the new dairy he had purchased three years before was looking at a lean year.

So it went on down the line. Each family had been hit in some way. Some, through no fault of their own, had been wiped out when a local bank closed its doors with no promise of ever opening again.

Doc and Molly Warne, on a two-year medical mission to Brazil, made no mention of the crash in their letters. They wrote only to tell of this needy family or that orphaned child or an epidemic of typhus in the shantytown outside the city of Rio. Perhaps his parents had not even heard of the American economic collapse, Ellis reasoned one evening at the dinner table.

Becky had another theory about the silence of her in-laws. Perhaps the everyday poverty and deprivation of the villages around the mission made America's plight seem like a picnic by the bandstand.

"If we could talk to your pop," Becky said, wishing that indeed Doc were around to counsel Ellis, "I think he would say that real trouble is a matter of perspective. To those folks down there in Brazil, the people here who are throwing themselves off bridges are killing themselves over the most trivial matters. They are wealthy and blessed by comparison."

"Don't be trite, Becky," Ellis snapped. "You don't know how badly people here are hit by this."

"No, no—I mean, of course I do. The Grahams are moving because Ted lost his job at the bank. But to kill oneself over something like money . . . I'm just saying that we see suffering differently than—"

"Simplistic hogwash. Like when we were kids and Mama used to tell us to clean our plates because there were kids starving all over the world. I used to wonder how my full belly made any difference to them. It didn't. Comparing us with them is trite and simplistic. You think it makes this easier? Just because there are parts of the world where the suffering is different?"

Becky exhaled and glanced at Boots, who sat with big eyes and her fork heaped with food that she did not eat. "You know that's not what I mean. We were . . . just talking about your mother and father. They see real problems."

"And I don't?" His voice trembled in angry defense.

"Ellis, please." Becky looked away before she broke into tears as she had a dozen times in the past months.

"Compare me with my dad? Doc Warne. Great heart. Out in the jungles of Brazil saving the souls of the natives while Americans—people here—are breaking apart and falling to pieces."

"Breaking. Over money," she retorted. "There are other, more important reasons for breaking. Only sometimes a person can't break. Sometimes a person has to decide what's really important, and he has to keep on going!"

She was speaking about the baby again. Reminding him that he had changed since the baby died. She was telling him that nothing meant anything compared to that.

"Why does every conversation come around to the baby somehow? Nothing is as big as our pain. There is nothing that matters but what we suffered. Is that it, Becky?"

Tears stung her eyes. How had they gotten into this? "Boots," she said calmly, "please take your plate upstairs. Your father and I . . ."

The stricken child started to rise. Becky knew that little Ellie had not heard her parents argue before. Becky and Ellis had always done that behind closed doors. Now the thing—the forbidden topic—had spilled out onto the table.

"Sit down." Ellis motioned for his daughter not to leave. "I . . . I don't know what . . . what's wrong with me."

Only silence greeted his words. Becky simply glared at him. He was a stranger to her. She could not understand him anymore. She did not know if she had the energy to try. "Let me know when you figure it out." Her voice was shaking with anger.

At this rebuke, Ellis grew darkly sullen. He glared at his plate of food and then, without eating, got up from the table and retreated to his office.

Becky watched him leave, and only then did she notice the tears rolling silently down her daughter's cheeks. The child still held her fork. The food on her plate was untouched.

"Boots." Becky was instantly remorseful. There were things she needed to say to Ellis, but not in front of the child.

"Why don't you leave him alone?" Boots sniffed. "He can't help that Howie died!" Sniffs erupted into a half-choked sob. "Nothing is the same anymore! I wish I had died instead of Howie! It wouldn't have been so bad if it had been me!" With a wail, she broke from the table and ran upstairs.

Becky sat there for a long minute before she slowly climbed the stairs to comfort her daughter.

Ellis had waited until he was certain that Becky was sleeping before he came to bed. Then he lay there, trying to figure out why they had argued. In the end, he was not even sure what the argument had been about. It was his fault, he concluded. He could not expect her to understand.

Finally he had given up trying to get to sleep. Two hours of tossing and turning had produced a terrific headache but no slumber, and his agitated movements were sure to awaken Becky.

He got up and heated a saucepan of milk on the stove. Bypassing the kitchen table and the parlor easy chair, he took a mug full of the steaming liquid into his office.

Keep your job or keep your principles—that's what Ellis Warne, MD, was struggling with this night. How could he continue to assist in Titan's underhanded scheme to lay off good men for no reason?

Still, good men were getting laid off all around Akron—around the whole country, if newspaper and radio accounts were to be believed. Titan didn't have to have a reason to let men go. He could fire the whole lot of them if he wanted. What Ellis and the other conspirators were being asked to do was to see that the union had no say in who stayed and who went. Was that so bad?

Besides, the bunch from the first shift at Plant One really *had* come to work with terrible hangovers, and that *did* make for hazardous working conditions, didn't it? Maybe Titan was right: Those who remained would be more careful and conscientious when they saw their coworkers disappearing from the line.

But Ellis knew it wasn't really so. Jack Daugherty had been one of the first to go, and Jack was a good, cautious worker, not a habitual drunk.

Fewer men on the line would mean heavier workloads and greater demands on those who remained. Since Titan wasn't about to spend money on improving the safety conditions, the speedup was bound to cause more accidents.

Lost workers meant nothing to Titan, of course. From the factory owner's point of view, workers were expendable, and injuries were a concern only as long as it took to get a new man trained. With thousands of laid-off employees, there would be no shortage of willing and able replacements.

Meanwhile, what about Ellis's own position? His family could not make it on the income from his little practice alone. And Titan could see to it that Ellis could not get on anywhere else either—not in Akron, anyway.

Ellis picked up the mug and took a sip. The milk was tepid, barely above the chilly temperature of the office. How long had he been sitting and staring at the framed copy of the Hippocratic Oath?

I will maintain the utmost respect for human life from the time of conception. Even under threat, I will not use my medical knowledge contrary to the laws of humanity.

Well, the threat was certainly there. Did making a fraudulent diagnosis of a nonexistent illness constitute a misuse of medical knowledge? Ellis knew the answer to that question even before his mind had finished framing it. Put more simply, he knew what his father would say.

"Good men are getting handed a raw deal," Doc would tell him. *"What are you going to do about it? Have those men ever hurt you in any way? Can you stand by and let them be treated like this, much less be a part of it? Put yourself in their shoes, Ellis."*

But that was the problem, wasn't it? Who was there who could stand in Ellis's place? Who understood what he was facing?

There was a scratching sound at the clinic door, the one that opened at the side of the house. Ellis glanced at the entry, then down at the undrunk mug of milk. Maybe the noise was made by one of the homeless cats that wandered this neighborhood. If so, it had managed to come to the right place. Ellis stood with the cup of milk in his hand and headed for the door.

As he opened the door, something fluttered to the ground outside and into the dark flower bed beside the walk. "Here, kitty," Ellis called, extending the mug. There was no cat in sight.

Stooping to pick up the scrap of paper from the ivy, Ellis heard the clash of gears from a car around the corner at the front of the house. He walked to the front yard to see but only got a glimpse of taillights receding down the block.

Ellis carried the paper inside and switched on his desk lamp. The outside of the folded sheet bore his name, printed in clumsy capital letters. He opened it and read:

WE KNOW ABOUT TITAN'S SCHEME. DON'T BE PART OF IT. TAKE THIS WARNING SERIOUSLY. WE KNOW WHERE YOU LIVE.

Ellis sat and stared at the note for a long time. When he heard Becky stirring upstairs, he quickly stuffed it into his pocket and resolved to say nothing to her about it. And that meant saying nothing to anyone.

Who was there to tell?

Max Meyer drifted in and out of consciousness. Buck Hooper's knife had punctured his lung, and even with the wound stitched up by Dr. Brown, there was some question whether he would survive. Breathing was an agony, and speaking was nearly impossible. He had managed to mutter these words to David one night: "Embarrassing . . . dodged the gang . . . the Feds . . . knifed by a hayseed. . . . Sorry, kid."

If Mary Brown, moving like a shadow in the background, overheard his feverish references to gangsters and G-men, she never showed the slightest curiosity about it. She did, however, take an interest in the apprehension of the hayseed who had knifed her patient. She telephoned the sheriff each afternoon in the hopes that Buck Hooper had been caught. It was her earnest prayer, she said loudly and often, that he would be locked in jail and the key thrown away.

But it wasn't that simple. The investigation into the incident involved questioning Boomer as a witness, so the facts of the case were unclear. Had Max grabbed the nail-studded board before Buck pulled his knife? If that was the case, then the stabbing would be a matter of self-defense. Boomer merely summed up his view of the fight with two words: *murder* and *blaspheming.*

The whole thing put a strain on Sheriff Potts, who had lost a good deal of money when he bet against Buck's winning the fight. In the first place, Max was not yet dead, so there was no case for murder. In the second place, he could not arrest Buck Hooper for blasphemy, as long as he had not blasphemed publicly and offended any of the fairer sex in town by doing so. Until it was all sorted out, it was presumed, Buck would be lying low somewhere up on Sugar Loaf Mountain, no doubt tending the fires of his whiskey still.

In the meantime, Mary Brown stoked the fires of her fury until she became a boiling cauldron of indignation about the entire thing. Heaven help Buck Hooper if she got hold of him before the law could lock him safely away!

The fact that Max Meyer now lay near death because she had danced with him spurred sweet Mary to exercise all her nursing prowess in seeing that he survived. She moved her sleeping quarters to the anteroom just outside the small infirmary on the bottom floor of her father's house. While David spent the night upstairs in her bedroom, Mary lay awake and listened to the ragged breathing of Max. Little Davey Meyer would not grow up an orphan if she had anything to do about it!

"He's no trouble," she had assured Trudy privately. "No, no! David must stay at our house. His presence might prevent his father from giving up on life. I have seen the very thing before in such cases!" Satisfied with that, Trudy had promised to care for Codfish and had returned to Shiloh without David. Daily reports of progress in the case were telephoned to Grandma Amos's Shiloh store.

David had opened up to Mary after the third day, telling her that he was an old hand around hospitals. After all, his mother had died in a hospital not long ago. "So it's just me and Dad now," he had said in a voice that made her heart twist and squeeze and ache for the widower and his son. Then, just when she regained her composure, David had quietly asked if she thought his father would also die.

"A thousand times no," Mary had promised him. But the truth was that neither Mary nor Doc Brown could be certain what the next hour would bring for Max. Who could say whether the infection would explode into an army of a billion bacilli to invade every cell of the handsome stranger? Max, who was sedated with morphine, did not experience half the torment that Mary Brown did. She had studied germs beneath a microscope, and her nightmares now included giant bacteria, all with the faces of Buck Hooper.

In her waking hours, when she was not dressing her patient's wounds or bathing or feeding him, Mary did her best to help David through the long ordeal. She listened patiently to long and tedious facts about the game of baseball. She also discovered that Davey was fond of gin rummy and poker. Would she like to learn the games?

In her life, Mary Brown had never so much as touched a deck of playing cards. But she cheerfully handed over a nickel, loaned David her bicycle, and sent him to Mr. Winters's drugstore, where he purchased a pack of red Hoyle playing cards. Before long, she knew the difference between a straight, a royal flush, and a full house. David seemed pleased.

In quiet moments, Mary softly read the Good Book to Max, just in case those bacilli got the upper hand. She did not know anything about

Max Meyer's spiritual state, and she did not wish to take that important matter for granted. With this on her heart, she recited the Gospels with the same thoroughness she planned to eventually use on unsaved Chinese souls. When working in the infirmary she sang hymns, knowing that music sometimes reached the heart where words would not. "'Love divine, all loves excelling. . . .'"

Often Max opened his eyes—such deep and soulful eyes—and whispered thanks to her before he drifted off again. Twice he took her hand and held it tightly for a few minutes before letting her go.

By the early morning of the seventh day, Miss Mary Brown was not only holding the hand of Max. She was holding the hope that both body and soul might be healed as well. Truth to tell, Mary Brown was also having thoughts about David's needing a mother and Max's needing a woman to take care of him. Was it possible, she wondered, to fall in love with an unconscious man?

Dr. John Brown, seeing the unusually soft glow on the face of his daughter, issued her a gentle warning that Max Meyer might be an entirely different fellow once his lung healed and he was taken off morphine.

"Most men are easy to love, Mary dear," Doc Brown said, "if they are more dead than alive. It's when they're awake that you have to worry."

Ever candid with her father, Mary reminded Doc Brown that she had seen Max awake. It was that chance meeting, after all, that had brought him here in his present condition. She had danced with him. Spoken with him. She had seen him cheerfully change the life of the schoolmarm Miss Price, who by now was probably engaged to wed Mr. Faraby.

Mary Brown might harbor tender feelings for the sick, sedated man. But she also liked what she had seen of the conscious Max Meyer.

CHAPTER TWENTY-ONE

Hard Times

For a time after the argument at the dinner table, the Warne household returned to a strained normalcy. In front of little Boots, Ellis was cheerful and laughed easily. He often stooped to kiss Becky on the cheek and comment about how pretty she looked. He offered no word of apology for his outburst, yet the next evening Ellis pulled the Ford out of the driveway and drove to the new Loews Theatre with his "two favorite girls." As if nothing had changed, they sat together in the dark Moorish splendor of the movie house and looked up at the star-studded ceiling and the painted drifting clouds and pretended that they were in Morocco instead of Akron.

When Ellis and Becky were alone, however, they made no attempt to pretend. She did not speak to him except out of necessity. In front of the patients at the day clinic operated from their home, they addressed each other with professional formality. In the privacy of their bedroom, she was hurt and silent. He was sullen and distant and defensive. Each turned inward to his or her own pain.

Ellis loved her still, longed to share his worry and fear with her, but he no longer felt confident that she loved him. He was convinced that to tell her the depth of their financial ruin would simply strike the final blow between them. She had trusted him, and he had lost everything. What would she say if she knew what he had done? Would she leave him for good? They had lost so much—too much—when the baby died. Maybe this problem was small in comparison to the death of a child, but he could not lay the additional burden on her. So he carried the truth alone. He pored over the books and juggled the bills and came to the same conclusion every time: He had to keep the Titan job.

Becky loved him, too. She ached for him to take her in his arms and make her believe that life could be good again, that they could have more children and begin to forget. At night she huddled in her corner of the bed they shared. She longed to touch him as he slept, to awaken him with the same fire that kept her awake. But she feared he would turn his back to her, push her away, perhaps even leave her, and she couldn't run that risk.

A dozen times Becky wondered if Ellis had somehow fallen in love with another woman. But where? And who? And how? Becky worked at his side in the clinic. The only times they were apart were the three nights a week he spent at the Titan plant. No. It could not be another woman that had driven a wedge between them. But what was it, then?

The warm glow of loving and being loved had cooled until only embers remained in the ashes. This was the reality that Ellis and Becky faced together—yet alone—every day.

The man who knocked at the side-door entrance to the Warne Medical Clinic was tall and dark-haired. A bit thin, perhaps, with a worried look in his eyes, but otherwise healthy enough to Becky's casual inspection.

Becky was acting in her role as Ellis's nurse, secretary, and receptionist when the man who identified himself as George Stepanov asked if the doctor was in. She turned from shaking her head over the sadly depleted state of the supply cupboard and asked Mr. Stepanov to have a seat. Then she went to fetch Ellis from the parlor.

"Good afternoon," Ellis greeted him. "What seems to be the trouble?"

"It's my heart, Dok-tor," said the man in a deep, accented voice that leaned heavily on the consonants. "My wife is scared my ticker's gonna quit. You check me, okay?"

The thermometer registered a normal temperature when Becky took the reading. Ellis passed his stethoscope over the man's chest, listened carefully, then repeated the operation again and again.

Unclipping the instrument from his ears, Ellis asked, "What makes you think there is a problem with your heart, Mister Stepanov? Have you been having chest pains?"

"You don't hear no *swish-swish-swish*?" Stepanov asked, surprised. "No sign of a moo-mur?"

"A murmur? No, none at all. Why? Do you have a reason for thinking you have one?"

"It's this way. I got one of those company phys-cals down at the Titan plant. You know the ones I mean, Doc . . . only I ain't on your shift."

Ellis started visibly. There was something familiar about the look he gave Becky—a mixture of guilt and surprise and a little fear. It reminded her of the way Boots looked when she was discovered playing with her father's instruments after being forbidden to do so.

"Becky," Ellis said suddenly, "is that Boots calling? Should you go check on her?"

"No, Ellis, she's at Teresa's house. Go on, Mister Stepanov."

"When Dok-tor Reynolds at the plant give me my phys-cal, he listens and right away he says 'uh-oh' and 'my, my,' you know? Then he asks me questions—do I get out of breath climbing stairs, do I ever hear the blood rushing in my ears when I lay down? And then he says to me, 'Stepanov, you got a heart moo-mur. Your heart says *swish-swish*. No more heavy lifting for you.' Next day, bang! I am laid off. My wife tells me, go see another dok-tor, but I don't have no other since I don't have the company doc no more. Then I remember you have office, so I come here."

Becky wondered why Ellis looked so pale and puzzled. Surely a heart murmur was a straightforward diagnosis. "Well, Ellis?" she questioned. "Is there a murmur or isn't there?"

"I . . . ah . . . it's not that easy to tell," Ellis mumbled. "Probably too faint for me to hear, but trust Reynolds to pick it up. He's sharp."

The mental comparison between the quiet of Ellis's office, where even the ticking of his desk clock could be heard, and the roar of steam presses and churning machinery at the Titan plant confused Becky even more. "Ellis," she protested, "Mister Stepanov has lost his job because of a condition he may not even have. What are you going to do about it?"

"Do? What can I do?" Ellis responded testily, jamming his stethoscope into a desk drawer. "I'm sorry, Mister Stepanov, but I'm sure Doctor Reynolds is correct. Good-bye." He stalked from the clinic back into the house.

Becky turned to the man whose face had fallen into a thousand lines of worry and unhappiness, as if the mirror holding his reflection had shattered. "Try not to fret," she urged. "A heart murmur doesn't necessarily mean anything dangerous."

Stepanov turned his deeply pained dark eyes on her. "Missus Dok-tor, it ain't for myself I worry. But there ain't no more jobs in Akron just now, see, and I got five kids. And with Christmas coming on . . ."

"Go home and try not to worry," Becky suggested again. "I'll speak to my husband. Perhaps he can check you again and do something for you at the plant."

Max's voice was clear, his mind seemingly lucid.

"Davey? Why aren't you in school with Tommy and Bobby out in Shiloh?"

David sat up abruptly and looked at Mary, who grinned happily back at him. This was a very good sign. "Because I wanted to stay with you."

"Hooky," Max said with a pleasant sigh. "Mary, darling, will you please call Trudy and have her come pick him up? He needs to be in school." With that, Max drifted off again into a deep sleep.

That little exchange was enough to cause a celebration over the breakfast table. Throughout the long days, Max had often called out for David to come to his bedside. Those requests had sounded unhappily like the last wish of a dying man. But for him to speak like a father accusing his son of playing hooky? Now here was reason for great hope! A man near death was not likely to wake up and demand that a beloved child get to school!

Mary made the call to Grandma Amos at the Shiloh store. The old woman shuffled out to her porch and clanged the iron dinner bell two long and one short—a signal to the Tucker family that a telephone message could be picked up at the store.

Neighbors recognized the Tucker signal and speculated that the ringing most likely meant Max had died. Suddenly there were reasons why folks needed to make quick trips to the store. Such calls always brought in more business for Grandma Amos. A considerable crowd had already arrived to purchase needles, thread, a quart of yellow paint, birdseed, bolts, a hammer, diaper pins, a pie tin. They lingered until Birch and Tommy arrived and retrieved the message from Grandma Amos.

Birch pleased each of his curious neighbors when he read the note to one and all:

"For Trudy and Birch
Praise the Lord! Max is better! Wants David in school with the
boys. Trudy and Birch, please fetch him home to Shiloh today!
From Mary Brown"

✳ ✳ ✳

Trudy reviewed the fourth-grade McGuffey reader with David that night and declared he would have nothing to worry about at school. It was plain, she said, that he was his mother's son, and Irene Dunlap had been among the best teachers in New York when Trudy knew her. Not only was David fluent in the chapters on grammar and spelling and reading, he was above his grade in some of these areas and far above average in mathematics.

All of this was said within earshot of Tommy and Bobby, who were also sons of a teacher yet not nearly so advanced as their newly discovered cousin. They eyed him with reproach, as though he were bent on humbling them in the eyes of their mother.

At bedtime, Trudy read a chapter from Grandpa Sinnickson's memoirs, then passed the heavy volume to each of the boys to read a paragraph. By the end of the section it was clear to all of them that David was a superior reader. He paused less and did not stumble over even one word in the account of the lynching of the Argentine miner. When he even pronounced the Spanish phrases correctly, Trudy patted him on the back and told him again that he would have no trouble whatsoever at Shiloh School.

After prayers, she tucked the trio in on the mattress they shared in the front room. Blowing out the lamp and retreating to the kitchen, she could be heard telling Birch, Jefferson, and Lily what a remarkably bright child David was. "He will not have a moment of trouble in school," she said once more.

David was feeling rather smug about showing up Tommy and Bobby. He smiled up at the dark ceiling. Then an elbow came crashing into his ribs.

"Show-off," whispered Bobby.

"You tryin' to make life hard round here?" Tommy snarled.

"Uh . . . just . . . no . . . ," David stammered.

"If you don't want your nose busted, you better tone it down at school, Davey. There are plenty of sixth graders who don't cotton to no Yankee fourth grader readin' better than they do and doin' ciphers like a seventh grader and generally makin' school harder than it is already." Another jab. "You get it?"

David got it, but he did not like it much. He felt he was being misjudged. Had he not been the most adept of his friends at playing hooky back in Philadelphia? Had he not made the life of his teacher miserable by a string of practical jokes for which the school outcasts got blamed? Had he not set the clock forward so that class let out early on a number of occasions? And now he had to start over, to win the hearts of fellow students by his bravado and daring and defiance. It didn't seem fair.

"Guess so," he mumbled.

"You better," Tommy warned. "Only girls read out loud that good."

"Yeah," agreed Bobby, who still got stuck reading words like *high* and *through* because the *gh* confused him. "You make us look dumb—that's all."

"Don't matter that our mama thinks you're swell. You'll prob'ly be a teacher's pet—that's what. It took us a lot of work to be one of the guys, and now you're likely to ruin it for us. Nobody likes a show-off. And I ain't gonna fight for you. Don't matter if we're related or not."

With this warning ringing in his ears, David went to sleep. His dreams were frightening ones in which Miss Price actually took a shine to him and thus ruined his new life in Shiloh.

But the dreams were not nearly as horrible as the reality of David Meyer's first day at Shiloh School. . . .

The eyebrows of Miss Price, which had once seemed knit into a single grim line, now arched pleasantly when she smiled. The fact that she was smiling was amazing in itself. She who had spent the days and weeks and months scowling and glowering at her pupils had rarely been cross at all since the widower Mr. Faraby had begun to court her.

Now it was the Faraby children who sat in sullen misery in the class-room. The smiling Miss Price would almost certainly wed their father, and who knew how long her smiles would last after that? This fear had put the brood of Faraby children in a lynching mood. None dared to tease them about the fact that Old Maid Price was soon to be their stepmama. No schoolmate dared comment on their poor bewitched father's goofy expression or mention the blush on Miss Price's cheeks. The fact that the teacher hummed when cleaning the blackboards and grading spelling papers was a forbidden topic.

The Faraby children had tolerated Miss Price much more easily be-fore she changed from the wicked stepsister into Cinderella. They had liked her better when they hated her.

And who had set this nightmare in motion? Why, it was the father of the new kid, David Meyer!

Privately it was believed that for his part in making the match between Miss Price and Mr. Faraby, the father of David Meyer deserved what he had gotten at the hand of Buck Hooper in the livery stable. True, these Yankee meddlers were relatives of Tommy and Bobby Tucker, and that was discussed. In the end, no one held it against either of the Tucker boys that their relation from New York had been fool enough to dance with Miss Price and thus attract poor Mr. Faraby to her like a trout rising to swallow a barbed-and-feathered lure.

Poor Mr. Faraby. Hook, line, and sinker he had swallowed, and she was reeling him in by patting the heads of his children and batting her eyes like a true Southern belle whenever the thought of marriage hit her over the head. The kids all knew when it happened. Right in the middle of arithmetic or geography, she would smile wistfully and blush and those eyelashes would begin to flutter. Everyone in the class would look this way and that as if to say, *"Poor Mister Faraby is dangling from her line again."*

This was the climate in the schoolroom the morning of David's first day. He longed to take his place in the very back seat nearest the door. But it seemed that this was the seat normally occupied by Dan, the eldest Faraby child.

"My seat, Yankee," snarled Dan, eyeing David as though he were something to avoid stepping in.

This same line was repeated in every empty seat in the room. David suddenly understood what was happening when he took a seat near the front and once again Dan Faraby towered over him. "My seat, Yankee," Dan asserted as he claimed the second desk and gave him a nudge.

All this was the stuff reserved for new kids, David realized. But he had been a new kid before, and he had always managed to come out on top after the first shoving match. This time he might have managed to overcome the general resentment of the entire class fairly easily . . . if it hadn't been for Miss Price.

Gushing and fluttering, the teacher swooped down and put her arms around his shoulders in greeting. She exclaimed loudly for one and all to hear that this handsome young man was the son of the unfortunate Mr. Meyer, who had been stabbed by Buck Hooper after the school dance. She then went on to comment about how she hoped Buck Hooper was not the standard upon which David judged all the citizens of Sebastian County.

"We are all very friendly and pleasant people to know. You shall see for yourself among the youngsters in this classroom! I am certain you will be the very best of friends. Perhaps you can even teach some of them better study habits by your own example."

One look at the sullen faces of his new classmates told David that Miss Price was too blinded by new love to see the truth. The students of Shiloh School were a pack of hungry lions, and he was slated to be their supper.

She was still gushing. "Welcome! Welcome, David Meyer! All the way from New York City! And your Aunt Trudy tells me that you are far advanced in your reader and ciphers, too. You shall keep us all on our toes. Your aunt says you are already reading above sixth-grade level."

David caught sight of Tommy, who winced at the fact that this information was now public knowledge. Aunt Trudy was a nice woman, but she had a big mouth sometimes. Tommy put palm to forehead in a gesture of exasperation, then laid his head down on the desk while Miss Price told everybody everything she knew about the new pupil.

She finished the monologue with a request that the entire class give David Meyer a round of applause to welcome him. The response was perfunctory, sounding more like sixty students swatting flies. She seated David in a place of honor at the head of the class and pinched his cheek affectionately.

Disaster! The damage would be hard to undo now. And all of this had taken place before they had even saluted the flag!

The recess bell rang like the opening of round one. David, deserted by his cousins, was last to leave the classroom. He walked out into the chill morning air to a colder group of students who waited with hostile faces to watch him walk down the steps and to the water bucket for a drink. The cup was knocked out of his hands by young Fred Woods, who then nudged Tommy Tucker, daring him to stand up for David. Tommy grinned sheepishly and shrugged in a way that said, *"Distant relation only—have at it."*

From that moment, David knew he was alone. If he did not do something dramatic to demonstrate his resistance to the attentions of Miss Price, he would be slaughtered before the day was through. But how, between the end of his first recess and the beginning of the next, could he demonstrate what a regular guy he was—in spite of the fact that his father had danced with the teacher and was a Yankee besides?

His stomach rumbled, not from hunger but from nervousness. But with that rumble he thought of food and of Lily packing lunches in the kitchen this morning. The idea came to him suddenly like a vision from heaven. . . .

"Pickles," he muttered, hurrying back to the cloakroom and his tin lunch bucket. He opened the catch and unwrapped a thick ham sandwich, which was seasoned with Trudy's famous pickle relish. Carefully David scraped off tiny bits of chopped pickles, which he placed in his handkerchief. *Desperate times call for desperate measures. . . .*

The bell rang. The students returned to class more reluctantly than they had left it. David was installed once again in his seat of honor. This was the reading hour, and Miss Price wished to use him as an example of how well even a fourth grader could read if only that fourth grader was smart enough and worked hard enough and applied himself. . . .

By the end of the speech, David could feel hatred radiating from his schoolmates. Miss Price balanced her reading glasses on the end of her nose and thumbed through her copy of Charles Dickens's *Hard Times*.

"Now, David, your aunt Trudy says that your mother was quite a reader. Quite fond of Dickens. Your aunt tells me that last night you read a passage of Dickens back to her flawlessly from the McGuffey. We would like you to give a demonstration. Please come forward." She smiled in a sappy way—the only one in the room enjoying herself.

David knew he must change that or he would never make it home alive! "Yes, ma'am," he answered primly, rising from his desk and approaching her.

"Your aunt Trudy said also that you are a young gentleman with good manners. An example to many, I am sure."

"Yes, ma'am." David took the book from her and inhaled deeply. "Where would you like me to begin?"

Miss Price, standing in erect dignity beside him, stooped to point out the passage.

In this instant, David seized his opportunity. He snatched out his handkerchief and exploded with a sneeze that no doubt could be heard all over Sebastian County. Shrapnel in the form of Trudy's famous pickle relish sprayed out with astonishing accuracy to hit the face and glasses of Miss Price.

She shrieked and fell back, knocking over the trash can and a stack of books. She whipped off her glasses and groped for a hankie to wipe her face. David offered his as an example of fine manners. This was refused, so the rag from the chalkboard was given instead. With white chalk dust powdering her face, it was difficult to tell if Miss Price was truly pale or just smeared.

The classroom was divided into two responses. The boys cheered and hooted, while the girls squeaked and moaned and gazed upon their green-speckled teacher with utter revulsion. As David pretended to grovel and begged her great pardon, Miss Price attempted to regain her composure. A patient, quavering smile cracked the chalk dust. She drew herself up and beat a hasty retreat out the door to the well.

At this, David opened his hankie and peered down into the cloth. He gave a sniff. He stuck out his lip in thought. "Pickles. I cleaned 'em up off the floor this morning. Must've forgot about it."

He then sat down to the cheers of newly won friends without ever having to read a word of *Hard Times*.

CHAPTER TWENTY-TWO

Where the Poor People Live

"But, Boss," complained the tinny, faint voice of Smiley over the long-distance phone connection, "there ain't nothin' here but greasy cowboys drinkin' beer. Nobody has any idea where this Tucker character is to be found."

Boss Quinn yanked his free hand away from the manicurist's attentions and gestured angrily for her to leave his office. "Smiley," Quinn said, strangling the receiver as if it were his henchman's neck, "these repeated failures of yours are becoming most repugnant to me. I find it difficult to believe that you are putting forth your best efforts."

There was a pause on the other end of the line. Even long-distance from Tulsa, Oklahoma, Smiley must have known that giving Boss Quinn back talk was likely to be hazardous to his health.

"I'm real sorry, Boss," he apologized. "I do got another lead, though. How's about I go straight to Akron, Ohio? You know, the other war buddy of Meyer's?"

Quinn considered the suggestion. This was really the only connection left to be explored. It would not serve any good purpose for Smiley to return all the way to New York before going to Akron.

"All right," he said more evenly. "But, Smiley," Quinn went on, "let us hope that Akron, Ohio, proves to be auspicious."

Hanging up the phone, he added, "For your sake."

★ ★ ★

It seemed that a forest of evergreens had magically appeared in downtown Akron. For blocks and blocks, in every direction you looked, the lampposts had been transformed into Christmas trees. Across every street corner, draped wires had been festooned with spirals of gold tinsel and hung with huge gold stars and enormous red bells.

Store windows all sported festive scenes, and toys were prominently displayed—red fire engines and roller skates, dollhouses and tea sets. A giant red-and-green jack-in-the-box that endlessly ground out "Pop Goes the Weasel" did double duty as an advertisement. The clown-suited figure that appeared held up a sign announcing Merry Christmas! Shop at Polsky's.

It was a time to forget troubles and unhappiness, at least for a while. Becky Warne found herself saying over and over again, "Look there, Boots!" and "See what's in that window!" Mother and daughter both giggled and *ooh-ahh*ed as they watched a giant banner unroll itself from the top floor of the department store. Stretching down four stories, it read Season's Greetings from O'Neil's.

Two more blocks of window-shopping in the chilly wind produced glowing pink cheeks on both Becky and Boots and convinced them it was time for a treat. A street vendor dispensing hot cocoa and cinnamon-sprinkled doughnuts had attracted a line of ladies in fur-trimmed coats and men with mufflers wound around their upturned coat collars. Across the street from him, a swarthy man turned tiny skewers of meat over a charcoal fire. The third corner of the same intersection boasted a yellow-and-white-striped umbrella that sheltered a silver cart. Kosher Hot Dogs! its sign proclaimed. Get 'Em While They're Hot. On the final corner was a hot-pretzel salesman. "Zee, kids," he demonstrated to eager and hungry onlookers as he explained the twisted dough, "de arms folded in prayer are."

Boots walked ahead of her mother with a cup of hot cocoa in one hand and half a doughnut in the other. "Look, Mom." Boots pointed, with a gesture that sloshed a drop of chocolate onto the toe of her red shoe. "What are they selling there? It must be really good. Look at the long line!"

An entire city block was surrounded by a board fence. A sign on the corner announced Coming Soon—Akron YMCA. And all along the boardwalk that stretched beside the fence stood a line of people. From Boots's perspective, the row seemed to disappear into the distance without end, and even from Becky's point of view it looked to contain a hundred or so people.

The men in the queue were mostly neatly dressed, but here and there a shoe sole flapped, and some jackets were too thin for the season. There were only a handful of women in the line, but none of them were wearing fur-trimmed coats.

The one thing they all seemed to share as Becky and Boots traveled along the line was an expression turned inward and away from others. Universally they stared at the ground, or if they happened to meet someone's eye they hurriedly looked away.

Boots tugged on Becky's coat sleeve. "What's wrong with ever'body?"

"Shhh, dear," Becky cautioned. "Come along."

At the head of the line was a truck. Out of its back, two men were passing out tin cups, into which two women ladled soup from a big kettle.

"Furnace Street Mission," Boots spelled out from the sign on the side of the truck. "Furnace Street," she observed. "Isn't that where the poor people live?"

☆ ☆ ☆

"I'm quitting school, Gramma." Harry Canfield raised his chin in defiance as Willa-Mae shook her head and pointed for him to sit down and quit talking crazy.

"No, you ain't! I gave my solemn promise t'your mama and daddy that me and your grampa'd look after you. I told 'em we'd see t'it you got schoolin' like your daddy never did have. Ain't no black man ever gonna be nothin' in this world 'less he go t'school! Now sit yourself down there like I says!"

Harry did not sit down. He stood, unmoving, like a tree rooted upright in the center of the little flat. She was a big woman, Willa-Mae was, but all the same she was short compared to him. If he sat down in her presence, then she would be bigger than him again. She would stand over him and shake her finger in his face. She would cuff him on the head if he argued and treat him as if he were an eight-year-old kid instead of a man grown up and nearly eighteen.

"I ain't gonna argue with you, Gramma," he began.

"Good! I'll say you ain't! You argue with me and I'll give you this, boy!" She raised her hand and whacked him on the shoulder.

He winced out of years of habit, even though the blow did not hurt him any more than a fly buzzing around a grizzly bear.

"Ain't none of my young'uns ever gimme no back talk! And if they did? Well, they knew what they'd get for it! You hear me, Harry?"

Woo-eee, she was mad as a wet hen! "Yes'm."

"Then set your backside down like I says," she growled up into his face.

"Gramma—"

"Hear me?"

"Yes'm, but—"

"Don't you gimme no lip, Harry! I ain't nothin' but an ol' woman, but I can still beat the tar outta you, boy!" She made her point with another whack on his shoulder. She always talked about beating the tar out of him if he didn't mind her, but the threat was all noise and smoke. Nothing ever came of it.

"Gramma, I got something to tell you."

"*You* ain't quittin' school! Such a thing'd just kill your grampa. Ain't you got no sense? Answer me when I'm talkin' t'you!"

"No'm. I got no sense."

"Don't you talk back to me!" *Whack!*

"No'm! I'm not! But it's true, Gramma!" he pleaded. "I got no sense! Now sit down, will you? If you sit down, I'll sit down. You *got* to sit down to hear what I'm going to tell you!"

He looked at his big feet. Size thirteen. Willa-Mae had worked hard to buy him those size-thirteen shoes. Did she know how much he appreciated what she had done for him? how much he loved her?

"Please, Gramma. You got to let me tell you."

"Did you git yourself in trouble down t'the school? 'Cause if you did . . ." She put her hand to her mouth as though she had seen a vision of something terrible. "You been down t'one'a them speakeasies, ain't you, boy? Been drinkin' that demon gin! Oh, Lord! Carousin' with them flapper gals! Lord, Lord!" She sat down hard. The chair groaned with the assault.

Harry sat down carefully on the worn sofa across from her. "Not that, Gramma." He could not look her in the eye.

"Then what? I raise you best I know how, and this is what you do! Git yourself drinkin' at a speak and run outta school when you ain't got but half a year left t'make somethin' outta yourself! Be a high school graduate like Nettie! Now this."

"*Gramma!*" He shouted to make her stop. "It ain't that! It—it's not school, Gramma. Not drinking. I don't go down to the speaks. You got to listen to what I have to tell you now!" Ashamed, he lowered his gaze to stare at her feet, which overflowed her scuffed leather shoes.

"Well then?" She glared across at him. "I'm waitin'. What you done so bad that you ain't goin' t'school no more?"

He cleared his throat and shifted in his seat. He tucked his chin and inhaled in an attempt to find the courage. "You know I been seeing Reverend Dale's girl . . . Rena."

Silence. Of course she knew. She had been plenty happy about it, too, that he would take such a sweet little thing to get ice cream and to the church socials and sings and such. Could this be the trouble?

"Oh my, yes, Harry. Little Rena Dale. Now tell me quick whilst I'm still a'breathin' . . . what you done?"

"I love her, Gramma."

"No sin in that. No reason t'drop outta school, neither."

He made a little moan as the news tried to come out but got stuck somewhere down in his chest. "Reason enough. We're getting married."

"She ain't but sixteen! You ain't but seventeen!"

"Gramma . . . I . . . we ain't all that young."

Did she understand?

Willa-Mae sat very still, her shoulders back and her chin lifted at a regal angle while all the pieces fit in together. "Y'all in trouble, then," she said in a weary voice. An accepting voice.

"Yes'm. My fault."

"I know it is," she replied without pity. "You done got that sweet little gal in the family way."

"Yes'm."

"So y'all gonna do the right thing and get hitched. There ain't nothin' else for it." She put a hand to her head. "Ah, Harry, I thought you was smarter'n that. What's t'come of you young'uns now? Done made a baby when y'all ain't more'n babies yourselfs. What a time y'all picked t'be dumb, boy! The world fallin' t'pieces!"

"Yes'm." He sat quietly for a while, wishing it were not so.

"Well, we'll make room." She glanced around the tiny space that Harry filled up by himself.

Make room where? he wondered. "We talked to Reverend Dale and Sister Dale last night."

"Hmmm. Bet that was somethin'." She shook her head, as if imagining the scene in Reverend and Sister Dale's little house. "Bet compared t'that, tellin' me what you done is a piece of cake."

"Yes'm."

"Well, it ain't gonna be so easy tellin' your Grampa Hock! He'll take a strop t'you."

"I told him first. He said I got to do the right thing. Said I got to be a man and own up to it. Marry Rena and get a job."

"Job? Huh!"

"I got one. Down at the Titan plant. They don't pay colored men even half of what they pay a white man. White men hate it. Won't work for what I was hired on for . . . fifty cents a day."

Willa-Mae just kept shaking her head. "It costs more'n that t'feed a mule."

"Yes'm. I know that. The man took a look at me. Said I was big as a mule. Told me I could haul bales of rubber for fifty cents a day. Said it was better than not working. I said he was right. I start tomorrow."

"Sounds like it's done, then."

"Yes'm."

"And I'm the last one t'know 'bout it."

"Yes'm. I didn't want to trouble you until I knew I had a job. Any job."

"Any job is what you gots, Harry. That won't hardly keep y'all alive."

"We're going to make it, Gramma." There were tears in his eyes. "At first I thought Reverend Dale was going to kill me. Sister Dale cried a lot. Kept saying I had ruined their baby. But then they got quiet about it. Reverend Dale said what's done is done. The blood of Jesus takes away my sin, but after that I'm going to have to be a good husband to Rena all my life and a father to our child. . . . I can do that, Gramma. I know I can. I watched how you and Grampa took care of all of us. How you worked and kept me in shoes and such. Y'all never seemed unhappy—not often anyway. If you and Grampa can be happy just living, then me and Rena can make it the same way. I'm sorry about the mistake, but I'm happy when I think about the baby and Rena."

"Well, yes." Willa-Mae nodded wistfully now. "There ain't nothin' in the whole world like a baby round the place. Long as y'all can keep a baby fed and dry and warm, he don't know the difference if you be poor or if you be king of the world! And by the time a baby grows up enough t'know that you the poorest folks there is—" she snapped her fingers— "then it's too late . . . that baby already love you, 'cause you be that little baby's daddy! Don't matter no more t'that young'un if you don't know where the next meal a'comin' from. That baby wouldn' trade you in for Mister Rockefellow and all the jewels and money in the bank! Babies don't need money—just a whole heap of love."

"I was hoping that's the way it is."

"It is."

"Then I ain't afraid of anything. I can live anywhere as long as I got Rena and our baby. Don't need much."

"That's good. 'Cause that's all there gonna be." She managed a smile.

"Reverend Dale says we can stay with them awhile until I get more settled."

"Well, that's good. Little Rena gonna feel better stayin' close t'her mama at such a time." She did not add that it would have been difficult to squeeze even someone as little as Rena into this place. Especially when she got big with that baby.

"I was hoping you and Grampa wouldn't mind me moving on over there. I mean . . . Rena thinks you're mighty fine, but all the same, she's got a room of her own and all."

"I hate t'see y'all go, but we're gonna manage."

"Thanks, Gramma." Harry gave her an embarrassed smile. "Can I stand up now?"

He embraced her and then hurried out the door to tell Rena the news that Willa-Mae was on their side.

Harry did not see the tears of the old woman as she wept for the loss of his future. She had hoped better for him than the drudgery of hauling bales of rubber like a mule all day long.

He was too young to know what lay ahead. And she would not be the one to tell him.

A dozen times, Max awakened to the same horrible nightmare of a thousand dead men, all bearing the face of his son. The gruesome image haunted him when he was awake. Today, when David rode here to visit on the back of one of Jefferson's mules, Max had to shake his head as the boy sat on the edge of the bed and told stories about Shiloh that were anything but grim.

Dressed in old denim bib overalls with mismatched buttons, David looked like a refugee from a Mark Twain novel. His blond hair had been trimmed according to Aunt Trudy's bedsheet-barrel-bowl-and-shears method. "She wraps me in a bedsheet, makes me sit on a barrel, then puts a bowl on my head and takes the shears to whatever sticks out from the bowl."

This description brought a delighted laugh from Mary in the other room, who often said that even her uncle the barber could not compete with the barbering mothers of Shiloh.

"It looks good," Max lied.

"It looks like every other kid's head in Shiloh." David sniffed. "I fit in with all the other bullet heads, anyway. I got us a baseball team going. Named it the Shiloh Bullets. I told the guys it was 'cause we could throw the baseball fast as a bullet out of a gun. They liked it fine. Nobody got it but me."

From there David progressed into tales of possum hunting with Codfish and the new red pup. Neither animal was much good at it, he confessed. But Codfish got the general idea. He had trotted off one morning and treed a railroad worker who had gone into the woods to relieve himself down by the broken trestle. Codfish had held the man in the hickory tree for an entire day until David and Tommy heard him sniveling when they took a shortcut home from school.

As for the red puppy, Aunt Trudy had banished her to the back porch because of one too many messes in the house. Then, when the poor thing had cried all night, Trudy had ended the solitary exile by moving a cot onto the porch and sleeping there to comfort the pup. Now the little dog slept in the bedroom with Birch and Trudy and toddled after Aunt Trudy like a baby duck after its mama.

Birch had argued with Trudy about it. He said Trudy was spoiling the critter for every useful use. He said there was no purpose calling it a coonhound anymore because it was nothing but a lady's lapdog, and he sure hoped Brother Williams never found out how spoiled it was! Jefferson said he was sure that instinct would win out in the end, and the pup would grow up to be just as good a hunting dog as Emmaline.

Bobby and Tommy paid no mind to any of it. After all, Codfish was big enough and ugly enough that he kept bullies away. And there was not much use for the hound puppy right now anyway, because anything worth hunting was hibernating for the winter.

Other news spilled out of David in carefree babble. He and his cousins had begun serious work on a tree house built from the lumber of the shattered barn. Baby Joe was teething and had bit the tail of the red pup. Miss Price had set the date for marrying poor Mr. Faraby, and Faraby's children were very unhappy these days. They blamed Max for everything, and this had at first been a difficult barrier to overcome, but David had managed to establish himself by his wits.

There was more. Old Grandma Amos got confused and made cookies with pure bicarbonate soda instead of sugar and passed them out to all the schoolkids who stopped by. Dreadful stuff, but the old woman claimed she might have invented a new cure for childhood bellyaches. She had instructed David to report this to Dr. Brown on his next visit, which David did.

David chatted on for more than an hour, reporting on Trudy's Christmas baking and Birch's plans for cutting down a tree. David already loved living in Shiloh. He thought Aunt Trudy was the cat's pajamas and Uncle Birch was a real swell guy. The conclusion was that David did not want to leave Shiloh. Not ever. When Max got well, he asked, could they stay on here all the same?

At this question, Max noticed that the clatter of Mary's work in the next room stilled in anticipation of the reply. Max had been giving this matter serious consideration during his recovery. He had often looked at Mary Brown and wondered what it would be like to marry and live out his life in such a place. But in spite of David's enthusiasm and Mary's charms, Max had always come to the same conclusion: He could not see any future at all for himself in Shiloh, Arkansas. David fit in easily, but Max stood out like a kosher dill pickle on a tray of corn bread.

"You can get a job here, Dad." David was ebullient.

"There's not a newspaper in the whole state of Arkansas that would hire me, I'm afraid."

"You could be a farmer. Like Uncle Birch. Plant cotton and goober peas."

Max gave a slight shrug. "I'm really not the goober-pea type, Son." There was nothing Max could do here in Sebastian County, Arkansas.

Max could feel the silence of Mary Brown radiating her disappointment from the next room.

Then David grew silent, too. He frowned at the scuffed toes of his shoes and hooked a thumb on the strap of his bibs in a Birch-like gesture. "Well . . . you could do something. . . ." His voice trailed off sadly.

Max suddenly felt very tired. "We'll see, David. Maybe we could work something out. We'll think about it."

"Sure," David replied.

In subsequent visits to his father, David continued to bring his Shiloh tales to the infirmary. He drank Mary Brown's tea and played chess or gin rummy with Max. But he did not speak again of staying in Shiloh. He had seen the thought flash in Max's eyes that maybe it was David who should stay here with Trudy and Birch while Max went away. That fear of being left behind crept into David's dreams, just as Max's nightmare of the thousand dead Davids had convinced the father that somehow he was no good for his own son.

CHAPTER TWENTY-THREE

Jack Daugherty Comes to Call

This week, Mrs. VanVonderen had paid her medical bill to Dr. Ellis Warne half in fresh eggs and half in canned tomato sauce. At the moment, the jars remained stacked outside beside the cellar door.

It was a remarkably warm and sunny Sunday afternoon. After church Becky suggested they pack a lunch and go for a drive. But Ellis declined. He was worn out, he said, and the coming week would offer no chance to rest. He glanced at the Sunday newspaper, noting the mention of layoffs at every factory around Akron. Then, with a pale and grim countenance, he limped upstairs and closed the door behind him.

"Does that mean Pop doesn't want to go for a drive?" asked Boots, peering after her father.

Becky sat silent until her lack of a reply threatened to tell the truth that something seemed very wrong with Ellis. "Your pop is just tired, Boots." Becky tried to sound unconcerned.

"He's tired a lot now, isn't he, Mom?"

"There are lots of sick people he has to fix up. Lots of hurting people. Not enough time to sleep. We'll let him rest this afternoon, and tonight we'll listen to *Amos 'n' Andy*. I've got some canned goods to put away in the cellar. You want to help?"

Unlike Ellis, Becky could not let herself have even one day of rest. Every hour had to be filled. To sleep meant she might dream. To sit awhile on the porch swing and relax meant time to think. To think meant worry . . . or worse yet, renewed grief.

It all seemed too much for her now. Not only had she lost her baby boy but also her husband and herself. Each day Ellis seemed more and more distant, and she felt more and more lost.

A thousand times she had tried to sort out the shattered fragments of her life. She had prayed, but there was no answer. She had inwardly raged against the silence of an unjust God. Then she had begged for some relief from the ache of her emptiness. She had reached out to the Lord, hoping to pick up the pieces and make some kind of sense out of the mess, but thoughts and emotions seemed to melt together and flow like water through her grasp.

So Becky filled her time with mundane tasks that required no thought or emotion to accomplish. *Just keep busy. Then there's no time to hurt. Blessed numbness.* This was how she survived.

With little Boots and Snowball trailing behind, Becky descended into the cellar with an armload of Mrs. VanVonderen's tomato sauce.

Becky stacked the jars on the shelf above Mrs. Peters's plum jelly and Miss Ruptke's strawberry jam. Very few patients came to the Warne clinic without some sort of payment in hand, but seldom was the payment made in badly needed cash. Now the shelves in the Warne basement were stacked full of canned food, kegs of cider, eggs, butter, even pickled pigs' feet and sauerkraut.

"There's enough to open a market," Becky muttered, hefting a crate full of Renata Miller's pickle relish as Boots stacked bars of homemade lilac soap into a tower on the basement steps. "What we will do with two dozen jars of relish I cannot imagine. At least we will not go hungry."

"I can use them, Mom," Boots replied as she studied her creation. "I can make a castle out of the jars."

From the patch of blue sky at the mouth of the stairs, a man's voice joined the conversation. "You could sell 'em, ma'am. I'll buy one jar for a nickel."

Snowball barked once and growled.

Becky straightened and squinted up at the light. The square silhouette of a powerfully built man blocked the entrance to the cellar. A coin was tossed down to clink and roll across the damp cement floor and come to rest at Becky's feet. The dog sniffed it suspiciously.

"One nickel, Missus Warne. Would you bring me up a jar of pickles, then?" There was a soft hint of an Irish brogue to the words, which had a pleasant familiarity to Becky.

Boots stared silently up, then looked at her mother expectantly before dashing over to retrieve the coin. "Yep. It's a buffalo, Mom," she cried. "Can we sell him a jar of Missus Miller's pickles for a nickel?"

Becky placed her hand on her daughter's shoulder in a protective gesture as the man squatted to peer down at them. "You could feed an army with all this," he remarked. "An army or a whole lot of hungry men. Lord knows there are plenty of hungry men these days round about Akron since the layoffs began. But I'll only buy that one jar of pickles, Missus Warne, for that is my last nickel."

Becky shook off the chill that coursed through her without reason. She gave a small laugh and grabbed a jar from the crate. "If that is the case, then we will be right up with your purchase." She felt an urgency to get out of the dank, cramped cubicle and up into the light of day, where she might face this stranger in full view of the entire neighborhood.

"So you have heard of Renata's pickles," Becky jabbered on. "She gave my husband this case and said it was her last until next summer at canning time. I told her we should start a pickle factory and become world famous and say it all started right here."

She was halfway up the steps when the man lowered his voice and asked, "Are you alone, Missus Warne?"

The question made Becky jump inside. Why would anyone ask such a question? She grabbed Boots tightly by the wrist. The child squeaked a protest as Becky dragged her the rest of the way up the steps and pushed past the man. Snowball rushed out into the yard.

The man was stocky, with a leathery face and deep blue eyes that gleamed beneath bushy black eyebrows. His jaw was set as though he were a fighter waiting to strike a blow or be struck one . . . only here there was no one to fight.

With relief, Becky caught sight of Miss Ruptke dragging a sack of rubbish around the side of her house. "Hullo, Miss Ruptke!" Becky gave her neighbor an unusually big wave, which made the woman stare curiously. "Unusually warm weather we're having today. Lovely day, isn't it?"

The man turned his back to the street and put a hand to his head as if to shield his face. "Missus Warne, is your husband home?"

"My husband is—is this a medical matter? His clinic hours are—"

"I need to speak with him, ma'am." His voice was soft but urgent. "Is he here?"

"Yes." There was an edge to Becky's voice that made Boots step behind her mother's skirt and peer around at the stranger.

"I do need to speak with him. I came to the front door and knocked. Was on my way to the back door when I spotted the open cellar door. Ma'am, I can't say how glad I am to find you at home. If you could help me locate the good doctor . . ."

The good doctor. Yes. So this fellow knows Ellis after all. "He is . . ." She started to tell him that Ellis was asleep. That this was his only day off and that, after the week he had had, unannounced visitors were not welcome. But there was something in this fellow's tone of voice, in his pain-filled eyes.

She thrust the jar of pickles into his hand. "Come along. I'll get him for you. Whom shall I say . . . ?"

"Jack Daugherty. He'll know me. From the plant."

Becky suddenly remembered. "You are John's uncle, are you?"

"That's right, ma'am." He sighed as though a great secret was out at last.

"Is everything all right with your nephew?" She led the way to the front stoop as Miss Ruptke stared with open curiosity. This was one occasion when Becky was grateful for her old-maid neighbor's propensity for nosiness! She waved again as if to let Miss Ruptke know that all was well.

"Our Johnny will make it even with one arm—thanks be to God and to your husband. I do not mean to be disturbin' him on a day of rest, but it is urgent that I speak with him. Beggin' your pardon, ma'am."

"Boots," Becky commanded as they entered the house. Her daughter's red curls snapped to attention. "Run and wake your pop. Tell him Mister Daugherty has come to call."

"Should he put on his leg, Mom?"

Becky smiled at the discomfort on Jack Daugherty's face. "Mister Daugherty will not mind if he leaves it off, I'm sure. It's his day off." She inclined her head to the Irishman and indicated that he should sit on the pale green sofa and wait. "You'll not be offended, will you? His souvenir from France. Now I'll go put on the kettle for tea."

Becky headed to the kitchen. She peered back toward Daugherty, who cast an uneasy look toward the windows as though he feared being seen from the street. Rising from the sofa, he furtively pulled the shades.

She called to him, "Do you take milk with your tea, Mister Daugherty?"

"Yes, ma'am." He resumed his place on the edge of the sofa.

Moments later, Boots clattered down the stairs. "Pop says you should come on up to his room, Mister Daugherty," said the child in a puzzled voice.

Becky turned from the kettle and tea tray to consider Jack Daugherty. When had Ellis ever received a visitor upstairs? "No, Boots," she corrected. "Your pop means in the office."

"No, Mom." Boots shook her curls. "Pop said—"

The voice of Ellis called down to settle the question. "Come on up, Jack."

The stout Irishman nodded uncomfortably toward Becky, hesitated a moment longer, then slowly climbed the stairs.

Ellis's weary voice drifted down. "Close the door behind you."

Then the bedroom door clicked shut.

Boots peered curiously up the stairs. "Is Pop sick or something, Mom?"

"Why don't you go play at Bertie's?" Becky busied herself with the tea and a plate of cookies on the tray as if there were nothing unusual about Ellis's taking a visitor in the bedroom. "You can take cookies and have a tea party on the stoop if you like."

Instantly the mysterious stranger was forgotten. Boots shrugged and gathered two dolls beneath one arm while she balanced a plate of cookies in the other hand and slipped out the door.

But Becky could not set aside the unexplained visit so easily. She stood listening as muffled voices penetrated the ceiling. Even at such a distance, it was plain to her that Ellis was angry.

☆ ☆ ☆

"I don't take kindly to threats, Jack," Ellis said heatedly.

"These men are fightin' for their lives. For their jobs."

"So are we all. You think I'm not hit by this?"

"You'll not lose your job, not so long as you do what Titan says. And we *are* losin' ours! Every day someone else is off the line. I was first . . . said I'm a drunk . . . said it was my fault about Johnny's arm. How'm I gonna feed my family now?"

"I have a family, too, you know. And now your union thugs are threatening my wife and child. This note . . . shoved under the door of my office."

A long silence followed, then, "None of my men would write this."

"Well, someone did."

"Doc Warne, I swear to you—"

"If you want my help, you'll not get it by threats. I promise you that."

"I'll find out who has done this. Your wife and kid won't be harmed. My solemn promise, Doc Warne. I don't know who done it, but I'll find out. I didn't come to make threats. I come to ask you for your help. See? The fellas with seniority—we're gettin' picked off one at a time, some of us for one reason and some for another. Every man still with a job is scared to make waves for fear it'll be him who gets the boot tomorrow. So them fellas who are left don't say or do nothin' to jeopardize—"

"This does not concern me."

"Ah, but it does. The rumor mill has it there's a list. This list has all the names on it—who gets the ax tomorrow and the next week and the week after 'til the plant is cleaned out."

"I don't know what you're talking about."

"Beggin' your pardon, Doc Warne, I'm thinkin' that you do. I think that you've seen the list, that you know what is happenin' here. Divide and conquer. Keep the men in line with fear. Whittle us down. Up production quotas. Cut personnel. Cut costs. You know about it, all right."

"I tell you this is none of my concern!"

"I was hopin' it was. I told the fellas that if there was such a list—a list namin' names of who was goin' to get the ax—that if we got the list, then we could get organized. I told 'em you were a right sort of fella. That if there was a list you could maybe get it for us."

"Is that why I get threatening letters? threats to my little girl and my wife?" Ellis began to quote from memory: *"We know where you live. . . ."*

"Look! I told you I'll nab whoever wrote that. Somebody desperate, Doc Warne! I'll pin this down. There ain't a threat to your family in this. I'm askin'—beggin'—for your help. Phony medical discharges. Trumped-up morals charges. And you doctors are helpin' Titan! We hear three thousand guys are goin' down if we don't get that list! Like lambs to the slaughter! One at a time! And you can tell us who is goin' to get it so they will wake up. Doc, you gotta help us stop it before it's too late."

"I don't know about any list. And if I did, no one could make me help by threats. You let your men know that, Jack! I am at the end of my patience."

"It's not threats, Doctor Warne. We're beggin' for your help with this. These are men with families like yourself—just men who've fallen on hard times. You have a heart. We all seen it. Please . . ."

Ellis did not reply. "I've got a lot to think about, Jack. Now call off your dogs. If anyone so much as looks wrong at my little girl . . . so much as a wrong word to my wife . . ."

"I promise. Just think about it. Think. We need your help. We know Titan's got you by the throat. Word is that you got cleaned out in the crash, too. Owe your soul to the bank. We know you need the paycheck same as anybody. So go ahead. Hand out those phony medical discharges just like he says. Nobody's gonna hurt your family . . . only get us that list! We'll take it from there!"

The footsteps of Jack Daugherty clacked across the floor and down the stairs. He left the house without saying good-bye to Becky. Ellis closed the door of the bedroom again and did not come out even when darkness came.

That night Ellis found himself sitting bolt upright in bed before he even knew what had awakened him. There had been a crash like splintering glass, then a thud as if something had bounced off a wall. Ellis wondered if he had dreamed it, in his sleep back in France again, reliving incoming German artillery shells.

But Becky had his arm, and she sounded frightened. "Ellis," she asked urgently, "what was that noise?" From Boots's room came Snowball's yaps to show that he, too, had been awakened.

"You heard it, too?" Ellis asked with sleep-induced stupidity. He wanted it to have been a dream, wanted to return to the slumber that had been so difficult to achieve of late.

"It came from downstairs," she said. "It sounded like a gunshot, and I think I heard a car drive away." Her voice sounded panicky. "Ellis, quick, go check Boots!"

A small, sleepy voice came from their bedroom door. "Pop? What was that noise? It woke me up."

"It's okay, honey," Ellis soothed, reaching for the crutches beside the bed. No time now to strap on his prosthesis. "You come get in bed with Mom. I'll go see what happened."

The curly-haired child padded silently over to the bed and slid onto the feather mattress without another word. Ellis wondered if she had even been fully awake.

"Be careful, Ellis," Becky urged.

Ellis picked his way carefully down the stairs in the dark. For some reason, he was unwilling to turn on the lights. Standing in the darkened entryway, he listened for any unusual sounds in the house. He heard nothing, and when he tried the front door, he found it locked just as Becky would have secured it at bedtime.

The mantel clock struck two as he entered the parlor. Moonlight coming through a crack between the curtains played on the wall opposite and drew a narrow line on the floor. In the thin beam, Ellis saw the glistening pinpoint reflections of broken glass. A cold breeze blew through the newly created hole in the window, stirring the curtains and revealing a jagged, fist-sized hole, but what had caused the damage could not be seen.

Ellis switched on the light then and looked around for something to gather up the shards.

"Ellis," Becky called down the stairs, "are you all right?"

"Fine. I'm fine," he replied.

"What happened?"

He found an unfamiliar black object lying underneath the sofa's edge. Above it on the wall was a round indentation where it had struck and then fallen to the floor. Ellis picked it up and unwrapped a clumsily knotted string that secured a scrap of paper to a chunk of cobblestone.

"Just some kids," he shouted back up the stairs. "Hooligans threw a rock through our window."

He unrolled the paper and squinted at the pencil-scrawled words: *Be warned—don't shill for Titan.*

Ellis heard Becky's footsteps coming and quickly crumpled the paper and string into his fist.

"Just some kids?" Becky asked. "Are you sure?"

"Yes," Ellis said hastily. "Some vandals waking up the neighborhood. Watch out," he urged, changing the subject. "Are you in bare feet? There's glass on the carpet."

Becky clucked her tongue. "What are things coming to? I'll get the sweeper and clean it up."

By the time Becky returned, Ellis had thrust the note deep into the pocket of his pajamas and was picking up the larger pieces of the broken window.

CHAPTER TWENTY-FOUR

The Empty Room

Becky had felt a growing uneasiness since the meeting between Ellis and Jack Daugherty. Now, as the clock on the mantel chimed five, she was troubled with a sense that something was not right.

Looking up distractedly from her copy of the *Saturday Evening Post*, Becky suddenly realized that Boots was half an hour late returning from a birthday party at little Millie Sable's. That was unusual. Not that Boots always came home on time, but Marge Sable never failed to call to say that Boots had pleaded to be allowed to stay a little longer and to ask if that was all right.

Rising quickly, Becky went to the phone and rang Central. When the operator came on the line, she asked to be connected to Sherwood-4900.

"Marge?" She hoped the pang of worry did not show in her voice. "This is Becky Warne. Would you please send Boots home now? She has some chores to do."

Becky's words gushed out in an almost angry tone, as if she were reproaching Marge for not calling to ask if Boots could stay. But of course it was not Marge's job to keep track of Boots, along with a dozen other neighborhood kids. Becky wished she had just made the walk down the street and hollered cheerfully for Boots to gather her things and get home.

There was silence on the other end of the line before Marge's perplexed voice replied, "The kids were playing on the porch after the party, but I'm sure Boots left half an hour ago, Becky. Are you sure she hasn't come in already?"

"Oh no, I'm not sure," Becky said with embarrassment. "I'll bet the little scoger snuck in while I was in the kitchen and went straight upstairs. She knows I have work for her, and she is probably hoping I'll forget about it if I don't see her 'til suppertime."

That had to be it. After all, the Sable home was only a block away, with no streets to cross. It was only a five-minute ride on a tricycle, even for a little girl who dawdled along the way, speaking to every dog and cat on the block.

Becky hung up the phone on that note and called up the stairs, "Boots! Come on down here, young lady! Time to set the table for supper."

There was no reply from the second floor. The ticking of the mantel clock seemed to echo, amplifying the emptiness of the house. Becky glanced at the magazine and chided herself for letting time slip away without realizing her daughter should have been home. If she had been paying attention, she would have been standing out on the porch, watching the sidewalk until Boots pedaled up.

Had Boots managed to make it in without being heard? Was she upstairs in her room—perhaps asleep beside her baby dolls? That had happened before, and the silence had terrified Becky then as well as now. A thousand desperate thoughts flew through her mind. Fears born of losing one child easily transferred to missing another. What if something had happened when Becky was not watching? What if something terrible had happened to Boots because Becky was careless even for an instant?

Becky recalled the angry tone of the muffled conversation between Ellis and Jack Daugherty. And the rock through the window . . . had it really just been vandalism?

Becky took the steps two at a time, all the while telling herself that Boots had just fallen asleep on her bed. "Boots?" she croaked out, pushing open the child's door to find the room empty. Dolls unmoved on the windowsill. The light of late afternoon dimming into evening. Snowball curled up asleep on the floor.

Boots! Not Boots! Oh, Lord, where is she?

Against her will, Becky relived the moment when she had come home from the hospital and walked into little Howie's room, only to realize he would never be coming home again. The crib, the stack of folded diapers, the toys scattered on the floor—they had all sat just as silently. Just the same as always, but empty—silent in the void left by a dead child who had filled the room with life.

She had lost more than her baby boy that day. Somehow she had lost Ellis as well. The Ellis she knew had never come home from the hospital either. Part of him had been buried with the baby.

How long had it been? *How long?* Their pleasant world had suddenly exploded, and they had spun off from each other like separate fragments of one planet, whirling into a black . . . despair!

Only Boots had kept Becky going. Only the life of her daughter had made it possible for Becky to face the ache of lonely nights when Ellis turned away from her or she turned away from him. *And now? What if something has happened to Boots?*

Becky forced herself to calm down. She stared at the open door of the nursery and told herself firmly that the emptiness of the baby's room did not mean something dreadful would also fall upon her little girl. Irrational fear gripped her again. The memory of what had been once more transposed its dark image over reality.

Becky closed her eyes and reasoned that the child was probably back in the clinic office, playing with Ellis's stethoscope again. But no, that couldn't be right. The outside clinic door was locked, and Becky would have seen if Boots had gone into Ellis's office from the house side.

She's just stopped to play with some other friend, Becky assured herself. *Why am I so jumpy over a little thing like Boots being late?*

For all the calm thoughts, Becky could not keep herself from dashing back down the stairs and onto the porch, ready to scour the neighborhood. But in her headlong rush out the front door she almost tripped over her missing daughter, who was huddled on the steps.

A wave of relief flooded over Becky, followed by an odd distress at having panicked so easily over nothing. All this was topped off by a rush of indignation that Boots had been so thoughtless as to make her worry. Becky tried to keep the tremor out of her voice when she asked, "Where have you been, young lady? Didn't you hear me call you? Did you know that you are half an hour late?"

The face that Boots raised to her mother's gaze was tearstained, smeared with chocolate cake, and puckered with unhappiness. Becky tossed away her resolve to be stern and sat right down on the porch and hugged her daughter. "Why, Boots, sweetie," she said tenderly, "what is the matter?"

"Mom," Boots said between little gasps,. "why does Pop get gummers fired down at the tire plant? Doesn't he know that it makes their kids real unhappy?"

"What are you talking about, Boots? Pop doesn't get people fired. You know he works as a doctor for the rubber company, just the same as he is a doctor here at home. He helps people."

Boots wiped her eyes on the sleeve of her sweater. "That's what I told Ralphie," she said. "But he was too mad to listen."

"Who is Ralphie?" Becky asked in confusion. "Weren't you playing with Millie?"

"Ralph is Millie's cousin," Boots explained. "He's ten. He says his dad got fired on account of a doctor at the tire company made up a story about him bein' sick when he isn't really, and they won't even have any Christmas at their house."

"But, Boots, dear," Becky soothed, "there are a dozen tire factories in Akron, and all of them have company doctors. Why did you think Pop had anything to do with it?"

"Because he said so! He said so in front of all the kids while we were eating birthday cake!" Boots wailed. "Ralph said his dad said if he could get his hands on the neck of that dirty Doctor Warne, he'd make that Doctor Warne sicker than anybody in Akron! I gave him a sock for it outside after, and Millie got mad at me and told me to go home!"

"Sounds to me like he deserved a sock for telling such a story!" Becky straightened the hair ribbon that was cocked off in Boots's hair. "Did he punch you back?"

"Nuh-uh." She raised her fist, and a flash of anger showed in her eyes at the memory. "But everybody thinks Pop is on the wrong side at the plant."

"Wrong side? Your Pop isn't on any side! He just takes care of the sick gummers. You know that. He's a swell fellow, your pop! You did right to punch any guy who says different. Only next time, wait until the party's over, will you?"

Becky tried hard to sound comforting and reassuring, but her own mind was spinning from the likelihood that here, at last, was the truth. Had she not heard the coolness in the voices of her friends? Had she not seen the sideways looks in church on Sunday? Yet no one had the courage to say aloud what was happening. Out of the mouths of babes, as it were!

Ellis is somehow caught between the union and management. No wonder he has been in such a black mood lately. And the other things that have been happening—this awful accusation, if true, will explain a lot.

But even as she thought it, Becky prayed that it wasn't so. "Come in and wash your face, dear," she said to Boots. "I'm sure it's just a misunderstanding. Pop will straighten it out. You'll see."

☆ ☆ ☆

Frank's mama paid the rent for another month in the little Howard Street flat. She brought home a paper sack of onions, potatoes, beans, and a little flour. But by the end of the week all the money was gone. Only two potatoes, one onion, a fistful of flour, and a little salt were left on the shelf. Just enough—only enough—to make potato soup.

The first night the leftover potato soup was thick. She had hopes of getting a little work that night, she told her boys. Even a little something and they could buy more groceries. Food was all they had to worry about now, since the rent was paid up. Trouble was, she explained, men at the plant were getting laid off, so they didn't have money to spare to pay her to go dancing with them. And those who weren't laid off had their hours cut, which meant they had to watch every dime. But maybe tonight would be different. . . .

It was not. Mama walked home because she did not have a nickel for the streetcar. She did not look like a movie star anymore. Her coat, dress, and hat were damp from standing in the cold all night and waiting for the shift changes. She had not been admitted to the speakeasy because she had no man to escort her. Trouble—that's what a single woman in a speak was, said the bouncer. He'd turned her away because he knew she did not even have enough money to pay the cover charge for one drink and because single women always caused fights.

The second night the leftover potato soup was thin and watery, but Frank still found a bit of potato in it. And the broth was good. He and Jim slurped it down while Mama fixed her makeup and tried to make her hair curl right. There were circles under her eyes tonight, and she was pale beneath the rouge on her cheeks.

"Gotta get lucky tonight," she said to herself in the mirror. "Somethin's gotta turn up."

Little Jim held up his bowl for more soup. Frank slapped his arm down and nodded at Mama's back. Jim had eaten his supper. Mama had not eaten in two days.

"Come eat your soup 'fore you go, Mama," Frank said.

She turned and looked at the pot on the hot plate and then back to her boys. "Naw. I'm not hungry."

It was a lie. Frank knew Mama was hungry. Nobody could go so long without eating and not feel it. "If you eat, you won't look so white, Mama."

She put a hand to her cheek and considered his warning. "Better eat," she mumbled. She poured a small bit of the broth into a cup and savored it as she sipped it slowly. There was just enough left to split the last bowl between Jim and Frank. She took her last swallow and gave the rest to the boys to finish.

"Somethin's bound to turn up," she said before she hugged them both. "Y'all know somethin' always turns up just when you think there ain't nothin' goin' to turn up."

With the usual warning that Jim must not cry and Frank must take care of everything, she slipped out of the flat into the cold winter night.

CHAPTER TWENTY-FIVE

Always
My Baby

Max was pronounced well enough to sit up on a day that the cold chill of winter briefly receded into beautiful warm sunshine. He was allowed a few steps to the chair in his room, which Mary had placed beside a window overlooking a small apple orchard.

The sun warmed him through the panes of glass. Outside, however, the apple trees held up bare, gnarled branches as stark reminders that winter was here and the glory of the day was only a momentary counterfeit.

Dry stubble of grass poked up around the roots, and leaves had been raked beneath every tree but one. That one tree was bigger than the others. Unlike its companions, it was surrounded by a litter of fallen fruit, and a few determined apples hung on its limbs to rot and wither through the frigid season. Max wondered why every other tree had been plucked clean of fruit and pruned while this one Old Man Apple remained so grizzled and unkempt.

Mary brought him a lunch of hot stew, homemade bread with apple butter, and apple fritter for dessert. These Browns were plainly apple lovers.

"What's wrong with the old tree there?" Max asked when Mary admitted that she had made the bread and the apple butter and the fritters and every gallon of apple juice he had drunk in the last few weeks.

"Wrong? Nothing. That's the best tree. The best apples."

"You've left the apples."

"We have enough from the other trees. Dad leaves those for the birds and such as need them."

"But why waste the best on birds, Mary?"

"Waste?" She frowned at the word as though she had never considered it in the context of the tree and the apples. "I suppose that's a matter of perspective. Waste. I guess that depends on how you feel about sparrows and such. I don't think Dad ever thought about it as a waste. We pick so many apples from the orchard—more than enough. I suppose he thinks it would be more of a waste if the birds starved through the winter for lack of apples." This was said in a matter-of-fact tone, as though she were instructing a child in basic scientific facts.

"Does it matter?"

"To Dad."

"Why?"

"Because it pleases him to feed the sparrows. That's reason enough." Raising the window, she let in the gentle chirping of the birds as they hopped among the spoils on the ground and then fluttered into the untrimmed branches of their gnarled host.

Mary closed her eyes to listen. A slight smile curved across her lips. "Dad says that old tree is like the Lord in a way. Dad can make up a hundred parables if you let him get going."

Max peered hard at the rough brown-gray bark, as if straining to hear the tales Doc Brown could create from such a mess. "Seems a shame to me, allowing apples to rot like that. When I grew up, I lived on a street in New York called Orchard Street, but there weren't any orchards anywhere near. If a kid was lucky, he could steal an apple like that every once in a while and get away with it. I'd grab mine off the pushcart and run like crazy to get away. I'd carry the thing around in my pocket for days until I got so hungry I would eat it—core, seeds, and all. Then I would do it all over again."

Mary did not take her eyes off the old tree. Sparrows chirped and popped among the weeds. She inclined her head slightly, acknowledging his story. "So all your life you grew up snitching apples, running away, and hoarding the things when this apple tree was growing here and you never knew it."

"Like I said. A waste."

"Maybe there's a lesson in the sparrows." She shrugged. "You've been looking for your apples in the wrong orchard—that's all. No need to steal, run, or hoard. There are apples free for the taking. More than you can possibly use. You just have to know where to look."

He grimaced and narrowed his eyes in amusement. "This must run in the family, this apple-tree thing, huh?" He laughed. "We're talking about things greater than apples and trees now, are we? Have I just heard a parable, Mary?" he teased.

"I don't know. Have you, Max?"

✳ ✳ ✳

Birch and Jefferson had left for Forth Smith early on a gray Monday morning. The Rock Island line was still torn up, so the two men took a wagon and mules to the big city. They had returned four days later with the taxes paid, a bill of sale drawn up for Jefferson and Lily's place, and the back of the wagon piled high with supplies ranging from seed to blue-checked curtains and new panes of glass to put in the windows of the old log house.

And there was one more important thing besides. When Jefferson Canfield smiled hello at Lily, sunlight had glinted on a mouthful of brand-new, gold-capped teeth. Yessir. Life had come around just about perfect as far as Jefferson was concerned. How could any man be more blessed than to have a wife, young'uns, a house, mules, and real gold teeth? It was purely a miracle.

This morning the sun shone bright and warm, drying the damp fields of Shiloh. Squirrels came out of their nests and played tag among the branches of the hickory trees. There were months of cold hard winter still to come, yet the sun and the sky and the warm earth reminded man and beast alike that there would be a spring at the end of it.

Now the work on the house was finished. Jefferson swept the last shavings from the smooth-sanded plank floor and leaned against the handle of the broom. He watched specks of dust swirl in the sunlight that streamed through the window. The rough-hewn log walls, the glass—each detail gave him the sense of another time and another place . . . life with his mama and daddy and his sisters in the old cabin in Mount Pisgah.

"Home," he said aloud, looking at the rafters. Jefferson remembered well the time he had told one of his little sisters that such specks of dust were really miniature worlds where tiny people lived—and that if she sneezed, she alone would be responsible for the deaths of millions. "And Mama whupped me good for that, too." He chuckled. "How that takes me back. How I wish my mama could see this place You brung me to, Lord."

He studied the bed frame that he had made with his own hands from the heavy timbers of the destroyed barn. Thick rope was woven to support a new feather mattress Miz Trudy had bought as a bargain from the Montgomery Ward catalog. It was a fine, big bed—big enough that even a man as tall as Jefferson could stretch out his full length and not hang off the ends but not so wide that his wife would be out of reach. The thought of sleeping in that bed next to his new bride made it hard to swallow. Soon now every dormant hope in his heart would reawaken.

Every good thing that had died inside his heart would once again live. This realization made him smile.

"It's a good bed; ain't it, Jesus? Me an' my Lily gonna make us lots of babies in that bed. I'm gonna learn all over again how t'love a woman— how t'hold her an' make her happy t'be mine. We gonna lay awake at night in that bed an' talk 'bout the crops an' the fields an' the young'uns. We gonna learn t'dream good dreams together an' pray together. Yessir, Lord, I'm askin' You t'make it a good bed for me an' Lily. I'll be grateful."

As if in reply, the breeze stirred the branches of the cottonwoods outside. Branches and dry leaves tapped together like clapping hands, and Jefferson felt the presence of a great cloud of unseen witnesses gathered around the cabin. Approving. Rejoicing for him. Cheering him on.

"My fambly," he whispered. "Is that y'all? Mama, can you see my heart done come to a place called home at last? . . . Lord, I don't know if they is alive or dead. Don't know if they sees me here or not. But I'd be mighty grateful, sir, if'n You'd tell my folks . . . say, *Jefferson is happy.* Tell my mama, Willa-Mae Canfield, that her boy has another chance t'live. Tell her that for me, Jesus, will You?"

Again the trees clapped their hands, and the rush of the James Fork sounded like the voice of a mighty crowd, cheering with the same joy folks had cheered the soldiers with when they had marched in the big parade after the war. Jefferson had fought another kind of war for ten long years, and now he was finally home.

"Thank You, Jesus." Jeff closed his eyes and whispered in reply to those who gathered around to rejoice now with his soul.

And so the house of Jeff and Lily Canfield was blessed before it had ever been slept in.

✳ ✳ ✳

There were a few things left on Jefferson's list before he could bring Lily home.

No flowers were in bloom this season of the year, so he borrowed from Trudy's stores of orange persimmons, yellow squash, and red apples. With these, he made an autumn bouquet, which he arranged in a basket on the window ledge. Building a fire in the enormous old stone fireplace, Jefferson carefully laid out his wedding clothes on the bed, then went out to bathe in the cold, clear water of the James Fork. He dried and dressed in front of the blaze, remembering this ritual from Sunday mornings when he was a child in Mount Pisgah. How he had hated washing in the icy water and getting dressed for church with half a dozen other youngsters, each vying for a warm spot by the hearth. Today he welcomed the freezing cold as a distraction from the excitement he felt.

A small, round, oak-framed mirror hung on the wall. Jefferson smoothed his unruly hair and straightened his tie. He smiled to himself as if he were smiling at Lily. Frowning at his gold teeth, he tried again, smiling with his lips closed.

"Welcome home, Miz Canfield," he practiced. "This here is our place, Lily. . . ." And again, "Hope you likes it." He tried a dozen different phrases, shaking his head at the foolishness of each of them. There really was no way to think ahead of all the things he wanted to tell her. "I fixed this place jus' for you, Lily, an' for our young'uns." He scowled. "Pitiful, Jeff. Jus' pitiful."

He was already feeling foolish when he heard the giggles of small voices outside the window.

"Who's he talkin' to?"

He lifted the edge of the blue-checked curtains to see Tommy, Bobby, and David huddled together, whispering beneath the window. Codfish sat a ways behind them. The dog was the only one who saw Jefferson. With a self-conscious wag of his tail, Codfish ducked his head and gave a halfhearted dog smile, as if to let Jeff know he had no part in this spying on Jefferson's dress rehearsal.

Very quietly Jefferson slipped out the door and circled around the cabin, coming up on the trio from behind. "What y'all doin' down there?" he asked softly.

The boys jumped and yowled with guilty surprise when he addressed them. Tommy fell backward. Bobby tumbled down on him. David ran a few steps away. They were caught in the act. But what act were they caught in?

"I ask you, Tom Tucker, what y'all doin' here sneakin' round my place?" Jefferson growled.

Tommy gulped and stood to brush himself off. He looked ashamed. Bobby grew very pale and blinked at Jefferson, then at David, who was stroking Codfish as if nothing untoward had happened at all.

Jefferson narrowed his eyes and picked up Bobby and Tommy by the backs of their bib overalls. "I ast a question, boys. Now, I s'pects I deserve an answer. This here's my place, an' I'll hafta have a word with your mama if'n y'all don't tell me what you's up to."

"It was him!" Bobby wailed and pointed at David.

Jefferson turned his menacing gaze on David. "What y'all up to, boy? Spyin', sneakin' round my place?"

David raised his chin coolly. "We weren't doing nothing wrong. Just out playing. No law against that."

Jefferson gave Tommy a shake. "Better tell ol' Jefferson the truth now. What was y'all up to here?"

Tommy, dangling several feet off the ground with his face at eye level with Jefferson, sniffed and said in a repentant voice, "It was him! *Davey!*"

"What you sayin'?"

"You shut up, Tommy Tucker! It was your idea as much as mine!" David shouted before dashing off into the woods with Codfish trotting happily after him.

"Davey, get back here! Chicken! *Coward!*" Tommy called after his fugitive cousin.

"Out with it, boy." Another shake.

"We didn't mean nothin' by it, Jefferson!" Bobby wailed.

"By what?" A double shake.

"David don't know nothin' at all!" Tommy exclaimed. "He said the palms of your hands is pink! Said the bottoms of your feet is pink. Said your tongue an' inside of your lips is pink, too."

"And so they is." Jefferson tried not to smile. "What of it?"

"He bet us two bits . . . he said . . . he bet . . . well, he ain't never seen no naked colored man b'fore, an' he bet us two bits that the only part of the colored folks that gets brown is the part that gets too much sunshine. He said your underside's pink, too! He bet us two bits that the parts of you that *ain't been in sunlight* was just as pink as any white man! Well, Bobby and me said you're dark brown all over . . . and two bits is *two bits!*"

Stricken by Tommy's confession, Bobby wailed, "We didn't mean nothin', Jefferson! Don't tell Mama! She'll take a willow switch to us."

Jefferson nodded gravely. "An' then y'all will have the pink backsides, now won't you?"

"Oh, Jefferson! *Please!* Don't tell on us! We'll give you the two bits!" cried Tommy.

Jefferson lowered them to the ground but held fast to the straps of their overalls while he spoke seriously to them. "Y'all ain't got no cause t'come sneakin' round mine an' Lily's house! It ain't polite. I tell you now, when y'all come to a man's house, come right on up t'the front door an' knock. An' wait 'til he says welcome an' how-do. If he don't, y'all get on back the way you come!"

"Yessir," the boys said in contrite unison.

"Now, I'll tell y'all somethin' else. *Listen up!* I say that Davey wins the bet. 'Cause all the outside part of me has been in sunlight one time or another, an' it's *all brown!* But the part of me that ain't seen the daylight is jus' the same as any white man. My blood jus' as red. My bones jus' as white. Under the skin you can't tell the difference 'tween any man.

"You remember this, boys, someday when some white man tells y'all different. Someday every person gonna be a bleached heap of bones standin' there in front of Jesus. We all gonna stand b'fore the Lord equal. Won't matter then what color my hide was—or yours either!"

Jefferson was enjoying himself greatly as the boys blanched and looked very concerned at this information.

"Yessir." They nodded.

Jefferson could tell from the looks on their faces that the boys were picturing millions of unhappy skeletons chattering in fear on Judgment Day. Serious business, this seemed to be—and all over two bits!

" 'Yessir,' they says," Jefferson snorted. "Y'all *better* say yessir. Then y'all better get on back an' remember that bein' nosy an' sneakin' around is pure *sinfulness!*" He gave them a shake that rattled their white bones inside and made their faces pucker with misery. Could Jefferson really be so cross with them?

"Yessir." Now they were very worried, and they were very angry at David for getting them crossways with good ol' Jefferson, who was never mad at them for anything. Jefferson! Who only smiled and sang and said cheerful things!

"And so's gamblin' a sin. Bettin' two bits 'bout the color of a man's backside is jus' as sinful as . . . bettin' on a horse race, playin' with playin' cards, or tossin' dice! Y'all give the ol' devil a vict'ry t'day!"

"Yessir." They hung their heads and stared mournfully at the toes of their shoes. Not only had they sinned. They had lost two bits to David Meyer.

"Now *git*! An' don't y'all come on back over here on this side of the creek unless you rings that little bell I set up over yonder on the far side of the log bridge! Then, when I says so, y'all can come an' welcome! Then y'all come an' Lily'll fix you bread an' jelly an' big glasses of buttermilk. An' ya'll will set like young gentlemens at the table, not go sneakin' round 'neath my window like thieves." One final shake. "Hear me now?"

"Yessir."

"YES, SIR, Jefferson!"

"You gonna tell Mama an' Daddy what we done?" Tommy asked quietly.

Jeffeson furrowed his brow thoughtfully. "Not this time. But if ever agin you boys sneak, I'll whup y'all myself!" He released his captives and patted them each on the head. "Now git. An' don't bother me an' Lily 'til I says you can come back."

One slight nudge, and Jefferson sent the young sinners scurrying on their way.

"Thank you, Jefferson!"

"Bye, Jefferson! You tell us when!"

✳ ✳ ✳

The wedding of Harry Canfield and Rena Dale was a small affair. Mostly just family members and a handful of high school friends came to wish the young couple well.

There was an afternoon potluck reception after the ceremony. Organized by the folks at the Missionary Baptist Church, the supper had all the signs of a rent party. Canned food for the couple was the price of admission. And there were gifts as well. A few small personal items were wrapped in tissue paper to be cheerfully given to the bride and groom. A down coverlet and a pair of pillowcases that had belonged to the grandmother of the bride were presented by Reverend and Mrs. Dale. Women of the congregation offered such items as mixing bowls and tea towels that had always been in the family. Most everyone wanted to lend a hand, even though everyone beneath the North Hill Viaduct was in equally bad shape.

A collection was even taken, raising the grand sum of fourteen dollars and sixty cents. This seemed a small fortune to Harry, who had already put in his first week on the night shift at the Titan plant. For six nights, eight hours a night, Harry had been paid three dollars. This gift from the congregation meant that he and Rena were starting with more than a month's worth of extra money.

As the afternoon wore on, the celebration and laughter erupted into singing and then prayers. After a short, impromptu sermon by Reverend Dale, the party ended at four o'clock in the afternoon. After all, the groom and his grandfather faced a long night shift that night.

Rena went home with her mama and daddy. Harry changed his clothes and headed off to Titan Tire with Hock. And Willa-Mae and Nettie walked slowly home from the church. The sun was shining after a week of overcast skies, and the world did not seem so gray this afternoon.

"The Good Book say that a man shall leave his mama and daddy and cleave only t'his wife," Willa-Mae said. "Reckon them two ain't gonna have nothin' t'cleave to 'cept each other and the Lord."

Nettie did not answer for a long time. She was thinking hard about something. Willa-Mae felt it in her bones—there was something Nettie wanted to say, but she could not get it out.

"What's troublin' you, chil'?" she asked. "What is it, Little Nettie?"

"I'm not little anymore, Mama. That is a good place to start. I'm a grown woman."

"Didn't mean no harm by it. You's my baby—that's all. The youngest, the last. So you always gonna be little to me, no matter if'n you grows outta them high-heel shoes and that skinny flapper dress and gets big as a barn. You know that."

"Yes, Mama. To you, maybe, but not to anyone else. I am a grown woman." Nettie talked just like any white gal in Akron. She had practiced speaking just so in her little curtained alcove. If Willa-Mae closed her eyes and listened, she would think that Little Nettie was a snowy-white dove of a gal. She sure enough did not sound like anyone else down at the church.

"What else on your mind?"

A brisk breeze shot up Howard Street, and Nettie pulled her coat close around here. Something had chilled her heart, and it was not the wind. "The college is closing down a number of classes."

"No school? Why's that?"

"It will stay open but—Mama, I know you and Daddy didn't notice, but Akron had a big election last week. Bond issues were on the ballot to raise money for the schools and . . . for everything. Every issue failed. Everyone is so scared because of the Wall Street crash. No one voted for the government to raise money. You understand? No money will be raised for hiring teachers or building schools. None for scholarships. Like mine."

"You can't go t'school no more?"

"That's it, Mama."

"Why, there ain't nobody gets as good grades as you do, Nettie. They can't cut you off. You the best, the smartest! They say so. Why, I got that letter from the president of the college sayin'—"

"Doesn't matter about my grades. I'm colored. They are cutting *my* scholarship first. They told me yesterday that they have no choice." Her face turned neither to the right nor the left as they walked. She gazed straight ahead without visible emotion.

"Oh, I know what that scholarship mean t'you, baby."

Why were there no tears? Nettie had set her heart on finishing college. She had worked her whole life to make something of herself. She had studied when other children played. Could the college cut her off now just because of the color of her skin?

Willa-Mae did not need to hear the answer to that question. When it came right down to it, Willa-Mae knew it didn't really matter how smart you were or how hard you worked. What mattered was whether you were white or not. White folks had to look out for their own first, which meant that Nettie came in last.

"I have a little money saved. Enough for a bus ticket to New York City. I'm going to live with Big Hattie for a while."

"With your sister? They gots no more room in their place than we does! Her and Philbert and them three little young'uns! Where they gonna put you?"

"I can help with the kids. I have already talked to Hattie. She says she needs help. She and Philbert have that band—"

"That jazz! Music of the devil, that's what!" Willa-Mae burst out. "Now, I put up with Big Hattie singin' in them speaks, but I ain't gonna have my baby Nettie in them dens of . . . sin and evil!"

"Mama, jazz is all the rage."

"Don't like my babies ragin'! Don't like my babies dancin' the Charleston and carousin'! I got no more t'say t'your sister about her changin' her name and callin' herself Fat Lady Band or whatever, but I can tell you—"

"Mama." Nettie turned her pretty face at last so Willa-Mae could see the sorrow in her eyes. Those eyes seemed much too old for her years. Nettie always saw the truth before Willa-Mae did. "There's nothing here for me in Akron. No job. Now no school."

"But me and your daddy!"

"I am not Little Nettie anymore. Not a child for you to fuss over. Not another mouth for you to feed—not the way things are."

She linked her arm in Willa-Mae's. "You've got to let me go now. You know I love you. You know I had better plans than this for all of us. I thought I might make something of myself—get a good job, take care of you and Daddy. But . . . it would be the two of you taking care of me, and I can't live that way. There is nothing for me in Akron. Hattie says that maybe she can help me find a job in Harlem. Things are still jiving down there, she says."

"Jivin'!" Willa-Mae spat. She was grateful that she felt angry so she would be able to hold off crying for a while. "Such talk!"

"There are shops in Harlem. Hattie thinks maybe I can get a day job because I speak polished. They like that, Hattie says. And then at night I can watch the kids."

"Work in a shop." This was not like being a chorus girl in one of the jungle-jazz shows. Not like being a cigarette girl or a hat-check girl either.

"Yes, Mama. And Hattie needs me."

"Hattie needs you?"

"Yes, she does. You and Daddy don't. I have to go."

It was settled, then. It had been settled for days, only Willa-Mae had not known it. Just like she had not known about Harry and Rena and that baby coming. "Guess that the way it is."

"It is."

"Then there ain't nothin' for me t'say?"

"Just say you know I love you, Mama. And say you love me, too."

It must have been an unusual sight as the streetcar rumbled by—two black women embracing right there on the street. One young and slim and pretty, weeping on the shoulder of another who was grizzled of hair and as broad as a bear.

"You always gonna be my baby, Little Nettie."

CHAPTER TWENTY-SIX

Some Things You Can Count On

The three boys were in the yard, sorting out broken boards from the rubbish heap and straightening bent nails. At the appearance of Jefferson, brushed and curried and decked out in his Sunday clothes, they froze in their work, looked up in unison, gulped, and gave him guilty grins. Their faces showed fear that perhaps Jefferson had changed his mind and thought again about telling Mama what they had done. Is that why he had followed them up to the house so soon?

"How-do, boys," Jefferson called in his usual cheerful way, as though nothing at all had transpired down at the cabin. Sunlight flashed on his smile. "What y'all up to?"

It took a moment for Tommy to find his voice. "We're buildin' us a tree house, Jeff."

"That's good." He turned to David, who looked more worried than his cousins because he had caused all the ruckus in the first place and then run away to let them take the rap. "Did they pay you your two bits, Davey?"

"Yes . . . sir . . . they did."

"That's good." Jefferson smiled and strode to tower over David like some living hickory tree. "Glad t'hear it." He stuck out his hand, pink side up. "Now you can pay me the toll. Mebbe you can run, but you can't hide from ol' Jefferson. That'll be two bits you owes me for crossin' over my bridge."

"What? That's nothing but an old log with rope for rails! That ain't even a real bridge! You can't make me pay you twenty-five cents for crossing over a log."

"Y'all should have read my sign."

"What sign?"

"Right there by the side of the bell I put up for y'all to ring if'n you wants t'cross my bridge." Jefferson's big hand remained out.

"That's nothing but an old cowbell!" David protested. "And we didn't see any sign."

Jefferson shook his head pitifully, then swept his hand over the air to illuminate an invisible sign. "It say right there, No Trespassin' Yankee Boys! Two Bits to Cross over. Southern Gentelmens Please Ring Bell."

"I didn't see any such sign, and I won't give you two bits either."

Jefferson tugged his ear and frowned down at David. "Well, them's my rules. Two bits for uppity Yankee city boys t'cross over on my side of the James Fork unless I'm feelin' like havin' comp'ny. Which I ain't. So . . . I reckon today you been behavin' like an' uppity Yankee city boy. If you break the rules I'll have t'have a word with your daddy 'bout them two bits you owes me."

At this, Tommy and Bobby jumped forward, grabbed their cousin by his arms, and begged, *"Pay him!"*

David did. He dug in his pocket and slapped the quarter into Jefferson's hand. "There. It stinks, though. Most anybody ever paid on a New York City toll bridge was a nickel!"

"This ain't New York. Jus' remember, boy. On my place, I makes the rules, an' I 'spects y'all t'respects them. Cost you two bits t'cross over my bridge unless you ask an' I says come over."

Confident now that he and Lily would have some privacy from the prying eyes of little boys for a while, Jefferson pocketed the coin, thanked them, and strode boldly to the front door of the Tucker house. He doffed his hat and smoothed his hair, then knocked as though he had never been there before.

Trudy opened the door and exclaimed, "Why Jefferson, you look dressed for church. Have you had lunch yet?" She held the door wide, but he did not go in. "Well? Whatever are you doing out here on the porch?"

Jefferson turned and gave the trio a warning look that made them duck their heads and return to preoccupied nail pulling and plank selection. He replied in a loud voice intended for them to hear, "Well, Miz Trudy, since Lily an' me are goin' t'have our own house now, I thought I should knock on your door like my mama taught me is the proper thing t'do." Then, in a normal tone of voice, "I come callin' t'fetch my Lily home."

"Why are you shouting, Jefferson? I am not deaf."

"Must be water in my ears, Miz True. I done took a bath down t'the creek, an' I must have got water in my ears." At this he gave the young villains a backward glance. They seemed to shrink as Jefferson hovered on the threshold of saying more.

"Well, come in. Mercy sakes. You would think you never set foot in the house before, the way you are dallying about with your hat in your hand."

"Thank y' kindly, Miz Trudy," Jefferson said, wiping his feet. Certain that the young sinners had heard the proper way to come calling, he went on in.

✳ ✳ ✳

"Miz Canfield." Jeff bowed slightly to Lily, who was folding towels and diapers in great stacks on the dining table. "I has come to take you home."

"You mean the cabin?"

"Yes, ma'am." He drew himself up proudly. "Ready and waitin' for my perty Lily and our babies."

Lily put her hand self-consciously to the yellow turban on her hair and then to her apron. "But I ain't ready. Didn't know t'day be the day. I ain't dressed proper." She glanced at her reflection in the mirror above the sideboard. "You didn't tell me, Jeff. Now here I be lookin' like I been pickin' cotton. You all fancied up like you come callin', an' look at me. An' beside that, I ain't finished the washin' like I promise Miz True."

"Go on, Lily," Trudy called from the kitchen.

"I ain't packed."

"What you got t'pack, gal? You come t'this place with ever'thing you own in one kerchief an' jus' the clothes on your back. Come on, gal . . . while it's still daylight, so's you can see it all."

"The babies is sleepin', Jeff. I can't wake 'em up now."

Trudy appeared in the doorway of the kitchen and put her hand on her hip. "Lily, the washing can wait. And I'll stay here with the babies while you and Jeff go to your new house."

Jeff inclined his head in dignified thanks. "Much obliged, Miz True."

Lily stepped back and leaned against the sideboard. Her chin quivered, and her eyes filled with tears. "My own house, he say! He come t'fetch me, he say. Oh, Miz True! I ain't dressed proper. It be like goin' t'heaven for me t'go t'a place t'call my home! I don't fancy goin' t'heaven lookin' like this! I ain't deservin' such a blessin'. Didn't think t'would ever come t'really happen." She burst into tears. "You shoulda gimme warnin', Jeff! Shoulda told me t'day was the day—that's all!"

Jeff's expression changed from pride to utter confusion and then remorse. He looked at Trudy and spread his hands as if to ask what he had done wrong. "I meant t'surprise you, Lily! Thought you'd like suprisin'."

"I ain't goin' t'my new home lookin' like an ol' field hand!" She sank down in the chair and buried her head to weep behind a stack of towels.

"Never saw no pertier gal than you, Lily. You look fine."

"No such a'thing, Jefferson Canfield! I look like I been pickin' cotton for a hundred years."

"What'd I do, Miz Trudy?"

"You go and wait on the porch, Jefferson," Trudy said sympathetically, nudging him out the door and following him outside. Then she whispered, "Your Lily has the blues—baby blues, as they say. Happens to us all, I'm afraid. It came upon me after Joe was born, and Birch said I looked pretty enough to dance with again. I caught sight of a fat woman in the mirror, and it was me! I thought I would nevermore fit into my dresses, let alone dance again. I am afraid I said some unkind things to poor Birch on that unhappy day—normal enough, but unpleasant. You will just have to be patient and try not to get your feelings hurt, Jeff. She would cry today no matter what you said to her. It is the nature of the curse, I suppose."

She hesitated, then went on. "Usually a man and a woman have time to . . . get to know one another before they have children. Your situation is a little unusual. But she wants to be pretty for you, Jefferson, and that is at the bottom of it."

"I never seen no woman as perty as my Lily," he said longingly. "I loved her when she was swelled up big as that little Jersey milk cow with them babies. Don't she know how I loves her, Miz True?"

"That is very sweet of you, Jeff." Trudy patted him on his arm. "Better not tell her the part about the cow, though. Sit there on the step and give us a few minutes."

Such things were too deep for Jefferson to attempt to understand. He nodded dumbly and sat down like an obedient child on the top step to await whatever discussion Miz Trudy had in there with Lily. He would go away entirely if she said so. He would hang up his Sunday suit and wait until Lily's blues passed. He would wait until spring came and court her with bunches of flowers and sit beside her in a porch swing. He would marry her again in church if she needed him to do such a thing. Jefferson had waited ten years to have a woman of his own to love and a home to bring her to. He had though he would never love again . . . not after what the Kluxers had done to his Tisha. He could wait a little longer if need be. It could never be said that Jefferson Canfield was not a patient man.

The boys had gone off to play in the woods beside the road. He was glad they could not see his miserable face and ask him what was wrong. Their voices and laughter carried through the trees, sounding like a flock of squawking guinea hens. He wished he were that young again. Wished that the mysteries of a woman did not fascinate him so. Thinking of Lily made him happy and unhappy by turns. It made him ache all over inside and then made him feel like he could bust wide open with joy when she looked at him in a kindly way or just put her hand on his.

It was all a puzzlement. His daddy had always told him that. Women as a race were about the most confusing creatures in all creation. Yessir. His old daddy had said that God should have rested a little longer before He made Eve, because maybe the Lord was plumb wore out from all the work He had done and put a few things together backward in her brain. Women had dedicated themselves to keeping menfolk in the dark from the beginning of time. Love was a hard row to hoe.

Jefferson looked at the slim ribbon of smoke rising from the stone chimney of his little house. If he didn't get back soon, the fire would die. The sun was sinking toward the treetops. If they didn't go soon, it would be too dark for Lily to see everything he had done for her in proper light.

He stood and brushed off the seat of his trousers as the clatter of wagon and mule and harness sounded in the distance. Birch would be back any minute, and Jefferson would take a ribbing for being all dressed up and looking like a foolish schoolboy come courting.

He turned to knock and ask Trudy to tell Lily they would see the house another day. Instead the door swung wide to reveal the smiling face of Lily.

"How-do, Jefferson," she said, as if there had been no tears at all. She was wearing her one blue dress and her new straw hat with the yellow daisies woven around the band. "I be ready t'go now."

"Lily . . ." He bit his lip as the ache of loving her rose in his throat, choking off his words. He wanted to tell her how beautiful she was. How it did not matter if she wore her old work dress or her yellow turban, because no other woman on earth could make him feel like this. But he was afraid to say anything for fear he would say the wrong thing.

"You ready now, Jeff?"

"Yes'm. Been hopin' you could come on down, gal. Got it all ready for you. You an' William an' Willa, too."

She took his arm. "Well now, ain't that fine? You an' me can go on down first. Miz True say she gonna pack up all the baby things. Her an' Birch'll come a'callin' on us an' bring the young'uns 'long after a bit."

Her warm brown eyes shone happily beneath the brim of her hat. She lifted her face and kissed Jefferson lightly on the cheek as they walked together arm in arm.

He let her do all the talking. He answered her questions and agreed with everything she said. This was also something he remembered his daddy saying was a wise thing to do when a woman was in one of the ways a woman sometimes got in.

By the time they reached the log bridge across the creek, Lily was laughing again, and Jefferson had altogether forgotten his recent misery.

"Mind your step," he said as he helped her cross.

When they reached the other side of the river she stopped, turned to him, and lifted both hands to caress his face. "Is this our own land, Jeff? Right here where we be standin'?"

"Yes, Lily. Our own land."

"Then kiss me here, Jefferson Canfield. My husband. Kiss me a kiss that will last for always. Here, where I first set my foot in heaven."

"Jus' as you say, Miz Canfield."

Not hesitating to marvel at the deep and unfathomable currents that coursed through his Lily, Jefferson kissed her as the waters of the James Fork rushed beside them.

Rain fell on the cabin roof like fingers drumming a soft rhythm on the shingles. Jefferson tossed another log on the fire and leaned against the heavy oak mantel.

Behind the curtain, he could hear the measured breathing of the babies against Lily's breasts. First William and then little Willa. Lying on the bed, Lily crooned their names as they nursed. "There now, little Willa. You sup your fill. Hmmm. William, you be hungry t'night. Sleep now, honey. That's right, baby. Mama right here, an' Daddy close by. . . . Y'all gots your own place t'sleep now. All warm an' safe, we is. Hmmm. Yeah. Ain't it sweet, chil'?"

Jefferson poked the fire with a stick. It was hot enough, stirred up enough, but he needed something to do. Something to take his mind off Lily. He closed his eyes and shuddered at the warmth of his own hunger for her. He envied the ease with which the babies lay against her. He longed for her hands to stroke his head while her voice whispered and hummed sweet things to him.

He wiped sweat from his brow. He had promised to care for her and the children. He had not asked, had not expected anything from her in return . . . at least not so soon. He would be more than happy with just a friendly, kindly sort of love is all he wanted. But tonight . . . in the shelter of his own house . . . with her so near and so womanly . . .

"I'm goin' t'split wood, Lily," he said.

"Split wood? We gots more wood split than near any place in Shiloh, Jeff." She laughed from behind the curtain. "Why you allus wantin' t'split wood when it be rainin' an' all dark out? You gonna catch your death'a cold, an' that's a fact, man."

"I say I is gonna split us some wood, woman." The words leaped from his throat like a bark. He had not meant to speak so sharply.

"Jeff?" Lily's voice sounded amused. "It be plenty warm in here."

He grimaced with the pain of wanting to go to her. "Little bit of cold rain ain't gonna do me no harm tonight."

Did she understand what he was saying? That he was surprised and alarmed by the depth of his longing? Cold rain might cool him off. Help him get through the night without improper thoughts. Without wanting to reach out and pull her close against him.

"Cold rain do a heap of harm if'n y' ask me, Husband." She was putting William and Willa in their cradles. He could hear the squeak of the rockers against the wood.

"Don't go out yet, Jeff." The curtain rustled. "Wait 'til it stop rainin'." Was she coming out? "Let's you an' me set a spell."

She emerged from the alcove. Her bare feet showed beneath the hem of the same white nightgown she had worn the night they were wed. A plum-colored shawl embraced her shoulders. The firelight flickered on her face. Lips were parted in a half smile. Dark eyes glanced from the flames to Jefferson's face, and the smile softened.

He could not speak. He dared not move. To take one step toward her might mean another step and another until he followed every step he saw clearly in his mind.

"What's got you, Husband?"

He tried to speak, but his words came out in a sort of moan as she came closer to him. Close enough that he could have touched her if he put out his hand.

"Jefferson." She said his name in the same crooning voice she used with the babies. All full up with love and gentleness.

"Ain't nobody . . . nobody say my name thataway for a long time, Lily." Again the little moan. His breath caught in his throat.

"Jefferson," she whispered and took his hands in hers. "Jefferson. Jefferson." She kissed his palms and then leaned against him with a sigh.

"Ah, Lily. Do you know how bad I wants you, gal?"

"We been waitin' a long time."

She raised her face to his. He saw himself reflected in her eyes.

"Jefferson . . ."

✳ ✳ ✳

"There's one thing certain, ol' woman," wheezed Hock Canfield as he and Willa-Mae returned home from seeing Nettie off at the bus station.

"Seems to me nothin's certain," Willa-Mae replied.

"That's what I was 'bout to say. The most certain thing 'bout livin' is that nothin's certain. Nothin' ever turn out the way I figger it gonna turn out." He sat himself down in the big, tattered, overstuffed chair beside the radiator. He stretched out his spindly arms and leaned his head back until his hat fell off onto the floor.

"I never figgered t'be livin' no place without young'uns all round," Willa-Mae observed. "I never figgered we was a'gonna be in no house all alone. Jus' the two of us without no chicks in the nest!"

"That's right. Me neither. You know we ain't been alone since nearly nine and a half months after we was married! Woo-eee, ol' woman, that's a long time!" He inhaled deeply, as if he were smelling fresh, clean mountain air instead of the musty odor of the tenement. "Peace an' quiet come t'us at last."

"Feels like the grave t'me." She sat down hard in her easy chair. "Ain't peace. Ain't nothin' like peace. Jus' feel lonesome t'me. Harry gone—up and married. And Little Nettie off t'New York City! A more wicked, crazy place I ain't never seen! They got a speakeasy on every corner! Loose womens and gigolos in fancy suits and white spats just a'waitin t'pounce on some pretty young gal like my baby."

"Well, now, ol' woman, you raised 'em up right. They knows the dif'rence 'tween right an' wrong! They knows the Lord, don't they?"

"Don't keep 'em from fallin'." She pouted as she kicked off her shoes.

"Well, if'n they falls, you ain't gonna be there t'pick 'em up no more, but I reckon the Lord can do it in your stead, Willa-Mae." Hock sat up and took Willa-Mae's foot onto his lap. He rubbed her toes and the bottom of her foot.

"Hmmm. Honey . . . that feel soooo good. I ain't walked so far since the old days when we walked everywhere in Pisgah. You know, we ain't rode a streetcar since I lost my job. That do feel fine, Hock Canfield. I know you love me, 'cause you rub my feet. I'm so fat I can't even reach 'em no more."

"Hush up now, ol' woman," Hock chided. "Sit yourself back." He smiled and went to work on the other foot. "Did I ever tell you? First thing I notice 'bout you was these feet. I said to m'self, 'Hock Canfield, a woman with feet so big gonna have a good under-standin'!'" He laughed at his own joke. "Feet this big mean a woman got a big heart."

"Uh-huh. You can say whatever you wants, long as you keep on rubbin'. Jus' remember I got a good memory, so don't get too insultin' now."

"Then I says to myself, 'A woman with feet that big—why, she gonna walk a long way beside her man. She ain't gonna get weary. Ain't gonna fall down like some other woman with little, dainty feet.' Didn't know that's what first 'tracted me t'you, did you, woman?"

"Go on."

"Then I seen the way you helped them young'uns that day when they was tryin' t'pull that little calf outta the bog. I seen the way you waded on in there inta the mud. . . ."

"I knowed I couldn't get stuck 'cause my feet was so big. That's all. Like snowshoes, they is."

"Well, I says t'myself, 'Self! Pay 'tention now! That woman have no fear. She got a big heart t'match them feet. She ain't 'fraid of troubles. Jus' wade right in up t'her—' "

"'Course I wasn't so fat back then. I'd of sunk right on down. Died there in the mud if'n I tried that now."

"Hush now, ol' woman." Hock got up and settled onto the arm of her chair. He put his arm around her and leaned down to kiss her cheek. "You jus' growed into them feet an' that heart—that's all. More of you t'love—that's what I was a'countin' on."

"More of me t'love, all right. Cookin' for them Weldons, eatin' ever'thing left over in the kitchen. Well . . . I'm an easy keeper. No need t'feed me no more. I could live off my middle for twenty years and still not die skinny."

Hock's leathery little face was beaming down at her. "Hush now, ol' woman. Don't you know how perty you is t'me?"

"How you go on, Hock Canfield!" She laughed and slapped her knee.

"What I'm a'tryin' t'say . . . now that we is alone . . . I'm tryin' t'tell you, Willa-Mae . . . it ain't gonna be all bad."

CHAPTER TWENTY-SEVEN

The Setup

"China food, that's what it is."

Six small, white-paper cartons were spread out on the top of the packing crate that Frank and Jim Penn used as a table. Their mama held up two pencil-sized sticks. "This is what you eat it with." She smiled, probing the rice with the chopsticks without success. "But we can use regular forks 'cause we ain't Chinee."

This was Frank's first experience with foreign food. It did not look like anything he had ever seen before. The "chow mein" stuff looked like worms. The slop Mama called "chop suey" did not look much better. Egg rolls fooled him altogether. He thought they would taste like cookies, but they did not.

He could not quite figure out what anything tasted like. Certainly not similar to anything he had ever tasted before. But he liked it all a lot. Right down to the fortune cookie, which Mama opened and read to him: *"Happy days are just around the corner."* She folded the paper carefully and tucked it into the pocket of her dress for luck.

Frank wished he knew which corner those happy days were around. He would get his crutch, grab on to Mama, take little Jim's hand, and they would be out of this place. They would leave Akron and go to California, if only that fortune cookie had told them which corner they needed to go around to get there!

"Now, wasn't that the best stuff?" Mama said when the last grain of rice was gone and the juice from the chop suey was mopped up from their plates. "Did you like it, Frank?"

"Yes'm." He really had liked it. This was the first time in a long time that his stomach had not been left partly empty and growling. Mostly he liked the feeling that he had eaten enough—only his belly ached a bit because it wasn't used to being full.

"Well, there's plenty more where that come from." She reached into her pocket and pulled out a five-dollar bill. "We're rich. For tonight, anyway."

"Where'd you get it, Mama?" Jim rose on his knees and reached across to touch the bill.

"A nice man give it to me for some work I done for him." Her voice sounded happy, but she looked away.

"What work, Mama?" Frank asked, looking at her eyes, which were not bright and cheerful like her voice.

"He took some pichurs of me." The five was folded and put away.

"Like a movie actress?"

"Just like an actress. He said I was pretty and . . ." Her hands were shaking as she began to clean up the mess.

"You gonna get some more pichurs, Mama?"

"That's right, Frank." She sounded almost cross as she answered his question. "He paid me in advance for tonight. I'm going to act in a little play tonight and maybe get enough to fix up this dump a little. Maybe get enough so we can eat chop suey every night, if we want to. And maybe I can stay home and tuck you in some nights if this works out."

Were those tears in her eyes?

Frank and Jim exchanged looks. "We don't need no chop—none of that stuff, Mama. Don't worry 'bout us," Frank said in a manly voice. "And I can tuck me and Jim in."

She did not reply. She dumped the empty cartons into a paper sack, but she saved the chopsticks. She gave one of the sticks to each boy. "Oh, I wish we wasn't here," she said, putting her arms around them. "Wish we was anyplace but here. It won't be this way forever. I promise. I'm gonna find some way. . . ."

"Like the cookie says, huh, Mama?"

"Yessir, Frank. My little man." The distant whistle from the factory made her jump a bit, as though it had frightened her.

"You okay, Mama?" Frank held her hand and looked up into her face, but she did not look back at him like she used to. She did not seem to see him anymore.

"I got to get going. They paid me in advance. Paid me extra. I got to go," she said.

"We'll be okay." Frank didn't know what he could do to take away the sad and frightened look from his mama's eyes.

Tonight was worse than usual when Mama left. She chided Jim when he began to cry. She told him not to be such a baby. It made no difference. Jim cried for a long time. Frank let his little brother suck his thumb all through the night. Frank felt bad, too. He wished there was something that could make him feel better inside.

The warm, full feeling he had gotten from the supper soon left him. Just like always, his belly growled and gnawed at him.

The scream of the factory whistle signaled the end of the shift at 3:00 AM.

Glaring lights shone on the gray walls of the Titan plant, giving the place the atmosphere of a prison yard. Ellis put on his overcoat, switched off the infirmary lights, and stood on the second-story landing to watch as grim-faced gummers poured out the doors of Plant One. Titan's speedup in production quotas was taking its toll on the men. Heads were bowed from exhaustion. Gone was the usual animated conversation between workers as they punched their time cards and filed past the dozen policemen who had been added to the security force.

Jack Titan was proving that his factory could indeed maintain production quotas at the pre-crash level with one-third fewer employees. But what was the cost in human suffering to those men now outside the gates and out of work? And what was the cost in morale to those gummers lucky enough to still have their jobs? They owed their souls to Titan Tire and Rubber Company. Homes, health, the food on their tables—everything depended on walking through the gate when the whistle screamed and then on spending the next eight hours meeting Jack Titan's production quotas.

And Ellis was no better off than any gummer on the line tonight. He walked slowly down the wooden stairs. His head was bowed as well. His shoulders sagged. He limped toward the end of the line of men and joined them as they spilled out the gates and moved against the flow of men coming in for the next shift. The crowd had nearly vanished by the time Ellis emerged on the street.

Brightly lit streetcars were packed with the homebound crews. Among the last to head toward the cars, Ellis fumbled in his pocket for his ticket. He did not raise his face to look any man in the eye until a hoarse whisper sounded from the shadow of an alleyway as he passed.

"Hey, Doc—Doctor Warne. You're the swing-shift doc, ain't ya?" The tone was furtive. A large man stepped into the light.

Ellis turned to face a broad, swarthy man with jet-black hair and thick black eyebrows. He was Greek, Ellis guessed, or possibly Italian. His nose was large and bent in a way that told Ellis it had been broken more than once. The dark streaks on the man's tan corduroy trousers revealed that he was a gummer.

"Are you the doc?" The man glanced over his shoulder as if fearful that someone might see him.

"I am," Ellis answered. The man was not a member of the swing-shift crew or he would have known at a glance who Ellis was.

The thick features of the man softened with relief. "I been waitin' here. Jack Daugherty says you are a good sort. A right sort of guy."

"You were on Jack's crew?"

"No, sir." The man stepped back out of the light as though he did not want anyone still at the gate to see him. "But I know Jack well enough. Trust him. Trust anyone he says can be trusted, see?"

Ellis was too tired to care. "That's fine, fella, but it's been a long night."

"Please . . . wait a sec, Doc. . . . I got trouble, see?"

"Everyone's got troubles. As for me, I'll have troubles if I don't get some sleep. And if I'm late again tonight, my wife . . ." Ellis turned to leave as the streetcars began to pull out.

"Wait a minute." Now a note of desperation sounded in the man's voice and stopped Ellis midstride. "There's a woman . . . trouble, Doc. I think she might be . . . gonna die. . . ."

A flash of anger swept through Ellis. "There are hospitals—plenty of doctors to call. It's three in the morning. I've been up since 6:00 AM yesterday!"

"Couldn't call no other doctor . . . not the hospital or the coppers either. I'm married, see? The woman—well, she ain't no lady. I picked her up down at Papa Tomano's place. She's one of the regular hookers who hangs around here at the gate waitin' for us gummers after quittin' time. She sees me tossin' back a few at the speakeasy. We start talkin', we go to a hotel . . . and she keels over. I dunno. I think first I'll just leave her. Then I think if she's dead maybe somebody will think I killed her. Please, Doc. Jack talks about you all the time. Says you ain't like the rest. I'm tryin' to do the right thing here. I mean, I can't pay you or nothin', but—"

"I get the picture. If you were trying to do the right thing, you would have gone home after work like I'm trying to do."

"You're right, Doc, and I'm sorry I didn't. But I didn't, and now I got trouble. She's just a block down the street."

"Right." There was no use arguing, Ellis conceded. He could not turn his back on the man now. He exhaled loudly as the warning bell clanged three times from the departing streetcar. Raising his hand, he waved the driver on. He would be late getting home again.

The building was not worthy of the name *hotel*. It was a sleazy, flea-bitten flophouse. In fact, Ellis thought that might be too kind a description for the dilapidated brick building. As Ellis rounded the corner with the man who had summoned him, he could hear the stirring of rodents in the garbage heaped at the side of the structure. Several drunks were sleeping it off in the alley as Ellis followed the gummer up the leaning back stairs to the second floor.

On the landing, a thin wooden door opened to a narrow, musty-smelling corridor. Two bare lightbulbs illuminated the water-stained plaster walls and the garbage-littered floor.

"This is better than home, is it?" Ellis remarked dryly.

"It's cheap. The hookers all use this place." The stink of rotting food mingled with the vague and nauseating smell of human waste as they passed a tiny closet with a toilet inside.

"In here." The big man stopped in front of a battered door that had once been painted red. Now only a few streaks of color remained on the splintered and faded wood. He turned the knob and stepped back, letting Ellis enter the tiny cubicle first.

The woman lay facedown, sprawled across the mattress of an iron bed, which was the only furniture in the space. She was half covered by a moth-eaten blanket. Her clothes lay neatly over the footboard.

"She fell just like that," the man blurted when Ellis did not go immediately to her. "I tried to wake her up. I didn't lay a hand on her, Doc. I swear I didn't. I just threw the blanket over her and ran to get you."

"Were you drinking?"

"A guy don't go to Papa Tomano's and not drink."

"Did she have much?" Ellis considered for an instant that this might be nothing more than a case of too much bad bootleg gin.

"Not so much as me." The man licked his lips and stared at her fearfully. "Is she . . . breathin'? still alive there?"

Ellis reached to take her hand. It was limp yet warm. No fever. Pulse normal.

"Alive? Yes." He looked up with disgust just as the man ran out and slammed the door shut. "Get back here," Ellis called.

His patient suddenly sprang to life. She grabbed his arm and pulled him off balance. He slipped and fell to one knee beside the bed.

"Hi, honey!" she cried. "I been waitin' here for you! Where'd you go? Glad you're back."

"Wrong customer." He tried to stand just as the door crashed open again and the bright flash of camera bulbs erupted. Another and another followed in a rapid succession of pops, blinding Ellis with the glare.

"What is this?" Ellis struggled to his feet. But he knew what it was. Titan was living up to his threat. The whole thing had been staged for the sake of photographs.

Behind the three faceless men with cameras who crowded into the room, a voice called out to him, "I'll tell you what it is, Doctor Warne. You've been caught in a raid on a bordello. Who knows? Your picture might even make the front page of the paper—that is, if they can make it decent enough to print down at the daily."

The woman pulled the blanket around her. "I'm sorry, mister," she muttered as she stepped around Ellis and grabbed her clothes, then disappeared behind a curtain.

"Fine, doll," remarked the amused voice from the hall. Then to Ellis, "A fine thing, eh? A nice young doctor like yourself being caught in such a place. Sure to ruin your reputation, you being a married man and all. You supposed to be a respectable doctor and everything. Trouble, yessir. You're going to have trouble explaining this."

Ellis's head throbbed. He squinted around the barrage of black dots that still swam in his vision from the flashing bulbs of the cameras. "No one will believe you!" he shouted.

"You're wrong, Doc. People love to believe this sort of thing. Human nature. And there's the evidence. Pictures. You on your knees beside her bed."

"We got some great shots, Boss."

Ellis could hear the sneer in that photographer's voice. He charged the man, grabbing the bulky camera and smashing it against the wall.

Somewhere in the building, a woman called, "What's goin' on up there?"

Hands grasped Ellis, throwing him back.

"You can't get away with this!"

"We already have, Doctor Warne." The man in the corridor laughed. "You can't smash them all." Then he added, "Go on, Mike. Take the film back to the plant."

"Sure, boss."

Again Ellis dove at his betrayers. This time he was knocked to the floor and kicked hard in the stomach. The breath exploded from his lungs with searing violence.

"I don't like to do that to a man who can't kick back," crooned the big man. "You only having one leg and all." Then another kick landed against Ellis's shoulder, knocking him against the iron footboard of the bed. "Look at that. Drunk, ain't he? Get one of that. He's drunk if ever I saw drunk."

As Ellis struggled for a breath, one final bulb popped and flared. He could not speak. Could not rise. The sour burning of his own vomit hung in his throat as the woman stepped over his legs.

"He's had enough," said the big man. The door swung shut, and they left him alone. He could hear their laughter all the way down the stairs and into the alley.

✵ ✵ ✵

It was just after sunup when Willa-Mae heard the shrill voice of the downstairs neighbor shouting at her boys to get out.

"Pro-fane," Willa-Mae said in disgust as she whipped the flapjack batter.

Hock yawned and stretched. "Me an' Harry seen her outside the plant last night. She up to no good, that woman. Jus' like that harlot in Proverbs, she out there en-ticin' them men into sinful ways." He lay back on the sofa. "When them flapjacks be done, woman?"

"Most anytime."

Again the fury erupted toward the two little boys downstairs. "Shut up, I said! I told you I'm tryin' to sleep! I'll kill you both if you don't shut up. Get out! Get out!"

Hock and Willa-Mae exchanged disgusted looks as the distinct sound of slaps preceded the crying of a child and then the loud slam of the door.

"Please, Mama!"

The woman's shouts began again, radiating up through the floor.

"Hmmm," Willa-Mae said, first stamping her foot, then picking up the empty skillet and letting it fall with a crash. Silence followed instantly. "That's better. Let that hussy know we's up here. Can't hear myself cook with all that a'goin' on."

Hock sat up and stared at the flakes of snow falling erratically beyond the windowpane. "She done turned them young'uns out, Willa-Mae," he said in an anguished voice. "That one with the crooked foot? Frank's his name. He ain't got but one shoe. If they go outside . . ."

She clucked her tongue and shook her head. "It ain't our business, Hock. You know what that hussy say about us colored folks. If we bring them kids up here and feed 'em and she finds out 'bout it, we're likely to get arrested for kidnappin'.'"

"Sweet Lord a'mighty, Willa-Mae. What kinda world this be when poor folk like us can't even feed flapjacks to starving chillens without we have t'worry 'bout somebody callin' the po-lice?"

Whimpering drifted up the stairwell from the landing. "Go get 'em then, ol' man. But Lord help us if'n that woman find out her chillens ate breakfast with colored folk."

Hock considered the matter a second time. "She'd let 'em starve sooner than have the likes of us feed 'em. It's mighty cold out there in that hallway. You know she don't feed them babies hardly enough to keep 'em alive."

She frowned and waved the skillet in the air. "Well, I done told you t'get 'em up here, didn't I? So go on, ol' man. They's hungry and cold. Don't matter if that loose dawg of a mother of theirs is the daughter of the Grand Wizard of the Klan! We'll feed them babies by and by. She is too drunk t'know anyway, ain't she? She too rotten t'care for 'em herself and too mean and selfish t'let anybody else take care of 'em. That's a bad woman, Hock, treat her own babies thataway."

"Put them flapjacks in the skillet." Hock looked suddenly relieved and happy at the decision. "Like tryin' t'feed a stray cat, ain't it? First we got t'let 'em smell the food before they gonna come close enough to eat. Mebbe they ain't gonna notice we ain't white if'n they smell them flapjacks first."

He put on his shoes and hurried out, leaving the door wide-open so the aroma would float down.

Willa-Mae cooked the flapjacks while she hummed softly. Ever so softly, because she did not want her voice to penetrate and awaken the dragon lady in her lair.

Presently Hock appeared with the Penn brothers in tow. He carried little Frank on his back. The crooked foot, bare and blue with cold, stuck out from under Hock's arm. Jim followed after with his thumb in his mouth. Both were dressed in ragged clothes, and Willa-Mae was certain they had slept in those clothes, too. Tears were fresh on Jim's face. Frank looked frightened yet hungry. The pink mark from where his mother had slapped him was bright on his cheek.

"Look what I found me, Willa-Mae." Hock feigned cheerfulness. "I was a'goin' down t'feed the chickens, an' I found me these two young'uns. I s'pose they was goin' out t'play, but I ast 'em t'come eat your flapjacks, since we got so much an' Harry ain't here no more. We don't want t'waste food."

"Why, that's fine." Willa-Mae pretended she had not known. Had not heard the ruckus. Pretended the boys were old friends. "How-do, boys. Frank. Jim. Y'all like flapjacks?"

Frank nodded vigorously. "Yes'm," he whispered.

The whisper told her he knew the barrier between the Canfield flat and his mother was too thin. "Our mama's sleepin' . . . ."

Willa-Mae lowered her voice as well. "Then we gonna be real quiet up here, ain't that right, Hock? We gonna be real quiet and let your poor, wore-out mama sleep. We'll have us a stack of flapjacks meanwhile, so she won't worry none 'bout you boys goin' hungry."

Willa-Mae did not expect that the woman would have worried about any such thing, but the pretense that she cared seemed to make Frank and Jim feel better. They each ate a stack and then another.

Conversation was slow at first, since their mama had told them not to talk to niggers. It took the boys a while to overcome her warning. But after a time they opened up and told Willa-Mae all about their daddy dying in the mine accident back in Coal Town. They talked about how their mama had come here looking for a job and how she had found one, only it was night work that she did not like. Frank told how sometimes their mama cried because she hated the work so bad, but times were hard and she had to do what she had to do. He was not sure about what sort of work it was, except that she came home tired and sad all the time now.

It was no wonder that woman didn't want her boys talking to anyone, Willa-Mae told Hock later. "They done told us ever'thing she don't want nobody t'know. Hmmm. Mebbe that gal's the scum of the earth, Hock Canfield, but there ain't no way I'm gonna think hard of her. She ain't but twenty-two, if my guess is right. Hardly growed herself. Takin' care of them two boys on her own."

"She ain't takin' care," Hock reminded her.

"Well, she need some help."

"She don't want no help."

"Yes, she do. She jus' don't know it."

"She don't want help from no colored person, woman."

"That gal wants help from *anybody*, Hock Canfield. A woman that sell herself t'keep a roof over the head of her babies can't afford t'be choosy 'bout who helps her with them babies." Willa-Mae stared hard at the floor. "You wait, ol' man. Even if she know them boys been up here, she ain't gonna stop 'em from comin' back. Mebbe she ain't gonna say yes, but she ain't gonna say no neither."

Willa-Mae was right about that. Flapjacks were only the beginning of many breakfasts with the Penn brothers. The next morning they were dressed in ragged but clean clothes. Their hair was combed and their faces were washed. They waited outside the door of their flat until Hock passed by, and this time there was no hesitation when he asked if they were hungry.

CHAPTER TWENTY-EIGHT

Warnings for an Apple Thief

It was not that folks did not get sick in Sebastian County, Arkansas. On the contrary, calls came for Dr. Brown at all hours of the day and night. Most of his patients lived. A few passed over yonder, as the saying went. But one thing held true regardless of the severity of the illness: Sebastian County folks liked to get well or die in their own beds and with their own kinfolk around them. For this reason, Max Meyer remained the only resident patient in Dr. Brown's small infirmary.

He paid the same rate that he would have paid down at the boarding-house of Miss Zelda Sue Brown, who, in spite of the name, was no relation to the blacksmith, the barber, or the doctor. Fifty cents a day was due to Dr. Brown for care at the infirmary . . . if the patient had fifty cents a day. If the patient was broke, then nothing at all was charged, but payment might be made in the form of a hog or a crate of laying hens.

As the only paying patient—the only patient—in the infirmary, Max had his pick of the five empty beds in the room. Ever since the day he first laid eyes on the old apple tree in the orchard and heard the parable of the free apples and the sparrows, he had asked for a bed beside the window. From that vantage point, he could see the gnarled old tree at all times of night and day. And as he lay on his bed and studied the grizzled tree, he thought about a lot of things he had not considered before.

He thought about his life—how he had indeed been stealing pleasure, like apples, from all the wrong places, and how no one thing had ever satisfied the appetite of his heart, no matter how he treasured that thing.

He also read from the Bible that Mary left open beside his bed. One passage spoke about sparrows—how God knew even when a single sparrow fell and so knew and cared about each person as well. This concept was an arresting one for Max. It also made him more aware of the birds that visited the old apple tree. He found himself staring out the window for hours until he could recognize each individual member of the avian congregation.

Some of the birds he saw were brash and pushy. Others were timid and hesitant. There were pairs, male and female, who clearly belonged together. They chirped and bickered sometimes, but they knew one another and feasted together. When a large black crow flew in to claim the tree as his own, the sparrows banded together and attacked like tiny fighting planes over the battlefields of France. Together they chased off the enemy and reclaimed what was theirs.

Like Dr. Brown and Mary, Max began to imagine other parables from the free apples as well. He was ready the afternoon that Mary returned from the shantytown outside of Greenwood. Her hair was tousled, her face smeared with soot. Her riding boots were muddy, but she was beautiful.

"You look tired," Max said to her. "You okay?"

"It's 1929," she observed grimly. "Things just shouldn't be the way they are—that's all. Not in the modern world. Primitive."

She shook off her heaviness and sat down next to his bed as had become her habit after a long day of house calls. "So. What have you been up to?"

"Reading." He held up the Bible and waved it like a flag. "Thinking of orchards."

This pleased her. She smiled hopefully at him. "Well? The old tree has got you too, has it?"

"In a way."

"You want to share?"

"Are you sure you want me to?"

"That has a less-than-holy sound."

"It depends on what you call holy."

She nodded, too tired for debate. "I'm game."

Max thumbed through the Bible and found the Song of Songs. *"As the lily among thorns, so is my love among the daughters . . . ,"* he began.

Mary chuckled and closed her eyes. "Trudy warned me about you. Said you know all the tricks."

"She said that?"

"Yes."

"Does that mean you don't want me to go on, Mary?"

"You think you're the first person to find that passage, Max?" she questioned, then began to recite the second chapter from memory:

As the apple tree among the trees of the wood, so is my beloved among the sons. I sat down under his shadow with great delight, and his fruit was sweet to my taste. He brought me to the banqueting house, and his banner over me was love. Stay me with flagons, comfort me with apples: for I am sick of love. His left hand is under my head, and his right hand doth embrace me.

She opened her eyes. Her warm gaze locked with his. Her voice lowered to a whisper. "You are leaving here, aren't you?"

"Someday."

"You are no apple tree, Max. No roots. No shade for a woman to rest in. No banner of love to cover me."

"Another parable for me, Mary?" Disappointment rose in his throat, choking out the desire he felt.

"This song is not for me and you, Max. It can't be. I can't love you now."

"Will you love me ever?"

"I mean . . . I *do* love you now. But I *can't* love you. You're still wanting to steal apples from the pushcart, Max." She stood and stepped out of his reach. "I will not be devoured, core and seed, to fulfill your appetite, so you can go on and steal again. I'm waiting for something else—something, somebody, permanent. Waiting for roots and branches and shade and nourishment. And then I'll give everything. I want to give."

"You're looking for perfection, not reality," he scoffed. "Mary . . . no man is . . . can be . . ."

"You're *wrong*, Max. You've been living your life as a thief so long you can't see that there is another way to live. And I won't feed your appetite. It's like a fire."

"Yes, it is!"

"Fire consumes the wood, leaving only smoke and ashes. I want much more than that when I give myself to a man."

"When?"

"When the time comes. And don't be so arrogant as to believe that you are my only choice."

"Buck Hooper," he spat.

"Don't be ridiculous."

"Then who?"

"Someone with roots planted in deep soil."

"I can't live here forever."

"I'm not talking about *where* you live, but *how* you live. Who and what you live for. . . . Max, you live only for yourself. I know that now. Maybe you have half heard what my heart was saying, but now you've turned it all around. You have translated everything into some formula for getting me into bed with you."

"Blunt, aren't you?"

"Truthful. I have that reputation around here. It makes a lot of enemies with people who do not want to talk straight. But life is too short for me to end up being one apple stolen off a pushcart by a greedy kid, when I can be a whole crop to some loving man someday." She shrugged. "You're getting well enough to make a pass. I'll tell Dad you'll be moving down to Zelda Sue Brown's boardinghouse as soon as your stitches come out." She smiled coolly. "She's no relation, by the way."

With that, she left him alone in the room to stare out at the old tree and try to figure out where he had gone wrong.

The Shiloh mail arrived late. And the letter from Montreal was the only thing in the Tucker box down at Grandma Amos's general store.

The voice of Grandma Amos became distant as Trudy scanned the precise handwriting of her mother on the crisp page. Everyone was well, business not bad, the weather cold . . . and something puzzling had happened recently:

> *First an American police official dropped by to ask if we had seen Max. He told me that we must be vigilant in trying to find him because he is in danger of being harmed by American gangsters who are attempting to find him and his son. Imagine! Max having a son and not telling us about it.*

Trudy frowned and glanced quickly at David, then returned to the script:

> *I am certain now that what the agent said is true. Shortly after this fellow left, a smallish, rather wicked-looking man came into the store. He claimed to be an old army friend of Max, but I did not believe it. He became quite agitated when your father asked him questions, and he left us in a hurry. Perhaps he was one of the gangsters? I do hope our Max is going to be all right.*

Trudy felt the color drain from her face at the news. Max was in no shape to run. He had nowhere he could hide.

"That Emmaline," Grandma Amos's voice rasped on. "If that there pup is half so good as her mama—" The old woman peered at Trudy.

"Why, gal! You're white as a sheet. Need t'sit down, Trudy gal?" She toddled around to the other side of the counter as Trudy hastily shoved the letter into the pocket of her coat.

"I'm fine. Fine, Grandma Amos."

"That letter bad news, gal? Your fam'ly alright? Mama and Daddy still livin'?"

"Everything is fine. Really."

The old woman took Trudy by the arm as though she did not believe it. Birch had said it was wise not to mess with the old woman, because she could detect a lie when she heard one. She had a message from the Lord every time she turned around.

"You sure now?"

"Nothing about my mother and father. A family member is in some trouble."

Grandma Amos stuck out her lower lip. "I figgered it were somethin' of the like. Either that or you got yourself in the fam'ly way agin, gal." She patted Trudy's arm affectionately. "Best take things easy awhile 'til you see for shore."

Then she turned abruptly from Trudy and stooped down to eye level with David. "How's your daddy, boy?"

"Better. He's gained some weight."

"He proposed t'Mary Brown yet?"

"I—I don't think so, ma'am."

"Well, he will." She mussed his hair. "Just tell him t'watch hisself, will you? Tell 'im Grandma still got this leetle old house down here by the crick if'n he needs a place t'live after he's up and at 'em. But most of all, he got t'watch his step. It ain't that Buck Hooper—no, t'ain't Buck. Don't rightly know what's set my teeth on edge." Her dentures clacked. "Anyway, he better watch out. You tell 'im that from me, will you?"

"Yes, ma'am," David answered respectfully. He looked at Trudy for help. The old woman made him nervous.

"That's real fine. Had a word from the Lawd." Grandma Amos closed her eyes and repeated her familiar warning.

"Hitch the mules to the wagon," Trudy instructed Birch when she and the boys returned home from the Shiloh store. "We are going to Hartford to a picture show tonight."

Trudy had expected rousing cheers from her little troop. Instead they looked at one another in astonishment and scratched their heads. They silently questioned if she was just joking or had gone crazy between the visit to the store and the walk home. Had she not reminded them just this morning that moving pictures were a waste of time and money and were purely frivolous entertainment for people who were too lazy to read? Had she not chided Birch for taking the boys' side when they declared that all they wanted in their whole lives was to see *The Big Trail*, which was not only a real talking motion picture but also a history lesson about the trek of covered wagons across the wide prairie? She had answered her husband sharply that if the boys wanted good history and entertainment, they would stay home and read Grandpa Sinnickson's memoirs.

"Well?" she challenged in an innocent voice this afternoon. "I am a woman, and a woman may change her mind."

"That is a fact," Birch agreed with a laugh. Then he spotted the glint of steel in her eyes and figured he had better just shut his mouth and hitch up the mules like he was told. He knew very well that Trudy had some alternate reason for going all the way into Hartford this late in the day.

Trudy, in yet another startling declaration, announced that they would also eat their supper at the café tonight. This was truly a miraculous change of heart. Trudy did not believe in wasting good money by eating food cooked in cafés and prepared by the hands of perfect strangers. Bobby and Tommy had never eaten out when they were with her unless there was some sort of emergency—and neither brother could remember the last time that had happened. When they went into town with their father, eating at the café was standard procedure. Birch saw cafés not as places to eat but more as places to sit and jaw with old friends. He did not mind if the food was up to snuff. He did not tell Trudy of his extravagance, however, and he cautioned the boys to remain quiet as well.

Birch stood gawking with the hames in his hands when Trudy spilled that great news. "Eat at a café?" he whispered as she charged off into the house to clean a mess of chocolate off of baby Joe. "Why, boys, are you sure you did not meet some great shinin' white light when y'all were walkin' home today?"

"No, sir," Tommy assured his dad.

"How 'bout you, Davey? Did your aunt Trudy fall down, maybe? Maybe hear a great voice from heaven? *Get thee to Hartford! Quit being such a spoilsport!* Huh? You didn't hear anything like that?"

"Naw, Uncle Birch. She just walked really quiet awhile. She said 'uh-huh' no matter what we said to her. So I figgered she wasn't listening."

Bobby verified Trudy's strange behavior. "I tried to tell her that baby Joe had stole a chocolate bar from the store and ate it with the paper on and then spit it out in his hands and—"

"He was just sitting there in the little wagon while we pulled him

along. He was wiping chocolate in his hair and giving it to Codfish,"
Tommy finished. "And all Mama said was 'uh-huh.' She didn't even
hardly notice. I thought sure she'd wallop somebody for not telling her,
even though we tried."

"Is that so?" Thoughtful, Birch stuck out his lower lip. "Well, boys, we
better not hesitate. She can change her mind back the other way just as
quick. Get a move on and get ready."

There was no time to take an all-over bath, so the boys stripped naked
on the back porch and doused one another with buckets of icy water from
the well. There must be some pain with such pleasure, they reasoned.

And so they left for Hartford. Trudy continued saying "uh-huh" all
the way. Only once did she sound cross, however. That was when she
informed Birch that she absolutely *must* have a word with poor Max as
soon as they got to town. Birch worried that they might be late for the
picture and asked if they couldn't stop at Doc Brown's on the way back.
Then Trudy drew herself up in the way that meant, *"Do not try my patience!"* She insisted that *after* would be too late, that before they went to
the café or the movie, she *had* to have a word with Max.

It was rare that Birch could ever induce Trudy to be so frivolous with
money as to sanction a night on the town. For this reason, he agreed to
her every condition in the hope that she might really enjoy seeing a talking moving picture, and perhaps she would let them waste money in
such a way more often. He had taught his sons this truth: When your
mama is agreeable, *don't rock the boat*!

In spite of the late hour, Birch drove the wagon up the lane to
Dr. Brown's house. He set the brake and nodded pleasantly when Trudy
insisted that she go in alone first to see if Max was feeling well enough
for company. There they sat in the wagon for half an hour as the clock
ticked closer to showtime. But nobody dared run up and pound on the
door for fear of breaking the spell that Trudy seemed to be under.

The letter from Trudy's mother lay open on Max's bed. Max could not
meet Trudy's direct gaze. He had not told her the whole truth. Did she
sense that there was much more to the story?

"So now you know." He summed up his tale with a convincing sigh.
"Are you surprised? I'm a reporter. Stick with this job long enough and
you're bound to make a few people mad."

Trudy managed a smile. "Seems to me that irritating people is
something you always had a knack for, Max." She glanced around the
infirmary to make her point.

"Just so happens that the gent who is mad at me is Boss Quinn, who runs most of the bootleg-liquor business in Manhattan. He would like to see me dead."

Trudy studied him and added, "Buck Hooper almost saved him the trouble. You should have given us the straight story, Max. I do not know if I should be flattered that you came here or insulted." She managed a faint smile.

"You were the only person I could think of. . . ."

"And Shiloh is at the ends of the earth." With a shrug, she sat back in resignation. "Why not go to the FBI? Surely they would protect you until you could testify."

"Do you know how many G-men have been bumped off the last few months, right along with rival mob members? They can't even protect themselves. There were threats made against David's life if I didn't fall in line with Boss Quinn. I couldn't take a chance on the kid getting hurt."

Trudy nodded and placed her hand on Max's arm. "What will you do now?"

"I mailed my résumé at every whistle-stop between New York and Kansas City. Dozens. Replies will hopefully be rolling in to a pal of mine on the *Times* staff. Europe. Asia. The Middle East. There are newspapers in places in the world where Prohibition gangsters do not do business. If I can get a job . . ." He paused. "But David—he's happy here with you and Birch. I was hoping he could stay with you for a while. Just until I get settled. Long enough for me to see that the heat is off. That I have not been followed. See?"

Trudy bit her lip in thought. "He is a bright child. He loves you very much. We would love to have him, but have you thought how he might feel if you leave without him?"

"I don't want to lose him, Trudy. It won't be for long. Just a few months maybe. A year at the most. I'll explain. He'll understand. He'll have to understand."

There was a profound silence in the room. Trudy looked toward the door by which Mary had left moments before. "Not everyone will understand if you leave."

Of course she was speaking of Mary. How could Max answer that? He had thought about asking Mary to go with him. Always he had come to the same conclusion. "Mary has her own plans. They do not include a chump like me."

"Have you asked her?"

"Not in so many words."

"Be careful with her." Now there was an edge to Trudy's voice.

"Careful?" He repeated the word as though he did not know what Trudy meant.

"Do not play with me. I have seen enough broken hearts in your wake to know. She cares for you deeply."

"She'll get over it."

"This is not Manhattan. People don't have an affair here and then walk away to another one. Around Shiloh, folks fall in love. Settle down. Raise their children. People get old and end up side by side down at the Shiloh churchyard. Max, you are handsome. Intelligent. Charming. Like a river, you look a mile wide at first glance, but you are about an inch deep as far as knowing how to love a woman."

Was that restrained anger in her tone now?

"I like Mary," Trudy said.

"So do I."

"Then why don't you ease up on the charm?"

"She likes me, too." He felt defensive. What right did Trudy have to butt in?

"Too much."

"That's for her to decide, isn't it?"

"You're leaving."

"So is she. To China, as I understand it. I won't get in her way, and she won't—"

"Get in your way?" Trudy stood and glared at him. "I love you, Max, but you are a cad where a woman's heart is concerned. David's mother—"

"Leave Irene out of this." He felt the color rise to his cheeks.

"Have you told Mary about all that? She thinks you're a widower."

"Why don't you tell her if you think it will make some difference?"

"It has made a difference to your son."

"Davey is with me now, isn't he?" Max shot back.

Trudy considered his remark for a moment. "No, he is with me. And you're still putting other things ahead of people who need you."

The accusation stung him. How could she know how he was feeling? How could she guess the danger David could be in beyond the boundaries of Shiloh? Max had nothing but time on his hands to think about it. By leaving, he could possibly draw the fire away from the boy until it no longer mattered to anyone if Davey Meyer was alive.

How long would that be? The question turned Max inside out every waking hour. There was no way to explain what he felt for David or Mary. It was hopeless. Was this putting business before the people he loved?

"Yes, I guess I am." He turned his face away from Trudy and did not say good-bye as she left the room.

CHAPTER TWENTY-NINE

Deeper and Deeper

Ellis had been kept waiting outside Jack Titan's office for thirty minutes when the intercom on Mrs. Fremont's desk buzzed and Titan's voice questioned, "Is Doctor Warne there?"

"Yes, sir," the secretary responded.

"Well, then, send him in at once." Titan's voice sounded chipper, almost cheerful.

When Ellis entered, Jack Titan was looking out the tall window, his hands clasped behind his back. He was rocking up and down on his toes.

"Sit down," Titan instructed Ellis. A single straight-backed chair had been pulled up in front of Titan's desk, positioned to make Ellis feel like an errant schoolboy summoned to the headmaster's office.

Ellis was caught between rage and despair, and the net effect was abject misery. His lips tightened and so did his grip on the arms of the chair at seeing Titan's wicked cheerfulness, but he said nothing.

Titan picked up a manila folder from his desk and thumbed through it idly, as if Ellis were not even in the room. Periodically he shot a few glances in Ellis's direction, daring Ellis to move or speak.

At last he laid the folder down. "It should not be surprising, in an enterprise as large and important as this one, that we keep track of the personal habits of our key employees. We know, for example, Doctor Warne, that you have a problem with women."

Ellis almost came up out of the chair at that, but Titan's next words froze him in place again. "We also know that you are in a precarious financial position and that things have not been going well for you at home. . . . Well, small wonder that a man may seek comfort elsewhere. Still, there is the company reputation to think of, you being one of our own, so to speak. We wouldn't want the career of our promising young physician to be tarnished by scandal, now would we?"

Ellis clenched his fists in his lap. His head was down, and he could not raise his face to look Titan in the eye. After a period of uncomfortable silence, Titan answered for Ellis by saying, "No, I thought not. I'm sure you won't have any difficulty following instructions exactly, will you?"

The stubborn silence in the room allowed the rumble and vibration of the rubber-processing machinery to penetrate the paneled walls. "Do you hear that sound, Doctor Warne? Titan Tire and Rubber is in the business of molding raw, uncooperative material into useful, obedient products. That applies equally to rubber and to men. Again I ask you—you will follow orders, won't you?"

Ellis gave the smallest of nods, but it seemed to satisfy Titan. "Good," he said, turning back to gaze out the window. "You can return to your work now," he said in dismissal. "I'm certain you have some physicals to catch up on."

Ellis stared at the green-and-gold-lettered advertisement that stretched across the inside of the streetcar above the windows. Building Your Tomorrow Today, it read. First Central Trust Company. Next to this rectangle was one that proclaimed Quality, Price, and Friendly Service—You Get It All from Acme. Visit the Acmeteria. This sign was a splash of the same glowing yellow with which the Acme stores were painted. Ellis found the bright colors and the cheery exhortations irritating.

Not that he was consciously studying the commercial messages that ringed the streetcar. Mostly he glumly watched the streetlights pass in a procession of bright moments that marked the wet pavement with feeble streaks of light. It was apparent to Ellis on this predawn ride home from the Titan plant that there was much more darkness than light in the world, and that which seemed bright and colorful was false and unhelpful.

Like the lowering clouds that promised to drop more rain on Akron, the storm of Ellis's thoughts swirled around his head. He felt as if there were a tornado inside his mind, blowing his thoughts like vagrant leaves from one topic to the next without his being able to stop them or change their course—each more dismal and inescapable than the last.

The First Central Trust Company was the institution that held the mortgage on his home—the mortgage Becky didn't know about—from which Ellis had poured their home's security into the rathole called Wall Street. The mortgage payments required that he continue to be employed by Titan Tire and Rubber, which he hated, because to give up the job meant more than the loss of income. It meant being ruined. Those photographs! How could he ever explain? What would happen to his practice if they were published?

But how much longer could things go on the way they were? How soon would the threats against his family from the bitterest of the fired Titan employees begin again? Becky would want—would *demand*—to know why they were being attacked. Could he explain that he was helping ruin other men's lives to protect his own?

He thought about Johnny Daugherty lying in his hospital . . . about Jack Daugherty, with the label of drunkard hung on him. How would Jack ever get employment elsewhere?

"I can't even help myself," Ellis muttered aloud. "How could I help them?"

Outside the breath-fogged windows, the commercial district of Akron reared up. The four-story-high vertical sign that proclaimed O'Neil's and marked Akron's premier department store was still lit. Store employees were already at work festooning the Christmas display windows with additional red and white ribbon. *Christmas*, Ellis thought morosely. *I don't think I can do that much pretending.*

"Hey, Danny! Hold it!" Ellis yelled suddenly, startling the driver, who was the only other occupant of the car. "You let me miss my stop! We're all the way downtown!"

"Not my fault, mister," argued the driver, who was not Danny. "I don't even know you."

"No . . . no you don't. Sorry," Ellis apologized while staring at the man. "Where's Danny?"

"You mean the guy who got laid off of this run? Beats me. I just keep my mouth shut and do what they tell me. Now, do you want off here or what?"

Ellis nodded vaguely. "Uh, yeah, I guess so. I don't want to get any farther from home."

On the sidewalk, Ellis berated himself as the streetcar's bell chimed and it rattled off. He wondered if he was losing his mind. "I can't afford to," he remarked to his reflection in the window of Polsky's Department Store. "What would happen to Becky and Boots?"

Across the street, the windows of O'Neil's displayed Christmas scenes. In one, a mannequin family was enjoying a sleigh ride, dressed up in mufflers and fur coats with plaid lap robes. In another, the mannequins were grouped around a holiday table loaded with turkey and all the trimmings.

A trip downtown to O'Neil's was always a favorite excursion for Boots. She loved the high ceilings of the ultramodern store and the tables piled high with merchandise. A lot of happy memories were connected with that store, but none lately. Anyway, what value did memories have now? They couldn't release Ellis from the trap he was in.

Ellis tilted his head back, involuntarily repeating an exercise he and Boots always carried out when approaching the store: counting the floors. *"One, two, three,"* they would count, *"four, five, six, seven."* Boots had been able to count all the floors from the time she had been two years of age.

That had been the same year Ellis and Becky had taken Boots downtown to watch as the Goodyear blimp Pilgrim showed off its maneuverability by landing on top of O'Neil's. "Oh," Boots had shouted, green eyes wide and auburn curls bouncing, much to the delight of all the onlookers and the swelling pride of her parents.

Studying the top of the building now brought Ellis no enjoyment. The blimp was long gone, flown away like the happiness and the good times. O'Neil's now seemed good for only one purpose: to jump off of. Seven floors to the ground would be a pretty sure way to end it all; no doubt about that. One short step over the edge and Main Street would rush up to meet you.

Ellis looked at the storefront and thought about embracing the pavement at the end of the fall. But how could he leave Becky to face the mortgage with no income at all?

That's when he thought of the life-insurance policy his neighbor Fitzgerald had sold him. Ellis had hated the persistence with which Fitz had pursued the sale. When Ellis had tried to put off the tenacious agent for a few months in late spring, Fitz had remarked, "Death won't wait until August," and Ellis had almost thrown the man out of the house. But Becky had responded otherwise, insisting that they take the five-thousand-dollar policy. Later Ellis had also come to believe that he had done the right thing, the responsible thing.

Ellis turned the thought over in his mind. Five thousand dollars! More than enough to get them out of Akron, give them a new start somewhere. Then Ellis remembered: To get the money, he had to be dead. Ellis examined this consideration with a coldness that surprised him. What had the agent said about suicide? Didn't that void the policy?

Ellis took one more look at the rooftop ledge of O'Neil's, then turned his face toward home. He was a doctor, after all. There were ways it could be done and no one would be any the wiser.

✳ ✳ ✳

The empty building had, until the previous week, been used as a showroom for the popular Chandler automobile. Dubbed the "Marvelous Motor" for its ability to imitate pricier machines at more affordable figures, it was locally famous because of being built in Cleveland. The people of Akron had shown it an almost hometown loyalty.

But the showroom was not vacant because the dealer had moved to more spacious quarters. Following the Wall Street crash, the manufacturer had gone belly-up, and from factory to sales floor, all the former Chandler employees were out of work.

Bill Denton, pastor of the Furnace Street Mission, had acquired a six-month lease on the big open space to use as a soup kitchen for what he already recognized would be an increasingly critical need. Tonight's inaugural meeting was an appeal to the community for donations to get the newly expanded program up and running, and Becky Warne was in attendance. She had looked over the stock of pickles, jellies, canned corn, and preserved apricots in the Warne cellar and decided it was time to share from their larder. Now she sat with some fifty men and women who had gathered at the former Chandler showroom to hear Denton's plea.

"We need your help. No longer are the down-and-out confined to the limits of Furnace Street and North Howard Street. No sir! You've seen it already. It's your neighbors, your friends, perhaps even your relatives who are out of work and hungry. Brothers and sisters," Denton proclaimed, "we must demonstrate the love of Christ in real, concrete ways to those in need. It may be your hands that are the hands of Jesus, reaching out to care for someone when they think no one cares for them at all."

Everyone knew that Revered Denton was genuine. No scam artist seeking to make a quick buck from a sad story, he had been preaching to "the least, the last, and the lost" of Akron's red-light district throughout the 1920s. Once a disgruntled pimp had threatened Denton with a pistol. Coolly, Denton had closed his eyes and prayed aloud, "Lord, You know this man's intentions. But let them take my dead body out, rather than me quit yellow for Jesus and not preach the gospel on this street." When Denton finished praying, the man had left.

This story and others about similar threats made the audience take Denton seriously. He was one who had put his faith on the line. Now he was challenging them to do the same.

"I'm not just speaking of your money or the excess from your pantry," he said—Becky looked down at the apple crate of canning jars at her feet—"although the Lord knows we need both and are grateful. But what I am also appealing for, brothers and sisters, is you—your hands and your labor. We need volunteers to work here and in other kitchens around Akron. *The harvest truly is plenteous,"* he quoted, *"but the laborers are few."*

Denton paused and looked around the assembly. Becky felt his eyes on her, and she felt the challenge deep in her soul . . . a stirring in her heart to look past her own grief.

"Believe this," he said. "The situation is going to get much, much worse."

Brown's Boardinghouse of Hartford was a large white Victorian building one block off Main Street. Green paint was peeling off the trim and shutters. The brick chimney leaned a bit, as did the front steps and the veranda. Grass and weeds grew up around the posts that held the weathered sign in the yard. The picket fence had not been painted in a number of years.

Once the private residence of Colonel Robert C. Brown, the building had been inherited by his spinster daughters upon his death in 1911. Since the good colonel had drunk up all his savings, his daughters had been forced to convert the home into Hartford's only boardinghouse.

In the early days, the Brown sisters had no doubt thought to snag themselves husbands through this enterprise, reasoning that even marriage to a stray traveling salesman was better than remaining single. Miss Zelda Sue Brown was once rumored to say that she would actually prefer marrying a man who spent most of his life away on business. After all, men were more trouble than use, but it was a fine thing to be able to call oneself "Missus." And the younger sister, Minna, had eventually achieved her matrimonial objectives. She had fallen in love with a farmer from Charleston and moved away, leaving the business to her less successful sister, Zelda Sue.

The rooms were full only on rare occasions, such as the time five years earlier when the James Creek trestle burned down and the Rock Island locomotive had been delayed, stranding twenty passengers who needed lodging for the night. Occasional dances and social events in town also brought in farmers from outlying areas who lodged at Brown's, and cotton-ginning almost always meant a full house. But occupancy was an ongoing problem for Miss Brown, so she welcomed Max Meyer to her establishment.

Max Meyer was still convalescing, so Miss Brown often brought his supper to him on a tray in his room. He was a quiet tenant who kept to himself and received no visitors except for family. In fact, he seemed to have no vices except for an extraordinary passion for discussing politics with various traveling salesmen, who invariably brought terrible news about growing soup lines and soaring unemployment in the outside world. Miss Brown considered this last tendency a vice only because it usually led to angry shouting matches between her tenants, and she liked to run a peaceful house at all times.

In all other situations, this Max Meyer seemed a lonely, thoughtful man. He took long walks in the evening and began to regain his strength. He used the telephone now and then to call Shiloh and pass a message to Birch and Trudy.

Once, when the mail was delivered by plane from Fort Smith, he invited the pilot to have a drink and talk awhile. But this was the only time Miss Brown was aware of any drinking. Having run a temperance house since before Prohibition, Miss Brown had reprimanded her guest at that time, but Mr. Meyer had graciously put away the bottle at her request. Lack of alcohol had not dampened the conversation of the two old veterans much, and they had talked far into the night about France and war reparations and the pilot's hope that there would be yet another war for him to fly in.

All of her boarders' comings and goings, taken together, kept Miss Brown richly supplied with gossip to pass along. She was also able to squelch some of the juicier rumors that kept surfacing. She had heard all about the suspected romance between Miss Mary Brown and this handsome stranger, but now she was certain the lowdown had been incorrect. Mary had not come round to see Max Meyer even once since his arrival. He made perfunctory visits to the house of Dr. Brown to have his wound checked, but there seemed to be no other connection between them.

This was disappointing to all the women of the surrounding area who had looked at Max Meyer and compared him to Rudolph Valentino. Most had imagined such a man as this carrying cool Mary away to some steamy tent in the desert sands, as Valentino had done in *The Sheik*. Now it seemed that such drama was reserved only for the movie screen.

There was one additional item of interest. Max had sent a large bundle of letters off with the mail pilot, Wildman McKinney. Miss Brown had heard him instruct the aviator that each letter should be dropped in the post box of a different town. The reason for this curious command was a matter of serious speculation among the ladies' Methodist Sewing Circle that week. No definite conclusion was reached.

CHAPTER THIRTY

Good Dogs

The frosty breath of the quiet group crowded around the back of the Furnace Street Mission truck mingled with the steamy wisps swirling upward from the broth in the shiny kettle. Just over fifteen minutes before, North Howard Street had been completely empty except for a skinny dog rummaging through a garbage can and getting his nose caught in an empty sardine can after licking up the last drops of oil. Now there had to be a hundred people, black and white, standing around the rear of the truck.

Becky thought it was just like magic, the way the crowd had gathered. Preceding the van's turn onto Howard was the gospel bus. As soon as the two vehicles pulled up at the curb beside a shabby row of tenements, the electric bells on the bus had begun to peal, and heads had poked out windows four blocks away. Shortly after, folks began to gather in the street, and by the time the organist started pumping out "Joy to the World," the first cups of soup were being ladled into eagerly extended bowls.

Becky saw the same guilty looks on the faces of those in line that she and Boots had noticed before. Being out of work seemed somehow shameful, almost as if the jobless had brought the trouble on themselves.

A man whose suit was out at the elbows and whose shoes had not seen polish in some time kept his eyes down but tugged politely on his ragged cloth cap. He mumbled his thanks when Becky passed him a cup of soup. Behind him was a trio—a heavyset black woman and two little white boys, one of them riding in a toy wagon.

The woman held one small boy by the hand, while his other fist was locked against his mouth. The black lady was pulling the wagon with her other hand. The boy in the wagon did not try to get up even while they waited in line, and Becky noticed that he had a twisted foot.

When the three came to the head of the rank, the woman extended a tin kettle that looked like a miner's lunch bucket. "If you could jus' put the soup in here, we'd be much obliged."

Becky complied and passed the container back, along with a loaf of bread.

"Here, Frank," said the woman, handing the kettle to the boy in the wagon, "you is in charge of seein' it don't spill." She turned back to tell Becky, "Thank you." Then she addressed her two companions again. "Ain't the Lord good, boys? Let's go set the table."

"Wait just a moment," said Becky. She rummaged in a crate at her feet and came up with a jar of canned peaches. "Perhaps you could use these as well."

The black woman's face split into the biggest grin Becky had ever seen. Real joy seemed to overflow from her and light up the air around her.

"Lord bless you," she said with delight. "Lord bless you real good!"

✲ ✲ ✲

"Well now, Trudy." Grandma Amos clicked her false teeth with pleasure at seeing the Tuckers enter the store. "Y'all got an interestin' letter today. For Jefferson, care of y'all, from Kansas City. If'n you would carry it to him."

"We ain't seen Jeff lately," Tommy offered.

"Why? Has he lit out or somethin'?" asked the old woman.

"He and Lily moved into the old cabin at last," Trudy explained with a wink. "They have not been receiving company. Posted a sign to keep out small boys with an itch to go possum hunting."

"Well, now, can't say I blame 'em. Young boys with dawgs and red puppies can be bothersome." The old woman squinted out the window to where the puppy frolicked in the shadow of Codfish. "Y'all cotched any possum with them huntin' dawgs?"

"No'm," Bobby answered seriously. "Brother Williams said we got to start her easy-like. Soak a rag in possum grease and have her track it some."

"Well now, Brother Williams knows 'bout hounds, all right. Y'all best listen to 'im. How 'bout that big dawg there?" She turned her watery eyes on David. "That be yourn, ain't it? Half bear, ain't it? That a huntin' dawg, Davey?"

"He got a blue jay yesterday," David answered seriously.

"Well that's somethin', all right. Them jays'll peck the apples right off the tree. Yessir. It's good t'have a critter t'keep them jays off the orchard."

Grandma Amos handed Trudy the letter and then opened the jar of lemon drops and tipped it down for the boys to take a piece of hard candy. She often did this when young'uns came into the store, and by this small gift she had won the friendship of nearly every young'un in Shiloh. None dared call her a witch, even though her skin was as puckered as a dried apple and her nose was long and droopy.

Grandma Amos rambled on to the boys about dogs she had personally known in her lifetime. Good dogs and bad dogs. Brave dogs that would face a bear and cowardly dogs who would run the other way at the scent of a raccoon.

"Now, y'all weren't round here a few years back, but that Brother Williams and Emmaline, the mama of that little pup of yourn, she cornered a catamount—mountain lion—up that old pine tree down t'the school. Figured that ol' lion was just a'waitin' for some chil' t'come by, an' then—" She made a grab for David's belly, which made him jump back. "So, Brother Williams didn't have no gun. An' he tells ol' Emmaline t'hold that lion up there in that tree until he come back. . . ."

It was half an hour before Trudy managed to leave the store and start back to the farm with Jefferson's letter.

There had been no word from Jefferson and Lily since the day they moved to their cabin across the James Fork. Tommy, Bobby, and David, remembering Jefferson's stern warning, had carefully stayed on their own side of the water.

"No reason to bother them," Trudy had remarked each day. "They've got a lot of catching up to do." She did not explain what it was they needed to catch up on, but the boys figured she knew something they didn't know. So Jefferson and Lily had been left alone to catch up, and no one had gone near them until the day the letter arrived.

Trudy fished the envelope out of her apron pocket and slapped it against her palm. Birch paid her no mind, even though she had the look of a woman about to explode with curiosity. She paced the kitchen while he sat at the table and read a well-thumbed copy of the *Saturday Evening Post* that had been passed from house to house.

"There is no return address on it," Trudy mused, eyeing the letter, "but it has a Kansas City postmark. What do you think it means?"

Birch sniffed and sipped his coffee. "I suppose it means it was mailed in Kansas City."

"Well, I know that," she fussed and stared hard at the white envelope, as if glaring would enable her to see through it. "What I am saying is, I wonder who mailed it."

"Hmmm." Birch turned the page of his magazine. "Just clear as anything, to my way of thinkin'."

"Well, what?"

"Has to be that old friend of Jefferson's from Mount Pisgah. Washington Young. Lord knows Jeff has written a letter every week tryin' to track the man down in case he might know where Jeff's family settled."

"But Washington Young was a cook in Little Rock. This letter is from Kansas City."

"Well, maybe this Washington Young fella moved from Little Rock. Lord knows there ain't any more reason to live in Little Rock than there is to live in Kansas City."

"Stuff and nonsense," she fumed. "This is a woman's handwriting."

"Well—" Birch shrugged and scratched his head curiously—"if you say so, True. But I don't know nobody else that would be writin' Jefferson Canfield care of me in Shiloh, Arkansas, except for Washington Young. Maybe he writes like a woman. He's a cook, ain't he? If he cooks like a woman, then maybe he writes like one, too." He grinned hopefully as Trudy went to the kitchen window to gaze across the valley at the thin ribbon of smoke that rose from the cabin chimney.

"How long have they been down there?" she asked in a voice that let Birch know they had been down there long enough.

Birch squinted out the window. "Now we know they ain't dead, because there's that smoke from the chimney. Although a man can die from bliss, I hear. Well, they been down there burning wood these two weeks and a little more. And the boys ain't dared to cross the creek."

Birch shook his head in amazement. "I don't know what Jefferson told those kids, but I wish I had his knack for making threats stick like that. If I'd told them not to cross the creek for two whole weeks, they'd have been over that log in the first afternoon."

"Well, we will just have to disturb them is all. This might be news for Jefferson about his mother. About his family. He will want to know."

"What if it ain't good news, True? It's been a long time since that man had a few days in a row that ain't had trouble. I hate to bother him if it's bad news. Bad news can wait."

"Birch!" Trudy contradicted his reasoning as if he had gone insane. "Jeff *has* waited. He has waited for years. Now here we have this letter. It may be the first word he has had in ten years about the whereabouts of his folks, and you are saying bad news can wait?"

"Just a thought." Birch raised his hands in surrender. "You want to take it yourself? That way, you can know right away if Jefferson's letter is good news or bad news or if maybe someone's tryin' to sell him insurance."

"You are insulting." She raised her chin indignantly.

"And you, wifey dear, are nosy."

She threw a biscuit at him and pocketed the letter again as Codfish lumbered over to lap up the crumbs of her missile. "All right. I am nosy. But we will go together. I'll take some fresh eggs and a pie."

"Good. That will give us reason to stay until the letter is read and its contents known."

There were no more biscuits, but Codfish looked up hopefully as Trudy declared, "You hypocrite! You want to know as badly as I do!"

"I never denied it." Birch closed the magazine and reached for his coat.

The Kansas City letter was neither good news nor bad news. And Trudy had been correct in her assessment of the handwriting. It was indeed that of a woman.

Jefferson's letters had been received by Washington Young, who was still a cook in Little Rock. From there, they had been forwarded on to his mother, Bertha, in Kansas City.

Jefferson read through her reply silently the first time and then again out loud for Lily, Trudy, and Birch while baby Joe banged on the washboard with a wooden spoon. Jeff raised his voice to be heard over the racket until the reading and the banging sounded like a sort of celebration.

"Dear Jefferson,

Praise the Lord oh my soul! And forget not even one of His little bitty benefits!

So you is alive! God be praised! We all give you up fer ded many year ago. When Washington send me your letter I think I'm gonna bust when I reads it. You be looking fer yer mama and daddy and sisters your letter say. I spose we all gonna have a reunion in heaven with Jesus, but fer now I got to tell you I don't know where most the folks from Pisgah has got to. Your mama and daddy pick up and leave some months afore The Man died and his young nefew take over the place and send us all packing. Your mama and daddy head way up north last I hear. But I hear that 8 year ago. Now I don't keep touch with nobody cept for Delpha Jean Jones who come back

*to Arkansas soon as she get her a new husband. Delpha Jean might
know where your mama and daddy be living becuz they was always
like sisters them two. . . . "*

At this point Jefferson raised his eyes to Trudy. "You remember
Depha Jean? She was the wife of little Billy Jones, who got himself
hanged by the Klan back in Pisgah. She had a heap of young'uns down
t'the school where you was teachin'. Every one of them chillens spoke
well of you. You remember them young'uns, don't you, Miz Trudy?"

Trudy nodded. Of course she remembered how the widow of Billy
Jones and her children had been turned out of their farm in Mount
Pisgah. She had never forgotten the faces of the Jones children and the
empty benches in the little school after they had moved away. None of
the remaining pupils had ever sat in those vacant seats in the classroom.
The absence of the Jones children remained a constant reminder of the
injustice of their banishment and the murder of their father. The death
of Billy Jones had only been the beginning of sorrows for the people of
Mount Pisgah. Faces and names and the grief of those times were as fresh
in Trudy's mind as if it had all happened yesterday.

"I remember, Jefferson," Trudy replied, wresting the spoon from Joe's
grasp. "I remember Delpha Jean didn't want to leave that farm and go
north—to Chicago, I guess it was. I am happy that she married again and
came back home. Her children were bright. Eager to learn."

"We all learned hard lessons that year, didn't we, Miz Trudy? Miz
Young say Delpha Jean is livin' in Pine Bluff. She say if anybody know
'bout where my folks is, Delpha Jean will know. She gimme this here
address." He waved the paper like a little flag. "Reckon I can find her all
right."

"It ain't a far ride t'Pine Bluff," Lily added hopefully. "I reckon you
best get on down there an' speak t'this Delpha Jean. It take too long
t'write a letter, send it, and mebbe not get a letter back. I say you saddle
up Ol' Bob an' get on t'Pine Bluff so's you don't be pinin' away for your
folks no more. Mebbe this Delpha Jean gonna tell you where they is!
Mebbe she got some kinda address or somethin' so's you can write your
mama an' tell her you gots a wife an' young'uns an' a place of your own
t'live. Don't wait." Lily was already on her feet, packing food enough for
the journey. "Your mama be somewheres in this wide worl'. She be
a'prayin' for her boy Jefferson right now, mebbe. Jus' think how she
gonna feel when she hear you be alive, Jeff! You gots t'hurry up an' find
her!"

Jefferson scanned the letter once again. "I reckon I'm goin' t'Pine
Bluff, ain't I?"

Birch helped Jefferson saddle up the old mule. Lily ironed two shirts, and Trudy rocked the twins while baby Joe played on the floor of the old cabin. It was noon when Jefferson kissed his wife and babies and rode away from Shiloh.

And so ended the sweetest time in the lives of Jefferson and Lily Canfield.

Ellis Warne paused outside the closed door that led into the private office of Dr. Keller. He took a deep breath and glanced over his shoulder for the twelfth time in the last minute. As bad as things were, it had occurred to Ellis that there was still one way for them to get worse: He could get arrested. If that happened, then all of the things he feared would come about, but he would have no way to do anything about any of them.

Reminding himself of the need to hurry, Ellis juggled Keller's key ring, sorting the key to the office door from the rest. Ellis had gone in to see the chief medical administrator earlier in the shift to have some forms signed and had simply picked up Keller's keys while the older doctor was laboriously adding his signature to an order for more laxatives.

Keller was always losing something—his gloves, his glasses, his cigarette case. So Ellis was not surprised when no great outcry followed Keller's discovery of the loss. Undoubtedly it was expected that they would turn up tomorrow, which is exactly what Ellis intended to happen. By tomorrow, of course, it wouldn't matter to Ellis one way or the other.

In the meantime though, Ellis needed to get on with it. He had sent Giselle out for coffee and doughnuts, remarking that it was a slow night and they could use something to wake them up. The nurse had given him an odd look. The request was out of character for Ellis, especially after the morose turn he had taken recently. But she had complied without argument. And this gave Ellis perhaps ten minutes—more than enough—to do what he had planned.

It should be easy. If someone in need of medical attention should arrive in the clinic, Ellis would return shortly with the explanation that he had gone to use the restroom, which was on the same corridor as Keller's room.

Another deep breath, and Ellis inserted the key in the lock. There was no real need for silence, since the medical building was completely empty, but the sound of the tumblers clicking and the slight creaking of the door seemed as loud as a siren. Ellis slipped in and shut the door behind him.

The air in the room was heavy with the stale aroma of the Chester-field cigarettes that Keller chain-smoked. Under that odor, but not com-pletely hidden by it, was the smell of bourbon that Keller's shaking hands had dribbled onto the coil rug.

Ellis almost switched on the light, catching himself just in time. Keller's office had a window, and it would not do to give notice that someone was moving around the room in the middle of the night. If the object of Ellis's breaking in was where he expected, then light was unnecessary.

The manila folder containing the master list of employees to be dis-charged for fake medical reasons was in the center drawer of Keller's desk. Ellis knew this because once in each of the past few weeks he had been summoned into this office to receive his week's assignment of workers to be eliminated. At every one of these meetings, Ellis had watched Keller withdraw the folder from the desk drawer, flip it open to long lists of names, and copy down by hand the names of those whose time had come to leave Titan Tire.

Ellis walked around behind the desk. As he did so, his shoe pressed down on something that rolled under his artificial limb, almost throwing Ellis against the wall. He caught himself on the back of Keller's desk chair and reached down to remove the hazard. It was an empty shot glass.

Pulling the desk chair away from in front of the drawer, Ellis confi-dently pulled on the handle. The drawer refused to budge. He rattled it, thinking it must be stuck on some papers, but no, it was actually locked. Ellis had never seen Keller use the lock on this drawer. Why had he cho-sen tonight of all nights to start?

Ellis felt the key ring in his pocket. It had to contain twelve or fifteen keys. Surely the one that would open the desk must be among them. He tried to hold the ring up to the faint light that came from outside the window, but it was no good.

Feverishly Ellis tried several keys in turn: too big, too long, right shape but wouldn't turn. Ellis lost his place on the ring, didn't know which he had already used and which were left untested.

No time! Ellis tossed the keys onto the desk with irritation. This couldn't wait until the next shift Ellis was on duty either. It had to be over tonight! He had reached the decision to steal the list after great delibera-tion. Who knew if his resolve would last? Tomorrow he might draw back from the planned suicide that was the only possible resolution to this mess.

Ellis picked up the keys again, almost weeping with frustration. As he did so, his fingers brushed a manila folder lying on top of the desk. Could it be? Was Keller really so forgetful?

Even in the blackness, the list of names in three neatly spaced columns per page was easy to make out. Ellis snatched up the folder and stuffed it inside his lab coat. He urged himself to hurry. Giselle would be back at any minute.

Ellis felt suddenly very content. He had the list—the great, wicked list—and it would soon be with those who would use it to stop this injustice. Tonight no one would be the wiser. Of course, tomorrow would be another story, and the disappearance of the folder would have an effect like throwing a rock at a hornet's nest. Titan and his cronies would certainly think to come looking for Ellis, but by then it wouldn't matter.

He was outside with the door closed and headed back toward his office when he put his hand into his coat pocket. Keller's keys! He had brought them away with him instead of leaving them behind as he had planned. This was bad—very bad. If the keys were found outside the chief medical administrator's room, someone else might be blamed for Ellis's crime.

He struggled with the keys again. Where was the right one now? In his flurry to reopen the door, the folder fell out from under his jacket, spilling the lists across the floor. Ellis bent down, hurriedly shoving the papers back into place.

There was still one more piece of paper to get. This page had fallen and slid halfway under Keller's door. Ellis stooped awkwardly to retrieve it, bending stiffly across his bad leg.

"May I help you, Doctor?" a voice said from behind him. It was Giselle.

"What? Oh, I—no, thank you, Nurse. Doctor Keller, he just . . . well, he . . ."

Giselle gathered up the final errant piece of the evidence. She took the manila folder from Ellis's stiff fingers and straightened the sheaf of pages inside before adding the last one to the stack.

"God bless you," she murmured. "I was hoping you'd do this before long."

⚹ ⚹ ⚹

The nurse who saw Ellis come onto the third floor of People's Hospital glanced up, recognized him, and went back to her chart. Then a thought struck her. She studied the large wall clock behind the nurses' station and frowned. Five in the morning.

"Oh, Doctor," she called, "can I help you?"

Ellis did his best to sound businesslike and professional. The truth was that he was out of breath and trembling all over. Even the most innocent questions had taken on sinister implications in his mind. Ever since leaving the Titan plant, he had been expecting a hand on his shoulder and a rough voice demanding his surrender.

At least he had anticipated this particular query and rehearsed his answer. "It's quite all right, Nurse. As you know, I'm the doctor who accompanied Johnny Daugherty here right after his accident. I need to look in on him, but my schedule for today is such that this is my only opportunity. I'm going to be unable to return later."

"I understand, Doctor, but I'm certain he's asleep. His chart calls for heavy sedation at night. He has been waking up with nightmares."

Ellis well understood what that meant. "I'll only be a moment, Nurse. I just want to look in on him."

"Of course, Doctor," she said, turning back to the forms she was completing.

The ward was dark, and the sound of steady breathing came from all corners of the room. Ellis wanted to make this quick, but he had come too far to make a mistake now. Standing beside Johnny's bed, Ellis looked around once more, then down at the sleeping face. In slumber, the lines of pain and fear had smoothed, and Johnny's color was no longer a twin to the pillowcase.

Ellis bent low and cupped his hand around Johnny's ear. "Johnny," he whispered urgently. "Johnny, it's me, Doc Warne. Wake up."

A groan and a stirring of the covers answered him, but that was all.

"Johnny," Ellis urged again, "open your eyes!"

Johnny's eyelids fluttered, then pulled back halfway. "Doc?" he queried in a groggy tone.

"Shhh!" Ellis hissed. "Don't talk, just listen." He extracted the manila folder from inside his overcoat. "I got the lists," he whispered. "The lists from Titan. You understand? I want you to give this to your uncle."

"Sure, Doc," Johnny said, suddenly awake. "I got you."

Ellis nodded at the comprehension in Johnny's words. "I'll slip this in the drawer of the night table, under your Bible. Tell Jack I'm sorry it wasn't sooner."

Ellis turned to leave, but Johnny struggled to bring his arm out from the covers and gestured for Ellis to return. The young man extended his hand and grasped Ellis's. "God bless you. You're the best."

"I . . . I have to go," Ellis muttered, fearing the effect that kind words would have on him right now.

"Thanks for telling me to never give up," Johnny continued, squeezing tightly. "It helps me to think about you and what the Lord has brought you through."

Ellis wanted to jerk his hand away. Johnny's grip seemed to burn him with fire. Gently, but as quickly as he could, Ellis broke free and backed away from the bed. "Don't forget the list," he said unnecessarily. "I . . . good-bye."

Stumbling out of the ward and back to the elevator, Ellis's eyes clouded. He kept his head down and passed the nurse again without speaking.

One half of his resolution was completed. Now the other half—the dark half—remained.

It was not cowardice that prevented Ellis from taking his life that night. After all, dying would take no courage at all. In fact, killing himself would be the ultimate act of cowardice. Running away from everything that threatened him would be the easiest thing, would it not? Paying his debts with his own blood was simpler than facing bankruptcy and a ruined reputation. To have the facade stripped away and risk losing the love of his family, to go on living without them—facing that possibility would have taken a braver man than Ellis.

Ellis did not fear death, although he knew that death was a fearsome thing. And he did not fear God, simply because he had forgotten God somewhere along the way. What little he thought of God was in the context of his own anger and loss. Why had God deserted him so completely? If there was a God, then why had so much tragedy come into his life? Like Job in the Bible, he cried, *"The thing which I greatly feared is come upon me!"* But unlike Job, Ellis could not look past his troubles and say of God, *"Though He slay me, yet will I trust in Him!"* It was easier to kill himself and get it over with.

What was it, then, that kept Ellis from committing suicide the same night he stole the Titan list? Not a miracle. Not a glimmer of hope. Not a shining revelation from heaven. Just an accident.

He stepped from the streetcar and walked slowly toward Florida Avenue. The wind was sharp. It howled up the roadway into his face. At the far end of the block, headlights swung an arc around the corner and beamed into Ellis's eyes. At that same instant, Ellis spotted the furry white form of Boots's dog, Snowball, as the animal trotted out of the Benjamin yard, across the sidewalk, and onto the road to greet Ellis—directly into the path of the car.

The horrible screech of brakes shattered the peacefulness of the quiet neighborhood. A split second later, the small animal yipped in pain as it hit the bumper and was slammed beneath the automobile.

In spite of the late hour, all the neighborhood was roused. After all, what household did not have a dog to worry about?

Windows flew up. Tousled heads poked out, each shouting to learn whose dog had been hit. Becky and Boots sprinted onto the porch. Barefoot and dressed in their nightgowns, the two ran to the edge of the sidewalk as Ellis muttered the name of Snowball and knelt to remove the limp little body from beneath the car's running board.

That night, it was no great miracle that kept Ellis alive. It was the tears of his daughter as she cried, "Daddy, is he dead? Daddy, can you save him?"

An odd thought flashed through Ellis's mind as he carried the little dog into his clinic. He could not bear to see his daughter hurt over the loss of her pet. Surely it would be too much for the child to lose her dog and her father on the same night.

This event alone was responsible for the fact that Ellis continued living. He stayed up until full light working on Snowball. By then he was too tired to think of anything but sleep.

UNVANQUISHED
WAR

part three

Stand ye calm and resolute,
Like a forest close and mute,
With folded arms and looks which are
Weapons of unvanquished war.

PERCY BYSSHE SHELLEY

CHAPTER THIRTY-ONE

Connections

It was late afternoon when the clanging of Grandma Amos's dinner bell resounded over the Shiloh countryside to announce that there was a telephone message for the Tucker household.

Birch hammered a final nail into the frame of the new barn, then paused to hear the same impatient ringing.

"Y'all got some telephone call down t'Grandma Amos's." Brother Williams, one of the men who had gathered to help, wiped sweat from his brow.

"I hear it." Birch spit and dropped the hammer into the leather loop of his tool belt. "I was hopin' I didn't hear right, but I heard."

The third call sounded from the old woman's bell, indicating that the message was important.

Trudy stepped onto the porch to shade her eyes against the sinking sun. "Birch?" she hollered.

"A bother, if you ask me—these telephones. It will be the end of all peace if we ever get 'em in every house."

"Birch?" Trudy called a second time.

"I heard it!" He waved her back into the house. "I'm goin'."

A good-sized crowd of shoppers had gathered by the time Birch arrived at the store. Grandma Amos was doing a brisk business, but she had breath enough to reprimand Birch.

"T'was Sheriff Potts on the line," she announced. "He had important news, too. Said you was t'call soon's you got here."

There was a murmur repeating the name of Sheriff Potts a dozen times among the bystanders. What could it mean?

"What is it, Grandma?" Mr. Woods whispered.

"Trouble," muttered the old woman.

"What variety?"

"The two-legged kind, I reckon," came the reply as Birch made his way behind the counter and into the clutter of the back room that Grandma Amos called her "office."

The crowd fell silent as Birch rang Central and asked for Sheriff Potts.

"What is it, Grandma? Have they caught up with Buck Hooper?" asked Harriet Pickens in a shrill voice.

The old woman waved the suggestion away as if the matter of Buck Hooper was of no account compared to what she knew. "Buck ain't nothin'." She held up a bony finger for silence. Sometimes, if no one dared to breathe, the other side of the conversation could be heard all the way out in the store. And Sheriff Potts, it was well-known, had a trumpet of a voice. He could outbay a coonhound on a good day.

"How-do, Sheriff Potts," Birch began with a touch of irritation in his voice. There was no escaping the fact that everyone in the community was about to know every shred of his business.

"Afternoon, Birch!" The lawman's voice could be heard even louder than Birch's. Folks nudged one another and nodded happily at the plainness and clarity of the sheriff's words.

"Well, I hear you called."

"That I did! How are y'all down there?"

"Fine." Birch stuck his head out from the curtain and asked the assembly, "Y'all heard Sheriff Potts, didn't you? He's askin' a question."

At that, everyone spoke up and hollered that they were fine and hoped he was the same.

Birch grimaced and ducked back behind the cloth partition. "Well, Sheriff, all of Shiloh is down here to find out why you have called me away from buildin' my new barn. You might as well speak up so's the ones in the back can hear, too."

"Yes? Well now, Birch," Potts roared, "I got some good news for y'all and some bad news."

"I am surrounded by friends and neighbors, Sheriff, so give it to me straight. I can take it."

"Are you settin' down, Birch?"

"No, I ain't."

That did not seem to matter to the sheriff. He rumbled ahead, heedless of Birch Tucker's sitting or standing state. "I just got a long-distance phone call from Oklahoma."

Utter silence hung in the store as folks waited for Potts to get on with it.

"Yes, sir. We're listenin'," Birch urged him on.

"Well, you know how we was out after the twister hit? How we was all lookin' ever'where for the dead body of your cousin J.D.?"

Something inside Birch began to sink. "Yes, sir. Half the search party is right here."

"Well, the reason we didn't find the dead body of your cousin J.D. is 'cause he ain't dead!"

A murmur of amazement rolled through the little space, threatening to drown out the rest of the conversation.

Grandma Amos flung up her arms for quiet. "Lord have mercy! I hope that's the bad news."

Birch did not reply. His sentiment was that this *had* to be the bad news. But wait. There was more!

"You hear me, boy? Your cousin J.D. is alive and well! He had left Shiloh that same mornin' on his way to Oklahoma to fetch back that Sheriff Ring on account of he says he knows where that escaped convict is, and he wanted to collect the reward himself. So off he goes. But then he took sick—got himself a case of pneumony that almost killed him. He's been abed in Siloam Springs near two months. Outta his mind with fever. When he come round, he found he lost all his money and his farm in the stock market. Then he heard his beloved Maybelle done got killed by a twister. Well, he figgered he needed that reward more than anythin', so he went on ahead to Oklahoma, where he and Sheriff Ring done give me a call."

Silence from Birch, then, "All right. Now what's the good news?"

"Why, boy, that *is* the good news. Your cousin J.D.'s alive and well. Now, if ever there was a man who needed his soul saved before he met his Maker, it is your cousin J.D. So the good news is that he ain't in hell yet—though Lord knows he deserves to be." As an upstanding member of the Methodist church, Sheriff Potts was doing his Christian duty and putting the best face on J.D.'s survival.

Somehow Birch was not cheered. "Well then, Sheriff, what's the bad news?"

"Bad news is that . . . J.D. had that reward on his mind. And he has convinced Sheriff Ring over there in Oklahoma that Jefferson Canfield is the fugitive in question. They got a warrant for his arrest. I'm supposed to bring him in and keep him right down here in the jail until they get here for that Sheriff Ring to see that Jefferson ain't that Cannibal feller at all."

A collective moan arose from the crowd. Most everyone knew that J.D. had always been mean and no good and greedy, but this took the cake. Didn't he know that Jefferson Canfield was a family man? Two babies and a wife and a good worker for Birch Tucker for these ten years?

How could J.D. sink so low? He should have stayed dead—that's all. Things were just fine around here without his rotgut hooch and his schemin' and his yapping dogs. . . .

Birch knew the folks of Shiloh were thinking all these things, even if they were not spoken aloud. "Well now, Sheriff, you know the truth of who Jefferson is. You can't mean he has to go to jail and just wait until that Oklahoma lawman comes along and says J.D. picked the wrong man." Birch did not mention the fact that Jeff was gone.

"Naw. It don't matter to me. I just wanted to let y'all know Jefferson shouldn't go nowheres. The sheriff done come down with whoopin' cough now, but we'll get this all straightened out by and by. Soon as that loony J.D. gets the Oklahoma law back here, we'll get it all straight. If we're lucky, they'll haul ol' J.D. off to the nuthouse, and we'll be shed of him once and for all."

"Amen to that," said Grandma Amos with a shake of her head.

"Think positive, Birch," the sheriff urged.

"I'll try." But Birch had a horrible sinking feeling.

"Just doin' my sworn duty, y'all. Now don't hold it agin me."

Nobody at the store held the problem against Sheriff Potts. Most held it against J.D. for surviving. Of course, the woods were full of riffraff who would rejoice at the news that their favorite bootlegger was not dead. After all, word was out that J.D. had died owing everybody money because he had gambled it away in the stock market. Wasn't it a blessing that he was coming back to Shiloh?

✴ ✴ ✴

With news that J.D. was alive and well, Birch and Trudy concluded that it was wise for Lily and the babies to come back up to the house to stay until Jefferson got home. And after that? It was plain that Jefferson could not remain in Shiloh.

Birch and Trudy did not say this to Lily. Trudy continued to speak to her about the future and their little house and the fact that babies have a way of growing up fast. But all the while, Birch and Trudy were thinking that Jefferson would have to pack up those dreams and turn and run again as fast as he could go. If he found Willa-Mae and Hock, perhaps he and Lily could flee to some distant safety with them.

In the meantime, Birch nailed a note on the door of the cabin telling Jefferson that his wife and family were once again at the Tucker farm. Each day Birch looked for the arrival of his cousin J.D. and the Oklahoma lawman, and he prayed that Jefferson would arrive first and then leave Shiloh forever before J.D. came back.

✳ ✳ ✳

Pine Bluff was a sleepy little town on the Arkansas River. A cluster of red-brick storefronts and white frame houses, it looked much like Hartford at first glance, only larger. A fine Baptist church and a Methodist church sat substantially near the center of town. Main Street presented a movie theatre, a barbershop, a café, a feed store, a dry-goods store, a cotton gin, a mill for grinding grain, a bank, and a boxy-looking building that had once been a hotel but had declined into a rundown rooming house. There were Model T Fords about, but Pine Bluff still provided hitching posts in front of every store. The curbs were built up high in case too much rain brought the river over its banks to flood the streets.

The surrounding countryside showed the remnants of a few grand plantations, but poor rock farms predominated—lean livestock in pastures owned by lean and sunburned men. How far the proud South had fallen!

Forty miles downriver from Little Rock, Pine Bluff had once been a center of commerce. Its docks had swarmed with slaves rolling bales of cotton onto boats bound for the Mississippi and beyond. Jefferson had heard that his great-granddaddy, bound in leg-irons, had been unloaded from a riverboat on this very dock.

Riding into town, Jefferson looked at the wide, muddy water flowing by and imagined he was seeing it through the eyes of his ancestor. It wasn't that hard to imagine. Jefferson, too, had learned something about the weight of leg-irons in his lifetime. He knew what it felt like to look over the land and not be free to walk across it without permission. A lot had changed in Pine Bluff, to be sure, but the old feelings were much the same.

Jefferson tied his mule up in front of the dry-goods store at the edge of town and looked for some likely passerby to whom he might show the slip of paper with the address of Delpha Jean Jones. He dared not speak to the white woman just coming from the store. She looked at him fearfully and pulled her young son around behind her as she hurried away. Best wait for a man . . . hope that a man of his own color would happen by.

He spotted an old black man shuffling toward him like a living skeleton. His coat was flimsy in spite of the cold air blowing up from the river. He wore a shapeless hat and held a cold corncob pipe, the bowl turned down, between his lips.

Jefferson brightened and raised his hand in greeting. "How-do."

"How-do," said the old man as if he knew Jefferson, or as if he thought he ought to know him. "You be—you that Johnson man, ain't you? What you doin' here in town? Don't you know you ain't allowed in town these days?"

"No sir. I come a far piece. I'm lookin' for kinfolk." Jefferson fumbled in his pocket and pulled out the paper. He held it out hopefully to the old man, who squinted at it and shook his head.

"I got no schoolin'. No, I do not. But I can quote the Good Book chapter an' verse." He tapped his temple. "I learnt it by my boy. He read it t'me ever' day 'til he go off t'that old war. Long time ago." The old man appeared to be in a mood to reminisce.

"Like I say," Jefferson interrupted gently, "I be lookin' for these folk. Mebbe y'all know 'em round these parts. Her name . . . Delpha Jean Jones. She got a farm—I reckon it's a farm—right near Pine Bluff, so I'm told."

The little man lowered his voice. "None of our kind got no farms no more. Run us off, man. Hard times, you know. White folks don't leave no room for niggers when there be hard times."

"But . . . I know they be here. Delpha Jean Jones is her name."

"White folks lets me stay round, though, 'cause I live on down back behind the *ho*-tel. Used t'groom the fine horses. Polish the saddles. Shine the boots of the rich folks. So . . . I been there so long they lets me stay on. But no coloreds allowed on the streets in Pine Bluff no more. There's typhus on out t'the shantytown. Nigger Mountain they calls it, an' now there be typhus there. White folks don't take kindly t'no strange coloreds here walkin' round town. Typhus. Yessir. That's what the doctor say killin' off ever'one out on Nigger Mountain. He say ever' black man but me ought t'stay on out of town else the white folks get it, too."

He squinted his filmy eyes at Jefferson. "So how come you here?"

"I come lookin' for. . . ." It was no use. The old man did not seem to understand anything except the jumbled thoughts running through his own head. Now Jefferson noticed that white folks were indeed looking at him with angry stares.

Across the street, a farmer in his wagon shouted, "Get on outta town, nigger! Ain'tcha seen the signs? Y'all got typhus, an' we white folks don't want it!"

"That's right," called a woman from the front step of the bank. "Get on back where you b'long!"

Jefferson looked down as if he were stupid and ashamed of his stupidity. To meet white resentment with an open stare or a word of explanation would be considered definance. And black men had been lynched for less reason than a typhus epidemic and straying into a town off limits to blacks!

"Yes'm," he called. "I'm goin'."

"Then *git!*" retorted the farmer.

"Which way to the shantytown, ol' man?" he whispered as he mounted the mule.

"Nigger Mountain be yonder." The old man extended his bony arm, and the breeze flapped through his tattered coat.

"*Git* out outta here, *nigger!*" The barber stepped from his barbershop as Jefferson rode past at a stiff trot.

The cry was repeated a dozen times before he reached the outskirts of the town and the dirt road that led to the low hill of shanties called Nigger Mountain.

Black smoke from a large fire rose to blend into the gray winter sky above the shantytown. Jefferson saw the smoke long before he reached Nigger Mountain. To the side of the rutted dirt lane was a graveyard surrounded by a dilapidated picket fence. Mounds of freshly turned earth and crooked wooden crosses bore silent witness to the devastation that waited up the road.

Jefferson raised his head and sniffed the smoke, which only partially covered the stink of death. He remembered this smell from the battlefields of France, where the rancid scent had oozed from graves dug too shallow and in haste. He shuddered and halted old Bob beside the cemetery. He fought the urge to turn back as he tried to count the new graves and the crosses. There were too many to number easily.

Typhus! The very word made Jefferson's skin and scalp prickle and his stomach churn. Carried by lice, the germ had infected and killed thousands of soliders and prisoners on both sides of the line in the war. He had seen an epidemic wipe out a thousand men in one week along the western front. The sickness had begun with an intolerable headache, a skin rash, and then a high fever, and almost always it had ended in death. Jefferson had carried the memory of that epidemic in his nightmares like a vision of the Grim Reaper stretching his scythe to harvest young men without warning. Typhus was one of a hundred ways death had swept away young soldiers in the trenches. But somehow Jefferson had not considered the disease as something that could reach out and kill common folk or fill a small country graveyard until every inch of ground was churned up.

"Oh, Lord!" He bit his lip and looked at the smoke. He thought of Lily and the babies and then of the tiny lice that leaped unseen from the body of one human to another to spread the sickness. Did he dare ride into a place infected with lice and typhus? Could he carry even one of the tiny white demons away in the folds of his clothes? Such a small thing, yet it could kill a man as big as him. It could kill Lily and the babies. It could spread through Shiloh.

"You know this ain't no place I want t'be, Lord. Death an dyin' all round this place. But if I'm gonna find my mama, I got t'ride on up that road. Got t'find Delpha Jean if she be there among the livin'."

He closed his eyes in an attempt to shut out the vision of graves in France that had become somehow superimposed over this place and this moment. There was war here, too, just like on the battlefields of France. Death was all around, all the way up the road to the place called Nigger Mountain.

But maybe news of Willa-Mae and Hock was there. For ten years he had longed for word about his folks. Such longing could not be stopped by fear of death—not if there was hope of finding his family!

Jefferson exhaled loudly and clucked the mule on. He felt his hands trembling as he held the reins, and he muttered the same psalm he had prayed on the battlefield when artillery and mustard-gas bombs had whistled over his head and exploded behind him: *"Though I walk through the valley of the shadow of death, I will fear no evil. . . ."*

He said the words, but the fear did not leave him. After all, he had so much to live for now! Lily. William. Little Willa-Mae.

The smoke grew stronger, burning his eyes. In the distance he could see that the hillside was crowded with shacks and shanties built of packing boxes, discarded lumber, and tin. Small plots of ground displayed the remnants of gardens. Chicken coops and a few stock pens were visible.

There were dwellings for several hundred people, yet only a handful of ragged men could be seen standing in the road, their hands stretched out to the warmth of a smudge-pot fire. Jefferson could not tell the ages of these men. Each was as thin and gaunt as the other. Those who stood on the far side of the fire appeared to be standing in the center of the flames.

All looked up at the clop of the mule's hooves against the road. Their eyes were weary and haunted. Skin like dark parchment stretched across the bones of their faces as they stared sullenly and considered the full face and healthy features of their visitor.

Twenty yards from the fire, Jefferson pulled Old Bob up. The mule seemed to sense that something was wrong. He took a step or two back and nodded his great head as if to say he did not want to enter the shantytown either.

"How-do," Jeff called, trying to sound unafraid. The men exchanged glances and waited for someone among them to reply. No one spoke.

"How-do, I say," Jefferson tried again. His voice quavered against his will, betraying his fear.

They knew about fear. A man whose face was hidden in the shadow of his hat spoke in a raspy voice. "What you want here, man? Ain't nobody tell you there be death here? Typhus."

"Yes. They tell me."

"Then what you want? You lookin' t'die, man? Don't take nothin' t'die of the typhus."

"I be lookin' for somebody. Mebbe y'all can help me. I need somebody who can help me find my kinfolk."

"Man, if'n you got kinfolk here, they most likely dead. Else they be sick. You best be gittin' on," said another of the group.

"Her name's Delpha Jean." Jefferson rose in the stirrups. Sweat beaded his brow in spite of the cold. "I come a long way to find her. Name's Delpha Jean Jones."

Now all heads turned to look at one man. His image was distorted as he stood behind waves of rising heat. He did not raise his gaze from the fire. He rubbed his hands as though he had not heard Jefferson's request.

"Delpha Jean Jones be the name of the woman I be lookin' for, y'all. Do y'all know somebody here'bouts by that name?" Jefferson's words were plaintive.

Now the man shimmered in the heat. He raised his eyes and glared resentfully at Jefferson. "You done come too late," he croaked. "Delpha Jean be dead. Buried her two weeks ago—her an' two of the chillens aside of her."

Jefferson moaned and lowered his head in grief at the news. But he told himself that perhaps he was no farther from finding his folks than he had been two weeks ago. Maybe Delpha Jean had not known where Willa-Mae and Hock were. Maybe this had only been false hope, anyway.

"How you know my Delpha Jean?" asked the man in reply to the stricken Jefferson.

"She was . . . I was . . . I growed up next to her in Mount Pisgah, mister. I knowed her since I were a young'un. Her and my mama—well, they was real close. I come hopin' Delpha Jean could tell me where my mama be."

Silence. The flames crackled like mocking laughter. "Come a long way, did y'?"

"From near Forth Smith."

"What the name of your mama, man?" Now the figure stepped away from the barrel. He inclined his head with curiosity.

"Willa-Mae." Jefferson fought the disappointment that threatened to erupt in weeping. "Willa-Mae Canfield."

"An' you be?"

"Jefferson Canfield."

"Why fo' you don't know where your own mama be?" The man asked as he turned back to the fire.

"I been gone," Jefferson managed. "Long time. Locked up in the white man's jail. Now I come back . . . t'nobody."

There was a long pause. The grim congregation knew a thousand stories like Jefferson's.

"When my Delpha Jean passed, we done burn the house where we live. Burn it t'the ground like the white doctor say t'do. Burn up ever'thing in the house. Nothin' left now 'cept ashes." The man narrowed his eyes and squinted as if he saw the fire and the smoke and the ashes of his life rising even now. "We burn up all Delpha Jean's letters. All them sweet letters she get from folks she love. Ol' folks she knowed back in Pisgah b'fore Billy got lynched."

He sighed. "The fire take all the letters. Ever'thing. Understand? The letters your mama write—they all gone with the rest. There ain't nothin' left. You be too late."

"My mama!" Jeff cried. "Willa-Mae Canfield! She wrote Delpha Jean! She wrote letters?"

"They all gone. Nothin' left, I'm tellin' you." Now the man began to weep silently. He wiped his cheeks with the back of his hand and mumbled about smoke in his eyes.

"Where my mama write from?" Jefferson lunged out of the saddle and started forward. "Where those letters mailed from? Y'all got t'help me! Ten year I been wond'rin'!"

"Don't come near, man! Don't you know? GET BACK!"

Jefferson stopped midstride. His big hands fell limply to his sides. "Please. I is beggin'. Try to recollect somethin'."

"All them letters. All them addresses . . . burned up."

Jefferson dropped to his knees in the dirt. He raised his fists in rage and frustration. "Lord! Do not forget me! Do not send me away empty agin! Hope! Lord? I need . . ." His cry fell away as he bowed in the dust. "I need some hope."

No answer came from heaven. There was only the sound of the fire and the sound of the wind.

Then there was a stirring among the men who warmed their hands and waited to die.

"He come this long way."

"Come here even with the typhus."

"Sometime it easier t'die than not know nothin'."

"Can't you remember, Ismel?"

"Ismel? In the name of God, man . . . can't you recollect where them letters come from?"

Then the voice of Delpha Jean's widower quickened as if some forgotten pleasure had awakened in him. "Lord, Lord! They was . . .

somewheres . . . up north. She a cook. He work in a tire fact'ry. Ohio. That's it! Way up north. Akron, Ohio, it were!"

Jefferson raised his head. There were smiles on the faces of these living dead men. They had touched life outside. They had glimpsed hope. They could send Jefferson from this place, and if they lived, they would remember this moment and wonder if he ever tracked his folks down in Akron, Ohio.

✶ ✶ ✶

"Akron, Ohio." Birch stretched his hands to the warmth of the cookstove as he spoke in quiet tones so he would not awaken the sleeping boys in the parlor. His voice echoed as he spoke, the way voices did late at night when a house was not supposed to be awake and words were not meant to be spoken.

"That's all the message Jeff left with Grandma Amos when he called down to the store. Wish I could have had a word with him about J.D. before he comes home. He said to tell Lily he'd be back directly and that his folks are somewhere in Akron, Ohio. No address for Willa-Mae and Hock, he told her. But they are somewhere in Akron."

"Ain' it somethin', Miz True?" whispered Lily. "I been tryin' t'remember where that place was on that ol' map we had in the schoolhouse where I went once when I was a chil'." She frowned. "I couldn't quite picture it. Jus' the big shape of the whole, big United States, but I couldn't see that Ohio in my mind at all. You know where this place is?"

Trudy hurried to retrieve a large, thick book that lay beneath the Sears catalogue on the bottom bookshelf in the parlor. *Atlas of North America.* The boys snorted and snored their protest at the disturbance.

"This should set us straight." Trudy laid the *Atlas of North America* on the kitchen table and opened it to the United States map. As Lily crowded in, Trudy drove her finger firmly onto the page as if to pin down a bug. "There it is . . . Akron, Ohio."

Lily beamed. "Jefferson's mama be right in *there*—what you think 'bout that?"

In reply, Trudy traced the Ohio River into the Mississippi and continued down until the slim blue thread on the page merged with the Arkansas River in the south. "Just think," she whispered. "Jefferson could stand on the banks of the Arkansas River down here and reach out and touch the same water that flowed by his family up north."

"Mebbee he could drink the same raindrops they hear fallin' on the roof a their place." Lily closed her eyes and breathed a sigh of relief. "I used t'wonder about it, when Jeff tol' me 'bout his folks. When I seen the lightnin' in the sky, I used t'wonder if that same light was a'touchin' the faces of Jeff's mama and daddy. Yes'm. I used t'wonder such things. An' now I knows the truth. I done look at a map an' know a man could just catch a steamer north on a river, an' with a coupla zigs and zags he end up in the right place, all right. Akron, Ohio. Mebbe we can get on up there when Jeff get back. Is it far from where we is, Miz True?" Lily scanned the map. "It look small. It don't look like it very far at all from where we is."

"It's the end of the world from here," Birch answered. He sat down and gazed solemnly at the book. "Akron, Ohio. Funny. All this time Jefferson has been wondering about his mama and papa. Where they were. If they were still livin'." He gave a laugh. "I know a little about Akron. It's a big ol' place. They make tires for automobiles."

Lily studied the map. "Funny how when you look at a little dot on a paper you can't see all the folks what live inside that dot. Ain't it, Miz True? Big or small, all these here dots look the same t'me. Thousand little dots an' millions of people in the worl'! All them folks has their own troubles. An' the Lord keep track of all of 'em. My, my, He is a *big* God, ain't He? It's somethin', ain't it? I mean, all this time Jeff's folks been alive an' well in that little dot. Only he didn't know which dot they was in. Now Jeff knows where they is, an'—"

Birch repeated a warning that she should not get her hopes too high. "Akron is a big place, Lily. Great big." At this, Birch raised his head. "But at least he has narrowed it down to one dot on the map."

Lily nodded solemnly. "We might be close, but we still ain't won no cigar. Close enough is gonna be when Jeff's mama sit right across from me in a room like your kitchen, Miz True. Close enough t'hold my babies an' sup a cup'a tea with my Jefferson. Now, how we gonna make that happen?" Lily scowled the at lines and dots and dark green patches that were mountains. "They's all c'nected up," she whispered. "All them lines an' dots. Roads an' rivers an' things. . . . Now, when folks lives down there in one of them dots, folks don't see how their dot is hooked up t'all the other ones. But lookit here. Ever'thing is c'nected up, ain't it? See, Miz Trudy?"

"What are you saying, Lily?"

"Well, Jeff an' his folks is jus' like them dots. Hooked up some way that mebbe we can't even see. But the Lord be up here. See? He be a'lookin' down t'the map, an' He see how we is hooked t'one another. He see how one skinny little thread of a line is a'gonna get us where we needs t'be. Well! Don't y'all hear me? Jus' 'cause we can't see God's map don't mean we's are lost! He know right where Jefferson's mama be. He know where Jeff be. An' He know how t'get him from here t'—"

"Akron!" Trudy exclaimed suddenly. "Birch was in the war with a man who lives in Akron. He lost his leg in France." This had nothing to do with anything, but Trudy's mind was just spinning out every bit of information it held about Akron. "His name is Ellis Warne. He's a doctor. We get a Christmas card every year, an occasional note. They lost their baby boy last spring. . . . He was little Joe's age. Sad. I haven't even written to tell them we've moved to Shiloh." She frowned. "I suppose I should write them."

Her outburst silenced Lily, who had been thinking deep thoughts about the all-knowing, all-seeing, all-powerful One who kept the map and knew the names of all the people in the little dots.

"Yes'm, Miz True," she murmured distractedly, "y'all won' get no Christmas card if you neglect to tell them folks where you is. . . ." Her focus drifted a bit. "Hmmm. I know I was a'tryin' t'say somethin' 'portant 'bout the Lord."

"You were close, Lily. But it's so late. None of us are thinking straight." Trudy stared hard at Akron, Ohio. "I should write the Warnes," she muttered as she closed the atlas.

CHAPTER THIRTY-TWO

Smiley's Luck Changes

The shopworn red sign above the telephone in Winters' Drugstore hung right at Max's eye level. In faded gold letters, it asked, Do You Have Tired Blood? Since the advertisement appeared to have been already hanging on the wall when the phone booth was built around it, Max was not sure if the promised cure, Livingston's Liver Tonic, was still being made or not.

"What's that, Operator? You'll have to speak louder, please. Yes, I'll wait."

It seemed to Max that his shouts might reach New York City without the aid of the wires. They certainly reached the ears of the ready-made audience standing around the store. Brother Williams, who had been arguing with Dr. Brown about the merits of Ferrabie's Fireball Liniment, stopped to listen, as did the doctor and Mr. Winters. When Max glanced over his shoulder at the trio, he was trying to suggest that they go on about their business. There was no need for such complete silence. They nodded back pleasantly but remained absolutely quiet.

"Harry?" Max bellowed into the phone. "Yes, I know I sound like I am at the end of the earth. That's because . . ." Max looked again at the three interested onlookers and left the rest of his comment unspoken. "Have you gotten any replies to my letters?"

There was a long pause and a rustling over the phone as Harry Beadle fumbled through a stack of mail addressed to Max.

The little audience in the drugstore discussed tomorrow's weather in hushed tones as they waited for the conversation to resume. The instant Max began to speak again, the weather ceased to be important and the group fell silent.

"Wait a minute; I want to write down the editors' names." Max patted his pockets in a futile search for a pen. There was a slate hanging next to the phone and a piece of chalk attached to it with a piece of twine. "Okay, go ahead."

Brother Williams wandered over behind the phone booth. He examined with seeming interest a display of buttons and one of artificial flowers that just happened to be in a direct line with the chalkboard.

The chalk squeaked a protest as Max scratched it across the tablet. "London *Times*," he repeated to Harry Beadle as he wrote the name. "Wilfrid Hyde-Smith. Got it."

Dr. Brown looked at Mr. Winters and raised his eyebrows. This was bad news. Max heading for London? London was on the other side of the world from Mary. Could this mean that the only man Mary Brown had shown an interest in had given up on her?

"Next? *Palestine Post*. That's Terrence Spencer, right?"

This likewise brought grim looks from the observers. Doc Brown's mouth turned down as he furrowed his brow and shook his head in resignation, obviously seeing his spinster daughter's last chance at matrimony slipping away.

"And . . . say it again, Harry. *Shanghai Courier*. Sam Underwood."

At the mention of Shanghai, Brother Williams turned and gave Dr. Brown a broad wink as if to say that he knew Shanghai was in China . . . and wasn't China where Mary was going to the medical mission? China was a mighty big place. But if Max Meyer took a job with a paper in China, at least the two would be on the same continent! This scenario could be discussed at length in the barbershop later, with all sorts of plot twists and romantic endings added to the speculation. Yes, this was much more hopeful than Max in London or the Middle East!

"Thanks, Harry. You're the best. No, no trouble here at all. I'll be in touch." Max hung up the phone and turned around to the concerted inspection of his listening audience. "Newspaper work," he explained lamely.

"I hear China is the new land of opportunity," offered Brother Williams helpfully. "Ain't that right, Doc?"

Dr. Brown cleared his throat. "I'll wager Mister Meyer doesn't want to discuss his private business, do you, Max?"

Max just grinned and shook his head. "Probably nothing will come of any of these. I'll probably end up writing obituaries in Boise, Idaho."

But Idaho was never mentioned as a possibility that night when the discussions about Max, Mary, and far-off places swirled through all the dining rooms of Hartford, Arkansas.

A stack of unaddressed Christmas cards was heaped on the table. Becky considered the chore before her. How could she write cheerful notes to everyone on her list when gloom was the prevailing mood of her life and marriage?

Ellis had barely spoken a word to her in days. Distracted and depressed, he retired to the privacy of his office at every opportunity and emerged only at mealtime. When his brother John called, Ellis had sounded right enough. He could muster up some of his old optimism on occasion, but it was all a charade and Becky knew it. She had tried to jolly him out of the darkness and had been met with anger. She had made an attempt at sympathy to draw him out, and he had simply gotten up from his chair and said he did not feel like talking. She had become angry, and he had glared at her so coldly that she ran weeping to her own room and slammed the door.

She rested her head wearily in her hand and stared resentfully at the lovely Christmas scene on the cards—baby Jesus smiling happily in the arms of His mother. The image sent a twinge through Becky's heart. Why had she chosen these cards? Out of every picture in the stationery store, why had she purchased the one with the baby in His mother's arms?

This would be Becky's first Christmas without her baby. Had Becky chosen this picture to remind herself that her arms would not hold her son this year?

"Joy to the world," she muttered, shoving the stack away. There was plenty of time yet to think of something to write before she had to mail the cards. Maybe things would change for Ellis. Maybe he would look at her the way he used to. Maybe, somehow, they would find a shred of joy again.

She was unaware of the passage of time as she sat, unmoving, at the table. The clock chimed the noon hour, and the neighborhood dogs started their usual ruckus as the mailman made his rounds. Letters whisked through the mail slot in the door.

The sounds of normality jerked Becky back to the present. Had she really passed two hours doing nothing? She gathered up the scattered mail and told herself that worrying was not doing anything. She had worked as hard as a ditchdigger this morning, unearthing every fear and every worry she had felt since little Howie had died. *A real archaeologist,* she chided herself.

She checked the mail for anything that might bring good news. There was a letter from her brother, Howard, who was off in Palestine digging up artifacts of more significance than her own. Hoping for good news from him, she tore open the envelope, which bore a postmark already six weeks old. Far from having good news to report, Howard wrote about the Arab Mufti and the riots that had just taken place in Jerusalem. People he knew had been killed.

It was a terrible time for the Holy Land, he wrote. There would be no peace on Earth this Christmas within the boundaries of the British Mandate. He asked Becky to appeal to the church for old clothes to send to the poor of the Holy City. Ragged Arab vagabonds were flooding in, and they had nothing to eat, nothing to wear. He had ended his letter with *Hope you are all well in good old Akron!*

Becky tossed his letter across the table. "Thank you, Howard," she replied aloud. "Things are not well in good old Akron. Haven't you heard? If there are any clothing drives this year, the stuff will be given to the people in the streets right here in town. And as for jolly old us . . ."

Three bills among the stack seemed more appropriate to her mood. She did not open them. Why rob Ellis of the pleasure of opening them himself? He seemed to have no greater pleasure these days than glancing at the electric bill, growing pale, then walking around the house switching off lights and railing about Becky's carelessness with electricity.

But here was something that might really cheer her up. Becky recognized the neat handwriting of Trudy Tucker immediately. Although she had never met Trudy face-to-face, the two women had managed through years of correspondence to keep their husbands in touch. Ellis was notoriously bad at letter writing. Trudy claimed that Birch was even worse. And so Becky and Trudy sent the news through the post about twice a year. How the babies were growing. What Birch and Ellis were up to. Plans for this project or that.

This letter carried a different postmark than the last: *Shiloh, Arkansas.* So the Tuckers had moved back to Birch's birthplace. The envelope itself was full of news. Really good news, too, from the look of it.

Becky opened the letter and scanned its contents. Yes. The Tuckers were back in Shiloh. A tornado had touched down, destroying the barn, but all were well. Shiloh was a tiny place, but because the rail line had been destroyed, it now had airmail service. It might be wise to write on onionskin paper then.

Trudy's cousin Max, who had saved Ellis's life in the late war, had come to visit with his son. Did Max have a son? This was news to Becky, who thought she knew most everything about Max Meyer. Ah, well. Another surprise.

Max had been injured in an altercation but was going to recover. And last of all, there was a fellow by the name of Jefferson Canfield, a black man, who worked for Birch and Trudy. He had somehow lost touch with his family, but had last heard that the Canfields could be in Akron. Had Ellis and Becky heard of these folks? It was such a small world, after all. One never knew, did one?

Ellis came home early from his rounds. He gave the letters from Howard in Palestine and Trudy in Shiloh no more than a cursory glance.

Like Becky, he had not heard of the Canfield family. He remarked, without a trace of humor, that it was interesting to imagine a man like Max Meyer in a place like Shiloh, Arkansas. That, knowing Max, there were no doubt a lot more sons than he was telling. That probably Max's fight had been over a woman.

Then Ellis had turned his attention to the bills, forbidding Becky to any longer leave the light on in the kitchen when she was in the front room.

☆ ☆ ☆

It was late morning when Boots called from the front door, "Pop? Do you know what kind of auto has six lights on its front and lots of chrome? Do brand-new cars ever get busted?"

"Hmmm?" murmured Ellis from behind his newspaper. "What?" Ellis had strapped on his wooden leg, but he was still wearing his bathrobe and pajamas.

Becky instructed, "Let Pop read his paper."

"Okay, Mom," Boots agreed. "I'm out on the front porch playing jacks. I made it all the way to fivesies."

The door slammed, and quiet returned to the Warne home. The distant *bump, scrape, bump* of Boots's game floated into the parlor. Becky went into the kitchen to clean up the breakfast things.

Ellis was buried in the *Akron Beacon Journal*, but his thoughts were far away. He had grabbed up the paper in order to avoid getting into another angry conversation with Becky. Hiding behind the front page, he was thinking about Jack Titan and Johnny Daugherty and how caught in the middle of everything he was.

Ellis had considered it all and resolved nothing when Boots returned. "Pop," she said again, "I think that car is busted or something. It's sitting there and sitting there. The man doesn't move or get out. Do you think he's sick or something?"

"A car? What man? Boots, what are you talking about?"

"Pop," the child replied with exasperation, "weren't you listening?

The man in the shiny brown car across the street is just sitting there. Staring at me. What do you—?"

Ellis grabbed Boots around the middle and carried her toward the kitchen. "Becky! Keep Boots with you!" He stuffed the surprised child into a kitchen chair and clumped angrily toward the front door, muttering, "Jack Daugherty! He promised he'd put a stop to this! I've had enough!"

Ellis pulled aside the pale yellow curtain over the window in the front door and peered around it. Sure enough, a brand-new Stutz Blackhawk was parked directly across the street. While Ellis studied the car, the man in the driver's seat studied the Warne house. The watcher's features were not visible because of the shadows in the car and the hat brim pulled low across his face, but from the tilt of his head it was clear that his attention was focused on Ellis and Becky's front door.

"Probably thinks he can scare us just by sitting there," Ellis grumbled. "I think it's time I sent them a message in return!"

Ellis flung open the front door and stomped down the steps. His wooden leg made a dull thumping noise on the sidewalk, and his bathrobe billowed around him. "Hey, you!" he shouted. "What do you think you're doing?"

From inside the car, pale eyes blinked with astonishment at the speed of Ellis's attack. Ellis saw a shade flutter in Miss Ruptke's front-room window and knew he had at least one onlooker.

The driver fumbled with the ignition. It was clear that he was already trying to retreat, but Ellis was not ready to let him go so easily.

"Not so fast, pal." Ellis reached through the open window and grabbed one of the man's wrists. "I need you to carry a word from me to your bully-boy friends!"

The man's sharp features registered alarm, and the hand that had been struggling with the ignition reached across his chest and inside his jacket. As the coat swung open, Ellis caught a brief glimpse of the butt of a revolver protruding from a shoulder holster.

Instinctively, Ellis thrust both his hands upward toward the man's neck. The line of a purplish scar disappeared under Ellis's grip as his fingers dug into the man's throat.

The driver's own hands tried to pry loose the chokehold that was pressing him toward unconsciousness. "Wait . . . Warne," he managed to choke out. "Just trying ta find Max. . . ."

Ellis stopped abruptly and released his grip, but the man had already passed out. "Well, now I've done it," Ellis fretted, looking toward the space between Miss Ruptke's shade and her window.

The man in the car groaned, and his head revolved drunkenly. Ellis prudently removed the pistol from the shoulder holster and tossed it into the backseat of the car before slapping the fellow on both cheeks. After all, this guy might wake up mad!

The pale eyes blinked in the light as they opened, and there was a momentary struggle before they focused on Ellis's face. "Is that da usual form of greeting in this burg?"

"I . . . I'm sorry," Ellis stammered. "I thought you were someone else."

"I would not wish ta be that party, whoever he is."

Ellis apologized again. "Perhaps you should come in and let me see that you're all right. I am a doctor, but then you knew that already, didn't you?"

"No." The man sat up slowly. "I am all right now. The reason I did not come ta da door is because I am seeking for someone, see, but I did not wish ta disturb youse if youse was not da person who could help."

"You mentioned Max? Would that be Max Meyer?"

"Da very same. I need ta find him, see, ta pay him some money I owe him, but now he has vanished to nobody knows where."

"You're in luck," Ellis said, grateful to be able to make up for his terrible error. "We just heard from Max's cousin, Trudy Tucker. The Tuckers are living in a little place called Shiloh, Arkansas. The letter mentioned that Max was there for a visit."

"This is most certainly interesting information, and I will not trouble youse no further." The man started the car and shifted the gears. He raised his hand in a gesture of peace, then rubbed his fingers gingerly over the scar on his throat.

Ellis stood in the middle of Florida Avenue and watched as the Stutz disappeared around the corner. "Why didn't he just phone me?" he murmured. "And why was he carrying a gun?" Ellis shook his head at the thought. Nothing where Max Meyer was concerned should surprise him. This additional mystery was altogether too much to add to his other concerns.

Shaking his head once more, he straightened his shoulders and his bathrobe and attempted to rearrange his dignity before climbing the front steps.

✴ ✴ ✴

Smiley rubbed his neck again and thought about the new information he had received. Meyer at last, and no doubt the kid, too! No bootleg information this, about who might have seen Max Meyer or who could possibly, maybe, once have known where Meyer was hiding. No, this was the genuine article. As recently as—Smiley counted the mail time on his fingers—three days ago, Meyer had been in some place called Shiloh, Arkansas.

Smiley could hardly wait to call Boss Quinn and report success at last. He pulled the Stutz up next to a phone booth and hurried inside. He had already lifted the receiver and was about to ask for long distance when a thought struck him and he replaced the phone. What if this information turned out to be wrong after all?

The grin faded and was replaced by a worried frown. Smiley's last conversation with Quinn had left no doubt that this time the boss expected results, not just another page of travelogue. Besides, Smiley was not clear on any geography west of Philadelphia, but he was fairly sure that Arkansas was someplace close to Oklahoma. He had better not tell Boss Quinn that he had been close to Meyer in Tulsa and then gone all the way to Ohio! At least he had better not mention it until the problem of Max Meyer was settled for good. Then it wouldn't matter.

Smiley wriggled his shoulders and readjusted the revolver in the holster. Picking up the phone again, Smiley asked for the Akron train station. "I wish to inquire," he said in good humor, "how one would come to a place called Shiloh . . . Shiloh, Arkansas."

CHAPTER THIRTY-THREE

He That Seeketh...

The selection of toys that Max Meyer was inspecting at Winters' Drugstore was neither large nor diverse. Max quickly rejected jacks and marbles. Briefly he considered a slingshot. Then a mental image of Trudy glaring at a broken window persuaded him to discard that thought as well.

The question of how to choose a Christmas present for his nine-year-old son loomed large in Max's mind. He had never before had to select a present for a child of any age. Even gifts to the children of relatives and friends had taken the form of monetary remembrances. And Max had never claimed to have real insight into the mind of a young boy, especially one living in the country. After all, growing up on Orchard Street as he had, his games had been stickball in the gutter and eluding the pursuit of the fruit-cart merchants.

So this gift, his first ever Christmas present to his own son, took on a special significance.

There was another reason why this gift felt so important, why it had to be so right. Max had made up his mind that he could not stay in Shiloh. He fit in about as well here as corn bread and pickled pigs' feet would have fit at a society matron's party in Manhattan. As soon as Max decided which response to pursue from his swarm of résumés, he would be off to some new corner of the world. But David would not be coming with him. Globe-trotting was no way of life for a nine-year-old.

Max had seen how well David was settling in to life in Arkansas and how good it was for the boy to have a loving family like Birch and Trudy and the cousins. He was convinced David would be better off in Shiloh. So this Christmas present had to be more than just a fumbling attempt on the part of an untrained father. This Christmas present would be his way of saying good-bye.

He was studying a Parcheesi set without enthusiasm when he spotted a kit to build a model plane from balsa wood. *It Really Flies!* the package promised. The top of the box pictured a Curtiss JN-4, a "Jenny," with its rakishly uptilted wings and its bicycle-tire landing gear. The illustration showed the aircraft decorated as it had appeared in the Great War: wings with white stars on blue circles and a red-white-and-blue-striped tail.

The model was a good idea, but it brought an even better thought to mind. Nothing had excited David more than the flight from Forth Smith. No subject came up more often and no figure loomed larger in David's imagination than flying Wildman McKinney style.

Max located Wildman McKinney's plane at the edge of town. The pilot was filling the fuel tanks by cranking a hand pump. He looked up at Max's approach. "Hey, city boy," he called, "you had enough of country life yet?"

Max agreed that it was almost time to leave.

"So when do you want to go?"

"The day after Christmas," Max said.

Wildman studied Max's somber face and guessed the cause of its seriousness. "Only one passenger this trip, right?"

"You got it," Max said. "Listen, there's something else. It's about my boy's Christmas present. He's pretty taken with the idea of being a pilot himself someday, and . . . well, I was wondering if I could buy your flying gear off of you. You know—helmet, goggles, scarf—the works."

Wildman retrieved the articles from the rear cockpit of the three-seater plane. "You mean this stuff? I don't know. It's my lucky gear, you know. I had an oil line bust and squirt all over my face and goggles."

Max could tell Wildman was warming up his most hair-raising tale as a way of boosting the price.

Wildman plunged in. "There I was at five thousand feet, wiping my eyes like mad and looking for a place to set her down before the engine seized up—"

"How much?" Max asked.

Wildman scratched his head. "I can see you're in no mood for haggling, and I can't say as I blame you. How does ten bucks sound?"

"Done," Max agreed. "And one more thing: nothing to anybody about this or my travel plans."

✭ ✭ ✭

It was cold tonight. The sky looked heavy, as though it might snow in Hartford.

Max took the evening meal alone in his room. He had been warned by the men in the barbershop that Zelda Sue Brown was not much of a cook. Perhaps, they speculated, this was why she had not caught herself a man. Too-heavy dumplings, tough chicken, lumpy mashed potatoes, an apple pie with crust like cardboard—it would take a man without taste buds to want to marry such a cook, Sheriff Potts had declared.

But tonight, Max thought, any meal would have been bland and tasteless. Dinner at the Waldorf would have been without interest to him. He was alone again. No longer did he look in the mirror and see in the face reflected there the possibilities of fatherhood and settling down.

Trudy was right. He was a mile wide and an inch deep.

Mary was right. He had no roots.

Max had spent his life living for himself. How then could he change the habits of a lifetime? How could he expect to make everything different just because he suddenly had a son?

He was a liar. He had lied to himself and to Mary and to David. More than all of that, Max Meyer hated what he had been and what he was and what he was likely to remain in the future.

He shoved the tray of food away, knocking a heavy, leather-bound Bible onto the floor. Every room at Miss Zelda's rooming house had a Bible, but Max resented it all the same. It was as if the volume had been put right out in plain sight to remind him of Mary's words. Now it had fallen open, and the passage leaped into his vision. He was reading the verses in spite of himself.

Ask, and it shall be given you; seek, and ye shall find; knock, and it shall be opened unto you: For every one that asketh receiveth; and he that seeketh findeth; and to him that knocketh, it shall be opened.

Max stooped to pick up the Bible and continued to read as though the words were food to fill the hunger of his soul. Although his mind rebelled, he adjusted the light and settled back to ponder the meaning of such things.

What man is there of you, whom if his son ask bread, will he give him a stone? Or if he ask a fish, will he give him a serpent? If ye then, being evil, know how to give good gifts unto your children, how much more shall your Father which is in heaven give good things to them that ask Him?

Max closed the book but left his finger to mark the place. Glancing at David's neatly wrapped gift of flying gear, Max considered the passage he had just read. Old memories swirled up in his mind. He had been so young when his father had died that it was difficult to picture his face. Had Papa ever given him a gift?

Yes. Something! What was it?

Max had a mental picture of large hands holding a present out to him. White cuffs sticking out from the sleeves of a blue serge suit. He could clearly see the package, wrapped in red tissue paper and tied with blue ribbon. *"For you, Maxie . . . ,"* the voice echoed. *"Take it. Go on, Maxie. I got it special for you, Son."*

Was the memory real, or was Max simply dreaming of it now to fill in the giant holes in his life?

"What was it?" Max asked aloud, unable to remember more about the gift than the fact that it was offered. What had been beneath the bright wrapping? What had his father picked out for him? Had he chosen it with the same care and hope with which Max had chosen this gift for David?

"I can't remember." Max felt a sorrow he had not imagined still existed in his soul. Could he still long for his father after a lifetime of living without him?

Max put a hand to his face. His cheeks were wet. Crying. Thirty-two years old, sitting in a boardinghouse in Arkansas, and missing a father he had hardly known. Crying like a baby for a man who had drowned twenty-five years ago! "You're losing your grip, Max," he chided himself, but still the tears came.

Max closed his eyes and tried to remember what it had been like when his family was still alive. Brother. Mama. Papa. What was it that frightened him now when he thought about them? Was it being left alone? And what frightened him about the fact that he now had a son of his own?

The unnamed agony boiled up inside him. Loneliness! How he hated it! Why could he not picture their faces or hear their voices? Why could he not remember what was in the gift his father had given him?

The image of fire and smoke rose in his mind. The screams of women and children, the shouts of men and the whistle of the steamer, *General Slocum*, as it burned and foundered on the East River! The strong arms of his father carried little Max down the stairway to the crowded deck. Where was his mother? Where had his mama and brother gone?

"Where were you?" Max choked out the question now. "Why did you leave me? Why didn't you let me go with you, die with you? Where did you go, Papa? Why did you put me in the lifeboat and make me go without you? Papa, you left me! You left me and made me go on living without you!"

Max laid down the Bible and sat with his head in his hands as all the images of that day returned to him in horrible clarity. Mothers screaming for lost children. The cries of the drowning in the water. The desperate faces of the people in the lifeboat as they beat back the dying who clung to the sides and threatened to swamp the packed vessel. And in all of that, where had his father been?

Max did not know how long he sat with these memories before Miss Zelda Sue Brown called for the untouched tray of food. "Mister Meyer!" she exclaimed. "You have not eaten a bite, and you look a sight. Are you ill? Should I call the doctor?"

He assured her that he was only tired. She left and closed the door quietly behind her as Max rose, turned to the window, and looked out at the dark night. Across the rooftops he imagined the branches of the old apple tree at Doc Brown's reaching up, the roots reaching deep into the soil, the fruit growing thick and ripe to feed the birds.

"She's right," he whispered, and the whisper was a prayer. "I have no roots. My own father left me, see? Died. I read this stuff about You, God, about how You will answer if I ask. The book said You will open if I knock. That You will give me . . . some good gift if I ask. But see, I don't know what to ask for or what door to knock on. I just . . . I need a father so I can learn to be a father to my boy. Otherwise I'm doing just what my dad did, aren't I? I'm throwing David into a lifeboat while the ship goes down around me, and I'm leaving him . . . like my father left me."

Max sat down wearily and gazed a long time at David's gift beside the Bible. "If I know how to give good gifts to my son, then how much more will You give me, God, if I ask You? That's what You're telling me, isn't it? I got this stuff for David because I knew he would love it. He hasn't even imagined what I got for him, but I really want to make him happy. Is that the way You feel about me? I admit it—I've heard about You, but I don't know You. Are You there?"

Picking up the Bible, he held it to him. "So. Maybe You have all the answers before I even know the questions. This is crazy, but I'm going to ask. I need something. I've failed in all the important things. Loving. Being loved. So I'm asking now, God. I need a father. I need You. You said if I ask . . . so I'm asking. Help me?"

There was no lightning flash in the sky. Max did not know for certain if his prayer was heard, but he began to read as if he could find questions and answers carved onto the thin onionskin paper of the leather-bound book. And somehow page after page seemed a love letter written to his heart. *I will never leave thee nor forsake thee.* Why had he resisted doing more than just glancing through this book? What pride had kept him from exploring such wisdom and power and love?

When at last he closed his eyes and slept, he dreamed of the hands of his father. He took the gift from him and opened it. Inside the package was the same well-thumbed Bible that lay beside him on the pillow.

"Take it, Maxie. It's for you. Just for you. . . ."

For days, the thought of tiny lice carrying a dreaded disease made Jefferson's flesh crawl as he rode nearer home. His scalp suddenly itched uncontrollably, and he thought he felt the prickle of invisible insects up the legs of his trousers.

He rode awhile, then bought a gallon of coal oil at a small country store. Fearful of the lice that he imagined in the dust of the shantytown, he burned the clothes he had been wearing and rubbed himself and the hide of the mule down with the coal oil. Then, his skin raw and burning, he sat naked in the brush beside a swollen creek through a long, cold day and a night. He did not eat or drink, instead letting the cold night air and the gnawing hunger take his mind from the tragedy he had witnessed and his own fears.

When the sun rose, he burned the blanket he had covered himself with. Every other scrap of fabric went into the flames except for a new pair of bibs and a shirt that Lily had wrapped in waxed butcher paper and packed in his saddlebags. Once more he rubbed fresh coal oil onto his skin and scalp. The sting he felt was like salt in a wound. But if his flesh was so raw and tormented, he reasoned, then surely any stray lice that might have jumped on him would be destroyed.

Finally, on the morning of the second day, he washed in the icy water of the creek. The ache of the cold was a relief compared to the searing sting of the coal oil. Again and again he plunged beneath the current until numbness eased his pain. Urging Old Bob into the stream, he scrubbed the mule thoroughly. Only then did he put on the remaining clean clothes that Lily had sent with him.

"Akron, Ohio," Jefferson said to the mule. "Don't recollect that I ever heard of that town before, mule." Jeff had pondered the question as he sat beside the creek. Now as he headed toward Shiloh, another concern entered his mind. What if there was not such a place? What if Delpha Jean's widower had been mistaken? Had Jefferson come all this way for nothing?

"Can't be. Of all the menfolks in shantytown, I come acrost the one who was married t'poor Delpha Jean. That ain't no accident, now, is it? God don't play jokes on His chillens."

His doubts eased a bit. Relaxed in the saddle, Jefferson closed his eyes and dozed awhile as Old Bob plodded steadily to the northwest. He dreamed sweet dreams of his mama and daddy, Little Nettie and Big Hattie, and all his sisters back in Pisgah. Would his sisters all be in this Akron place as well?

In his dream he saw Miz Trudy standing in front of a yellowed wall map that had hung in the front of the classroom in Pisgah. . . .

Miz Trudy pointed a long pointer at the map, which seemed to have no lines or borders or names of towns on it.

"Little Nettie?" she asked.

Nettie, gangly and scrawny, popped up from the bench. "Yes'm?" The child rocked on her heels and tugged on the spiky braids that exploded from her head.

"Can you tell your brother, Jefferson, where Akron, Ohio, is?"

Nettie screwed her face into a scowl. "Ain't no such place," she said in a pouting voice, then sat down.

Miz Trudy shook her head. "You did not study your lesson, Little Nettie." She held out the pointer and touched the red-hot top of the potbellied stove with the tip. Suddenly the end of the stick burst into flames.

Jefferson tried to warn her, but he could not, because he was asleep in the back of the classroom. He could not raise his head or open his mouth or shout that she should be careful.

Miz Truly did not see the fire licking the stick. She turned and slapped the brittle fabric of the map hard with the pointer. "There it is," she said, and the place on the map blackened and curled back in a small circle.

Then, with a roar, the whole map dissolved into fire, while Miz Trudy seemed not to notice. Smoke billowed from the map and encircled Miz Trudy. Children in the class began to cough and choke. Jefferson, still sleeping, yet aware of the disaster in his dream, looked up and saw that the ceiling was on fire. He glanced down, and flames were licking his boots. On either side of his seat, great towering flames leaped up to engulf the Pisgah school and all its children.

Through it all, Miz Trudy kept talking. "Akron, O-hio. Up north, it is, Little Nettie. Right there. . . ." She stretched her hand into the inferno. "Wake your brother, Nettie. Tell him where it is. Tell him where you are."

CHAPTER THIRTY-FOUR

Jefferson Stands His Ground

It was late at night when Jefferson finally arrived at his cabin, but no friendly lamps were burning to welcome him. No wife and chillens were sleeping within. The place was empty.

By the light of a match, he read the note that Birch had nailed to the door:

Welcome home, Jeff! All is well. Lily and babies up to our place. Come on up. Birch.

✴ ✴ ✴

Birch was asleep but heard Jefferson coming across the field and staggered out to greet him. He did not mention the fact that J.D. was alive and well and headed back to Shiloh with the law. There would be time enough for bad news. Instead Birch led Old Bob into the new barn while Lily ran out to embrace Jefferson and pull him into the house to see how big the babies had grown while he had been gone. Trudy brewed strong coffee and heated a pan of persimmon pudding.

Birch wondered how Jefferson would react to hearing that he had at least one more mountain of troubles yet to climb.

"It'd be good for y'all if we could find your family, Jefferson," Birch began, trying to broach the subject of J.D. "You might even want to think about goin' on up north for a while."

"No sir, Birch. I couldn't do that to y'all. You an' Trudy done ever'thing for me an' Lily an' the young'uns. Now we got that place of our own. . . ." He faltered and looked at Lily curiously. "How come you ain't home, gal?"

Lily lowered her eyes.

Birch cleared his throat. "Me and True thought it would be best if she was up here with us while you were gone."

"Somethin's happened," Jefferson guessed.

"Yes," Birch replied simply. He took a sip of coffee to fortify himself for what lay ahead. "We got news while you were away."

"News?" Jefferson looked from one to another as though their faces could tell him what was wrong.

"Jefferson," Lily began, "honey, you know it don't matter none t'me where we is, long as I got you."

"What y'all tryin' to say? It's mighty late, an' I wish y'all would just say it."

Birch nodded curtly and got to the point. "Jefferson, J.D. is alive."

"Lord," Jefferson said miserably. "I ain't one t'wish a man dead, but that is one man I was not sorry t'see gone."

"Well, he ain't gone, and that's the problem. Seems like he went to Oklahoma like he promised and . . . Jefferson, he's got the law with him. They're comin' back here to Shiloh."

"For me." Jefferson reached out to take Lily's hand. "Gonna take me back."

"Sheriff Potts telephoned. They got a writ that says if you're the man, then they can take you back over the state line. That's what it says."

The room was silent. Lily closed her eyes and squeezed Jefferson's fingers hard. "We can go most anywhere, Jeff," she repeated in a childlike voice. "You know it don't matter t'me 'bout where we be long as—"

Jeff gave a shake of his big head. "No, Lily." He replied sadly. "Me and my folks done been run off our land before, gal. An' I just come back from seein' what happens to colored folks what got no place t'call their own." He shuddered.

"But Akron," Trudy offered hopefully. "If Willa-Mae and Hock are there, Jefferson . . ."

"No, Miz True." He flashed a sad smile, and the lamplight glinted off the gold of his teeth. "We can't leave." He tapped his tooth. "This here is the only pocket change I got. The Lord done give me an' Lily our own place through y'all. I ain't gonna turn yeller an' run because of J.D. an' Sheriff Ring. No, ma'am. Folks like me an' Lily here—if we don't stay put in our Promised Land, then we ain't gonna have no more chances.

"Folks like us is dyin' out there," he went on. "Y'all don't see 'em 'cause they been run off t'live like animals way out of sight. But I seen it, Miz True. I got me two young'uns t'raise up. An' I ain't gonna cut an' run an' watch 'em die in no shantytown. No, ma'am. If the sheriff take me back t'prison, then I reckon Lily an' little William an' little Willa will be better off stayin' right here in that cabin." He inclined his head to Birch. "Even if I can't buy the place from y'all like we planned . . . mebbe you could see your way clear t'let my wife an' babies stay on in the cabin, Birch?"

As one, Trudy and Birch jumped to reply that Lily and the children would always have a home with them if they wanted it. It was never a question, but politeness required that Jeff ask, all the same.

Lily tried to argue. "But, Jeff, we can get on up north. Mebbe find your mama an' daddy. . . . We be fine up north, an' nobody know who you is up there."

"Lily—" Jefferson rubbed the scars where manacles had long ago rubbed away the flesh of his wrists—"I seen a lot of hell in my day. Lived in the middle of it, gal, an' lived through it with the help of the Lord. Now I got t'tell you, what I seen down in Pine Bluff is a worse kinda hell than what I seen in prison. If they come an' take me away, I can go on livin' if I know that my Lily an' our babies gonna be here in this piece of heaven waitin' for me t'come home. I'd rather do that than take y'all away from here an' risk the chance that my wife an' babies end up in some place like what I seen down in Pine Bluff."

"But we wouldn't go no place like Pine Bluff."

"Lily . . . gal . . . don't you see? It ain't Pine Bluff I'm talkin' about. Things is bad all over for colored folks."

"How you know that, Jeff?" she begged.

"'Cause things is bad all over for white folks, Lily. And if that's the truth—an' it *is* the truth—then folks like us ain't hardly gonna get through this alive. Akron ain't no different than what I see down there. Up north, white folks is standin' with tin plates in their hands an' beggin' for soup an' bread. I done read it in the papers. It's bad up there, too."

Jefferson had always been a big man, but somehow he looked stronger, more powerful than he ever had, sitting there in the Tuckers' kitchen.

"I ain't gonna take my fambly away from here. If I go t'prison, I'm still gonna have this place an' these folks t'think on. My friend, Birch. His Trudy. Them little boys. My Lily an' them two babies growin' up right here in Shiloh. I'll pray for the crops an' pray for the folks round here who been so good t'us. Y'all will write me, an' I'll get letters at mail call. I'll keep preachin' 'bout the mercy of the Lord t'them who have nothin' t'live for an' no heaven t'die for. An' all the time, I'll know there really is a little bit of heaven right here on earth."

"Oh, Jefferson!"

"The Lord ain't cruel, Lily. This ain't some dream I'm gonna wake up an' find gone. No, it ain't. You're my dream. Those babies are my dream. The mountains an' the fields an' that little cabin are all my dream. An' even if I gotta spend the rest of my natural life in jail, I'm gonna know that it ain't no dream at all but the real thing. Heaven. Right here, waitin' for me."

Jefferson rose before sunup the next morning to stir the fire and sit awhile beside the hearth. Uneasiness churned inside him, a foreboding of what was ahead for him and Lily.

J.D. comin'. Bringin' the law back to Shiloh so he can collect the reward an' pay off his debts. Yes. That is trouble comin', all right.

Jefferson stared at the soft orange flames licking the wood and wondered if he was a fool to stay here by the fire instead of packing up and clearing out while he could. Then he remembered Nigger Mountain once more. Remembered the lean, angry faces of unemployed white miners he had passed on the road. No, it was best to keep Lily here. If his dreams of a good life were about to end, then at least he could leave her knowing she would have a roof over her head and food to eat as long as Birch Tucker was still alive!

Jefferson read the Good Book some and prayed on the matter. Gradually the sky began to lighten, but his spirits remained heavy. He felt as if a mountain of worries rested on his shoulders. And no matter how he prayed, the weight of it did not lift.

"You say, Lord, that if I have faith small as a mustard seed I can say t'that mountain t'get into the sea. But I ain't got even that much faith, sir. I can't see this trouble goin' away no time soon. An' it feel t'me like there be no more miracles left in my life. So I guess I jus' accept whatever You is gonna bring my way. I can't move this mountain on my own, so I guess I got t'leave it t'You, then."

Hope depleted, Jefferson prayed for courage, asked for the strength not to run from the baying hounds that he sensed were near his heels even now. Lily slept on peacefully, and Jefferson did not wake her. He would have liked to hold her close once more, but perhaps it was best if she dreamed sweet dreams awhile longer.

He walked over to the cradles where baby Willa and little William slept side by side. They were so tiny. They would not remember him if he was gone long. Jeff was sure he would be a story-man they heard their mama tell about. They would grow up loving the story but not knowing the man.

Watching these young'uns grow up was what he would miss the most, he reckoned. It was a miracle he had wanted to be part of—like planting an orchard and waiting for years 'til the young trees matured to bear fruit.

Once again he thought of the road. He pictured himself and his little family running far away to the end of it, to where there was no J.D. to trouble with. But young'uns, like trees, needed a place to put down roots. What would come of them if they were on the run?

This vision of flight made his heart pound fast, and beads of sweat formed on his broad brow as though he were actually running. To take to the road, to run away would mean facing a thousand different fears every day. He prayed again to strengthen his resolve. And gradually, as his decision to stay became rock solid, he began to feel the nearness of the Lord.

"Thank You, sir," he whispered. "You got to take care of my fambly when I'm gone. That's all I'm askin', sir."

After his long time in prayer, Jefferson was prepared when he heard the distant jingle of a harness and the clatter of horses' hooves against the road. He washed his face and dressed to be ready when they arrived. It was Birch Tucker's voice that called out to him. Other men, a half dozen or so, coughed nervously. Horses stamped and snorted, blowing steamy breaths into the pale blue morning air.

Lily awoke in confusion and sat up at the familiar sound of Birch's voice. "Jefferson!"

Jefferson looked at Lily, then at the door.

"Why, Jeff," she said in a sleepy voice. "You got your Sunday clothes on. You an' Birch goin' t'pull stump this mornin', or what?"

"Don't worry none 'bout it, gal," Jefferson looked long at his wife and then stooped to kiss her gently. "I reckon we be goin' in t'town."

"But, Jefferson, you ain't had breakfast."

Birch called again; then the big voice of Sheriff Potts followed. "Jefferson? This here's Sheriff Potts."

Lily gasped and covered her mouth with her hand. In an instant she sprang from bed and grasped Jefferson's hand. "Don't go out there, Jeff!"

"Got to, Lily," he said in a whisper. "Stay back now, gal. Think of the babies an' stay outta this. I aim t'go in peaceful."

"Jefferson!" It was Birch again. "Doc Brown is here, and Miss Mary Brown and Trudy and the kids. We have come to help so Lily can go with you into town. And the Reverend Adams."

"And me!" It was the unmistakable cry of Brother Williams. "We come with Sheriff Potts to escort you into Hartford for the hearin'."

Potts added, "That's right, Jefferson. We done called Judge Flowers over in Charleston. He says it ain't legal they take you back to Oklahoma unless we have us a hearin'. He's comin' t'Hartford t'preside over the matter himself." Potts cleared his throat and spit as though the whole thing was distasteful to him. "No need for you t'be a'feared to come along into town. Them Kluxers ain't likely t'be nowheres along the road with these good folks ridin' with us."

"Jefferson!" Lily pleaded, wrapping her arms around his middle and holding tightly to him. Tears began. "Do we have to go?"

"Now, let go of me, gal." He gently pried her arms loose. "Don't let nobody see you cry. You know how folks talk. Don't want them t'think we was scared. Think on the Lord. It'll be all right."

He looked at the door again. "I heard the squeak of Birch's FAMOUS wagon. Reckon that means they brought it t'fetch you an' Willa an' William back up t'Doc Brown's house. It won't be so bad." He gazed around the little room as if he was seeing it for the last time. How long would it be before he saw it again?

"Get them babies ready, gal. I got t'get me t'Hartford jail before those friends of J.D. hear what's goin' on an' come out here for a different kind of visit."

Jefferson greeted the impromptu posse cheerfully. He patted Codfish and scratched the chin of the red pup. He offered the posse coffee, which they all declined. No time, they said. Best get on back to Hartford before the snakes came out. J.D. had wired from Fort Smith that he and Sheriff Ring were on the way. A federal warrant had been issued to take the escaped convict back across the state line. Sheriff Potts had no choice but to serve it and take Jefferson in for a hearing.

Old Bob was saddled. Lily came out with the babies. Jefferson made his final farewell to the cabin, then locked the doors. Birch and Trudy helped load the wagon for Lily, and they left Shiloh surrounded by the posse of neighbors, friends, kids, and dogs.

While Lily, Birch, Trudy, and the children settled into the house of Mary and Doc Brown, Jefferson was taken to jail.

The two-story jailhouse was the oldest building in Hartford. Built of hewn logs during the Civil War, it had originally been intended to serve as detention for prisoners of war. There were bars on the windows, but the eight cells on the second story were divided by log walls, which created individual rooms.

Because it was the strongest, warmest, best-built structure in the area, the victorious Yankees had turned the building into barracks for the Union Army. History recorded that the Rebel prisoners had been herded together into a barn nearby and guarded like animals in stalls while the Yankees enjoyed a luxurious stay at the jail.

The office of Sheriff Potts had been converted from one of the cells. Now family pictures and needlepoint Scripture verses hung on the walls carved with the initials of former Union soldiers.

DO UNTO OTHERS AS YOU WOULD HAVE THEM DO UNTO YOU.

This was the basis of all law to Sheriff Potts. There it was, cross-stitched in red letters above his desk, and he did his best to live it. He had used his sidearm only twice in the memory of local residents. One occasion had been to shoot a mad dog that had cornered Boomer down at the livery stable two summers before. The other time had been after the beating and near lynching of an Indian by the Kluxers down near Hooper's cotton gin last fall. Potts had pointed the revolver and called each one of his hooded neighbors by name, saying that he would sure hate to have to shoot a friend and send an unprepared sinner into eternity, but he would fire if his duty so demanded.

This had proved a tense moment for the Kluxers, who liked the sheriff well enough. Since they did not consider hanging an Indian worth losing his friendship and maybe getting a bullet hole or two punched through their sheets, they had dispersed without further trouble. The Indian had left town in a hurry all the same.

Only rarely did anyone in Hartford require locking up. Sheriff Potts usually left the matter of bootlegging to the federal officers. He made no arrests to enforce the Volstead Act unless moonshine sales were made right out in the open. No use looking for trouble, he reasoned. Sheriff Potts also allowed an occasional drunk to sleep off a hangover indoors rather than leaving such a person out in the rain.

It had been years since there had been reason to lock a cell in his jail, and the sheriff informed Jefferson that he would not resume the practice now. Jefferson was here for his protection, Sheriff Potts explained, lest he be taken from Sebastian County without benefit of a hearing. The keys remained on the hook, and Jeff's cell door stayed unlocked.

The sheriff explained further that prisoner Jefferson Canfield was on his honor when it came to his personal hygiene. An additional cell in the jailhouse had been converted into a bathroom with a flush toilet and a sink, but there was no lavatory for coloreds in the building, and although Sheriff Potts was a broad-minded man, he would not fly in the face of convention. The local Kluxers would have burned down the historic Hartford jailhouse if a black man had been permitted to use the same facilities as the white prisoners. So Jefferson would be obliged to go down the back stairs and into the alley to use the separate outhouse reserved for colored people and Indians. The lawman trusted him to come and go as he pleased without supervision.

Guests were also free to come and go as they pleased—and they did. Grandma Amos, upon hearing the news of Jefferson's whereabouts, brought him a mincemeat pie from her Christmas baking and an encouraging word from the Lord. Lily, with the help of Mary Brown, carried the babies down to the jail to visit their daddy for most of the day. Mary Brown made apple dumplings and fried up a chicken. Brother Williams, smelling the chicken as he sat with Sheriff Potts, paid a call on Jefferson and ended up staying through the noon meal. Reverend Adams brought spiritual nourishment by way of practicing his Sunday sermon on the captive audience. Mr. Winters accompanied Dee Brown the barber, who gave Jefferson a free haircut and a shave so he might look his best before Judge Flowers at the hearing.

And so it went, as all of Hartford and Shiloh awaited the arrival of J.D. Froelich and the sheriff from Oklahoma. Nearly everyone despised J.D. Those who were counted among his friends did not like him much because he was a liar and a cheat. His enemies did not like him for the same reasons.

The town was divided on the issue of Jefferson Canfield, however. The Kluxers were certain that, being black, Jefferson was guilty of something, even if they were unclear about what it was. At any rate, he was taking up land that could be farmed by a white man, and therefore it was hoped that Jefferson was indeed the fugitive.

Most everyone else in the area knew that Jefferson Canfield was the man who had risked his life to save the boys of Birch and Trudy Tucker during the tornado. Even if the evidence of Jefferson's identity was cloudy, they thought he deserved a fair hearing and that he ought to be able to stay with his family while awaiting his day in court.

All of this was argued at length in Dee Brown's barbershop until the issue became so volatile that Dee, fearing for his mirror and windows, forbade further discussion. It would all be decided by the hearing, he declared. Until then, he closed his shop and pulled down the shade.

A large room beneath the jailhouse was designated as the site of Jefferson's hearing. The same chamber had been used by the Union Army as a courtroom for the judgment of local secessionists. Nowadays the room was used as a meeting place for the local Grange, the Masons, and, on alternate Sundays, the First Church of Holiness in God. And now it would be the setting where Jefferson's identity was established.

Through the day, Birch and Trudy, along with Max Meyer, Mary Brown, and Doc Brown, made frantic efforts to establish that Thomas

Jefferson Canfield was not—could not be—the escaped convict whom the lawmen of Oklahoma so desired to take back to their prison. This task seemed impossible, since they knew Jefferson was indeed that man.

And Sheriff Ring and J.D. Froelich were on the way to Sebastian County to prove it.

✮ ✮ ✮

A subdued Ellis Warne escorted Mrs. MacAfee and five-year-old Sean to the door of his clinic. "Give him only some clear broth tonight, and he should be all right tomorrow, Missus MacAfee."

"That's real good," Sean's mother said. "Say, Doc, about your fee. You know the laundry business ain't been comin' in so good lately, and I was wonderin' . . ."

"It's all right," Ellis said. "The charge is one dollar. Pay me when you can."

"Thank you, Doc," Mrs. MacAfee said, grasping Sean by his much-abused ear. "Things just seem to be gettin' tough all over. And so fast, too. Why, folks that—"

Mrs. MacAfee's comments were interrupted by Boots's sudden and violent arrival. The little girl flung open the outside door to the medical office with a crash and dashed in. "Pop, come see," she called in a breathless voice. "Three police cars!"

"Boots!" Ellis reprimanded her. "You know better than to charge in here when I have a patient. Now apologize to Missus MacAfee and Sean."

The look on Boots's face indicated that offering an apology to Sean MacAfee, who was known around the neighborhood as a brat, was not going to come easy. But Boots was bright enough to recognize that she was not going to be allowed to deliver her important news unless she complied with her father's order first.

"Sorry," she said quickly. "Three police cars, Pop!"

"All right, now," said Ellis, holding the door open for Mrs. MacAfee and son, "what's all this about?"

Boots grasped her father's hand and dragged him toward the front yard. "Suzie and I were playing hopscotch when this police car drove by," she explained, "and then another and another. We thought maybe they were after gangsters!"

"Boots," Ellis said with weariness showing in his tone, "you've seen police cars before. Why is this so important?"

"Because . . . ," Boots said emphatically, tugging Ellis out to the side-walk. "Because they stopped right there!"

Sure enough, no more than half a block away, three dark blue, long-bodied patrol cars hemmed in the front of the Fitzgerald house as if to keep the little green home from escaping.

Mrs. MacAfee weighed in with her opinion. "It's sure to be either alcohol or gamblin'," she stated with conviction. "For the boys in blue to roll three cars for this occasion means a raid of some kind. Or else maybe an ax murderer like him over in Cincinnati."

"Missus MacAfee!" Ellis remonstrated. "Don't go spreading gossip like that! That's where the Fitzgerald family lives . . . fine folks. Fitz is my insurance agent."

"That is as may be," said Mrs. MacAfee, "but just you look there." She waved a meaty hand toward the recently painted forest green door of the Fitzgerald home, which was opening as they spoke. Three burly police-men appeared, followed by a handcuffed Fitz Fitzgerald. Another patrol-man accompanied the insurance agent down the white-brick steps. He was followed by a man in a three-piece suit whose air of authority indicated he was the officer in charge. Around the whirlpool of the scene floated the whole crew of little Fitzgeralds, ducking and bobbing like twigs on the edge of the current that was sweeping their father away.

Fitzgerald kept his head down as he was loaded into the back of a patrol car, so perhaps he did not see that, all up and down Florida Ave-nue, friends and neighbors were watching him being arrested. The police cars filled up again. As they whizzed past, Ellis caught the briefest glimpse of Fitz's stricken face.

"Mark my words," said Mrs. MacAfee knowledgeably. "It'll be some kind of racketeering. For shame! Him bein' a family man and all!"

Ellis regarded her sternly. "I'm certain it's some kind of mistake. Fitz would never do anything to get arrested for."

"Ah, Doctor Warne," said Mrs. MacAfee with a shake of her ponderous head, "you're a babe to be sayin' such. Who knows what wickedness men may conceal in their hearts? Come along then, Sean."

"Are you all right, Pop?" Boots wanted to know as Ellis stood looking from the departing MacAfees to the Fitzgerald house. The four Fitzgerald children had watched the police cars until they were clear out of sight before dragging themselves back inside. It seemed to Ellis that the home had a pathetic, forlorn look now, even though nothing in its physical appearance had actually changed.

Becky met Ellis at the front door. "Go upstairs and get washed up, Boots," she commanded. When the girl had obeyed, Becky drew Ellis aside and told him in a whispered tone about a telephone message she had just received. "It was Missus Benjamin who called," she reported. "Mister Fitzgerald has been arrested for larceny. He's accused of taking insurance premiums and never turning them in to his company. Even money collected from people on our block—our payments! Missus Benjamin says she heard he played the market with the money, thinking he'd pay it all back, and now he's lost it all! Isn't that terrible that our policy is no good? It's just awful."

Ellis wondered if Becky would have understood how profoundly he agreed with her. It was truly the most awful thing he had yet heard.

CHAPTER THIRTY-FIVE

Better Dead

There was only one lawyer in Hartford. He had done a fine trade in his day concerning minor legal matters—drawing up wills, settling estates, and the like. With the help of Dr. Brown, he had managed to track down Birch Tucker after the death of his father. But Hiram Jones, attorney-at-law, was eighty-three years old, and he had suffered a stroke last August. The matter of Jefferson Canfield was far beyond him at present.

For this reason, the defense of Jefferson had somehow come to rest squarely upon the shoulders of Max Meyer. This fearful responsibility crashed down on Max after he foolishly mentioned having witnessed a similar case of mistaken identity in the courts of New York City.

"You mean you witnessed the trial?" exclaimed Doc Brown.

"I covered it for the *Times*. It involved a man who was high up in a brokerage firm and—"

Max was not allowed to finish his story. He had been a close observer in a courtroom in a case that was similar to this. Did that not make him more expert than anyone else in Sebastian County? An educated man, Max understood the proper legal lingo with which to address Judge Flowers: "Your honor." This skill alone would put Max miles ahead of everyone else in the room.

Upon protesting vigorously that he was no more than a glorified scribe who had been around some interesting places, Max was told that not even Judge Flowers had ever been in a courtroom in New York City. Trudy added the information that Max had won honors in debate in college. Was not a hearing simply a matter of debate?

So Max was trapped. He swallowed hard and organized his legal team to discuss the defense of a man whose very face would condemn him the moment Sheriff Ring laid eyes on him.

✱ ✱ ✱

There was the writ for Jefferson Canfield's extradition, and there was a Wanted poster with a poor sketch and a description of him:

WANTED!
DEAD OR ALIVE
ESCAPED CONVICT
JEFF FIELD
ALIAS CANNIBAL
$1,000 REWARD

All of that paled in significance beside the fact that Oklahoma law-man Myron Ring was coming to Sebastian County to personally retrieve the man who had managed to escape his net. Ring would take one look at Jefferson and bring out the leg-irons. Could the word of the sheriff be disputed when it was widely known that Jefferson Canfield had appeared in Shiloh just about the time the Cannibal had disappeared? What good was the word of Birch Tucker in such a case? How could the scars from shackles and handcuffs be explained?

This was all quietly discussed among the small group that gathered in Doc Brown's office. Lily, Birch, and Trudy were joined by Doc Brown, Mary, Max, and Reverend Adams. The writ was passed from hand to hand. The poster was studied as though staring at it could change the description or alter Jefferson's appearance.

"The days of slavery are over," commented Doc Brown in a firm and thoughtful voice. "Or so it is supposed to be. How can we let them take Jefferson back?"

" 'Jeff Field,' the poster says." Max held the paper to the light. "They have that much wrong."

"But the name is all they have incorrect," commented the reverend grimly. "This will be difficult to argue with, even before a man as fair as Judge Flowers."

Max furrowed his brow. "But that much *is* wrong, all the same. It might be something to go on. Mistaken identity, maybe."

Everyone cast doubtful looks at Max. Only Lily looked hopeful, but her hopefulness was born of wishful thinking.

"Well, if we can prove that Jefferson is not Jeff Field, not the Canni-bal," Max continued. "Remember, Judge Flowers has never seen him before. Then it becomes the word of Ring against proof of Jefferson's identity."

"I'm listenin', Max." Birch sat forward. "Just how can we prove who he ain't?"

"By proving who he is," Max replied. "He's Jefferson Canfield. A war hero, wasn't he? Legion of Honor, you said. Such things do not go unno-ticed, no matter what the color of a man's skin."

"He didn't come to Shiloh packin' medals," Birch said. "War hero or no, it didn't make any difference to those Kluxers and lawmen ten years ago. They threw him in the prison camp and added two years to his sen-tence every time he tried to get away. That's the facts of it. No matter what they call him by, that's the way it happened. Every word we speak at the hearin' we have to swear on the Good Book."

"Legion of Honor," Max continued stubbornly. "Such things were won by Jefferson Canfield, not this Jeff Field fella—if we can prove they are not the same man."

Reverend Adams nodded. "Our Jefferson is in need of a miracle, friends. And we are certainly in need of wisdom."

✳ ✳ ✳

"Hey, Maxie!" The voice of Harry Beadle was jubilant through the crackle and hiss of the long-distance telephone wire. "Boy, is this your lucky day!"

"Listen, Harry . . ." Max overrode his friend's enthusiastic greeting. There was no time for conversation about anything but Jefferson Can-field. "I need you to do a little digging into something for me . . . a little research . . . and I need it wired to me as soon as possible."

"Where are you?"

"Arkansas."

"Where are you really, Maxie? Listen! You can tell me! The heat is off. Boss Quinn got himself murdered yesterday by the O'Farrell mob in a chop-suey joint! You hear me, Maxie? You and the kid can come home! Boss Quinn is now a stiff down at the county morgue. The coppers do not care to interview either you or the kid about a guy who is already dead and so will not need a trial or need to be zapped in the electric chair. You are a free man, Maxie! Come back to Manhattan and do your own research."

"No time." Max spoke matter-of-factly, as though the news of Boss Quinn's death meant nothing to him.

"Time? You have now got the rest of your entire life, which will now be a very long time."

"Harry!" Max began to lose patience as all heads in Mr. Winters's drugstore turned to stare. "Just listen to me! This is what I need. You got a pencil?"

☆ ☆ ☆

Lily sat with her head leaning on Jeff's shoulder. His big hand pressed gently against her hair, holding her close. "Don't worry 'bout nothin' gal," he soothed. "Ever'thing be all right."

Lily sighed deeply. She wanted to believe Jeff's words, wanted to trust, but she could not bear the thought of being parted from him. Even glancing at the barred windows of the Hartford jail sent a shudder through her that she could not restrain.

The heavy clump of boots echoed down the hallway in the direction of Sheriff Potts's office. "Where's that nigger of mine?" a harshly sullen voice demanded. "I come to fetch him."

There was the noise of a chair being slowly scraped across the floor, then the dry tones of Sheriff Potts. "You'd be Ring then, I reckon. Hullo, J.D. See you made it back."

"Where is he, Potts? Trot him out here quick." J.D.'s bellowing voice made Lily stiffen and grab tightly to Jeff's arm. He cautioned her with a gesture to remain still and listen.

"Well, now, let's be clear," Potts said. "He ain't *your* nigger nohow, and he may not even be the right man. That's for the hearin' to decide."

The incredulous snorts of J.D. and Sheriff Myron Ring blended into one. "What hearin'?"

"Judge Flowers. You can't waltz in here and demand that the sovereign state of Arkansas, Sebastian County, send some poor soul back to Oklahoma without no hearin' first."

J.D. swore fiercely, and there was the crash of a fist slamming down on Potts's desk. "See here, Potts. I am goin' to collect that reward, and you ain't gonna stop me."

"You'd have a mighty tough time spendin' it inside a cell," Potts threatened quietly, "which is where you'll land if you don't control that public blasphemin'."

"Shut up, J.D.," commanded Ring. "When's this hearin' gonna be?"

"Tomorrow night."

"We want everythin' to be legal, now, don't we?" Ring's voice cautioned J.D. "We can wait." He nudged J.D. toward the door, then wished Sheriff Potts a good day.

✴ ✴ ✴

Birch paid the boys a nickel apiece to curry down the mules and feed them at Brother Williams's livery stable. Boomer, the chief groom, did not take kindly to being displaced in his chores, so he called directions to his rivals from his perch in the hayloft.

"Tommy TUCKER! Git on out from 'hind that ol' mule! He'll kick your head right off. . . . Git on outta there!"

"Aw, Boomer, this is Ol' Bob. This mule don't kick nothin' no more."

"NAW!" Boomer boomed. "I seen it! I SEEN it! That ol' mule is the kickin'est mule! Kick a head clean in! Git! Leave his tail be!"

Old Bob always liked having his tail combed, but Boomer's yelling made the chore unpleasant, so Tommy rolled his eyes and moved along to the next animal.

The livery stable was the best place in Hartford for kids and dogs to play while parents took care of business. David followed his cousins to this sanctuary, where sweet-smelling hay and the pungent aroma of horse manure mingled with the smell of leather and saddle soap.

Rosey, the red pup, was pleased to see her mama again, although Emmaline snarled at her and rolled the puppy on her back when she tugged the old dog's ear. Emmaline bristled at first sight of Codfish and stood stiff and still while the big dog circled her. Then with a snort and a sniff the two were friends. They lay down side by side in the dirt while the boys climbed into the loft and swung by the rope to drop into the haystack while Boomer hooted and cheered.

A corncob fight rounded out the day, and somebody had the idea of staying the night in the stable with Codfish, Rosey, the mules, and Boomer. Tommy was confident that the adults would approve this plan, since all they wanted was to have the boys out from underfoot so they could have their meetings about Jefferson and the hearing. The plan was voted on and passed unanimously. Boomer was allowed to vote as well so he could not change his mind, as he often did, and throw the boys out.

Then, with that important business taken care of, the cousins perched on the edge of the loft to observe the regular goings-on of the livery stable and to listen to the gossip. This way they heard all the discussion firsthand about what had befallen their good friend Jefferson. The subject of the upcoming hearing took precedent over all others. The weather, Christmas, who was well and who was ill—none of these usual topics even came up. All talk was speculation about Jefferson and J.D. and a rehashing of stories about the desperate convict who had escaped from the Oklahoma lawman last September.

Could it be Jefferson Canfield?

Some said it most definitely was. Others disavowed it as nonsense. Bobby and Tommy knew the truth, of course, and they remained out of sight whenever anyone came into the stable. They had their story down: "Tommy is named after Jefferson . . . Thomas Jefferson, like the president. Dad and Mama have known Jefferson ten years."

It was a good story and a true one, but they did not want anyone to ask them more than that. High in the loft like observing angels, they fell instantly silent at the sound of voices.

"Well, J.D. don't look none the worse for wear." That was the father of Fred Woods.

"Mean as ever and twice as ugly." This was the crackling voice of Grandma Amos. "He's a cussed thing, ain't he? Where's Brother now? Boomer! Where's Brother? I got me a load of freight t'haul next Tuesday if the Lawd don't come first. Way things is goin', I s'pect the Lawd any time. Now where is that Brother Williams? Boomer!"

And so it went through the day. A half hour later the boys heard from Brother Williams that meek and mild Sheriff Potts had sent Sheriff Ring out of the jail empty-handed. J.D. had blasphemed Potts and called him a nigger-loving fool. Potts declared that J.D. was the biggest fool ever born and that if J.D. did not watch his mouth, Potts would throw him in a jail cell and actually lock the door.

J.D. had not liked that much. He had left with Ring and gone out to Shiloh to see what was left of his place—which wasn't much. After calling at the church to visit the grave of Maybelle, which was J.D.'s solemn duty, J.D. and Sheriff Ring would be staying at the boardinghouse of Miss Zelda Sue Brown.

This information made David glad he would not be spending the night under the same roof as such a sinister man as J.D.—although David did wish he could see what J.D. looked like. Sort of like seeing a dragon, it would be. David did not want to get too close to J.D., but he wanted to know if a man so dark inside looked any different from other men on the outside.

As for the rest of the news? Judge Flowers was coming to Hartford tomorrow afternoon. The hearing was scheduled for tomorrow evening at eight o'clock. It would be held in the large room on the first floor of the jailhouse. The outcome did not look hopeful for Jefferson Canfield.

The tap at the clinic door at the side of the Warne home was so faint that Ellis thought he imagined it. He continued scribbling with a pencil, adding up columns of figures.

The way things were going, his practice could not be sold. Nobody would buy a business whose chief income was home-canned foods and IOUs. Still, his instruments should bring a hundred dollars, and all the furniture perhaps three hundred more. Throw in his clothing and his medical books and there was maybe, barely, five hundred dollars in all.

Ellis circled the figure of five hundred on his scratch pad and stabbed it so hard with the pencil that the point broke off.

Becky and Boots would need the money to move away and start over. Maybe they could move back to the farm and find some peace of mind again, while Ellis simply faded out of their lives and memories. Becky would want to leave him once everything was out in the open. He could not ask her to stay and weather the storm that was soon to break over his life. Five hundred dollars was all they would have.

The tap at the door came again, still faint and hesitant and fearful-sounding, but more distinct. Ellis got up from his desk, glancing at the door into the house to see if Becky had heard, but she was upstairs out of earshot.

The door opened to reveal Jack Daugherty. "I came to thank you, Doc, for Johnny and for the list and all. Thank you by warnin' you. I don't want to alarm your missus, but there's trouble comin' tomorrow night. At the plant, I mean. Best you stay away."

"How can I do that, Jack? They are already suspicious of me. If I miss work the same night something breaks loose, they'll know for certain."

"Be on your guard, then. We aim to be peaceable, but there's those on both sides of this fight who'd rather throw the match on the gasoline. There'll be blood spilled tomorrow, I'm thinkin'." Daugherty nodded curtly as he stated that fact. "You been good to us, Doc Warne. Kind to my family and to the men at the plant. I'd hate to see you hurt in this. You've got a nice missus. T'would be a shame to make her a young widow."

"Perhaps that would be merciful," Ellis said in a hoarse whisper. Then he asked, "That list . . . have I done this, Jack?"

"It would have been done without the list. Without you. We got to work. We got families to feed. It ain't just here, Doc! You know that. It's happenin' to men at the steel factories in Pittsburgh and at the packin' sheds in Chicago. Look at the breadlines. Growin' every day. Are we supposed to just lie down and take it? The wheel is turnin', turnin', Doc. And it ain't goin' to stop until the country turns with it."

There was nothing Ellis could say to change it. Terrible forces had been set in motion, and there was no preventing the battles. Deep down, Ellis knew they would sweep across the nation.

Like all wars, this one had begun almost imperceptibly. Jobs lost one man at a time. Dreams and lives smashed to pieces on every block and in every neighborhood in Akron. And now there was an army of angry men joined together to break down the gates of the Titan Tire and Rubber Company. There would be other workers shut out of other factories, too. Millions of men would become like Jack Daugherty before the country turned around. Thousands of others would die in the cross fire. In a vision that made him shudder, Ellis saw clearly that what was coming at the Titan Tire plant tomorrow night was only the beginning. . . .

Ellis thanked the messenger, although the message was grim. At that, Daugherty slipped out the door. He looked up and down the street before pulling his hat brim low over his eyes and hurrying away.

Hock's hands were trembling like dry leaves as he spoke to Willa-Mae. She thought that she had never seen him look so old and brittle. A strong wind might have easily picked him up and carried him away. And now Willa-Mae could hear the strong wind of trouble roaring toward them.

"Trouble, Willa-Mae," he rasped and coughed. "You know I don't pay no mind t'what the white folks be doin' down at Titan. I tell myself there ain't no cause t'get mixed up in all that."

"It's good you don't, Hock Canfield. You and Harry? Y'all will get tangled in a web if you choose sides."

"But they ain't gonna let us stay outta this, Willa-Mae! That's what I'm tellin' you, woman!"

He paced the length of the little flat to the window and stared down on North Howard Street. "Them union men, they got the list of fellers due to be laid off. A thousand already gone down—one man at a time, they jus' gone off the line. There wasn't nobody gonna speak up real loud about it, 'cause ever'body was scared it would be them get fired next. But now they got that list of ever'body who is gonna get the ax. It's all the fellas who got the most years an' get the most pay. It's all the men who b'lieve in the union . . . those men who go t'the meetin's most regular an' such."

He shook his little head and sighed. "That list be copied an' passed t'every gummer on every shift. Now they know there weren't no call t'turn those other fellas out on account of medical reasons." He coughed hard. "Here I was thinkin' somebody gonna hear me hackin' an' I was gonna end up out on the street. But bein' sick or well don't have nothin' t'do with all this. Titan jus' got his mind made up 'bout men he thinks could cause trouble. He gonna turn them men out t'starve."

Willa-Mae sat up very straight in her chair. "But you ain't on the list, Hock?"

"No, I ain't. It's 'cause I'm too black an' too scared t'go to a union meetin', an' I don't make so much as half of what the lowest gummer makes on the line. I ain't no account t'nobody . . . like some ol' dawg they keep round the place an' feed sometimes. I clean up their messes, scrub the toilets, trim the hedges, mop the floors. . . . I ain't no account t'nobody."

"Then you got t'keep it that way," Willa-Mae said firmly. "Stay outta the way of them union men and stay outta the way of Ol' Man Titan, too. Keep your mouth shut, do your job, and don't cross nobody."

Hock turned to face her. With the light from the window shining in behind him, she could not make out his expression, but she heard a quaver in his voice that sounded like fear. "Don't you know what happens to ol' dawgs when men is starvin'? Men shoot the dawgs, that's what, so's the men can eat the scraps the dawgs was livin' on."

"Don't go on so."

"It's so. You know it is. Them folks is desp'rate. Got wives an' young'uns t'feed. Sooner or later they's gonna look up an' see me. Someone gonna see me an' Harry walkin' outta the plant after our shift. They gonna say t'each other that we ain't got no business bein' there an' gettin' scraps when they got nothin'."

"Stop it, Hock."

"It's true, ol' woman. You know well as me that there's as many Kluxers here in Akron as there is in the whole state of Arkansas. They're even on the city council. Look what happened t'Nettie's scholarship. You know they already been burnin' crosses down t'the end of Furnace Street. They throwed a young colored man off a streetcar on Twenty-first Street, too."

"What we gonna do? We come as far as we knew t'come. We made us a life here. Ain't a fancy life, but it was good for a while. Church and friends. Raised up the young'uns. I had work. You got a job. I thought troubles was all past us now that we be growin' old."

He did not speak for a long time, but she knew that, in his silence, he agreed with her. They had lived humble lives—so humble that the next level down was destitution, homelessness, starvation, and death.

"The union men is all talkin' 'bout a big strike. If me an' Harry go along with it, then we gonna lose our jobs with Titan. But if we don't go along with it, me an' Harry gonna be the dawgs that gets caught in the middle an' shot over the scraps we get. That's the truth as I see it. I got no choice either one direction or t'other."

"Where we gonna go now if the whirlwind is a comin' after us again?"

"It ain't a'comin'. It already landed smack-dab in the middle of us!" His shoulders sagged. "I got no answer, ol' woman, 'cept that you an' me have had a fine life together, ain't we? Raised our babies the best we knowed how. Learned 'em 'bout the Lord. Taught 'em right from wrong. I ain't never amounted t'nothin' much in my life, but I have loved me a fine woman and raised me up a fine family. . . ."

His voice broke. He bit his lip and turned back to the window. "In the end it's gonna be the same for that Mister Titan as it's gonna be for me. In the end it don't matter that I been poor an' he been rich. In the end mebbe Jesus gonna look at me an' say I done the best I could. Mebbe Jesus slap me on the back an' say I done good. Then He gonna turn round an' kick Titan down the stairs for what he's a'doin'. . . . But it's gettin' from this hard hour all the way to the end of things that has me stumped! It ain't that I don't trust that the Lord is gonna sort things out in the end. It's the *now* that has me scared. From this minute t'future glory seems a mighty long way off, and I wonder if I can jus' keep on puttin' one foot in front of t'other. I find myself wishin' that today was Judgment Day 'stead of jus' another Thursday. Then I wouldn't have t'worry nor fight no more. I jus' wish the Lord would tell me, *Hock Canfield, lay down your sword, boy. Time to lay it down an' rest.*"

"What's the matter with us," Willa-Mae suddenly chided. "Don't you go talkin' thataway, Hock Canfield! Times is a little rough, and we forget ever'thing the Lord has done for us b'fore. Jus' like the Hebrew chillens grumblin' how they was better off in Egypt."

She placed her fists on her ample hips. "Well, now—it ain't over! We got grandbabies to love. We got each other. We gonna have us a great-grandbaby when that little one of Rena and Harry's gets born. Life always gets better after it gets so bad you can't stand no more. You know that. We done buried our babies in that field in Pisgah. We lost Latisha and then we lost Jefferson and never knowed what come of him! We got throwed off our farm! We seen more grief in a year than most folks see in a lifetime."

She shook her head sadly. Then the fire of determination burned even brighter within. "But we come back. Yessir, it turned round for us! I got happy t'be alive again. That's what old age does for you. You learn that life is terrible lots of times, but that don't matter 'cause sooner or later life is gonna turn round and smile at you again. Then you're glad t'be alive."

Willa-Mae raised her hands heavenward. "You look up and thank the Lord that He didn't answer you when you was askin' Him to take you outta the fight and feelin' like you wanted to die. You say, 'Thank You, Lord Jesus, that You did not answer that foolish prayer. I'm mighty glad t'be alive! I'm glad I didn't miss this.' Now ain't that so? Take the bad with the good—that's what it means t'be livin'. I ain't ready t'give this up.

Ain't ready t'lay down and die. I don't mind these troubles so much. I seen enough that it makes me kinda excited because I know God's gonna do somethin' if I wait long enough! He gonna make some miracle we ain't thought of yet. He gonna take all our sorrows and turn 'em into blessin's. That's what you got t'keep tellin' Harry so he don't fall into despair. The old have got t'teach the young that lesson. Bad times always pass! *Lift up your heads; for your redemption draweth nigh."*

When Hock hung his head and cried a bit, Willa-Mae knew she had gotten through. Hock would keep hanging on, so Harry would see it and learn from it. Hock would not lay down his sword until the young'uns learned clearly that in this hard old world there was hope.

"You done preached a sermon better'n Reverend Dale." Hock blew his nose. "I feel better, even though the worl' still look like a basket of eggs dropped from a high cliff. I can't sort nothin' out, can't put the goo back in the shells. It's gonna be interestin' t'see what the Lord can cook up for His chillens outta this scramble."

The gleaming black and chrome of Jack Titan's chauffeur-driven McFarlan Coach-Brougham was easily recognized passing through the owner's private entrance into the tire plant. It was also easy to recognize the aristocratic qualities in Titan's choice of vehicle: At a time when a brand-new, reliable Ford could be purchased for $425, the McFarlan was reported to sell for $10,000 or more, depending on the purchaser's selection of hand-rubbed walnut interiors and solid-silver door handles.

But it was not the McFarlan's ostentatious arrival that caught Ellis's attention. Instead he was focused on the car following Titan's limousine. The dark green body and black roof of the five-passenger Locomobile were partly obscured by the figures of the two brawny men standing on the running board on either side. This was Ellis's first view of Titan's bodyguards. He watched with fascination as a solid phalanx of seven two-hundred-pound bruisers in identical dark blue suits surrounded the company president and hustled him from his auto directly into the office building.

As a flurry of rumors about strikes and labor violence swept through Akron, Titan had surrounded himself with more protection, Ellis supposed, than President Hoover would ever have. So fearful was Titan of "Bolshevik-led violence" that he no longer went anywhere without his guards. Ellis had even heard that when Jack Titan and his wife dined at the exclusive Mayflower Hotel, two additional tables were required to accommodate his muscle.

If Ellis had pondered Jack Titan's frame of mind, he might have realized that the little tyrant was less frightened than he appeared. Certainly, the man had reason to be afraid of the mounting hostility, but the flamboyantly obvious protection was also good publicity for Titan and a knock against the union. After all, few of the good people of Akron wanted anything to do with a Bolshevik-style revolution. Already the *Beacon Journal* had weighed in with editorials deploring labor violence and union agitators.

But Ellis spent very little time thinking about what was going on in Jack Titan's mind. He was too wrapped up in his own thoughts. Had he done the right thing in stealing the list?

Through another window, Ellis could see the main gate through which the workers passed as the shifts came and went. Gathered outside the high fence were several hundred unemployed workers, the men recently discharged on moral grounds or for medical reasons. So far there had not been any outbreaks of violence, but the number of silent watchers was increasing. Today they were passing out some sort of handbills to the men entering the gate.

What good had his action accomplished? Either Titan would win and the fired employees would drift away to seek other jobs or else something would ignite the smoldering anger and Ellis would be the cause of injuries, perhaps even deaths.

And his own future? It was odd to be depressed because he still had one. With the life-insurance policy no good, suicide was out of the question, but the ruin he had feared now loomed more certain than ever.

Ellis wondered why he had not been arrested. After all, Titan must know by now that the union had the secret list. The company would not have to look far for suspicion to fall on Ellis. Maybe the blame had temporarily fallen on Dr. Keller. The man was almost constantly inebriated these days. Perhaps Titan believed that his chief medical administrator had misplaced the list himself.

But Ellis knew that his was only a brief respite at best. Slowly he realized that he probably would not be arrested at all. For that to happen, Titan would have to admit there had been a secret list in the first place. Instead Ellis's fate was bound up with those faked blackmail photographs, and their publication would not be withheld much longer. He leaned his forehead against the grimy glass pane and closed his eyes. It was all so terrible, with no hope of escape. Worst of all, would anybody ever understand?

There was a hand on his shoulder—heavy but not menacing. "You did the right thing," Giselle said. "No matter what happens now, you did the right thing."

* * *

It had been mighty quiet lately around the Fort Smith train depot. Some said it was because folks were too broke these days to travel far. Others said it was just a lull before the holidays.

No matter. Leroy Johnson, as the head redcap at the station, had had to lay off two of his nephews. Even after that, there was still barely enough work to go around. Tips were few and far between, so Leroy had taken on toting heavy loads again in hopes of earning enough to keep his family fed.

Tonight his back ached because of a steamer trunk he had hefted off the train for an old white woman from New Orleans who had come to Fort Smith to visit her sister through Christmas. She told Leroy all about it as he grunted and groaned and tried to act as if the load were nothing at all.

"She done her Christmas shoppin' 'fo' she come." Leroy winced as he explained the origins of his aching back to his oldest nephew. "Hope her kinfolk 'preciate that ol' woman bringin' that stuff all the way to Fort Smith! I ast her what did she buy her kinfolk for Christmas . . . was they gittin' a sack of bricks? Then she laugh an' she tell me that she bought 'em books! That's why that trunk was so heavy! Books—pract'ly a whole lib'ary. Pert near broke my back! Heavy as them stone tablets Moses carried down from the mountain, they was! Then that lil' ol' white woman ast me if I ever reads books myself or does I jus' carry books? I tell her I don't know one book from 'nother, but I'll carry 'em, all right, long as it pays enough!"

"Did she give you a good tip?"

"No suh, she did not. Offered me a stick of Beechnut gum is all. I figgered totin' all them books was worth a nickel anyways, but jus' a stick of Beechnut is what I gots for all my trouble! Now I ain't worth shootin'. Down in my back so bad I can't hardly push the hand truck."

"Well, Uncle Leroy, you ain't gonna be worth nothin' if yo' back don't git stronger. Best let us young'uns carry the heavy stuff. From now on we'll put all our tips in yo' hat at the end of the shift and split it. You take half since you give us this job, and we'll share the rest 'tween us."

This seemed a smart idea. After all, if Leroy lost his job because of an injury, how long could all his nephews stay on with the railroad?

When the 11:17 from St. Louis pulled in, Leroy assigned the arriving passengers to his redcap nephews. Most of the travelers were plain folks. Families moving from one town to the next. A shoe salesman carrying a scuffed leather case with a picture of a shoe stenciled on the outside. Two grim men who looked like federal revenue officers.

Last off the train was an odd-looking man carrying a battered valise. He was dressed like a bootlegger. Leroy had seen enough to know. The suit was new. Shoes shined. Tie knotted just below an ugly purple scar that looked like a tight-lipped smile on his neck. Leroy hobbled toward him, since gangster types were usually generous with tips. The man's fedora was of the finest felt. Eyes were hard and cold like a snake's eyes beneath the shadow of the brim. Such types were often seen at the spas up in Hot Springs. Why had this fellow come to Fort Smith?

"How-do, suh." Leroy tipped his hat. "Have a good trip?"

"Ain't over yet," the man growled.

"You goin' on down the line, then?"

"I am tryin' to get to a place called Shiloh, Arkansas. Youse ever hear of it?"

Leroy considered the appearance of the man before him. This did not look like the sort of fellow who would be going to Shiloh. Didn't talk like one, either. "Well, yessuh, I hear of it all right. Ain't nothin' there 'cept a few farms. One school. A Baptist church and a Methodist church and a store."

"That may be so. All the same, I am lookin' for a certain fellow I heard may be livin' in this Shiloh place. For his health. He likes such quiet, out-of-the-way places as this Shiloh place. Exceptin' now when I arrive here wheres I am supposed to change trains, I am told that there ain't a train no more to Shiloh, on account of a tornado that ripped up the tracks out there a while ago and they ain't got it fixed yet."

"That be the truth of it, suh." Leroy wrested the small bag from the man's hand and started walking slowly toward the lobby of the terminal. Sometimes information and sympathy were better for tips than carrying big bags. "It is the slowest re-pair I ever seen. I declare! They been flyin' the mail on out to Hartford three times a week since the track got tore up, but freight go by wagon and truck, and I reckon that's all the way there be t'get there."

"Not many regular citizens go out that way, then? And I suppose that anyone who come by train would come right here to this depot, same as me?"

"If someone come by train, then he come through here. That's right, suh. Ain't no other railroad station, 'less you count the stockyard loadin' dock. Them's freight trains down there. Plenty of folks hoppin' freights these days, I hear, but this here is the only reg'lar depot this side of the river."

"And if a guy was goin' on to this Shiloh, Arkansas, this would be the train station he would leave from?"

"Yessuh. Use t'be. But not since the twister took the rails. Now, somebody wants t'get on out thataway, I tells 'em go on over to the Gold-man Ho-tel. Best ho-tel in Fort Smith. Got a radio tower right on top of it."

"And have many people gone out there to this Shiloh place from here?" The man halted and rummaged in his coat pocket for something.

"Not so many, suh. And nobody goin' there tonight. Like I say, ain't much out there." Leroy spotted the ominous bulge of a shoulder holster beneath the man's overcoat.

Pulling out several dog-eared photographs, the man fanned the pictures like a poker hand before Leroy's face. "I'll give youse ten bucks, old man, if youse seen these two. A well-heeled gent and a little kid 'bout so high. They was travelin' wid a dog. Would have been six weeks ago. Maybe more."

"Well, I'll be." Leroy's eyes lit up because he did indeed recognize the pair, and ten bucks was a lot of money just for saying so.

"Now, for ten bucks, youse might tell me youse seen 'em and I might believe youse. Ten bucks is a lot of dough. But if youse was to be found to be lyin' to me, I am givin' youse fair notice that I will be leavin' this town through this very station just like I am arrivin'. So I am advisin' youse to think hard and give an honest answer. Do youse recognize this man and this kid?"

"Yessuh. They come through here 'bout the time of the big rain, when the moon was full. The gen'l'man was a Northern gent, and he ast about Shiloh. Jus' like you. Tracks tore up, I tell 'em. They went to the Gold-man Ho-tel, jus' like I was tellin' you to do."

The expression on the face of the seeker was intense. Dangerous, somehow. "If youse is lyin', old man . . ."

"I ain't!" Leroy cried as the man grabbed the sleeve of his uniform threateningly.

"The dog. Tell me about the dog."

"Big and black it were! Biggest ol' dog I ever seen. Like a bear."

Ten dollars was shoved into the hand of Leroy Johnson. Then the man snatched his case away and sprinted toward the exit of the building, where a taxi waited outside at the curb.

By the hiss of the lantern light, David, Bobby, and Tommy played draw poker with Boomer on a crate in the hayloft. Using matchsticks to bet with, Boomer, who had turned out to be some kind of natural genius when it came to a deck of cards, was beating them handily. His heap of matches on the upturned crate made him chuckle with glee and slap the knee of his holey britches each time a card was dealt. This made the game more of an irritation to the boys than fun.

David had a straight. Five consecutive cards—five, six, seven, eight, nine. He bet his last matchstick, only to be beat by Boomer's four queens.

"Well, that's it for me." David sat back in disgust as Boomer howled happily and awakened Emmaline and Codfish with the ruckus.

"Me too," said Tommy, relieved to be finished.

"Yeah." Bobby slapped his cards onto the crate and flung himself back onto the hay in exhaustion. "I'm tired." He closed his eyes.

"NAW!" Boomer hollered. "Y'all ain't DONE! Gotta win back yore matches! How y'all gonna light that?" He patted the hot lantern. "Gotta win them matches back."

"You sure you never played poker before, Boomer?" David lay back on the soft hay and considered the stablehand suspiciously.

"Just TONIGHT! Sure, lots of . . . I like it lots. Too bad. TOO bad." He gathered his win into his pockets as though he had won gold coins instead of wooden matchsticks.

Boomer's chortling was interrupted by a curse ringing from the entrance of the stable.

"Where is that idiot?"

Tommy blanched. "It's J.D.," he whispered and scooted back as J.D. shouted up to the rafters again.

"Boomer! You stupid idiot! Where are you?"

Boomer's lower lip jutted out in a pout. He did not like J.D., did not like the names J.D. called him. He patted his match-filled pockets and blew out the lantern.

"I know you're up there, Boomer." J.D.'s words were slurred—a sure sign he had been drinking.

Tommy put a finger to his lips, warning Bobby and David to keep quiet. Everyone knew J.D. could get mean when he was drunk. Best to stay out of his line of vision.

J.D. swore again. "He's got no brains. Stablehand. Horses is smarter than he is."

Who was he talking to?

At that insult, Boomer called out like an avenging angel, "WHO'S THAT? WHO'S BLASPHEMIN' IN BROTHER WILLIAMS'S STABLE?"

"Why, Boomer!" J.D. sounded amused. "So you're up there, huh? Come on down here. Take care of our horses."

"I ain't comin' down," Boomer declared. "Not 'til I know who's down there. Y'all sound like the devil to me."

"It's your old friend J.D., Boomer." J.D. laughed. "You remember me—J.D."

Boomer spat off the loft, bringing fresh curses from those below. "NO! You—you ain't J.D.!" Boomer stammered, although he knew well that it was indeed J.D. "If you's J.D., why ain't you dead? We was all real glad that you was dead and gone. No. If you's J.D., then you's a ghost, mebbe. Or mebbe somethin' worst."

"I ain't dead, Boomer," J.D. said in a soothing tone. "Just take a look. It's me."

Boomer threw an armful of straw over the edge. "Why ain't you dead? Things was nice round here since you died and Buck Hooper run off. No trouble! Ever'thing quiet!"

"You moron! Get yourself down here and take care of these horses, else I'm comin' up and I'll drop you on that brainless head of yours!"

Boomer sat for a long moment, then muttered something about the devil and descended the ladder.

Now the three boys scrambled forward to peer from the darkness down at the two disheveled men waiting with their mounts for Boomer.

In a barely audible whisper, David asked, "Which is J.D.?"

Tommy pointed to the short, bullnecked man in the heavy canvas coat and midcalf boots. His face was lost beneath the shadow of a drooping hat brim, but David imagined that the look in his eye must be as mean as the sound of his voice. J.D. laughed, gave Boomer a shove that spun him around, and booted him in the rear, sending the stablehand sprawling on the floor.

"That'll teach you to hide when I say come!" Boomer lay there a moment, then picked himself up as J.D. caught sight of Bob, Jefferson's mule. He passed the reins of his horse to Boomer and staggered toward Old Bob's stall.

"Why, that's my mule!" he exclaimed, whacking Bob hard across the rump. The animal jumped forward against the manger at the blow and looked around uneasily, ears cocked and laid back at the nearness of J.D.

Boomer spat. "That's Jefferson Canfield's mule. He got that mule from Mister Birch. And don't go whackin' him like that or he'll kick."

Another blow to Old Bob's rear. "It's my mule, I say! I got him from Birch's daddy when he died. Payment for my kindness to the ol' man, you might say."

"Don't hit that mule!" Boomer bellowed, waking up the rest of the stable. Nervous whinnies and kicks could be heard in the stalls.

The other man stepped forward. "Come on, J.D. It ain't worth it. We'll take the nigger back to Oklahoma on that mule, and then you can do what you want with it. Let's get on to bed now. I'm all done in."

J.D. considered this a moment, then shrugged. "Those what argue with a fool is a fool themselves. Don't matter none. It'll be straight to-morrow." Backing away from Old Bob, he warned Boomer to take good care of the horses.

The two men left as Boomer led the animals to the back of the barn, muttering, "It was better when he was DEAD!"

CHAPTER THIRTY-SIX

Still Standing

Frank noticed that his mama's hands were ice-cold as she combed his hair this morning. There were dark circles beneath her eyes, and she seemed especially tired.

"You okay, Mama?" he asked her.

She nodded only once, as though the question disturbed her thoughts. "I gotta go out today," she said in a hoarse voice. "Gonna look for a job. I mean, a real job." She was not speaking to Frank, but to the air.

"Sure, Mama," Frank said.

Little Jim looked worried. He plugged his thumb into his mouth and considered his mother as she turned away and slipped on the same dress she always wore. She always said she couldn't find a job unless she had a decent dress, but she couldn't buy a dress unless she had a job.

"Y'all get on up to Missus Canfield's. Don't be no trouble to her. I gotta get me a job, Frank. I got to. . . ."

★ ★ ★

There were no jobs to be had for the likes of Frank's mama. She stood in line with two hundred other women waiting outside Polsky's to fill one opening in the cosmetics department. She was turned away before the queue had advanced two yards up the sidewalk.

Twice she entered small cafés and asked to speak with the manager. She was pretty enough that she drew a second look, and for a moment her hopes rose. All she needed was a job. All she wanted was work. The aromas of real food made her head spin and her stomach churn with hunger. She would work for leftover scraps of food, she said.

But one look at her and the managers sent her away. She was too lean and hungry to be a waitress. Carry a plate of meat loaf, and she was likely to devour it herself or keel over before she got it to the table.

Waitresses needed a certain quality about them. It was important that they be cheerful and look well fed. And Frank's mama was neither. Her delicate features were painted with desperation. What customer would appreciate a meal served by one so frightened and pale? Besides, her clothes were wrong. Waitresses were required to provide their own uniforms. And it was plain that Frank's mama could not feed herself, let alone buy a waitress dress.

And so Frank's mama came to the end of another endless day without hope.

Carburetor trouble had delayed the usual departure of the mail plane from Fort Smith to Hartford. Smiley was in a dark mood by the time the yellow Curtiss lifted off. The pilot had warned that there was a possibility they would be unable to land in Shiloh due to the lateness of the hour. Smiley had hoped to have his business settled by this time. He had planned to be back in Forth Smith and on board the 7:10 Northern tonight. That now looked doubtful.

Wildman McKinney squinted at the setting sun and flew along the double line of the railroad tracks like a giant arrow launched from Fort Smith and headed for a bull's-eye in Hartford. The three-seater plane was full to capacity. One seat contained the pilot, one was occupied by the mail sack, and the remaining seat held Smiley.

The outlines of Hartford appeared, with a single row of brick buildings marking the business district. Smiley almost lost his hat as Wildman made a sudden banking turn and swooped across the dirt road that paralleled the tracks. Wildman pulled up sharply over some hickory trees, then repeated the diving reversal, crossing the road once again to make sure there were not any cows, horses, or pigs in the way.

Satisfied at last that there were no barnyard obstacles on the makeshift runway, Wildman made a final gut-wrenching turn and dove for the road. By the time Smiley had managed to sit upright again, Wildman was taxiing along the roadway, his prop wash throwing up dust. Turning aside into a clearing just at the edge of town, Wildman spun the plane so it faced the road again, then killed the engine.

Smiley crawled out from the cockpit and pried up the hat he had jammed down over his ears. He scanned the dirt streets and the mules in Brother Williams's corral. "I cannot recall ever seeing a more backward-looking place."

"And you ain't even seen Shiloh yet," Wildman said and grinned. "It's another few miles up that way." He hefted the mail sack out of the plane and gestured toward the mountains with it.

Smiley was disgusted with the way of life in Arkansas. "Do youse mean to say it is less of a place than this? Will we get there today?"

"You can hire a horse at Brother Williams's stable tonight or wait and go tomorrow with me. After I get this mail delivered, it'll be too dark tonight to chance playing tag with a big old oak tree."

Smiley did not fancy riding a horse. The closest he had ever gotten to a horse was walking past a mounted policeman in Central Park. Besides, he had hired this pilot to take him to Shiloh and to wait until Smiley's business was completed, then return him immediately to Fort Smith. This Wildman fellow was well paid for his trouble. And he had said there was no trouble with waiting, although he would not fly after dark or in a thunderstorm.

In a place as tiny as Shiloh, Smiley figured it would be no trick to find where Max Meyer and his kid were located. He would finish them off quietly, then simply step into the little plane and fly away before the bodies were cold. No hired horse could provide the getaway that an airplane could.

Smiley could wait. One night in this Hartford place would provide him with the time and opportunity to pinpoint the exact location of Max and the kid.

"Come on. There's one decent boardinghouse in town. I'll take you to it."

McKinney commented that the gang of boys who usually ran out to greet his arrival had not appeared. "Bet they all went to the picture show. There's a new Western playing."

Miss Zelda Sue Brown's boardinghouse looked as antique as the rest of Hartford, but at least it was clean. McKinney introduced Smiley to Miss Zelda, then left to deliver the mail sack.

"Will you be staying long, Mister Smith?" Miss Zelda inquired, using the alias Smiley had offered.

"That remains to be seen. I am searchin' for a friend from the war. I been told he's been stayin' nearby in Shiloh, which I understand is like a suburb of this city."

"Oh my, yes. Everyone in Hartford knows everyone in Shiloh, and everyone in Shiloh knows everyone in Hartford."

"The guy I'm lookin' for is one Max Meyer, by name. Do youse know him?"

Miss Zelda practically gushed with the news that not only did she know Mr. Meyer, but he was also a guest in her rooming house. "Room three at the end of the hall," she prattled on. "Tonight his son will be staying here, too!"

"Ain't that nice?" said Smiley. "Are Max and his kid here right now?"

Miss Zelda explained that the Meyers were at some sort of meeting, but that Max had said they would be back later.

Stepping close to Miss Zelda and lowering his voice, Smiley invited her to join in a friendly conspiracy. "Y'know, it would please me if I could play a little joke on my old pal Maxie. Do youse think we can keep my arrival just between us 'til I can spring the surprise?"

Miss Zelda eagerly agreed.

"This is most helpful of you," Smiley said. "I can promise you that it will be a really big surprise to Maxie. I'll just wait in my room 'til I hear him come in. Remember," he cautioned her as he bent to pick up his valise, "not a word to anyone."

Jefferson was alone in his cell when Max arrived that afternoon. In one hand Max carried two orange sodas; the other held a slim manila folder filled with a stack of telegrams and official papers.

"My friend in New York found your records," Max said triumphantly. "Legion of Honor. Honorable discharge. It's all here." He flipped open the file and extended it to Jefferson.

"I ain't thought about that much these last ten years," Jefferson said wistfully. "Thought folks burned all them old papers up or wrapped garbage in 'em."

"We keep copies of everything at the newspaper in a file called the morgue. You gave me the dates. Harry Beadle went to the files. And there you are: Jefferson Canfield, son of Hock and Willa-Mae." Then Max shuffled through the papers to pull out the twins' birth certificates. "And now you've named your baby daughter after your mother. That will help, Jefferson."

Jefferson leaned back against the rough log wall and studied little Willa-Mae's birth certificate. "It's good, ain't it?" he said in a whisper. "My name right there on that piece of paper. My young'uns."

"It will be good for our defense," Max said in a matter-of-fact tone.

"That ain't what I mean."

"There is reason to worry, Jefferson. You need to think about to-night."

"Can't think on it no more, Mister Max. My mind done wore out thinkin' on all this."

"You've been through a lot." The eyes of Max Meyer traced the scars on Jefferson's face.

"No more'n any man," Jeff replied quietly.

"A lot more, I'd say. A lot of battles. A war."

"Reckon every man has his own war to go through. This is my own. You got your own. Life ain't ever easy. It's good, though."

Max studied him as though he wanted to look past the scars to a soul that was not scarred or bitter in spite of years of hardship. "You can still say that?"

"I say it ever' day. One day at a time."

"Do you believe it—after everything? And now this? Just when things are going good for you, J.D. and the devil show up at your back door."

Jefferson nodded and closed his eyes. "I got this t'go on. Jesus said a lot of fine things. But He didn't just talk. He lived ever'thing He talked about. Not like most folks. He was the genuine article." He took a different tack. "Go inta a church an' see folks there on a Sunday. They's all worried 'bout ever'thing. Worry 'bout if it's gonna rain or not rain. Worry 'bout themselves an' their kids. Worry 'bout the country an' who's good an' who's bad. They complain 'bout their troubles. They ask how come they got troubles. Mad at God. Doubtin' God. Beggin' God."

"And you?"

"Sometime I'm like that, too . . . 'cause I forget."

"Forget what?"

"I forget that havin' religion ain't the same as knowin' Jesus. Then I got t'get back t'just who Jesus is. He had troubles. Had plenty of sorrows. Did right for folks. Loved 'em. Healed the sick. An' look what folks done t'Him." Jefferson gave a little laugh. "You got a copy of the Good Book?"

"In my room."

"Read the Gospel of Matthew. Chapters 6 an' 7. It's all there. The Lord's whole idea is right in them two chapters. I had me a fine Bible once where all the words of Jesus was in red. Them two chapters is all red."

"I'd like to see that," Max said with a smile. He had not known there was such a thing.

"Last thing them red words say is this: Folks who listens to them words an' puts 'em into practice is like a man who built his house on a rock. When the storm comes an' the rain comes down an' the streams come up, that house is gonna stand! Yessir! It ain't gonna be washed away in the flood! See? But the man that gets religion but don't do what them red words say? Why that man, he's built his house on sand. When the storm comes, that house come crashin' down!" Jefferson leaned forward, his eyes gentle and at peace as he put a hand on Max's arm.

"See, Mister Max? The Lord never said there wouldn't be storms. There's big ones. Big enough t'knock a man's house of dreams and hopes right down flat. We all got storms—you, me, ever'one. If we's alive, livin' is bound t'get hard sometimes. Where folks get off track is when they think Jesus is just gonna make ever' day clear and springtime. That ain't what He said. Not ever. Storms come. He said they would."

"Well, this is certainly one of those times, Jefferson." Max held up the extradition papers and turned his attention to the file. "Here is your storm."

But Jefferson was not finished. "I done built my house on the rock of Jesus. Not the sand of religion. Just 'cause there are clouds, I'm not gonna quit believin'. Thunder boomin'. Windows rattlin'. Door blows down. But I'm gonna still be standin' when this storm passes, Mister Max. No matter how hard it blow against me, I know the Lord got me an' my fambly right in His hand. When this storm passes, my fields be watered. The air be clean. Dirt washed off. The stream an' the pond be full! I ain't scared of nothin' no more—that's all. If Sheriff Ring take me back t'prison, well then, the Lord goes with me an' the Lord stays with Lily an' the Lord will see us through. He said it. I believe it. If I die tonight, I'll wake up in heaven an' I'll be standin' on that Rock."

With a knowing smile, Jefferson turned his attention to the matter at hand. "If it's true for me, then it's true for you, Mister Max. You go on back an' read them chapters. Things will be all right for y'all, too. I know it."

CHAPTER THIRTY-SEVEN

Present Sufferings

There were six brown eggs in the bowl. Two for Frank. Two for little Jim. Two for Frank's mama.

Tonight Frank's mama did not ask where the eggs came from. She knew they had been given to the Penn brothers by little Hock Canfield, who kept his chickens locked in a pen behind the tenement. Two months ago she would have returned the gift because it had been given by a black man. Such had been her pride and her prejudice when she first came to Akron.

But her pride was gone now, and self-loathing had left no room for prejudice in her heart. All pretense was gone. She had committed every sin to feed her boys. She had lied. She had stolen. She had sold herself for pennies. And she had ruined the life of a good man for money. Wasn't that something like murder?

She scrambled four eggs, which made them seem to stretch further. She cut mold spots from the crusts of the remaining five pieces of stale bread and dipped the slices in batter made without milk. There was no butter or syrup, but a pinch of sugar added sweetness to the primitive French toast.

It was a feast, this last supper. Frank's mama dished it up. More for Frank. A little less for Jim. A tiny bit for Mama, so Frank would not chide her for not eating something.

They sat together that final time around the packing-crate table, and she raised her eyes upward in a kind of prayer. "Thanks for these here eggs," she whispered. "I needed help. Y'all seen it, and I thank y'all for the kindness."

She had never said an open word to the couple, but she no longer spoke a word against them either. She did not call them niggers anymore. She told the boys to be polite when they went upstairs, just as if they were going to visit grandparents. She knew that Hock let them help feed the ten chickens and that he paid the boys a pretend salary in eggs. She knew that Willa-Mae fed them every morning. And she was grateful. . . .

Frank wished his mama would come upstairs, too. He wished his mama knew Willa-Mae like he and Jim knew her. Sometimes he thought his mama needed to be gathered into old Willa-Mae's arms and rocked on her broad lap and told stories out of the Good Book just like Willa-Mae did for Frank and Jim.

Frank worried a lot more about his mama than he worried about little Jim. Little Jim didn't cry so much anymore since they had begun visiting Willa-Mae, but Frank's mama cried a lot these days, and her eyes were always sad and hopeless like the eyes of folks in the breadlines. She was thin. Her coat was tattered. There were holes in the soles of her shoes, which she fixed with pieces of cardboard stuck inside. And tonight it was especially cold. Wind howled around the side of the building and rattled the glass in the windows.

"Don't go out tonight, Mama," Frank said as she stood in front of the mirror and smeared rouge on her pale cheeks.

She did not reply, but she did not turn from the mirror, and Frank knew she was going out anyway.

Little Jim finished his supper and held up his plate for more. Frank gave him a hard look. There was no more to eat except what was left on Mama's plate.

"Come finish your supper, Mama," he said.

She looked at him in the mirror. Her face was like a talking picture in the frame. "That's for you and Jim. I ain't hungry tonight."

The wind howled louder outside. Frank looked at Mama's worn-out shoes, which were lying beside the door. She did not have stockings to cover her legs anymore. The last pair had given out, and she had no money to buy more. It was things like her ragged dress and no stockings that made work so hard to get these days, she had told the boys. If it was so hard to find work, then why did she have to go out on a night this cold and dark? Frank wondered.

"I'm goin' to find work," she said. "I might be gone awhile, Frank." She did not turn to speak to the boys. Instead she talked to their reflections as though they were a long way off and she was speaking to them through a window.

Frank looked at her face in the mirror and then at her back. It was as though there were two of her—the one distant image framed in the glass and the one with her back to them. He wished she would turn around and look right at them, but she did not.

"Little Jim, don't you cry when I'm gone now. Frank, you be my little man. Take care of your brother. Do good. Do right. Mind your manners."

"Yes'm," Frank replied. It sounded as though she would be gone a long time. "When you comin' back, Mama?"

She did not reply. "I got to go see a fella." She did not look at them now, not even in the mirror. "That Missus Canfield upstairs . . ." Mama did not finish. "Y'all be polite."

"Yes'm." Frank turned as the windowpane shuddered against the force of the wind. "Will you be outside tonight, Mama?"

"Don't fret," she snapped, making his eyes fill with tears. "You always frettin' 'bout somethin', Frank!"

Why did she not look at him?

"Sorry."

"Don't be such a worrywart. Gets on people's nerves the way you worry all the time." She was still cross.

He ducked his head as though he had been struck a blow. "Yes'm."

"I got to go—that's all. So leave me go in peace." Now her voice was shaking. Her hand was shaking, too, smearing the lip rouge and making her more irritated.

"Sorry," he said again, wishing more than ever that she would turn around and look at him and take him in her arms like old Willa-Mae did.

"Just remember . . ." Her voice caught with emotion just as it had the day they told her their daddy had died in the mine. "Remember what I told you. . . . Keep care of . . . little Jim."

"Yes'm, Mama. I will."

She nodded but did not meet his gaze. Instead her eyes shifted from the faces of her sons to her reflection. She studied her face for a long, curious moment. Then she shook her head slowly as if she were having some silent argument with the stranger that was her. Turning away, she took two white envelopes out of her pocketbook and stared hard at the writing on the front.

"I got to go now." Her voice was barely audible. Stepping away from the mirrored image, she left the pensive faces of Frank and Jim alone in the frame. She did not look at Frank or little Jim. She did not say goodbye as she put on her coat and slipped out the door, not bothering to lock it behind her.

The streetcar clattered over the tracks with double its usual load of riders for this time of day. At every corner, it seemed, more were scrambling for places. Hock and Harry Canfield, who already stood on the rear plat-form where coloreds were always permitted to ride, saw the amassing of men and knew that something was up.

"Trouble," Hock breathed in Harry's ear. "I knowed it was a'comin', and it look like it be here today."

The men boarding the late-afternoon car headed toward Titan Tire and Rubber were grim-faced and serious. Some eyed Hock and Harry with dislike. "Anger fixin' t'bust out of ever'one," Hock observed quietly. "They jus' lookin' for somebody t'bust out at!"

The Canfield men got off at the next corner, even though they were still ten long blocks from the factory. Their places were immediately taken by more white men, who crowded onto the car.

"What do you s'pose is up?" Harry asked.

"Could be they's fixin' t'strike the plant. But they actin' like they's gonna tear it down."

"What are we gonna do?"

Hock could not answer for a time while a coughing spell racked his chest. When he could speak again, he said, "Nothin' else *to* do 'cept show up for work. We both got folks dependin' on us, Harry, so we got no choice."

Harry looked up the street toward the plant. The gloom seemed to thicken with the anger and malice of the night. The cold flurry of wintry air seemed to carry the odor of violence. "Grampa, let's go home."

Hock shook his head. "If they is gettin' rid of white folks like they is, you think they'll keep a raggedy old black man like me if I miss my shift?"

The young man tried to argue, but his grandfather had already squared his narrow shoulders and was marching resolutely toward the Titan plant. Harry had no choice but to follow. But out of every side street and alley, more white men were gathering. None of them smiled or spoke to Hock or Harry, and Harry's uneasiness increased with every step nearer to the Titan gate.

Hock had been gone to work for an hour when Willa-Mae heard the tread of footsteps on the landing. Slow and measured . . . there was the sound of weariness and grief in those footsteps. Willa-Mae did not raise her eyes from the Scripture in the book of Romans, which she had been reading since Hock left.

"For I reckon that the sufferings of this present time are not worthy to be compared with the glory which shall be revealed in us. . . ."

She read the words aloud, then said, "If that's what You say, Lord, then I'm gonna believe it. But that glory gonna have t'really be somethin' if it's gonna make us folks forget the sufferin' of this old worl'."

At that, the footsteps stopped outside the door. There was a long pause, then a faint, hesitant knock . . . a pause and then another knock.

"Now, who could that be at such an hour and on such a night as this?" Willa-Mae left the well-thumbed Good Book open on the chair as she shuffled to the door.

"Who's that?" she called through the panel.

After a long pause, the voice of the woman from downstairs answered. "It's . . . Frank and Jim's mama," she replied as though she had no name of her own, no identity but that.

"Well now!" Willa-Mae smiled and unbolted the latch. "Come on in, honey," she said, throwing the door wide.

Before her stood the woman whom she had only passed in the shadowed corridor of the building. She made no move to enter the warmth of the flat, in spite of the invitation. She was painted like a clown, yet beneath the makeup Willa-Mae could see that she was young—very young indeed—and childlike in her demeanor. Her black hat covered light brown hair. Her eyes—like little Jim's eyes, except green—seemed to hold the sorrows of the world. Her cheekbones were high, her features aquiline like Frank's, and she was far too thin beneath her ragged brown coat. Standing there in run-down shoes, she looked vulnerable and small and frightened.

For just an instant Willa-Mae thought she might have come up to chide the Canfields for looking after Frank and Jim.

"You are Missus Canfield," she said in a quiet, almost frightened tone.

"Yes, I am, honey. And you are Miz Penn."

The young woman looked up as though the title startled her. "S'cuse me. I ain't been called by that since we left home. I'm Mama to the boys, and don't much anybody else call me by name."

"Well, come on in and warm yourself, Miz Penn." Willa-Mae stepped aside to let her see the light of the lamp beside the overstuffed chair and the shelf of knickknacks beneath the window and the picture of Jesus holding His light and knocking on the door—all welcoming sights. But the woman did not step into the Canfield apartment.

"I got to go, Missus Canfield." She did not meet Willa-Mae's gaze.

"I got me a job and . . ." She paused. "What I mean is . . ." She could not look at Willa-Mae's face.

Willa-Mae waited. She understood. She saw the shame in the young woman's face—the shame that she knew the boys had told Willa-Mae what she had said about colored folks.

With a hard gulp, Frank and Jim's mama began again. "Well, Missus Canfield, what I come for is . . . I want . . . want to thank y'all for the way you've looked after my boys some. I mean the eggs and all. The way you got bread for them when the mission truck come through."

"That's nothin', honey." Willa-Mae waved away the compliment with her big hand. "I've raised me a passel of young'uns myself. I knows what it is t'fall on hard times."

Now green eyes lifted to search the mahogany face of the old woman, as if to ask, Did Willa-Mae Canfield know? Could she possibly know just how hard times were? "Well, ma'am . . . y'all been kind—" she lifted her chin—"and I want to thank you."

"Think nothin' of it, gal." Willa-Mae wanted to take her by the too-thin arm and pull her in and feed her corn bread and milk, but she did not. This was hard for Frank's mama. Willa-Mae could see how it humbled the young woman to come here like this.

There was also another reason the young mother had come, and she was trying to get it out. "I . . . I have this job. . . ."

"That's real good, honey. Jobs is hard t'come by. Near ever'one in the neighborhood is outta work."

"Yes'm." She looked at the toes of Willa-Mae's shoes. "Well, I'm scared I'll lose it if . . . well, I got t'leave town for a few days. No more'n a week. Going to model cosmetics at a department store in Cleveland. And I need help with the boys."

Willa-Mae's smile faltered. She looked at the ragged countenance of Frank's mama. How could she model anything at all? "A job . . . ?"

The head snapped up, and words gushed out to counter Willa-Mae's doubts. "Oh yes. They got us little uniforms to wear. It's a good job, even if it don't last long. But I got to show up at the train station. I told them I'd be there even though I didn't know what I was a'gonna do about the boys. I got no one to watch Frank and Jim while I'm gone. And . . . I thought of you, Missus Canfield." She held out three one-dollar bills, which looked like wilted lettuce in her hand. "It ain't quite fifty cents a day, but for a week . . . three dollars . . . ?"

"Don't need no money t'watch them young'uns, Miz Penn. Good boys they is, both of 'em. I don't need no money from you."

"Please . . ." Frank's mama took Willa-Mae's hand and shoved the bills into it. "Please . . . it makes it easier for me."

Willa-Mae had her guess about how that money had been earned. "I don't want no pay."

"I ain't a beggar." A flash of pride reared up in her eyes. "Take it . . . please."

"All right, then." Willa-Mae accepted the offering with the thought in mind that she would take the boys to Kress and buy them new underthings and socks with the money.

That Willa-Mae took the money seemed to soothe the young mother. She nodded and stepped back. "I thank y' kindly." She fumbled in her pocketbook and took out a letter. "There's gonna come a man here to pick up this here letter. Then somebody will pick up the boys for me."

"You ain't comin' back yourself, gal?"

There was a long, thoughtful pause. "No, I ain't comin' back here." Another pause as though she was considering how this would work and what she should explain to Willa-Mae. "I'll get me enough for two child's-fare tickets, and then I intend to send for the boys and we are goin' to California." She repeated this as though she had memorized it. "There'll be somebody come to take the boys off your hands." She passed the envelope to Willa-Mae. "When those folks comes here, make sure they get this letter. Then ever'thing will go easy."

The young woman sighed, and the sigh became a shudder. "I didn't want to tell the boys . . . tell them I'd be gone awhile. I didn't tell 'em nothin' about it. They like y'all a lot. Little Jim don't even cry no more when he's around you. Just give me a little time to get gone, and then go on down and fetch them up here, will you?"

The three dollars, the letter, all the plans . . . and still Willa-Mae did not feel easy letting that young woman walk out of the tenement. She wished she might have brought Frank's mama into the flat and mothered her the way she loved on those young'uns.

Willa-Mae stood in the dark hallway for a few minutes before she went down to fetch the brothers. "Oh, my Lord," she muttered as the outside door opened and Frank's mama stepped out into the windy night. "It will take a heap of glory t'make up for the sufferin' of this ol' world. The sufferin' is so big."

* * *

The wind cut through the thin coat, but Frank's mama barely noticed the aching cold. She dared not look back at the old white tenement. She felt the presence of her sons behind her as they stood framed in the window and looked down on their mama's progress. She knew they saw her lean into the wind as she crossed the street. They saw her stop beside the big green mailbox on the corner, remove a letter from her pocket, and slide it into the slot. She checked to make sure that the envelope dropped, then walked on with the certainty that the letter would arrive within a day at 1064 Florida Avenue.

It was not the only good thing Frank's mama had done in her life, but she knew it would be the last.

Tears streamed down her cheeks, freezing in the cold wind as she walked toward the high bridge of the North Hill Viaduct. She did not look back. Not once did she look back, although she knew Frank and little Jim were waving good-bye to their mama.

A steady stream of people moved toward the Hartford jail and courthouse. As on opening night at the movie theatre, nobody wanted to miss the drama about to be enacted between J.D. Froelich, Birch Tucker, and Birch's hired man, Jeff Canfield.

Pop Lyle, the proprietor of the Hartford theatre, had planned to run *The Big Trail* as scheduled. But when he saw the way the flood of interest was running, he refunded the only two moviegoers their two bits and locked the doors. Tossing an apologetic wave of farewell to the movie poster of the young film hero, John Wayne, Pop Lyle joined the crowd headed for the hearing.

Outside on the steps leading into the downstairs meeting hall, J.D. Froelich stood like a dignitary at the head of a receiving line. He bragged to one and all about how he'd located a dangerous criminal named Cannibal and how he was about to get his reward. Very few of those attending stopped to speak with J.D. or shake his hand, and Grandma Amos waved her Bible in his face and told him he most certainly would be getting his just reward if he didn't mend his ways. "How can a man be spared the wrath of the Lawd in a twister an' still be so wicked?"

That set him back some, but only momentarily. Bunched together in a tight knot were Trudy Tucker and her sons, with David Meyer, Doc Brown, and Mary Brown holding a tiny black infant, followed by Lily Canfield with another baby. At the back of the group, shepherding them along, was Birch Tucker.

J.D. could not keep still any longer. "Hey, Birch," he crowed. "What do you think will happen to a man who harbors an escaped nigger convict?"

Birch made no reply and tried to pass his cousin without incident. But J.D. would not give up. "Shelterin' his whore and her whelps, too," J.D. continued. "Or is she your—?"

Birch's sudden spin brought his right hand arcing down toward J.D.'s face. With a crack that Brother Williams later claimed to have heard half a block away, Birch flattened J.D.'s nose and felled him like a pole-axed hog.

"Did you see that?" J.D. gibbered from the ground, his shirtfront spattered with blood. "He attacked me! My own cousin! Right on the courthouse steps! Did you see that?"

Dee Brown, the barber, handed J.D. a handkerchief to press to his dripping nose, but he spoke for the crowd when he said, "No, J.D., you just slipped on the steps and knocked yourself silly. And nobody saw anything different neither."

A swelling rank of men stood along the outside of the fence at the Titan Tire and Rubber Company. Silently they passed out handbills to the shift coming to work. A few of the gummers stopped to read the papers. A few more refused to accept them. But the majority thrust them hurriedly into their pockets and continued past the baleful stares of the guards.

Arriving ahead of the shift as usual, Ellis had seen Jack Daugherty among those passing out leaflets, but Jack had been careful not to approach Ellis in any way. Of course, Ellis already knew what the paper said. It confirmed the existence of a secret dismissal list and that the union had a copy. It also urged attendance at a union meeting but cautioned against violence.

Ellis had been expecting a police officer and a crowd of reporters to be waiting to question him while a grinning Jack Titan waved a sheaf of photographs, but it had not yet happened. Sleepless nights and brooding waking hours had finally convinced Ellis that he had to locate the girl in the blackmail trap. She had been paid, certainly, but maybe there was a shred of decency in her somewhere. If Ellis could find her, talk to her, maybe he could convince her to tell the truth. If she would just tell Becky what had really happened, maybe Ellis could live with whatever else came. A foolish thought, most likely, but it gave Ellis a small purpose to go on living, at least for a time.

Meanwhile it was business as usual at Titan Tire and Rubber. Or was it? The grime on the windows hadn't changed, nor the stench of rubber in the air, yet something was up. Ellis could sense a mounting tension. He had ignored it on the crowded streetcar and avoided thinking about it as he passed through the silent gallery of discharged employees who stood outside the gate.

There had been more men at the gate than usual—perhaps a hundred men. But it was the knots of men he'd glimpsed in the alleyways and standing on the street corners as if awaiting a signal that increased Ellis's apprehension. More were arriving by streetcar than just the upcoming shift. Still more were arriving by foot . . . rank upon rank of grim, silent men, intent on something as yet unexplained.

And when the factory whistle screamed and the tide of men exiting the plant flowed toward the gate, there was not the hurried step to get off the grounds that usually marked quitting time . . . no dash for the streetcars, no rush to find a speakeasy out of reach of Titan's finks. The outgoing sweep of workers washed up against the crowd outside the fence and rebounded, like a wave hitting a seawall.

The guards at the gate tried to move the men along, waving and pointing. *"Incoming shift,"* their gestures said. *"The rest of you, out."* One of the guards disappeared in a swarm of workers, and nobody seemed to be leaving. The other made a hurried exit from the road, retreating inside the guard shack.

He must have gotten on the phone and sounded panicked, because no more than thirty seconds passed before Jack Titan's bodyguards emerged from the main office building. They formed a row across the doorway, but they made no move to go to the aid of the guards at the gate.

A mass meeting was being held right under Titan's nose. And undoubtedly the little man was viewing the scene from his office window and shouting orders to his flunkies to call the police or the National Guard.

Giselle joined Ellis at the window looking toward the main gate. The shadows of night were collecting in the spaces between the just-lighted streetlamps, and a cold breeze was whipping at mufflers and coattails.

"I've cleared off the desks to use as extra examining tables," she said. "We have only two stretchers, and they are sitting by the door. All the bandages and splints we have are along the front of the shelves, where we can get them easily."

Ellis nodded his agreement without speaking and turned to again study the mass of men outside the fence. It was no longer possible to see past the gloom around the wire to the street outside. Ellis guessed that the crowd was ten or twenty men deep. It extended in both directions until it disappeared behind the buildings that reached out to the road.

The stream of men coming through the gates to join the shift just now going to work had slowed to a trickle. In fact, as Ellis watched, a group of twenty who had already passed the guard shack reversed direction and headed back outside. A wave of cheering erupted from the crowd.

A half dozen workers from Plant One came out of the calendering floor to see what the noise was about. The cheering from the throng outside the fence changed to chanting, offering advice to the workers inside the fence: "Shut it down! Shut it down! Strike! Strike! Strike!"

The six men from Plant One held a hurried conference that was watched with interest by the crowd, by the guards, and by Ellis. They seemed to be divided about what they should do. Five workers pointed toward their fellows outside, while the remaining one, a tall man with fiery red hair, gestured toward the building. As Ellis looked on, the argument grew more heated, with much arm waving.

A man in favor of joining the strike put his hand on the arm of his redheaded coworker. It was shaken off angrily. The redheaded man started to stalk back into the plant. Then the striker must have called something to him, for he whirled around and made a broadly obscene gesture that took in the whole mob outside the fence.

The striker jumped in, and the other four urged him on. Punches were thrown, and both men went down in a tangle of kicking legs and flailing arms. A guard blew his whistle shrilly and ran toward the fight, waving a nightstick. But before the guard even got near the two men wrestling on the ground, one of the others from the calendering floor knocked him down and ripped the club from his hand.

☆ ☆ ☆

Hock and Harry Canfield arrived in front of the Titan Tire main gate in time to hear the chant begin: "Shut it down! Shut it down!"

They stood by a lamppost on the corner across from the plant and watched as scores and then hundreds of angry men pressed forward, shaking their fists and shouting. A flatbed truck roared up out of the twilight, scattering the men in the street. The truck stopped in the middle of the intersection, and two men began rolling barrels off the truck to smash on the road. The barrels were full of ax handles. From all around, individuals rushed forward to claim an ax handle and wave it toward the Titan factory.

As Hock and Harry looked on, some men tried to argue against the wielders of the ax handles. "This is a protest," they shouted, "not a riot! Are you trying to prove that Titan was right? that he was just eliminating the troublemakers?"

The voices of calm were roughly shoved aside. "We've taken all we're going to take! Let's teach Titan a lesson he'll never forget!"

Hock saw one man near the gate who was trying to calm things down. "We don't need this," he was arguing. "If we stand united and prove to Titan that we mean business, he'll have to give in. But if we burn the place down, nobody'll have a job!"

There was a momentary lull as if some of the newcomers were actually considering what was said. Then a cry rang out from the fence: "The guards—they're clubbing our boys!"

The pots of stew simmering on the stoves of the Chandler Soup Kitchen filled the air with a wholesome, warm smell. From her place behind a giant kettle, Becky Warne could see that the breadline stretched far down the street.

Tonight the former automobile showroom was packed with hungry people. Not only were there out-of-work gummers in line, but men, women, and children from every age-group and social strata. An elderly woman in an ankle-length dress stood beside a young flapper whose stylish drop-waist frock would have seemed more appropriate for dinner in the Mayflower Hotel dining room. Behind her was a haggard, pale young mother with three toddlers in tow. A second glance at the gaping coat and the swollen abdomen told Becky that soon this woman would have another mouth to feed. Former bankers stood beside bricklayers who had been laid off when work on the Masonic Temple halted after the crash. Mechanics and shopgirls chatted amiably, while former socialites and college men tried to pretend they were not really here. Not really hungry. Not really desperate.

"I passed out from hunger on the streetcar, and the motorman told me about this place."

"Haven't eaten in three days."

"Preacher Denton's out there serving up a main course of hellfire and brimstone to the crowd," remarked a young man who looked fresh out of a college philosophy class. He held a cold pipe between his teeth. Becky guessed that he had no tobacco to fill the bowl, or on a night as cold as this the thing would have been lit to warm his hands at least.

"Good for Denton," replied a young man whom Becky had seen a dozen times at the kitchen. He wore the same ragged clothes and always brought his own pie tin and spoon. "It's cold enough these days that I need a little hellfire and brimstone to keep me warm."

"Not a substitute for coal."

"That's why they serve hot stew." The ragged man banged his pie tin and smiled. "Best stew in town, too."

Bread and stew made a simple meal, but it was enough to keep penniless socialites and former salesgirls from keeling over on the Akron sidewalks.

As for the stuff that Pastor Bill Denton was dishing out, it was nourishment of a different sort. Despair had blown through the city like a plague of locusts to devour the souls of those who lost hope when they lost their jobs and their savings.

Most who stood in this line tonight believed that they had somehow brought this suffering on themselves. Guilt and shame hung on nearly every face, speaking their own message: *"I am hungry, broke, and out of work. It's my fault somehow, though I don't know how . . . but I'm not worth feeding. If my belly didn't hurt so bad, maybe I'd go ahead and starve. At least then my soul wouldn't hurt so bad."*

This was starvation of a different sort than the hunger that brought people to the breadlines, but it was just as deadly. Becky knew that from her own life. To live without hope was to die by inches every day. And after the example of Jesus, who fed five thousand hungry people while He preached about the Kingdom of God, Bill Denton's Furnace Street Mission was endeavoring to meet both needs. Hope and bread—there were times when the two could not be separated. This was one of those times.

Like the meal, the message Pastor Denton preached was a simple one. Becky ladled up stew while he dished out hope to the hungry crowds. His voice boomed over the loudspeaker and carried both inside and outside. But he did not preach inside the warmth of the room. He stood in the freezing cold of the blustery night. His face was chapped raw by the wind, and his lips were cracked. Had he stood in line with his ever-moving congregation, he would have looked like any of them. His shoes were run-down, his coat worn-out at the elbows. The difference was that, unlike so many in the breadline, Pastor Denton's soul was not lean and hungry.

At the moment, Pastor Denton was engaged in lively debate with a grizzly, barrel-chested man who looked like a wrestler who had lost his last match.

"Bunk and hogwash, Denton!" the big man argued. "If there's a God, how come I'm out of work and standin' in a soup line?"

The answer boomed over the loudspeaker. "Why, brother! If there wasn't a God, you'd be outta work and there wouldn't be a soup line to stand in, nor soup to eat!"

"That's a load of bull! We can get fed without God or your preachin'—down at the army recruitin' center!"

"That may be so, brother, but I've eaten army chow in my day, and the stew the Lord cooks up is a lot tastier than anything you can get in a mess hall!"

"Amen to that, Preacher," shouted the ragged young man near Becky. He raised his tin plate and banged it hard in approval.

Denton laughed, bringing smiles to faces that had not laughed in weeks. "God's no slouch when it comes to good food. He brought some of the best cooks in Summit County together to feed you folks." He drew in a deep breath. "Smell that, will you? Real meat in that stewpot, brothers and sisters! Real potatoes, carrots, beans, and beets! Real butter on your bread, too. Not like down at that other soup kitchen—no sir! What the Lord does for His children He does right!"

Then Denton's face grew serious. "You got troubles?"

"You don't think we'd be here in this breadline if we didn't have troubles!" scoffed the wrestler. "If your God loves us so much, how come we're here?"

"Well, maybe the Lord directed you here, friend . . . just so you could taste the real feast He's got for you! Maybe you been standin' in the wrong line all your life, and it takes a bitter taste to get you to move on over to the Lord! Scripture says, *All things work together for good to them that love God, to them who are the called according to His purpose.* Well, you look big as an ox and stubborn as a mule to me, brother! You've been eatin' at the devil's café long enough! The devil serves up cow dung that looks like meat loaf, and you've been gulping it right down because you thought it was the only meal in town! Well, have I got good news for you! Now the Lord has made you really hungry. Cow-dung meat loaf isn't enough to fill your hurting soul anymore! Only the Lord can fill you with hope again! So the stubborn-mule part of you will just have to move on over to God's kitchen to get fed!"

All of this was greeted with "amens" from the believers in the line, and the cynics soon fell silent. None could deny that there was a hunger inside that ached far more than the pain of an empty belly. For a few short minutes, believers and cynics alike moved forward toward the soup pots.

There was a disruption at the far end of the block, and two uniformed policemen pushed through the crowd. They started for the platform and were met by one of Denton's assistants. A whispered conference took place; then the assistant signaled for Denton to join them. "Excuse me," he said to the crowd. Expectant rumor buzzed through the queue.

Becky watched as Denton listened carefully and gave an emphatic nod of agreement. Back up on the small stage, he said to the crowd,

"You'll have to excuse me, brothers and sisters. Brother Lowell will take over for me. It seems there is an urgent matter I must attend to."

When Denton was almost to the patrol car, he turned suddenly and headed straight for Becky's kettle. "I understand that you are a nurse. Is that correct, Missus Warne?"

When Becky agreed, Denton added, "I wonder if you would be willing to accompany the officers and me?"

Becky felt a nudge on her elbow, pushing her forward. She nodded quickly, almost involuntarily. "Of course, Pastor." She took off her apron and started to hand it to the other worker, the one who had urged her to agree, but no one was standing that close behind her. She shrugged and laid her apron on a nearby table.

Outside, the wind was howling. Becky pulled her coat close around her and got into the backseat of the patrol car. The police vehicle set off at once, its siren screaming back against the wind, as Pastor Denton explained.

"There is a young woman on the North Hill Viaduct," he told Becky. "She intends to jump."

The evening breeze sifted through the partly open window and rustled the curtains at Smiley's back. It flavored the air with the spicy aroma of woodsmoke and the acrid scent of livery stable. These odors of the country only increased Smiley's desire to finish this job and get back to civilization.

Flexing his fingers till his knuckles cracked, Smiley stretched out his hand to touch the .38 caliber revolver lying on the table beside the rocking chair. Standing there in the darkness, Smiley practiced grasping the pistol quickly and soundlessly.

Smiley had entered Max's room through the unlocked door. Nobody locked things in Arkansas. Grinning to himself at how absurdly simple the catch was after the complications of the chase, Smiley reviewed his plan once again.

At the end of the corridor, just a few steps away, was a door that opened onto a second-story landing. There an outside staircase led down to the rear of the boardinghouse.

Once Smiley had his gun pointed at David, he had no doubt that Max would cooperate. Smiley would take them down the stairs and into the woods that clustered close around. A short walk to a suitable spot and everything would be done. What could be simpler?

Smiley sighed with contentment. By this time tomorrow he would be

on a train far from this place and headed for the approval and reward of
Boss Quinn. Even if he had to shoot them down right here and flee out
the window, nothing would stop him now!

The line of bodyguards outside the Titan office building made no move
to assist the gate guards who were involved in the brawl, even though the
security men were getting the worst of the fight. But when the mob
crashed through the gate and poured over the opening like a stampede
of club-wielding wild animals, the situation changed.

To Ellis's horror, he saw the bodyguards reach into their suit coats, and
each drew a revolver from a shoulder holster. With cold precision they
awaited the rush of the horde, then began firing into the mass of men.

The sound of gunfire that reached Ellis was a chorus of cracking
sounds, like the limbs of a grove of trees breaking from the weight of ice.
For some it would have been hard to connect the innocuous popping
with death, but the staccato rhythm carried Ellis back to the killing fields
in France.

The patches of brightness where the pavement was illuminated by
the floodlights were separated by intervals of dark. The effect this had on
viewers like Ellis was to create a sense of theatre about the bloodshed.
Players would run into the spotlight to club or be shot and then dash out
again as if relinquishing center stage to some other performer in a pre-
sentation of death and maiming.

The courtyard inside the main gate of Titan Tire was littered with
bodies just moments after the phalanx of club-wielding men ran into
the gunfire of Titan's bodyguards. Some of the fallen screamed with the
agony of their wounds or called out for someone—anyone—to help
them. Others were ominously silent, while all around them the fire-
storm of rage continued to surge.

Ellis froze in place at the infirmary window. Unfolding right in front
of him in Akron, Ohio, was a replay of what he had seen and endured in
France. The furious assaults into point-blank gunfire lacked only uniforms and barbed wire for the similarity to the Great War to be complete.

The overwhelming numbers of the attackers closed around the
guards, and the fighting was hand to hand. Someone kicked over the
smudge-pot fire where the guards had warmed their hands. A dozen others followed, running in to snatch smoldering fragments of scrap wood
from the ashes. As these makeshift torches roared into flame, piles of
tires were ignited. Black serpentine coils of rubber coughed up orange
flames and vomited thick, oily black smoke.

All this took only seconds, and then a man was struck in the leg by a bullet. It happened directly in front of the infirmary window in the glare of a floodlight. Ellis saw the bullet's impact. Saw the man flung to the ground like a discarded puppet. Heard his cries for help. A fountain of blood spurted into the air.

Ellis shook his head to clear it, as if waking up from sleep. Grabbing a handful of cotton and gauze, he turned to dash outside.

Giselle stopped him. "You can't go out there now!"

"I can't stand here and watch him bleed to death." Ellis thrust her aside.

Outside, Ellis commandeered the first man he saw. "You!" he said with authority to a tall man with a scalp wound of his own. "You come with me!"

"Ain't you the doc? Hey, are you gonna help me?"

"If you want help, then do exactly what I say," Ellis ordered. He forced the man to kneel beside the worker with the leg wound. Ellis stuffed a handful of cotton into the wound and closed the tall man's hand over it. "Squeeze right there and don't let go," he ordered. Scanning the courtyard for other assistants, he rose awkwardly on his prosthesis and started away.

"Hey!" the tall man yelled. "What about me?"

"I'll be back to take care of you. But if you leave before I tell you to, that man will die and then I'll hunt you down and kill you myself!" Ellis spoke these words with such ferocity that the tall worker gulped and nodded, then hunkered down as small as possible.

"You two!" Ellis shouted in the faces of two brawny warehousemen. "Come here and carry this man!" One of the two snarled and swung his club at Ellis, who fell heavily while lunging out of the way.

The other man stopped his friend from closing in. "Don't, Bill! It's the doc!"

Ellis dispatched the two to carry the wounded man into the infirmary. He had the tall worker trot alongside, still keeping pressure on the leg wound.

But he did not accompany them into the clinic. Ellis scanned the combatants for more of the seriously injured and more who could be pressed into service as stretcher bearers.

One of those he came across was Jack Daugherty. Jack had been struck over the head. He was unconscious and bleeding from the ears. As Ellis knelt beside him, Daugherty's eyelids fluttered open. One eye stared upward, unseeing. The other struggled to focus. Garbled sounds came from his mouth, at first urgently, but fading away softer and softer. Ellis placed his ear close to the dying man's lips.

"Johnny . . ."

Ellis could barely understand the word.

"Help Johnny," Jack Daugherty whispered. And then he died.

Harry grabbed Hock and pulled him back from the mob. "Nobody will be working tonight! Let's get out of here!"

But their way was blocked by a large, black-haired man who slapped an ax handle against his palm. "Lousy niggers," he spat with angry menace. "You caused this. Takin' jobs from white men. Hey!" he yelled to other cowards who had not committed themselves to storming the Titan factory. "Let's teach these niggers a lesson!"

"We don't want no trouble, mister." Harry backed up a step.

"Yeah? Well, you already got it." The bully lashed out with the wooden handle, his swipe aimed at Harry's head.

Harry jumped aside and took the blow on his shoulder, but his arm went instantly numb and hung useless at his side. "Run!" he yelled to Hock.

But little Hock had leaped between Harry and the attacker. He threw a punch with a gnarled, veined fist that caught the man in the throat. The white man made a strangled noise and swung awkwardly at Hock, missing him completely.

Someone grabbed Harry's arms from behind, but he kicked up and back as hard as he could and heard a startled gasp. A fat man cried out and fell on the sidewalk.

Turning to help Hock, Harry saw the ax handle in the hands of the black-haired man swing around again. Hock stumbled, trying to get out of the way, but the club connected with the old man's chest. There was a splintering noise, like the sound made by a brittle heap of twigs when crushed under a boot.

Hock crumpled to the ground.

The black-haired man drew back his arm to launch another blow at Hock, but Harry flung himself onto the backswing and, with a convulsive twist of one hand, wrenched the ax handle out of the man's grasp.

"What the—?" the man exclaimed, whirling around. His turn was completed precisely at the right instant for the wooden club to shatter his mouth and nose.

Harry never looked to see how complete his victory was. Gathering up Hock in his good arm, Harry sprinted across the street into the riot. Somewhere behind the smoke and the fire and the fighting was the infirmary, and Harry was going to get his grampa some help.

Police sirens competed with the hoarse cries of men. By now the Titan warehouse had caught fire and the area was brightly lit, but the rolling clouds of black smoke made it even harder to see and doubly hard to breathe.

A new note entered the pandemonium of the night: the excited neighing of horses and the clatter of iron-shod hooves on brick paving stones. It seemed that only Ellis heard the approaching riders. The battle had dissolved into small knots of men fighting with fists and ax handles, wrenches and knives. Three workers near Ellis held a guard up between them, pummeling his head and body with their clubs. When the fumes swirled apart, Ellis could see across the yard to where a guard was kicking the bloody head of a striker who already lay unconscious on the ground.

Out of the dense smoke hammered the mounted patrolmen. They rode directly into the thickest part of the mob, scattering strikers and guards indiscriminately. The rioting workers, choking with the fumes of the burning tires, were not up to facing the hooves and clubs, and they broke and fled out of the courtyard.

Ellis continued commandeering men for assistance. To a policeman he shouted, "I'm a doctor! Get me a dozen able-bodied guys to help carry the wounded. And get me ambulances. I want a lot of 'em, and I want 'em here now!"

The policeman looked at Ellis's bloodied coat and black-streaked face and never even hesitated. "Right away," he said. "Franklin, Muldoon! Stop those men there." He pointed with his nightstick. "Round 'em up and bring 'em here."

"Doc! Doc!" a desperate voice called to Ellis from the direction of the street. "Can you give me a hand? It's my grampa. He's hurt bad." A young black man had a small, frail-looking form slung over his shoulders like a half-filled sack of potatoes.

"Take him into the clinic," Ellis ordered. "I'll be right there."

The North Hill Viaduct was a massive concrete bridge that carried foot, car, and streetcar traffic 135 feet above the valley of the Little Cuyahoga River. On a clear, warm day, it was an engineering wonder to be marveled at. On a bitterly cold night, with ice crusting the metal rails and turning even innocent-seeming paths treacherous, the viaduct was a fearful place.

In the stark glare of automobile headlights, the thin woman who stood on the narrow ledge outside the railing looked helpless and child-like. "Don't come no closer," she said to the officers who were trying to coax her into coming back to the roadway side of the rail. "Don't come no closer. I . . . I just need to think. I come here to do something, but I can't think if you crowd me."

"Take it easy, lady," said one of the policemen. "Nobody's tryin' to crowd you. Just hold real tight to that rail, okay?"

The officer looked over his shoulder at the approach of Pastor Denton and Becky, and Becky saw relief spread over his tense features.

"Hold on, lady," the officer urged again before moving quickly to meet the preacher. "Boy, am I glad to see you, Reverend. I'm not doin' any good here, and I don't know how much longer she can stay out there, what with the wind and the cold and all."

Denton nodded, sizing up the situation in a single glance. He lifted his eyes heavenward for an instant before stepping through the police barrier. He approached slowly, calling out well in advance to warn the woman. "Miss? It's Pastor Denton, miss. May I come and talk to you?"

Her eyes went wide, like those of a hunted animal cornered in a lantern's beam. "Don't crowd me!"

"It's all right," Denton soothed. "Would you like to talk? I'm a preacher. Lots of people come to me if they need to talk over something. Would you like to talk about it?"

The woman's too-thin face shook a sharp negative. "Can't help nothin' by talkin'."

"Would you like to talk to a woman?" Denton offered, gesturing for Becky to come up and stand beside him.

The only reply was a choked sob. The woman looked down and cried out, "I'm sorry! *So sorry!*"

Becky's heart was pounding hard, and her throat was constricted with fear. What if she said the wrong thing? What did she have to offer someone this desperate? "Would you like to tell me your name?" Becky took a step forward.

The young woman's face, its stark pallor showing through beneath heavy makeup, seemed to ponder this request. "I used to have a name," she said, "but I don't no more."

Becky looked at Denton for instruction. *"Keep her talking,"* he mouthed without voicing the words.

"Aren't you cold?" Becky asked, eyeing the girl's thin coat. "It is such a terrible, cold night. Would you like to have some hot soup to eat?"

The woman shook her head, a ragged tatter of light brown bangs escaping her black hat. "Won't be cold or hungry much longer. Just thinkin' here a minute. I'm so tired."

An image flashed into Becky's mind of the last leaf on a tree, its stem a tenuous hold at best against the sweep of the winter storm. Beneath her, the world fell away into the rushing waters of the Little Cuyahoga.

"Come in. It's always easier to think when you're warm. When you have something to eat. You're too tired to think out there. I'll get you a nice bed and a warm bath. I have a big kettle of stew on."

The girl made a half turn to look full in the face of Becky. But as she did so, her left foot slipped on the icy concrete. Her hold almost broke free from the railing, and her foot thrust out into space. A shoe flew off, sailing into the air and disappearing into the inky darkness below.

Becky gasped. There were shrieks and shouts from among the spectators who had poured from cars and streetcars to watch the drama play out.

The woman struggled to catch herself on the railing, barely managing to hook one elbow around the pipe. "Keep back," she screamed as Denton and the police rushed forward.

Denton slipped on the ice and fell to the roadway as two blue-coated officers dashed toward the rail.

With a shout, the woman pulled herself upright for an instant. Her eyes locked on Becky's face and then, like the last leaf of autumn, she gave up. She shook her head, trembled in the wind, and let go just as the policemen lunged to grab her.

Judge Flowers hammered his gavel for silence. The table where he sat was at the far end of the meeting hall and on a raised platform so that everyone in the large crowd could see.

"All right, settle down," the judge demanded. "Keep it quiet or I'll clear the room." The volume of noise dropped considerably, but the crowd continued to whisper. "These proceedings are to establish the identity of one Jeff Field, alias the Cannibal, for purposes of extradition back to the state of Oklahoma. Sheriff Ring, you claim your escapee is in this courtroom?"

"Yessir, Your Honor. That's him, right there." Ring leveled an accusing finger at Jefferson, who was seated near the left-hand wall at the front of the room. Sheriff Potts flanked him on one side and Max on the other. Jefferson stared back at Ring without flinching.

"All right, then, who will speak for the accused?"

Max cleared his throat and climbed nervously to his feet. "I will, Your Honor. Max Meyer is my name. I'm a friend of Jefferson's."

"Let me remind both parties," the judge explained, "that this is a hearing and not a trial. I will not permit cross-examination. I'll ask the questions I see fit to ask. Now, is everyone clear on that? Sheriff Ring, you may proceed."

"Your Honor, I was personally transporting the prisoner when he escaped from custody due to an unfortunate accident."

"When and where did this escape take place?"

"In September of this year, Your Honor, at . . ." Ring mumbled the end of his sentence so the location could not be heard.

"Speak up, Sheriff. Where did you say?"

"Not far from here, Your Honor. In the Devil's Backbone country."

"I see," said Judge Flowers, squinting over a pair of reading glasses. "In the state of Arkansas. Is that correct?"

Ring looked uncomfortable but agreed that this was correct.

"It is not pertinent to the matter at hand," said the judge, "but on another occasion we will examine why you were operating so far outside your jurisdiction. Now, what else do you have to say?"

Ring looked nonplussed. "Ain't that enough? I can personally identify the prisoner, and I have the extradition papers permittin' me to take him back!"

Judge Flowers gave Ring a withering look. "That may be enough for the way they do business in Oklahoma, but in Arkansas you have to satisfy *me* that your escaped prisoner and the accused are one and the same."

Ring was shocked. "Do you mean to say you might take a nigger's word—"

The gavel hammered down hard, and the table jumped. So did the spectators. This was getting interesting!

"You will refrain from either impugning the integrity or damaging the dignity of this court," Flowers warned, "or I will find you in contempt."

Half the onlookers asked the other half what *impugn* meant.

Ring sat down abruptly.

J.D., who was seated next to Ring, had lost his smug look and started frowning with unhappiness at the thought of his reward skipping away. He mopped his face with a bloody handkerchief.

"Mister Meyer," the judge continued, "it's your turn."

"Your Honor," Max began, "we will show that this is a case of mistaken identity. The man seated here is well-known in the community. He is Jefferson Canfield, and he cannot possibly be the prisoner known as the Cannibal."

"Do you have witnesses on his behalf?"

"Yessir, Your Honor. Birch Tucker knows Jefferson Canfield."

Birch took the stand, which meant that he sat in an oak armchair beside Judge Flowers.

"Since this is not a trial," the judge said, "just tell us in your own words what you know."

Birch began by explaining how he had first met Jefferson Canfield in France during the Great War. "And he won a medal over there, Your Honor."

"Can this be substantiated?"

Max produced a copy of a wire-service news release dated 1918. It reported that a company of Negro soldiers had received special honors from the French government for heroism in battle. Prominently mentioned was one Jefferson Canfield, who was awarded the Legion of Honor. The story gave the soldier's home as Mount Pisgah, Arkansas, and mentioned that his parents were Hock and Willa-Mae Canfield.

Sheriff Ring waved his hand to get the judge's attention. "That don't prove nothin', Your Honor. That happened more'n ten years ago."

"If it please the court," said Max, "we are not through yet."

Birch was allowed to continue. "Jefferson Canfield is a fine, upstandin' man. He saved my life once, and I named one of my boys after him."

This caused a ripple in the nearly all-white audience. But since Birch was respected in the community, it was generally allowed that it must be all right.

"And Jefferson is my hired man, as all the folks hereabouts know. What's more, he saved my boys from the tornado."

"Your Honor," Ring spoke up, "you can see that Mister Tucker has a personal reason to try and protect the accused."

Flowers chose to ignore this comment and asked Max if there was more.

"Your Honor," said Max, "we also have the evidence to be given by Doctor Brown and Pastor Adams."

Doctor Brown testified that he had delivered Jeff and Lily's twins on the night of the full moon and the big storm, the first week of November. Everyone, including Judge Flowers, did a little calculating on their fingers. If that was true, Jefferson could not possibly have been in prison when Sheriff Ring claimed he was!

Ring objected. "How does the doctor know they are his kids?"

Max was prepared for that question. He introduced Pastor Adams.

The preacher explained that he had been present at the naming of Jeff and Lily's children. "The names of the children are William and *Willa-Mae*," he emphasized. "Is it likely that a man would name someone else's child after his own mother?"

A murmur of approval rippled through the audience.

"Hold on a minute!" J.D. shot upright. "But they didn't come to Shiloh together! Ask 'em, Judge! She come after the Tuckers!"

Judge Flowers hammered for silence, but he did ask Pastor Adams the question. "That they were separated is a personal matter," the preacher explained. "But I will swear that they are husband and wife and that the twins are their children."

The courtroom just about broke up at that, since everyone knew that Pastor Adams would not—could not—lie. Flowers again gaveled for quiet and in fairness asked Sheriff Ring if he had anything else to say.

Ring unfolded a wanted poster from his pocket and asked if he could read it aloud. "'Negro. Thirty years of age. Six feet five inches tall. Face scarred numerous times.'"

Everyone in the meeting room craned their necks to examine Jefferson's features. An element of question crept back into the whispered comments.

Judge Flowers frowned over his glasses and studied the accused.

Max interrupted the judge's reverie. "Your Honor, ask him to read *all* of the description."

Flowers did so, and Ring complied with a smirk. "There's jest a little bit more. It says, *'Can be identified by condition of mouth. Teeth mostly missing, and remaining teeth broken and jagged.'*"

Max nudged Jefferson, telling him to stand and turn sideways so that both the judge and the crowd could see him clearly. "Your Honor," Max said, "even a description that sounds close is worthless if it isn't exact."

Jefferson opened his mouth to reveal a perfectly even row of shining gold teeth!

The crowd applauded. They'd known all along, they said. Birch Tucker's hired man who had saved the lives of his sons could not possibly be a desperate criminal!

Judge Flowers banged his gavel. "Clearly mistaken identity," he said. "Case dismissed!"

And the celebrating began.

It was like after a wedding or a baby dedication. Everybody stood around congratulating everybody. With the exceptions of J.D., who slunk off declaring he'd been robbed, and Sheriff Ring, who clapped his hat on his square head and left without speaking, most everyone stayed around to pump hands and slap backs.

Birch congratulated Jeff, who hugged Lily and got hugged by Trudy.

Doc Brown praised Pastor Adams, and Grandma Amos praised the Lord. And everybody wanted to shake Max's hand.

David looked at his father with renewed admiration and pride. His father might not be ideally suited for life in Shiloh or Hartford, but there were times when Shiloh and Hartford needed him.

When the crowd finally broke up, it was only to split into smaller groups and continue the discussion in parlors and around kitchen tables.

Jefferson drew Max aside. He stuck out his hand. "You gave me back my life. I can't never thank you enough."

Max grinned. He felt better than he had in a long time. But he also felt exhaustion beginning to settle in after the effort. "C'mon, Davey. Let's go up to our room. Unless you'd rather stay over with Boomer and the boys again."

The pride reflected in David's eyes answered for him. He was staying with his father tonight!

CHAPTER THIRTY-EIGHT

A Shot in the Night

Jefferson had just switched on the light in the spare bedroom at Doc Brown's house when the angry voice of J.D. Froelich called up from the yard below.

"Come out here, nigger! Get your black hide out here! I got Sheriff Potts with me! You done stole my mule, and I aim to have you back in jail!"

Jeff and Lily exchanged weary looks, the pleasure of their victory abated.

"He ain't gonna let us be, Jefferson," Lily said softly. "Don't matter none 'bout this hearin'. Long's J.D. is round here, we ain't gonna have no peace."

Jefferson nodded as a knock sounded on the door of the room. Outside, Sheriff Potts shouted at J.D. to shut his mouth.

With a sigh of exasperation Jefferson opened the door to Birch.

"It's J.D.," Birch said. "He wants Ol' Bob. Says that mule is his and that you stole him. Me and Sheriff Potts told him how it came about that you have Ol' Bob, but J.D. won't be satisfied until Ol' Bob and Alice are back on his place. He says if Potts won't do something, he's going to get the sheriff over in Mansfield and have you arrested for theft."

"Hate to turn that mule over to a man as mean as J.D.," Jefferson said. "But I'm weary of trouble, Birch."

"I figgered you'd say so. I feel the same about it myself. We'll get you another team. I'll tell Potts J.D. can take Ol' Bob, then."

J.D.'s harsh call resounded from the porch. "It's my mule, and I aim to shoot it! Try and stop me, nigger! My mule, and I'll do with it as I please!"

"He means to do it, just to provoke you. I know J.D. He's just that mean," Birch said quietly. "Ol' Bob is over thirty years old. He had a good life too, before J.D. got him. Reckon it'll be a mercy if J.D. shoots him instead of finishing his days mistreated."

"Just try and stop me, and you'll be right back in jail!"

Jefferson stared past Birch into the dark corridor. He pictured himself going down the stairs and thrashing J.D. But that was just what J.D. wanted Jefferson to do. That was what this was all about.

"Ol' Bob has been a good mule." Jefferson felt emotion choking him. "But I ain't gonna war no more, Birch. I ain't gonna get myself hung over a mule. Go tell Sheriff Potts that J.D. can take Ol' Bob."

Trudy and Birch stood together on the porch. Mary and Dr. Brown flanked them. They did not look at J.D., who continued raving about the "robbery."

The face of Sheriff Potts was pained and angry. "It's best, I think," he said in a low voice. "It ain't worth it, Birch. You know your cousin as well as I do."

"Well then—" Birch glanced toward the lighted window, where Jefferson and Lily waited—"me and Trudy will just go on down there to the livery stable with you and J.D. to fetch Ol' Bob. My boys are down there with Boomer and"—a hard look at J.D.—"I don't want them getting' in any kind of situation."

J.D., madness in his eyes, crooned, "Trouble? Why, Cousin, what you think—I'm gonna harm them boys? My own nephews? Just aim t'shoot me an ol' mule is all. Put it outta misery. Been mistreated by that nigger of yours, I hear."

Birch chose not to reply. He held tightly to Trudy's arm and felt her trembling with barely controlled fury.

"Shut up, J.D.," Potts warned again. "And hear me: You swear just once more, and I'm locking you up for profane behavior in public. Far as I'm concerned—"

"Don't matter what you think, Potts," J.D. crowed. "The sheriff in Mansfield ain't no nigger-lover like you. You mess with me in this, and that's where I'm headed. Shiloh is smack in the middle 'tween here and Mansfield. You know that lawman has just as much jurisdiction as you do. I'd fetch him back here right now, but all I want is to finish my business peaceable."

"If that's what you want, then you'll get out of town," Potts replied in a menacing tone.

"Get on with it," Birch urged quietly. They walked toward Brother Williams's livery stable, where the lantern still burned in the loft.

* * *

Miss Zelda's oak stairs creaked as Max and David took the steps side by side, Max's arm resting lightly on David's shoulders. Outside their room, Max fumbled with the antique brass knob, then pushed the door open into darkness. David preceded his father into the room.

Max twisted the light switch on the wall, but no answering gleam appeared from the hanging bulb. "Hold on, Davey," Max said. "There's a lamp on the table."

"Shut the door and stand still," ordered a voice from the deep shadows near the window, "if youse do not wish to suddenly develop a bad case of bullet holes."

"Who are you? What do you want?"

"Shut up and shut that door," commanded the voice. "Do it!"

Max obeyed. As the latch clicked, a wooden match flared and was applied to the kerosene lamp.

"Dad, what's going on?"

The pale features and the puckered scar across the throat left no doubt as to the intruder's identity. "This is Smiley," Max said. "He works for Boss Quinn."

"Bright boy." Smiley inclined his head. "Even knows my name. But being too bright can cost youse. Boss Quinn does not like bright boys who steal from him or bright kids who see too much."

"The joke's on you, Smiley. Quinn's dead—killed by the O'Farrell mob."

"That's a good one, scribbler. Youse had me goin' there for a minute."

"It's the truth," Max insisted. "Call New York and ask. You don't want to commit murder when there's no reason."

"Who was speakin' anythin' about murder? We are just goin' for a nice walk to a quiet spot. My employer simply wishes for me to find out how he can get his money back and to receive a promise from the kid that he will not play the rat." Smiley waved them over by the wall with his pistol and kept it pointed at David while moving to stand near the door.

"This is how we will proceed," Smiley said. "Youse, newshawk, will go first, followed by the kid and then me. Please note that a rather large lead slug travels faster than you, so no funny stuff. We will go down the back stairs very quiet and friendly-like."

✳ ✳ ✳

The voice of Boomer woke up half the population of Hartford.

"YOU! J.D.! You ain't killin' . . . you ain't gonna! Naw! I AIN'T LETTIN' YOU SHOOT THIS HERE MULE!"

J.D. brandished his gun and chuckled. "Tell this moron, Sheriff Potts. Tell 'im who this here mule belongs to."

Tommy shouted down from the loft. "Ol' Bob belongs to Jefferson! That's who."

"Yeah!" Bobby agreed.

"No, nephews." J.D. was clearly enjoying the stir he had caused. "This here mule belongs to me, Cousin J.D. And I aim to destroy him because he's so old. I'll get Alice the same way."

Bobby began to cry. "Dad! Stop him! Don't let him do it! Dad?"

Trudy stepped to the foot of the ladder. "Come on, boys. Come on back to Doc Brown's house."

"He ain't gonna shoot Ol' Bob, is he?" Tommy choked out the words, which ended in a sob.

Boomer leaped onto a hay bale. He brandished his arms about wildly and then crowed like a rooster. "NO! He ain't gonna shoot this mule! Ha! Ah-ha!" With that, Boomer snatched a pitchfork from the hay and pointed it at J.D.'s heart.

Emmaline began to howl, and Codfish barked and snarled.

"You'll see, boys," Boomer bellowed. "YOU, J.D.! YOU AIN'T SHOOTIN' THAT MULE IN BROTHER WILLIAMS'S STABLE!"

J.D.'s cruel grin changed to a scowl. "Call him off," he menaced, his eyes on the tines of the pitchfork.

But no one moved to stop Boomer or reprimand him. It was clear that J.D. would have his way eventually, but all who witnessed the scene were glad that Boomer was making it difficult for J.D.

Birch and Trudy, Doc Brown and Mary stepped back and watched as J.D. attempted to step around Boomer and the pitchfork. Each step sideways was countered by a move of Boomer's. He crouched and flourished his weapon like a broadsword, protecting the old mule's rear end.

Moments ticked by. "You ain't gonna be able to stand here forever, Boomer," J.D. cajoled. "Put it down. Remember, I'm your friend. I brung you a Nehi on a hot day. Remember?"

"Weren't no good!" Boomer responded. "Didn't have no fizz. Get back, you! GET BACK, J.D.! Ain't gonna kill this here mule! He been talkin' to me! This here mule says you are rotten! ROTTEN! Says he wished you'd got sucked up in that twister! Said he's gonna KICK YOUR BRAINS CLEAN OUT!"

"Well now." J.D. regained his composure, although beads of sweat stood out on his forehead. "See there. Ol' Bob don't like me, and I don't like him none neither. Did you say that 'bout me, Ol' Bob?" J.D. looked at the mule. He leaned his head close.

In that instant Boomer turned to listen to the mule, who was silent. "I didn't hear nothin'."

J.D. reached around and grabbed the handle of the pitchfork. With a wrenching motion, he pulled it from Boomer's hand and then kicked his adversary hard in the chest. Boomer fell sprawling backward, and the standoff was over.

While Bobby and Tommy wept in the loft, J.D. untied the mule from the stall and led him out past the small group of witnesses.

"Only reason I don't kill him here is that I don't want to leave a mess of brains for you to clean up." J.D. laughed. "See? I really am your friend." At that he led the animal off into the darkness of the alley.

Muffled voices and laughter drifted up from downstairs. Light showed from the cracks around other bedroom doors, illuminating the empty corridor as Smiley forced Max and David out of the room. Even J.D. would have been a welcome sight to Max at this moment, but no one appeared in the hall.

Max took the lead, carrying the kerosene lamp to light their way into the woods. David followed with the barrel of Smiley's gun pressed behind his left ear. Max had no delusions that Smiley only wanted to talk. "A quiet place" meant some deserted spot far enough from Hartford that gunshots would not be heard and bodies would not be found until Smiley was long gone.

Walking as slowly as possible to gain time to think, Max was three treads down the outside staircase when David stepped off the landing. The boy turned back abruptly to face Smiley's weapon as though it were a toy. "I forgot my coat," he said, hopping back up to the platform.

The sudden move caught Smiley off balance, and he turned awkwardly to grab at David's hair. "No youse don't, kid," he barked. But David's move turned the gunman's back to Max for an instant.

It was long enough.

Max whirled and threw the lamp at Smiley's head like a shot put.

Smiley ducked, and the glass globe missed, spinning over the railing and crashing on the ground below.

Shouting for David to run, Max lunged for Smiley's ankles.

"The gun, Dad!" David shouted.

Smiley took aim at Max's face. But as Smiley's trigger finger tightened, David leaped across the gunman's arm, ruining his shot. The .38 exploded, shattering the night with a blast that went wide as Smiley's arm struck the banister.

Max charged, tossing Smiley backward onto the landing, and the two wrestled for possession of the revolver. "Get away, David!" Max yelled. "Get Birch!"

Smiley threw a left-handed punch that hit Max over the ear; then his fingers ripped at Max's eyes. Max closed both fists over the gun hand and hung on as the two rolled over and the pistol blasted again.

Brother Williams, in his nightshirt, stumbled out to join the group in the stable. They clustered in a tight knot and spoke in low tones as they waited for the shot from J.D.'s gun that would kill Old Bob.

When it came, everyone jumped. Trudy gasped, and Bobby wept softly against her.

A second shot sounded.

Sheriff Potts held his head high as though sniffing something in the air. "Two shots," he muttered. "Sounded like a .38. J.D. don't carry a .38. He carries a .45 like me."

"Sounded like it was coming from Miz Brown's boardinghouse," shouted Brother Williams.

Suddenly the cries of young David Meyer split the night.

Max slammed Smiley's gun hand down on the planks, trying to knock the pistol loose. Smiley hammered at Max's face, then closed his clawlike fingers around Max's windpipe.

Struggling violently from side to side to dislodge Smiley's hold, Max flung the two of them against the lower rail of the landing. The board splintered, and Max and Smiley shot through the opening. In midair, the gun went off again, and Max felt a searing pain tear into his left arm.

A drop of ten feet brought the ground up with a rush. They hit a scant yard away from the pile of glass shards that had been the lamp, now blazing merrily like a small bonfire. Smiley landed on top of Max, who lay breathless and bleeding. Max felt the wound in his chest rip open again. His shirtsleeve was dripping blood.

The thump of the impact had knocked the pistol from Smiley's grip, but he recovered quicker than Max and retrieved it. By the flickering fire-light, Max could see Smiley standing over him.

"Good-bye, scribbler. Youse can die knowin' I'll be back for your kid." Smiley raised the pistol.

Around the corner of the boardinghouse at Smiley's back came Birch and Jefferson and Sheriff Potts with his gun drawn. The firelight silhou-etted the hoodlum perfectly.

"Hold it," Potts demanded. "Drop it!"

Smiley turned at the noisy approach, swinging the .38 up and around as he revolved. But the shimmering glow reflected off the gun barrel as he turned, and Potts fired first.

The impact of the .45 slug lifted Smiley off his feet and flung him backward. He landed across the remains of the lamp, snuffing out the light that had pinpointed him as a target.

CHAPTER THIRTY-NINE

No One Was Lost

The North Hill Viaduct suicide made only page 8 of the morning newspaper. It was an item of small interest compared to the front-page banner headlines describing the riot at the Titan Tire and Rubber Company: "3 Die, 59 Hurt As Rioters Attack Police!"

Numb from lack of sleep, Becky spread the issue on the dining table and studied the photographs of club-wielding police and workers caught in the flash of the camera the night before.

Ellis had been somewhere on the fringe of violence, picking up the pieces after the blows had fallen. He had called her at 3:00 AM with word that he would not be home.

Had she heard about the tragedy at the plant? he asked her. Did she know what had happened? In a voice trembling with rage and grief, he told her about the police and the horses and the guns and ax handles and his helplessness in all of it. Workers had turned against one another—those who wanted to cross the line and those who drew the line.

It was the beginning of a war, he said. Men had died before his eyes. Jack Daugherty had been killed. One man had bled to death while he tended another. There were so many wounded that the death toll was sure to climb. The world had all gone wrong. His life had all gone wrong. It was not supposed to be this way, was it?

His heartache had overflowed, and in the end he had said he wanted only to come home again . . . to see her again . . . to look at her and try to remember what was real and important about being alive. Was it too late for them? he asked. Could he still come home and find her waiting?

"I'm here, Ellis," she told him. "Come home when you can. I'll be here."

Becky hung up the telephone without telling him about the tragedy she had witnessed on the bridge. Now, hours later, Ellis still had not returned. Becky scanned the columns of newsprint to find the one small story about the suicide.

The article reported flatly that the woman who had thrown herself from the North Hill Viaduct was nearly rescued by two officers who missed her hand by inches and who tried to save her at great peril to their own safety. Her body had been recovered an hour later from the rocks beside the river.

As though describing an item in the Lost and Found, the notice ended with this:

> *There was no identification on the body, and the deceased may be identified and claimed at the Summit County Morgue. Brown hair. Green eyes. Blue dress. Brown coat. 5'5" and 112 lbs. Coroner estimates the age of the woman as between 20 and 25 years.*

To the editor of the newspaper, no doubt, this one more death seemed of small significance compared to the riots at Titan Tire. Becky knew that hardly a day passed without a suicide, that such events had become commonplace in the past few weeks. But this morning, in the cold blue light of dawn, Becky was able to put a face to the black-and-white statistic in the newspaper.

"You were somebody!" Becky whispered aloud. "Like me. You had a name. You had a name. . . ."

The waiting room at People's Hospital was crowded with family members awaiting word on the condition of the men injured in the riot. In one corner, the wife of a policeman sat surrounded by her four children. Her face was dull from exhaustion and worry.

Across from her was the family of a young gummer whose skull had been cracked by a police billy club in the fray. Mother, father, brothers, and sisters huddled together fearfully. Their faces lifted at every opening of the door. Their eyes followed the coming and going of each white-clad nurse.

Dozens of others shared the same fear for their loved ones. No matter that the men had been on opposite sides of the line last night. This morning they balanced on the same line between life and death. Some of them would not see another sunset.

There had been no word about Hock's condition since he was taken by ambulance to the hospital. Willa-Mae Canfield sat straight and tall on the bench reserved for coloreds in the hallway outside the waiting room. Little Jim Penn slept in her lap. Frank, his crippled foot tucked beneath him, dozed under her arm like a chick sheltered by the wings of a hen. Harry waited silently next to his young wife, and Reverend and Mrs. Dale kept the vigil beside them.

A dozen others from the church had come and gone as news of the tragedy spread, and their presence was a comfort to Willa-Mae. She was grateful that she did not have to be alone at such a time.

Hock was bad off, Harry had told her when he came to the apartment to fetch her. Hock had looked at Harry and whispered the name of Jefferson once before he lapsed into unconsciousness. Was it because Harry looked so much like Jefferson, or had Hock seen a vision of his lost son? There was no way to know the answer now. Hock was barely breathing on the stretcher bound for People's Hospital when Harry had left him.

Throughout the night, Dr. Warne had walked by the waiting family in the corridor, but he had not met the anxious gaze of Willa-Mae or Harry. Once, when Harry stopped him, the doctor had indicated only that Hock was hanging on and that X-rays had been ordered to see how extensive the damage was. There were so many seriously injured men and so many tests to do that it was unlikely anything would be known until morning.

The blackness of the night gave way to the pervasive gray of a reluctant dawn. The distant booming of thunder echoed across the city of Akron. Willa-Mae could see rain falling hard beyond the glass pane of the window at the end of the hall. She had no tears left to shed. Now it seemed as though heaven itself wept for her and for Hock.

Willa-Mae and Hock had weathered one storm after another and come through still standing. Were their years together finally to end here as the result of a fight that Hock had never wanted to be part of?

As if he heard her thoughts, Reverend Dale leaned down to whisper, "How you doin', Sister Canfield?"

"Weary, Brother Dale," she replied.

"I know you are, sister. Life's hard most times."

"Me and Hock seen troubles come before. Lost our babies. Buried young'uns. Stood beside their graves and said, 'So long.' Spent ten years grievin' for our Jeff. Reckon Hock be ready t'lay all them troubles down if the Lord wills it. But I don't like t'think on livin' without that ol' man."

"The Lord give us strength t'bear what we must, Sister Canfield."

Willa-Mae nodded and closed her eyes to hold back the tears that threatened. No use these poor little brothers seeing her cry, she told herself. They had enough sorrow to bear in their own lives. So Willa-Mae leaned her head against the wall and pretended to be resting as she thought about her life with Hock and conjured up memories of the good times. . . .

Babies born. The laughter of growing children in the little cabin in Pisgah. The scent of fresh air in the country morning. Tall cotton thick with white bolls shining like snow in the summer fields. Hock carrying a newborn calf in from the pasture while young'uns clustered all around their daddy to look on in awe. Sunday mornin' side by side in church. . . .

Willa-Mae's brow furrowed at this last image. Clear as anything she could see Jefferson standing at the pulpit and hear him preach. *"Rest in God's arms, Mama,"* he seemed to say to her this morning. *"Be His baby. Lay Daddy in the Lord's hands."*

"Yes. I will," Willa-Mae answered aloud and opened her eyes just as the doctor limped down the corridor toward them.

Dr. Warne was not smiling. His youthful face was lined with strain. What was in his eyes? Life? Or death?

Reverend Dale stepped back as Dr. Warne approached. Whatever the verdict, perhaps the waiting was over.

"Missus Canfield." He stood over Willa-Mae as though there were no one else in the hall.

"Yessir. You got word of my husband?"

"Yes, ma'am. Mister Canfield has four fractured ribs. He will recover from the blow."

This news was interrupted by a chorus of "Praise be!" and "Thank You, Lord!"

But when Doc Warne held up his hand as though it was not yet time to be thankful, Willa-Mae knew there was more. "Tell it all t'me, Doctor."

"The X-rays show that your husband is a very sick man, Missus Canfield. Tuberculosis. His case is not far advanced—some spots the size of quarters on his right lung. However, without proper care I cannot make any promises about recovery. It is certain that the factory smoke and climate make Akron the worst place for him to be."

Mrs. Dale gasped at the news. Reverend Dale reached out to grasp Willa-Mae's hand. What hope could there be for Hock now? This meant an end to his job. No matter that his case was light. Tuberculosis was a sentence of death for Hock, and each breath posed a danger to all those around him.

Willa-Mae looked down at the child sleeping in her lap. She stroked Frank's fair hair. Were these little ones at risk from the time they had spent with Hock and Willa-Mae?

Dr. Warne continued, "It is important that you be tested as well, Missus Canfield." Now his attention focused on the brothers. "These boys?"

"I watch 'em both."

"Have they been with you much?"

"They been round enough, I reckon."

"Then I'll arrange to see them." His eyes were kind and sympathetic, his voice gentle. He pulled a card from his pocket and presented it to Willa-Mae. "Call this number and make an appointment this week."

He smiled sadly and touched Frank's face with his fingertips. "Nothing to worry about. They look healthy and . . ." At his touch, Frank opened his eyes and shifted, revealing the grotesquely deformed foot. The doctor's smile faded. He looked hard at the child and then, as Frank sighed and returned to sleep, he asked, "His parents? Have they taken him to a doctor?"

Willa-Mae shook her head to let the doctor know that the situation for these children was as hopeless as it was for Hock. "Got no money for doctors. Daddy's dead. Their mama's poor. It ain't possible for some folks t'get well and be made whole. You understand what I'm sayin'? It ain't so easy as goin' t'see a doctor and gettin' advice on how t'fix what's wrong. My Hock don't have no air to breathe but this air in Akron. This chil' got no money t'make his foot straight."

At her words, Dr. Warne winced and nodded. His brow furrowed as he stared hard at little Frank's bent limb. Then he turned his attention to Harry. "It's important you all be tested for TB. There will be no charge, of course. Just a precaution. You may call at my clinic."

To Willa-Mae he said, "Your husband is in isolation. He would like to see you."

✯ ✯ ✯

Warned that a tribe of reporters waited in the lobby of the hospital, Ellis slipped out through the kitchen entrance. He had lost his hat somewhere last night, and he bowed his head against the surprising rush of cold.

The usual scent of burned rubber was absent from the rain-washed morning air, and it had begun to snow. Large flakes drifted down, creating a soft white veil that concealed smokestacks and muffled the sound of factory whistles and traffic. The sweet, warm aroma of oats from the nearby Quaker Oat factory awakened Ellis's appetite, reminding him that he had not eaten since yesterday morning. He lifted his face to the cold kisses of snow as he limped slowly through the alley toward the streetcar.

Rounding the corner, he could see Jack Titan's long, black limousine waiting at the curb. Titan, who had been cracked on the head by a bottle, stood surrounded by newsmen on the steps of the hospital. His words were shouted for all to hear.

"This is all, of course, the work of Communist agitators seeking the destruction not only of our company but of our country! This rumor of a layoff is totally false! Propaganda by the Reds, I assure you!" As he talked, Titan's face turned toward Ellis for an instant—long enough that Ellis expected him to shout out his name and shake his finger in accusation.

Ellis tucked his head again and hurried toward the streetcar. He paid his nickel, then sat down for the first time since the previous evening. And looked around him.

What was different? Everything looked the same, yet something had changed inside him.

The finality of death had awakened Ellis's mind like the shock of frigid air. He was still alive, and others were not. He considered those who had died—men like Ellis with wives and families, with a thousand reasons to go on living in spite of hard times. By tonight there would be more from among the injured who would never see another sunrise.

The ordinary world of Akron slid past the window of the trolley like some wonderful panorama on a screen. The snow fell harder, covering the soot with a blanket of pure white. Children smiled and pitched soggy snowballs as they waited on corners for the school bus. Outside the halls of People's Hospital, the faces of passersby were bright, as though they did not know what had happened last night in the factory yard. Cheerful bits of Christmas decorated lampposts and store windows.

Was it really Christmastime? Had he been asleep? he wondered. Had he been moving so long in the dark shadows of fear that he had not noticed the world around him?

"Yes," he whispered, suddenly remembering the endless rows of graves on the battlefields of France. Wooden crosses topped by battered helmets. When he was a young soldier who had barely begun to live, that sight had made him drink deeply of each moment. Then, as now, even the commonplace events of life had seemed miraculous. They *were* miraculous.

"Forgive me, God," he whispered. "So beautiful . . ." His eyes filled with tears as he watched the whole city become new and fresh and pure in a mantle of white. He had forgotten to look. Forgotten to be thankful. What if he had missed this instant? And what if there were not ten thousand mornings like this in his future? Winter snow. Summer baseball games. Nights with Becky in his arms. Little Boots growing up. Someday, perhaps more babies to hold and to love. And patients who needed him. A kid with a clubfoot and no money who might be able to run and play because of what Ellis could do for him.

It came to him like a bright light through his darkness. He had a lifetime of tomorrows in which to rebuild things that had been lost.

Things. He marveled at the emptiness of the word. Would he have given up his life for the loss of things? How foolish he had been! How wrong!

Suddenly he longed to see Becky's face, to hold her, to love her quietly, to know that she was all right. He would tell her everything. He would explain how he had gambled in the market and lost their money and the clinic, how no man had ever been such a fool as he had been. He would ask her forgiveness and tell her the truth that had come to him this morning. He realized now that he could lose everything and still go on as long as he did not lose Becky. Was it too late for them?

Thoughts mingled with prayers, and his hopes grew stronger with every passing mile. Ellis was hardly aware when the streetcar clacked to a stop on Twenty-first Street. He peered out toward the little houses on Florida Avenue as he stepped from the car, then hurried up the quiet street toward home.

Was Becky up yet? Had Boots left for school? Ellis took the steps at number 1064 in one bound, calling out for Becky as he threw open the door.

The front room was dark, and the ticking of the mantel clock was the only sound. He smelled coffee brewing in the kitchen.

"Beck?" His voice was a jarring interruption to the stillness. "Becky? Are you here?" There was no reply. An instant of fear gripped him. He made his way through the dining room and into the kitchen.

She sat still and pale at the table. The newspaper was open, displaying the headlines. She held a letter in her hands, and her eyes brimmed with sorrow as she looked up at him.

"Are you . . . okay?" she asked quietly.

"I'm okay." He sat down across from her and reached for her hands. She clutched the letter even as he touched her. "I don't know where to begin. . . . Becky . . ."

She bit her lip and searched his face with her eyes. "Here." She pulled her hand free and offered the letter. "Maybe this will help you. It came special delivery a few minutes ago."

Ellis took the crumpled sheet of lined paper without looking at it. What was in Becky's eyes? Was it reproach? accusation?

"Addressed to me. Read it, Ellis," she urged.

He nodded, suddenly afraid that she had heard everything before he could tell her.

The writing on the sheet was a childish scrawl. Printed carefully in pencil, the writer had pressed so hard that the lead had torn the paper in places:

Der Miz Warne,

Yor husban is been black mailed. I tryed to tell you once. Seen you in the yard but didn speak. Pleze come to 534-B North Howard Street Flat 3 on 3rd floor to see why and who has did it. Ther is a letter ther for you as proof to tak to police.

A friend

Ellis groaned and let the paper fall to the floor. He did not look at Becky. She reached across and rested her hand on his arm.

"Where is Boots?" Ellis asked.

"She spent the night with . . ." Becky's voice was gentle. "Ellis? You could have told me."

"I . . . you had so much . . . the baby . . ."

"You could have told me."

"There is more to it than this."

"You mean the fact that we're broke?" she probed gently.

Her statement startled him. "What do you know?"

"Nothing really, just suspected. The stock market. You bought on margin? lost it all?"

"How long have you . . . ?"

She shook her head. "What does it matter, Ellis? We have so much. If only you would look at me." Her voice cracked with emotion.

He raised his eyes to her face. He saw her. For the first time in months, he really saw her.

"Oh, Ellis!" A single tear escaped and coursed down her cheek. He rose and went to her, lifting her into his embrace. Stroking her hair, he kissed her forehead and bowed his face against her shoulder.

He did not know how long they remained that way. The clock ticked. The snow fell to cover Florida Avenue beyond the windowpane.

"I'm sorry," he whispered at last. "So sorry."

"I'm here, darling." She held him tighter. "We're going to make it. I know. . . ."

The sun was well up when Doc Brown emerged from surgery with news of Max. Solemn as ever, he crooked his finger at David and called him to his side.

"Your daddy will live, boy. He lost a lot of blood, and he'll be laid up awhile, but he'll live. Now let's get us some breakfast."

Tears of relief flowed freely among those who had stood the vigil in Doc Brown's parlor. Mary Brown seemed more relieved than anyone as she embraced David. Prayers of thanks were offered up.

Trudy and Lily volunteered to make breakfast, and then a holler sounded out in the yard. It was the unmistakable voice of Boomer.

"Hey! Hey, y'all! LOOK WHAT I GOT!"

The curtains were pulled back, and Sheriff Potts and Brother Williams exclaimed at the same instant, "Lord have mercy! It's that mule, and Boomer's with him!"

Birch joined them to gawk out at Boomer's beaming face. His presence in itself was some sort of miracle. Boomer almost never came out of the livery stable. But there he was in the cold morning light, holding Old Bob by the end of a lead rope. And slung across the back of the mule was the limp body of J.D. Froelich!

"Hey there, Jefferson!" Boomer called. "I brung your mule back! He come to the stable first thing this mornin' and told me HE DONE KICKED J.D. IN THE HEAD!"

Trudy and Lily kept the straining children inside while the men crowded out onto the porch. But even inside there was no missing the conversation with Boomer this morning. Most of Hartford heard it. Even Mr. Vibe, who was almost stone deaf, heard the news.

"It's J.D., all right," Birch muttered.

"Dead," Jefferson said somberly.

Sheriff Potts concurred. "Looks like his head's kicked in."

Brother Williams just clucked his tongue, while Doc Brown went down the steps to examine the body.

Then Boomer explained, "I told J.D. this mule DON'T LIKE HIM!"

"Yes, you did, Boomer," said Brother Williams in awe. "We all heard you tell him."

"He should have listened," remarked Doc Brown with a shake of his head.

"But that J.D. was a fool! Y'all heard me warn him what this mule said! Ol' Bob said he was gonna kick in J.D.'s head—that's what! He's an honest Christian mule! AND NOW HE DONE IT, ALL RIGHT."

Jefferson raised his eyebrows. "Good Book says a man should listen up when a mule is talkin' to him. That's right, Boomer."

"J.D. never listened to nobody. When Ol' Bob come back alone without J.D., I figgered what happened. I went on out. Follered them tracks back to the clearin'. Found J.D. cold and dead as a post. Got a mule footprint right smack on his forehead. I found his gun, too! Where do y'all want me to put him? He's REAL DEAD. I DON'T WANT HIM, AND NEITHER DOES THIS MULE."

Doc Brown patted Old Bob affectionately, then gave his head a shake. "Smith's Mortuary is going to be working overtime, what with that gangster fella down there, too. Just take J.D. on down to Smith's, Boomer—to the undertaker's. And tell Mister Smith I'll be along directly to fill out the death certificate on him."

Boomer beamed. He reached deep into his pockets and held up a fistful of matchsticks. "I'll do that, Doc Brown. And then I'll bring back Ol' Bob. And after that, me and the boys'll play us a game of poker in the loft. It's gonna be a good day!" He raised his face to the sky. "GONNA BE REAL FINE NOW!"

They could hear Boomer singing off-key and out of rhythm as he went his way with Old Bob following along like an old dog. "Some bright mornin' when this life is over, I'll fly a-wayyyy. . . ." His echo resounded from the brick storefronts like a second voice joining in. Not loud but plainly audible.

"SING OUT, OL' BOB!" Boomer cried happily, waving his arms, directing an unseen choir. As though in agreement, Old Bob nodded his great head to the rhythm as he plodded down the street.

Folks left Willa-Mae and the boys to themselves in the apartment. It was a good thing, too. Willa-Mae did not much feel like having company after the news she had gotten this morning. No matter that the doctor said Hock would get well from his broken ribs. Where would the two of them go after that?

Willa-Mae considered the alternatives as she scrambled eggs for Frank and Jim. Every one of the Canfield children was grown and living in a big city where the air would be no better than here. And all of them had young'uns of their own. Willa-Mae would not consider the risk of exposing them to Hock's illness. And was there anything worse than two old folks moving in on their married children? Willa-Mae fretted.

"Oh, my sweet Jesus. Oh, my." She tried to pray, but her prayers came out worries and gloom.

After breakfast she set up a game of Chinese checkers for the boys beside the warm radiator. They played happily enough without bickering as most children do. These were good boys, Willa-Mae knew. What would come of them now that their mama was gone?

Willa-Mae put away the morning paper, where the news of a woman's suicide was printed. By the description of the victim, Willa-

Mae knew the woman could be none other than the young mother of Frank and Jim Penn. Would someone be coming for them soon? How long should she wait before she called the authorities?

The thought of the two boys being taken to the county orphanage made her shudder. She would wait. Bad news and heartache could wait awhile longer anyway.

Fingering the letter the woman had left her, Willa-Mae slipped it into the pocket of her bright blue apron and busied herself with cleaning the apartment.

Willa-Mae looked out and shook her head in dismay. The snow fell fast and heavy outside, covering the shed and the roof of the chicken coop out the back window. It was going to be a long, cold, hungry winter.

The brothers played on, heedless of the tragedy of their own lives and the hardship that had suddenly fallen upon Hock and Willa-Mae. When their game ended, she sang them lullabies as she rocked them both to sleep on her broad lap, then tucked them into Little Nettie's bed. They were sleeping peacefully when the knock sounded at the door. Willa-Mae drew the curtain across the alcove and replied when the knock sounded again, "Hold your horses! I'm comin'!"

A twist of the knob, and suddenly the surprised face of Dr. Warne was there gawking at her from the hall. Willa-Mae moaned slightly, certain that the doctor and this woman had come to tell her that Hock had up and died in spite of the hopeful prognosis.

"Missus Canfield!" he exclaimed dumbly, as though he had no intention of being here.

"Is it my Hock?" She put a hand to her heart. "Has he passed on?"

"No. I mean . . . why, no! My wife and I have come here for . . . we were told we would find a letter for Becky here at this . . ." He looked at the door and then at Willa-Mae and then beyond her into the room.

"Third floor of 534-B North Howard Street," said the red-haired woman—evidently Doc Warne's wife—who looked to be not much more than a girl to Willa-Mae. "Have we come to the wrong place, Missus . . . ?"

"Canfield." Willa-Mae replied and stepped aside before all the warmth escaped from the apartment into the hall.

"Canfield?" Mrs. Warne looked surprised at the name. "An uncommon name."

"I reckon, Missus Warne. Y'all come on in here. Mighty cold outside. Good gracious. Y'all make house calls on such a day, Doc Warne? Them boys is a'sleepin'. All wore out from the fuss. I told you I'd bring 'em in. No need to come out here."

With everyone in the apartment, the door was closed. The couple looked at each other in confusion.

"Becky and I have come, you see . . . ," the doctor began.

"We were told you have a letter for us," explained Becky.

Now Willa-Mae peered at them in wonder. "Letter? Y'all knowed Frank and Jim's mama, then?" she whispered.

Another strange exchange of looks.

Willa-Mae pulled the envelope from her apron. "Then I don't feel so bad for them young'uns, if it's you two. Y'all know she was in a bad way when she left last night. Left them two babies here. She say, 'Miz Canfield, a good woman comin' to get this here letter, and after she reads it she'll fetch my boys.'"

Willa-Mae placed the letter in the hands of Becky Warne. "I reckon she meant you, Miz Warne."

"It's the same as the other letter, Becky," Doc Warne said. "Same envelope. Thicker."

Becky nodded and tore open the seal. There were several sheets of typed paper inside, but she picked out a single sheet of lined notebook paper and scanned the childish scrawl silently. Her eyes filled with tears as she handed the note to Ellis. She looked up searchingly at Willa-Mae. "Where are they?" she asked.

Willa-Mae knew she was speaking of the boys. She stepped back and pulled the curtain to show her where the Penn brothers slept curled like two spoons on the feather bed.

For a moment, Becky hung back. Then, with a shake of her head, she walked into the alcove and sat on the edge of the bed. She lifted the quilt to reveal the crippled foot of little Frank. Her fingers curled around his toes, and then with her other hand she reached out and brushed back the child's hair. His eyelids fluttered, and his mouth curved in a dreamy smile.

"It's all here, Beck." The doctor searched the papers and slid them back into the envelope. "Who did it and why."

"And why she was part of it," said Becky, her eyes never leaving the children. "We cannot be bitter, Ellis. These were reason enough for her. She was . . . without hope." And then, sadly, to Willa-Mae, "She did not sign her name, Missus Canfield. Did you know her name?"

Willa-Mae shook her head slowly. There was so much here she could not understand. "I jus' knew her as Miz Penn. Frank and Jim's mama."

At that, Becky stood slowly but did not move from the bedside. "I saw her last night," she whispered. "She told me she was sorry. So sorry. If I could have talked to her . . ." She looked up at her husband. "Ellis? Help me."

He cleared his throat. "The mother of these children has asked . . . she requested that I take little Frank as a patient, perform surgery on his clubfoot. Her payment was information that has saved my medical practice. I suppose she paid me with her life." His strong voice broke. "I would have done it for nothing." He could no longer speak.

Becky lifted her head, and with clear eyes she addressed Willa-Mae in a way that made Willa-Mae believe that this was a woman strong as an oak tree yet gentle as a soft wind. "We will take the boys home to our house now. But they will need someone familiar to come along, Missus Canfield—for a while anyway. We have two extra rooms if you are willing."

And so it was that Willa-Mae Canfield went to Florida Avenue to stay at the home of Ellis Warne, who had served in the Great War with Birch Tucker of Shiloh, Arkansas . . . the same Birch Tucker who loved Thomas Jefferson Canfield like a brother.

Jefferson Canfield. Son of Hock and Willa-Mae Canfield. In that house on Florida Avenue in Akron, Ohio, a map was unfolded, and all the little dots were connected by lines of roads and rivers. And suddenly no one was lost.

The body of mobster Smiley Crillo was laid out on a slab at Smith's Mortuary in Hartford next to J.D. Froelich. Wildman McKinney made a good deal of extra cash carrying passengers to the little town as newsmen flocked to snap a picture of Sheriff Potts beside the dead killer.

It was Max Meyer, however, who broke the story to the world. Sitting up in his regular bed at Dr. Brown's infirmary, the wounded reporter wrote the story out in longhand and then gave it to Mary to be wired to the *Times* in New York.

The news of Smiley's death wrote a conclusion to the rule of the Boss Quinn syndicate. Bold headlines across the front page of the nation's most prominent daily newspaper proclaimed the end of a desperate criminal at the hands of a brave lawman in a little town in Arkansas. Sheriff Harlan Potts became a household name. No mention was made of the fact that he had only drawn his weapon two other times in twenty-two years. He became the stuff that dime-novel heroes were made of. Known now as The Man Who Shot the Murderer of Fifty, Sheriff Potts would henceforth be asked to endorse soap and razors and chewing gum. His future was secure.

As for the future of Max Meyer? He was offered his old job at the *Times* with a raise in salary. Turning the offer down, Max cited personal reasons for this astounding decision. He had a son to raise. And he had fallen in love with a missionary to China. He had a yen to work in the Far East—in Shanghai—he informed them.

It was widely speculated among the newspapermen who knew Max that his injuries must have included a severe blow to the head. It was bad enough that he intended to raise a kid. But everyone knew Max Meyer could never be happy any place on earth beyond the boundaries of Manhattan.

And whom had he fallen in love with? A broad from the Salvation Army—like one of those drumbeating Bible-thumpers down on the corner of Broadway and Times Square? Impossible! Not Max Meyer. He always went for the society-type dames, didn't he? He plucked broads like ripe fruit from a tree, took a taste, and pitched the rest.

Max Meyer in love with a missionary to China from Arkansas?

Obviously he had lost his marbles, and they were nowhere to be found.

In early January of 1930, the whistle of the great Rock Island locomotive echoed once again across the snow-covered hills of Shiloh. Along the James Fork Creek, between Mansfield and Hartford, work on the new tracks was complete. Freight and mail and passengers traveled easily by rail from Fort Smith, eliminating further need of Wildman McKinney's air service. Rail workers and strangers caught the 12:40 back to Fort Smith, and from the porch of her store Grandma Amos looked out and saw the cloud of Trouble dissipate and vanish.

"Gonna be a mighty dull year," she predicted, puffing on her pipe.

This was good news to all the folks of Shiloh, who had seen excitement enough lately to last a lifetime.

"But is it gonna rain, Grandma Amos?" asked the farmers.

"Showers of blessin's!" she replied, and they believed her.

On February 3, as the smoke of the approaching train billowed into the gray winter sky, men and women looked upward and expected blessings and miracles. This morning half the population of Shiloh gathered beside the tracks beneath the water tower to await the arrival of Jefferson Canfield's mama and daddy. Grandma Amos had offered her little guesthouse to Hock and Willa-Mae in exchange for Willa-Mae's work as housekeeper and cook. After all, Grandma Amos wasn't getting any younger, and she could use the help.

Jeff and Lily and their babies were flanked by the Tucker family on their right and newlyweds Max and Mary Meyer on the left. Binoculars in hand, the Tucker boys scrambled up the tower ladder after David Meyer in his leather flying helmet and his silk aviator scarf. Once they were perched on top, the water tower sprouted wings and carried them over the treetops to where the stubby train huffed toward the reunion.

"What y'all see, boys?" Jefferson called as the distant whistle wailed again. "They'd be in the last car, I reckon."

The cold wind puffed David's scarf as he banked his imaginary plane and Tommy reconnoitered.

The windows of the Rock Island slid past the view of Tommy Tucker's field glasses to reveal two ebony faces shining through the frosted panes of the last car. With a holler that rivaled the joy of the train whistle, the boy called out, "I seen your mama and daddy, Jeff! Willa-Mae and Hock! Comin' home! Comin' home to Shiloh!"

Say to This Mountain

"Everything's new and wonderful to a kid. . . . They think they can sprout wings and fly. They believe everything they imagine is possible. . . . I reckon that's what the Lord meant when He said we ought to be like little children. They have faith still. They still believe they can move mountains." BIRCH TUCKER (p. 135)

What mountains loom over your life?

Do you feel lonely and rejected, like Ellis?

Heartsick and sad, like Frank and Jim Penn's mama?

Are you grieving for what you've lost, like Becky?

Have you waited a long time for joy—then had it snatched away from you unjustly, like Jefferson?

Do you wonder sometimes if anything good is going to come of the trouble in your life? if you have anything to live for, like Max?

All the characters in *Say to This Mountain* have mountains to climb. Mountains so high that it seems they cannot be overcome. Mountains such as the ones you face right now. But is it possible—as God says—for those mountains to be moved into the sea?

Absolutely! All it takes is that seed of faith . . . and the determination to wait for miracles, large and small.

Miracles like:

*Bringing Ellis, Becky, Willa-Mae, and the Penn brothers together

*Connecting the dots of the map between Jefferson Canfield and Hock and Willa-Mae, so they could all be home in Shiloh

*Creating the surprising love between Max Meyer, former Wall Street whiz, and a spunky missionary to China

*Joining Ellis's and Becky's hearts once again, after a long period of grief, loss, and darkness

If God can accomplish these mighty miracles, what might He accomplish in *your* life?

Dear reader, when troubles come, why not have the perspective of Willa-Mae Canfield:

> "I don't mind these troubles so much. I seen enough that it makes me kinda excited because I know God's gonna do somethin' if I wait long enough! He's gonna make some miracle we ain't thought of yet. He's gonna take all our sorrows and turn 'em into blessin's. . . . Bad times always pass! *Lift up your heads; for your redemption draweth nigh.*" (p. 359)

There may not be a lightning flash from the sky to prove God's love for you. But if you look in the pages of the Bible, you'll find a love letter written to your heart. A letter that says, over and over, *I will never leave you or forsake you. You are precious to me.*

Life will always be complicated. You will always face challenges that will affect your soul deeply. We trust that the following questions will help you dig deeper for answers to your own daily dilemmas. You may wish to delve into these questions on your own or share them with a friend or a discussion group.

Most of all, we pray that through this Shiloh Legacy series you will "discover the Truth through fiction." For we are convinced that if you seek diligently, you will find the One who holds all the answers to the universe (1 Chronicles 28:9).

Bodie & Brock Thoene

SEEK . . .

Prologue

1. October of 1929 was a catastrophic month (with the stock-market crash and the tornado in Shiloh, Arkansas). Have you ever had a "heap of trouble," as Grandma Amos would say, touch your life all at once (p. ix)? If so, when?

_____

_____

2. In what ways has experiencing this trouble changed the way you treat others who are suffering? How has it impacted the way you live now?

_____

_____

PART I
Chapters 1–3

3. When Max and David are traveling toward Shiloh, Max sees the light from a distant farmhouse. "Like a bright star, it gleamed to mark the spot that some man's heart called center of the universe. Home! . . . But for Max tonight, the light was simply a reminder of everything he had missed" (p. 8). Then he realizes that his "light"—the center of his universe—is right in front of him! "This boy—*his* boy—had suddenly become the beacon calling his heart home" (p. 8).

   What does "home" mean to you? What or who is your "light"— the center of your universe? Explain.

_____

_____

4. "Leroy had only a few years of formal schooling, but he had spent his life as a student of human nature. This was his hobby, his entertainment, his true calling. It was, he often told his nephews, a

gift from God, a great responsibility that the Lord had given him
to serve and observe folks and then to pray for them according to
what they needed" (p. 21).

    If someone asked you what your true calling was, what would
you say? Why? What proof would others see of this?

5. "What was to come of the world if a man like Mr. Weldon could
   do such a desperate thing?" (p. 30). Willa-Mae Canfield wonders.
   Have you ever done "a desperate thing"? If so, when? Looking
   back, would you change your action? Why or why not?

Chapters 4–5

6. To Frank and Jim's mama, neighbors Hock and Willa-Mae Canfield
   were not individuals but "niggers" (see pp. 37–38). She could not
   think of them as anything else, perhaps, because of her background.
   What prejudices, if any, have you grown up with? How do those
   prejudices affect your treatment of others who are a different race,
   religion, or gender?

7. Lily is lost in wonder when Trudy gives her a beautiful white-cotton
   nightgown to wear for her wedding. "Such a thing is too fine for the
   likes of me," Lily says (p. 46). When have you received a present
   you didn't feel like you deserved? Tell the story.

8. Lily and Jefferson carefully weigh the names for their twins, finally
   naming them after her deceased first husband and Jefferson's

mama (see p. 48-49). Little do they know how important these names will be to their future!

Are names important to you? Why or why not? Do you know any of the background behind your name? If so, what is it? How has this knowledge influenced you?

_____

_____

9. "I got me a reason to live," Jefferson realizes when he gazes at Lily and the newborn babies (p. 56). Even in the midst of difficult times, what reason(s) do you have to live?

_____

_____

Chapter 6

10. Although Ellis Warne plays well the role of a doctor as he encourages John Daugherty's distraught mother, "all the time, he was feeling just as false and hollow as his bum leg" (p. 58). Have you ever felt "false and hollow" when you encouraged someone—even though you were trying to do the right thing? When?

_____

_____

11. "What was the use of wishing things could be different? Nothing had turned out as Ellis and Becky had planned" (p. 59). When have you played the "I wish" game? Did it help—or make things more difficult? Explain.

_____

_____

12. Ellis was afraid to tell his wife, Becky, the truth about their lost investments. "Real fear settled on his shoulders until he felt as if he carried the weight of a mountain on his back. And no matter

what happened, he knew he must carry the burden alone" (p. 63).
What burden do you carry by yourself? What would you not want
others to know about? Why?

_____

_____

13. When Ellis stares at the photos of his brothers in baseball caps, he
realizes, "Back then there was only the joy of the present. He had
never imagined what the future held for him . . . he had not been
able to see into this bleak moment. If he had, he would not have
taken even one halting step toward his future" (p. 64). Would you
want to know your future? Why or why not?

_____

_____

Chapters 7–9

14. "'Why are they looking at Jeff?' [Trudy's] question was barely
audible.
    'Because he's there. That's all the reason they need to hate.
It's like asking a mountain climber why he climbs a mountain.
Because it's there. Ask these fellas why they hate a colored man,
and that will be their answer. Because he's here'" (p. 75).
    Do you agree with Mary Brown's explanation? Why or why
not? Where do you think racial prejudice comes from?

_____

_____

15. "We were poor then, but I loved him. Did he think I could not still
love him if we were poor again? . . . Everything is gone! . . . He
took it all with him! He left me to face it without him!" (p. 85).
Mrs. Weldon says after her husband dies. Have you ever been left
alone to face something? How did you respond?

_____

_____

16. When Brother Williams doesn't sell the red pup to the highest bidder, Mr. Winters says, "There is a God" (p. 88). Everyone is surprised. "It is not like Brother Williams to show any kind of generosity, but he saved that pup for them boys just the same" (p. 88). When have you been surprised by generosity?

Chapters 10–11

17. Everyone in Shiloh and Hartford has his opinion about what should be said about Maybelle at her funeral (see pp. 104–107). If you could choose the words, what would you want said about you at your funeral? In what way(s) does your life now reveal the truth of those words?

---

18. What conclusions does Trudy jump to when David and Max arrive (pp. 116–117, 126–128)? Which of these conclusions are right? Which are wrong? Frank and Jim Penn's mama jumps to conclusions about her black neighbors. Willa-Mae's neighbor, Euola Peck, jumps to conclusions about Frank and Jim Penn's mama, calling her "white trash." When have you jumped to conclusions? Were you right, wrong, or a little of each? Tell what happened.

---

19. "It wasn't Shiloh I brought him here to see," Max said. "It was you. Family, you know. Something I have never really had myself. I thought maybe you and Birch could teach us what it's all about" (p. 128).

     What does *family* mean to you?

Chapter 12

20. Bobby, Tommy, and David have a sleepover—a great adventure—in Jeff's cabin. What fun adventure(s) can you remember from your childhood? What made them so memorable?

_____

_____

21. "'This little old rock farm . . . it ain't much, I guess, but it's home. Gives me a chance to do better for my boys and for Trudy than my own father did for us. Guess I'm livin' my life now the way I wish it had been when I was a kid. Let them have some fun. Make sure they know I love them. . . . Just want to make it better—you know what I mean?'

    'Yes . . .' Max wanted to ask his friend where to begin. How could he make up for all the wasted time with David?" (p. 134-135).

    Who are you most like—Birch Tucker or Max Meyer—in the way you live? Explain.

_____

_____

22. "I think a kid . . . any kid at all . . . mostly just wants to do good. Sure, they ain't gonna do everything just right the first time, but that ain't a sin. That's just what learnin' is all about. Make a mistake. Try again. Do a little better next time—and better yet, the next time," Birch says (p. 135). If you put learning in the light of Birch's thinking, what would change about your life? the way you treat children? other family members? coworkers?

_____

_____

Chapters 13–14

23. "Willa-Mae had prayed enough years to know that the Lord did not often step right up in her face and shout directions in her ears. Most times she just prayed and prayed and began to feel easy in her soul, like a mountain of worry had been lifted away. That was answer

enough. It was like the Lord said to her, *Don't you worry none, Willa-Mae. You know I'm gonna take good care of you and yours"* (p. 141).

Do you agree with Willa-Mae's philosophy about prayer? Why or why not?

_____

_____

24. When Ellis talks to young Johnny, who has just lost an arm, he says, "It's how whole you are inside that counts." But inside he thinks, *What right do I have to talk about being whole on the inside?* (see p. 146).

Are you "whole on the inside"? Why or why not?

_____

_____

25. Jack Titan tells Ellis, "Your position here is secure . . . unless you choose to go your own way. You are free to do that if you wish, but I rather think you will see things our way. Am I clear?" (p. 154).

If your supervisor told you that about your job, how would you respond? What factors would you consider before opening your mouth?

_____

_____

Chapters 15–16

26. When Max suggests that he and Mary spend more time together, Mary pulls herself free from his arms. "We say some simple phrases the same here in Shiloh as a Yankee girl might say them in the North. Gentlemen on both sides of the Mason-Dixon line understand this one: Good night, Mister Meyer" (p. 166). How did you respond, as a reader, to Mary's action? Why is Mary's action important for a person like Max?

_____

_____

27. "He called you a Yankee and a Jew."

   "Well, I am both of those things, I suppose. If it offends Buck Hooper, I can't change it by fighting him" (p. 171).

   If you were Max, how would you handle the situation with Buck? with Mary?

   _____

   _____

Chapter 17

28. When Max believes he is dying, he has great regrets. "All the great things Max had achieved meant nothing. What use were degrees at a university? What use were honors? What did success matter now? All those things for which he had sold his soul were utterly without value here at the end of his life!" (p. 181).

   If your life were to end today, would you consider it well-lived? Why or why not?

   _____

   _____

29. Max realizes with great sadness and horror that he would have told Irene to get an abortion because a baby would have been too much trouble. And yet, ten years later, that baby—his son, David—is the one thing Max has to live for! *"I would have killed him without a second thought while I went chasing after things . . . just things . . ."* (p. 181). When have you found yourself chasing after things? putting things above people? What was the result?

   _____

   _____

PART II
Chapters 18–20

30. If you were asked to lie to keep your job (as Titan tells Ellis to do—
    see p. 191), would you do it? Why or why not?

_____

_____

31. As she mourns the loss of her baby, Becky goes through many
    difficult emotions—anger, grief, betrayal. Gradually she grows cold
    and numb (p. 198). She reads her Bible and prays for comfort, but
    it never arrives. So she merely tries "not to feel life too deeply"
    (p. 199). Have you found yourself doing this? If so, describe the
    circumstances.

_____

_____

32. "Most men are easy to love, Mary dear," Doc Brown says, "if they
    are more dead than alive. It's when they're awake that you have to
    worry" (p. 207). Do you agree with Doc Brown? Why or why not?

_____

_____

Chapters 22–24

33. Becky and Ellis both still secretly love each other, but they don't
    know how to talk any longer. "She was hurt and silent. He was
    sullen and distant and defensive. Each turned inward to his or
    her own pain. He loved her still, longed to share his worry and
    fear with her, but he no longer felt confident that she loved him"
    (p. 209).
        Are you holding yourself distant from someone you love? Are
    you "together—yet alone—every day"? How could you take a step
    toward reconciliation?

_____

_____

34. Max made a decision to leave Irene behind to pursue his career. By the time he knew she was pregnant, it was too late for their relationship. Harry makes a different decision—to go to Rena's parents and then to Willa-Mae and tell the truth. He says he is going to marry Rena. "I'm sorry about the mistake," he says, "but I'm happy when I think about the baby and Rena" (p. 224).

    Have you—or someone you love—had to make this difficult decision? What would you do—or advise your friend or loved one to do—and why?

    _____

    _____

35. "Becky filled her time with mundane tasks that required no thought or emotion to accomplish. *Just keep busy. Then there's no time to hurt. Blessed numbness.* This was how she survived" (p. 230). Can you relate to Becky now—or in the past? Tell or write about your experience.

    _____

    _____

Chapters 25–26

36. "Maybe there's a lesson in the sparrows," Mary Brown tells Max. "You've been looking for your apples in the wrong orchard—that's all. No need to steal, run, or hoard. There are apples free for the taking. More than you can possibly use. You just have to know where to look" (p. 244). What do Mary's words mean to you? Have you, like Max, been looking for your apples in the wrong orchard? Explain.

    _____

    _____

37. "The part of me that ain't seen the daylight is jus' the same as any white man. My blood jus' as red. My bones jus' as white. Under the skin you can't tell the difference 'tween any man.

    "You remember this, boys, someday when some white man

tells y'all different. Someday every person gonna be a bleached heap of bones standin' there in front of Jesus. We all gonna stand b'fore the Lord equal. Won't matter then what color my hide was, or yours either!" (Jefferson, p. 248-249).

Do you agree with Jefferson's words? If so, how do your actions and words reveal your beliefs?

_____

_____

38. "Women as a race were about the most confusing creatures in all creation. Yessir. His old daddy had said that God should have rested a little longer before he made Eve because maybe the Lord was plumb wore out from all the work He had done and put a few things together backward in her brain. Women had dedicated themselves to keeping menfolk in the dark from the beginning of time. Love was a hard row to hoe" (p. 259).

Have you ever found women hard to figure out (even if you are a woman)? Why?

_____

_____

Chapters 27–28

39. When Ellis Warne is set up by Jack Titan, Frank and Jim Penn's mama plays a leading role (see p. 269). How would you feel about "that woman" if you hadn't read about her home life? her desperate situation? How does knowing her background affect your judgment toward what she does to Ellis? toward how she treats Frank and Jim (p. 271)?

_____

_____

40. When Willa-Mae and Hock Canfield see the hungry Penn brothers, they make flapjacks (p. 273). How might you be "the hands of Jesus, reaching out to care for someone when they think no one cares for them at all" (p. 289)?

_____

_____

41. Max "thought about his life—how he had indeed been stealing pleasure, like apples, from all the wrong places, and how no one thing ever satisfied the appetite of his heart, no matter how he treasured that thing" (p. 275). In what area(s) is your heart satisfied? In what area(s) is it still longing?

_____

_____

Chapters 29–30

42. If you were Ellis Warne, would you have taken the list? Why or why not?

_____

_____

43. "Ellis did not fear death, although he knew that death was a fearsome thing. And he did not fear God, simply because he had forgotten God somewhere along the way. What little he thought of God was in the context of his own anger and loss. Why had God deserted him so completely? If there was a God, then why had so much tragedy come into his life?" (p. 303).

Have you asked questions like Ellis? If so, when? What has happened since?

_____

_____

PART III
Chapters 31–35

44. After ten long years of unjust imprisonment, Jefferson Canfield finally has a new life—a wife, two babies, land of his own. And he's now on the trail of finding his parents. Then all of a sudden, he's hit with his past—in the form of a pursuing sheriff and a vindictive J.D. (p. 310). It all seems so unfair!

    What do you do when life treats you unfairly? What has made you "glimpse hope" again (see p. 317)?

    _____

    _____

45. If you were going to give "a last gift" to someone you love (as Max plans to give to David for Christmas—see p. 330), what would that gift be and why?

    _____

    _____

46. "Trudy was right. He was a mile wide and an inch deep.

    Mary was right. He had no roots.

    How then could he change the habits of a lifetime? How could he expect to make everything different?" (p. 331).

    What would people say about you? If you were to look carefully within your soul, what would you see?

    _____

    _____

47. "I know God's gonna do somethin' if I wait long enough!" Willa-Mae tells Hock (p. 359). What has happened because you waited?

    _____

    _____

Chapters 36–38

48. "Religion ain't the same as knowin' Jesus. . . . I got t'get back t'just who Jesus is. He had troubles. Had plenty of sorrows. Did right for folks. Loved 'em. Healed the sick. An' look what folks done t'Him," Jefferson says (p. 371). What is the difference, to you, between religion and "knowin' Jesus"?

_____

_____

49. How does Frank and Jim's mama change in *Say to This Mountain*? Trace her attitudes and actions from the beginning (see p. 38) to the day there are six brown eggs in the bowl (see p. 373) to the day she visits Willa-Mae (see p. 377) to when she jumps from the viaduct (see p. 393). What do you think drives her to her final actions?

_____

_____

50. "Only the Lord can fill you up with hope again!" Pastor Denton tells the hungry men (p. 386). Has this happened to you? Has the Lord filled you with hope after a lean, hungry time in your life? If so, tell the story.

_____

_____

51. What kind of "justice" does Smiley receive? Jefferson? J.D.? the mule? How is this justice fitting of the Bible quote *All things work together for good to them that love God*? (See p. 386).

_____

_____

Chapter 39—Epilogue

52. When Willa-Mae discovers how sick Hock is, she hears Jefferson say, *"Rest in God's arms, Mama. Be His baby. Lay Daddy in the Lord's hands"* (p. 410). In what situation do you need to rest in God's arms?

_____

_____

53. "The commonplace events of life had seemed miraculous. They *were* miraculous. 'Forgive me, God,' [Ellis] whispered. 'So beautiful. . . .' He had forgotten to look. Forgotten to be thankful. What if he had missed this instant? . . . It came to him like a bright light through his darkness. He had a lifetime of tomorrows in which to rebuild things that had been lost" (p. 412-413).

What do you need to look for? be thankful for? How can you build for tomorrow?

_____

_____

About the Authors

BODIE AND BROCK THOENE (pronounced *Tay-nee*) have written over 45 works of historical fiction. That these best sellers have sold more than 10 million copies and won eight ECPA Gold Medallion Awards affirms what millions of readers have already discovered—the Thoenes are not only master stylists but experts at capturing readers' minds and hearts.

In their timeless classic series about Israel (The Zion Chronicles, The Zion Covenant, and The Zion Legacy), the Thoenes' love for both story and research shines.

With the Shiloh Legacy series and *Shiloh Autumn*—poignant portrayals of the American Depression—and The Galway Chronicles, which dramatically tell of the 1840s famine in Ireland, as well as the twelve Legends of the West, the Thoenes have made their mark in modern history.

In the A.D. Chronicles, their most recent series, they step seamlessly into the world of Yerushalayim and Rome, in the days when Yeshua walked the earth and transformed lives with His touch.

Bodie began her writing career as a teen journalist for her local newspaper. Eventually her byline appeared in prestigious periodicals such as *U.S. News and World Report*, *The American West*, and *The Saturday Evening Post*. She also worked for John Wayne's Batjac Productions (she's best known as author of *The Fall Guy*) and ABC Circle Films as a writer and researcher. John Wayne described her as "a writer with talent that captures the people and the times!" She has degrees in journalism and communications.

Brock has often been described by Bodie as "an essential half of this writing team." With degrees in both history and education, Brock has, in his role as researcher and story-line consultant, added the vital dimension of historical accuracy. Due to such careful research, the Zion Covenant and the Zion Chronicles series are recognized by the American Library Association, as well as Zionist libraries around the world, as classic historical novels and are used to teach history in college classrooms.

Bodie and Brock have four grown children—Rachel, Jake, Luke, and Ellie—and five grandchildren. Their sons, Jake and Luke, are carrying on the Thoene family talent as the next generation of writers, and Luke produces the Thoene audiobooks. Bodie and Brock divide their time between London and Nevada.

For more information visit:

www.thoenebooks.com

www.familyaudiolibrary.com

THOENE FAMILY CLASSICS™

✪ ✪ ✪

THOENE FAMILY CLASSIC HISTORICALS
by Bodie and Brock Thoene
Gold Medallion Winners*

THE ZION COVENANT
Vienna Prelude*
Prague Counterpoint
Munich Signature
Jerusalem Interlude
Danzig Passage
Warsaw Requiem*
London Refrain
Paris Encore
Dunkirk Crescendo

THE ZION CHRONICLES
The Gates of Zion*
A Daughter of Zion
The Return to Zion
A Light in Zion
The Key to Zion*

THE SHILOH LEGACY
In My Father's House*
A Thousand Shall Fall
Say to This Mountain

SHILOH AUTUMN

THE GALWAY CHRONICLES
Only the River Runs Free*
Of Men and of Angels
Ashes of Remembrance*
All Rivers to the Sea

THE ZION LEGACY
Jerusalem Vigil
Thunder from Jerusalem
Jerusalem's Heart
Jerusalem Scrolls
Stones of Jerusalem
Jerusalem's Hope

A.D. CHRONICLES
First Light
Second Touch
Third Watch
Fourth Dawn
Fifth Seal
and more to come!

THOENE FAMILY CLASSICS™

✪ ✪ ✪

THOENE FAMILY CLASSIC AMERICAN LEGENDS

LEGENDS OF THE WEST
by Bodie and Brock Thoene

The Man from Shadow Ridge
Riders of the Silver Rim
Gold Rush Prodigal
Sequoia Scout
Cannons of the Comstock
Year of the Grizzly
Shooting Star
Legend of Storey County
Hope Valley War
Delta Passage
Hangtown Lawman
Cumberland Crossing

LEGENDS OF VALOR
by Luke Thoene

Sons of Valor
Brothers of Valor
Fathers of Valor

✪ ✪ ✪

THOENE CLASSIC NONFICTION
by Bodie and Brock Thoene

Writer-to-Writer

THOENE FAMILY CLASSIC SUSPENSE
by Jake Thoene

CHAPTER 16 SERIES
Shaiton's Fire
Firefly Blue
Fuel the Fire

✪ ✪ ✪

THOENE FAMILY CLASSICS FOR KIDS
by Jake and Luke Thoene

BAKER STREET DETECTIVES
The Mystery of the Yellow Hands
The Giant Rat of Sumatra
The Jeweled Peacock of Persia
The Thundering Underground

LAST CHANCE DETECTIVES
Mystery Lights of Navajo Mesa
Legend of the Desert Bigfoot

✪ ✪ ✪

THOENE FAMILY CLASSIC AUDIOBOOKS
Available from
www.thoenebooks.com or
www.familyaudiolibrary.com